Lin Treadgold returned to the UK [...] in the Netherlands. To support h[...] she resigned from her self-employ[...] Now retired and living in Devon, Jack Russell terrier, Dylan, while the rest of her family pursue careers.

Since writing her first book in 2012, *Goodbye Henrietta Street*, nominated for the RNA Joan Hessayon Award, Lin has spent her time writing two more novels. *The Tanglewood Affair* is her second book, published in 2018. *The Trail to Freedom*, her third novel, although a work of fiction, powerfully evokes her father's WWII Prisoner of War experience through his letters.

Lin is the group organiser for the *Romantic Novelists' Association, Exeter Chapter*, and enjoys art and wildlife. Years of global sailing adventures in her youth gave her the experience to draw on for her novels.

Also by Lin Treadgold

Goodbye Henrietta Street
The Tanglewood Affair

THE

TRAIL

TO

FREEDOM

LIN TREADGOLD

SilverWood

Published in 2025 by SilverWood Books

SilverWood Books Ltd
14 Small Street, Bristol, BS48 1UH
www.silverwoodbooks.co.uk

ISBN 978-1-80042-304-6 (paperback)
Also available as an ebook

British Library Cataloguing in Publication Data
A CIP catalogue record for this book is available from the British Library

Page design and typesetting by SilverWood Books

Hope

Within the cool mountain air,
I hear whispers of a war
that never seems to end.
Decked in tattered khaki,
soldiers find comfort in letters
kissed with lipstick,
or face the dreaded
'Dear John' from home.

I asked her to wait
as thoughts fell into my empty cup.
Will freedom come tomorrow?
Always tomorrow…

(Lin Treadgold)

In loving memory of Private Harry Twidle (1920–1995). He escaped Campo 78 in the face of enemy-occupied Italy and wandered the Abruzzo mountains on a desperate mission to return home.

For Lorna and Martin.

Part One

The Pre-War Years

1936–1939

Chapter One

Summer 1936, Saltburn-by-the-Sea

Harold hesitated and checked his watch. Two minutes to seven. He pressed the doorbell and heard muffled tones from within.

'Mam, someone's at the door.'

A voice from upstairs yelled, 'Aggie, answer the bloody door, for God's sake.' Cough, cough.

Harold guessed the shouting from upstairs was Ellie's father, since the window was open.

'It's alright, Ern. I got it. You rest now.'

'Mam, answer the flippin' door!'

'Yes, yes. I 'eard it.'

That's got to be Mrs Brownlee. Harold sighed, wishing he could change his mind.

He buttoned his jacket and checked his watch for the umpteenth time. As a shadow loomed, their identity remained obscured by the frosted glass, but a muffled curse broke through from behind the door before it opened with a jolt. He tightened the grip on the dog lead hanging around his wrist.

'Bloomin' door, it always sticks after I've washed the step. Oh! Harold Dean. What can I do for *you*?' Agnes Brownlee's gaze bored into him, a storm brewing in her eyes; he braced himself for her anger. Instead, she relented with a half-smile, which Harold took as acceptance.

'Hello, Mrs Brownlee. I've come to call for Ellie. I thought it'd be fun for her to walk down with me and the dog to the beach before it gets dark.' The sound of his thumping heart seemed to drown out everything else, and he pleaded that his voice wouldn't betray him as it wavered with the changes of puberty. Realising he'd startled her, he pushed his leg forward to stop the excitable dog entering the house. He hoped he'd done the right thing by calling for Ellie. She'd said it was fine. 'Well…we've left school now, and Ellie likes our Sammy. I thought she *might* like to come for a walk.' He looked down at the Jack Russell panting at his heel, half to acknowledge his canine friend, the other half because he found himself unable to meet Mrs Brownlee's eyes.

Ellie's mother unfolded her arms. 'Erm. As long as she's home no later than nine o'clock. Behave yourselves. Walk only as far as the beach, close to town, right? Do you hear me?'

His excuse sounded feeble, but it could be too late if he didn't see Ellie today. Her new job at the hotel and his new placement in the offices at Cargo Fleet meant time apart for both of them. He pushed back his hair and smiled. 'We will, thank you.'

'Nine o'clock, then. And don't go to the end of Huntcliff in case the tide comes in and no going down the woods either,' she warned. Her voice whipped through the house like a tornado. 'Ellie – it's young Harold Dean! He wants to ask you if you want to walk the dog. Hurry up, I can't stand here all day.'

A disapproving snuffle, or so Harold thought, came from Mrs Brownlee as she reacted. Even though she was aware of his friendship with Ellie, he found her strict and a tad formidable. His mother often said that his smile melted hearts; would Mrs Brownlee think that too? Most Yorkshire folk were friendly, but standing here, he wasn't sure. He waited on the step, holding Sammy. Mrs Brownlee was more authoritative than his mother. 'Mistakes teach lessons,' she'd often said, but Ellie always seemed so under her mother's thumb, and he'd never understood the reason. Kind, sweet, and clever at school, he'd admired her. He shrugged, a nonchalant movement of his shoulders, guessing some parents were just like that.

'Hurry up, Ellie,' Agnes called.

Harold stifled a chuckle as she squeezed along the narrow hallway, pressing her mother into the coat pile on the hanger.

'Scuuuuse me, our mam.' Ellie perked up at the thought of

getting out of the house. 'Oh, hi!' She grinned. 'What a surprise!'

'Harold's walking the dog on the beach, and he's invited you to go.'

'Can I, Mam?' Ellie gave a deliberate, wide grin.

Agnes nodded, despite her reluctance.

'I'll grab my jacket. It'll be chilly on the beach.' Ellie seemed to reply before her mother changed her mind.

'Now, you behave, young lady, and don't be long, d'ye hear?'

'Of course, I'll behave.'

Agnes frowned, looking as if she regretted her decision.

Halfway down the street, Harold turned to Sammy and noticed that Mrs Brownlee was still standing at the gate, her gaze fixed on them. His eye-roll betrayed his annoyance at the mistrust.

They followed the path down the hill, passing by elegant Victorian terraced houses, until they reached the lively promenade.

'This is great! Thanks for calling for me, Harold.'

'You know, it wasn't easy for me asking your ma, El. She's a lot stricter than mine.'

Ellie paused to reflect, a sigh escaping her lips. 'Yeah, I know, but she has an awful lot to cope with. You know Dad's sick again? Getting up to Lumpsey Mine every morning has been too much for him. He gets breathless, and when the bus doesn't always turn up, it kills him having to walk. He's often late for work and the boss gets annoyed. I don't think he'll return to work any more – Ma's got her worries now.'

As Harold gave a half-smile, his expression resembled that of someone unravelling a tangled web of thoughts.

'Mind you, she's always bossing him around, but he's too sick to do anything. Sometimes, she's obsessed with his illness. She won't let him do anything for himself. The problem is she's so secretive and never tells me a thing. It's as if she's carrying the whole world's weight on her shoulders. Our Tommy isn't the perfect kid either, but he's doing all right at school.'

Harold patted her arm and leaned away from her long brown

flyaway hair. 'Sorry to hear that. I can't imagine how you must feel. Come on, let's keep walking.'

Surrounded by the serene tranquillity of the sea, Harold cherished these moments in the company of Ellie. Despite his lack of romantic experience, he found comfort in his hobbies and the camaraderie of his school friends, a group that always made him feel included and accepted. Ellie gave him hope for a change of heart. He loved her naive personality and took pleasure in helping her when she didn't know the answer to a question.

'Anyway, what about this new job of yours, El?'

She hesitated, unsure what to say. 'Don't know really,' she murmured. 'I had dreams of using the money however I pleased – but no. Mam said last week I had to contribute more than half toward my living expenses.'

'I guess you have to help when you're working,' Harold said.

She reminded herself not to complain as she struggled to suppress her frustration, but after all, her dad was ill. 'I hope she was joking. I don't want to feel worthless for the rest of my life. Flippin' 'eck, is there anything left these days? Is that all there is? Cleaning up after everyone at the hotel? One day I'll get married and have ten kids, and that will be that! Oh dear, I'm sorry if I sounded like I complained, that wasn't my intention. It's just…this job doesn't sound very stimulating.' Ellie wrinkled her nose.

'Aw, don't think like that, Ellie. I understand, but at least you don't have to travel far. Meeting people at the hotel will be fun. I have to catch the train daily to the steelworks at Cargo Fleet, which isn't very scenic, but at least the wages are pretty good for my age. Not only that, but our William leaves school within two years, and Peter is still a kid. I expect William will take over the shop when Pop retires.'

'Didn't you want to work in the shop?' Ellie said. 'Your dad's lovely.'

'No, I only do it for pocket money. I help Pop on Saturdays when William has band practice. I wish I could do something more adventurous, like travel.'

'Me too. There's an entire world out there, and then there's the likes of you and me just starting out. Our mam always says, "Be careful what you wish for."' Ellie tutted and rolled her eyes. 'I expect she means well.'

They walked on until they reached the end of the road, when Ellie felt the need to say more but admired Harold's new jumper instead.

'Did your mam knit that tank top? She's clever, isn't she?'

They peered down at the Victorian cliff lift and heard rushing water echoing as it emptied from the tanks.

'Let's go down the steps. I haven't got any money with me for the lift. We'll be on the beach before it reaches the top again,' Ellie said.

'Me neither.' Harold patted his trouser pockets. 'I didn't think we'd need any as we were only walking. Come on, Sammy, stop sniffing.' He tugged at the dog's lead and looked at Ellie. 'Things'll be better when we start work.'

They reached the clifftop and strode down the steps to the beach. Sammy pestered Harold for the ball in his pocket, and he let him off the lead. The Jack Russell jumped up, then ran away as he often did when the call of the sea invaded his nostrils.

Ellie changed the subject. 'You know Vicky Empsall?'

'Course I do. She's a bit too...you know, forward, if you get my meaning.'

'What's wrong with that?'

'She knows too much about all that man-and-woman stuff, and flaunts it. I think she's a bit of a flirt.' Harold scoffed. 'I like her, but I wouldn't walk out with her.' He gave a coy smile.

'Don't tell anyone, but Vicky has a boyfriend. She doesn't want gossip in case her mam finds out. Vicky's a good person, and she's always been kind to me. I think she's often misunderstood.' Ellie smiled.

'I don't see anything wrong with having a boyfriend, Ellie. I mean, I'm your friend, aren't I, so what's the difference?'

As Harold descended the last step, he flung the ball, watching it soar through the air before plunging into the rolling waves for Sammy to retrieve. The dog chased it along the wet sand like a torpedo, his body straight and narrow as his stubby legs propelled him onward.

Ellie took in a breath of sea air. 'I see what you mean. Anyway, Vicky's good fun.' Once again, her hair blew across her face, and Harold watched her push it behind her ears.

'Come here, let me fix that for you.'

With a smile on his face, he ran his fingers through her silky hair, happy to secure the loose ends of her ponytail. Sammy returned with the ball in his mouth and Harold stood aside to throw it.

'Here, catch this, Ellie. Sammy wants it.'

As Ellie caught it and tossed it back, Sammy's high jump added to the excitement of the moment.

Continuing their leisurely stroll along the beach, leaving only foot and pawprints in the sand, they couldn't help but admire the imposing Huntcliff that loomed above them. Harold checked the tide, listening to the crashing waves in the distance. Aware of the consequences, he heeded Mrs Brownlee's warning and made sure not to get caught out by the incoming tide.

Today appeared changed as the conversation mirrored the colourful sunset, full of anticipation.

'I'll be turning seventeen soon, El. I feel like I'm getting like my pop,' Harold quipped.

Ellie gave a heavy sigh. 'I wish I were seventeen.'

Sammy returned the ball to Harold. He hurled it toward the surf, and the dog leaped into the murky North Sea.

'Come on, Sammy, this way,' he called.

Sammy returned dripping wet, and Ellie was taken by surprise as he playfully leaped up from behind and nudged the back of her knees, causing her to stumble over a stone.

'Oh heck, Sammy. Stop it! Ouch!' Ellie cried.

'Are you okay, El?' Harold's voice filled with concern. 'Honestly, you're such a silly dog,' he chuckled.

Ellie's face went from shocked to amused as she attempted to stand up, but the gritty sand clung to her knees and socks. She brushed herself down and rubbed her wrist. 'You're a naughty boy,' she laughed.

Harold bent to her side, and she seemed more settled when he placed his arm around her waist to comfort her. At least she was smiling. Being with Ellie in that moment provided a fresh feeling of togetherness.

'Oh dear. My jacket's wet.'

'El, I'm so sorry. Sammy's got an awful habit of jumping up.' Harold slipped his hand into his pocket and offered a clean handkerchief.

She wiped her wet hands and returned the dog's ball. 'Thanks, that's kind,' she said with a gleam in her eye.

They walked in silence as Ellie rubbed her wrist again. As she approached the rock pools, the distinct aroma of seaweed transported her back to carefree days spent collecting seashells, building sandcastles, and finding moulted gull feathers.

'I often came here with our Tommy and my parents when I was small. You know, when things were easier and Dad's breathing didn't trouble him. We used to build sandcastles here, put a feather on the top, and use shells for the windows.' Ellie smiled.

'Yeah, we used to do that too, and burying Pop in the sand so his head was poking out always kept us laughing.' Harold put his arm around her shoulder and comforted her. 'Let me see your hand. Listen, El.' Harold paused, biting his lip instead of letting the words fall freely. 'I want to ask if we can go out together more?'

'You mean…?'

'Well, you know, now we've left school.' He gave her a meaningful squeeze.

'Gosh, Harold, our mam would have a dicky fit, and Dad doesn't seem to care any more.'

'Yeah, but your ma knows we're only school friends having a nice time, just as it's always been with you and me. I'd have liked to have called for you more, but I know how it is with her. We don't have to show her we...you know, *like* each other in front of her, do we? I mean, you do *like* me, don't you? Like boyfriend and girlfriend, *that* kind of like?'

Ellie took a breath. 'Course I do. I didn't expect... It sounds like fun,' she said, smiling. 'Perhaps it's something I need now. Life hasn't exactly been normal recently, with Dad being ill and all that.'

Seeing her fragile situation at home, Harold felt a strong desire to protect and care for her. There was absolutely nothing amiss with Ellie; everything was as it should be. She was friendly and kind, always looking for someone to lend an ear, especially now that her dad was ill. He'd only hoped to add a touch of sunshine to her day, to make it a little brighter.

'We could go to the pictures, eat fish and chips down the prom, and tell each other about our new jobs. Would you like that?' Harold leaned in and nudged her elbow, his face close to hers.

Ellie glanced toward the sky. 'I would, but it's just...if our mam finds out, she'll kill me.'

'El, you're grown-up now, starting work, starting life. You can almost do what you like.' He hoped his intention to show Ellie some affection hadn't been misunderstood and come across as harsh.

'Not until I'm twenty-one, I can't!'

Harold noted the defeat in her voice. Every time she tried to prove she had grown up, her mother would bring up the twenty-one topic, as if it was the ultimate measure of adulthood. It was strictly against the rules for her to get married or have a boyfriend. Harold's liberal upbringing left little room for him to understand Agnes's controlling attitude.

'But that won't stop us from being friends, will it?'

Ellie shrugged. 'I suppose not.'

Harold's eyes gleamed mischievously as he slipped his hand into hers, their fingers interlocking.

'I do like you a lot,' she confessed, her voice overflowing with sincerity.

As she said it, he could see shyness in her eyes, and gave her hand a soft squeeze.

His gaze immediately fixed on the stunning sunset as it transformed the sea into a canvas of beautiful shades of orange and gold. 'What a memory of our first proper date,' he said, trying to be romantic.

'Isn't it wonderful?' she confessed, mesmerised by the crashing waves and the sight of herring gulls and kittiwakes nesting on the cliffs. 'Actually, there's something I should tell you?' Ellie smiled. 'You mentioned about going to the picture house.'

Harold felt a stab in his stomach. What was she going to say next?

There was a deliberate pause, like she was struggling to find the right words before they tumbled recklessly from her lips. 'I've never been inside a picture house. Our mam calls it "the fleapit", but maybe we can – if she lets me,' she said, before bursting into nervous laughter.

Her comment took a moment to sink in and Harold finally released the breath he had unknowingly been holding. Despite the not-so-dramatic admission, he refused to let go of her hand. It felt warm, soft and welcoming, like home; he wanted to hold on to her forever.

'My parents taught me a lot when I was growing up. Is your ma always so stern?'

Ellie shrugged, her shoulders rising in a gesture of indifference. 'She's always been like that with Tommy and me.'

Harold, mindful of avoiding conflict, gently proposed that they head back to her house. Unwilling to attract the attention of any bystanders, he reluctantly let go of her hand.

'Yeah, there's too much gossip around here,' Ellie chuckled. 'I daren't be late. I wouldn't want to spoil things. There'll be hell to pay if our mam finds out.'

Chapter Two

Agnes checked the clock in the hall and stepped outside, her eyes searching down the street. No sign of Ellie yet. The aroma of the incoming tide wafted toward the house, recalling memories of her life with Ernest and how much it had changed her all those years ago. She had also gone to the beach for walks with… Oh yes, life was very different then. How could she forget the sadness she'd felt until Ernie came along, sweeping her off her feet? She'd had no option but to accept his offer of marriage, but it had taken her time to accept his love. Tragedies after the Great War, the loss of loved ones and the Spanish flu, had caused much insecurity, and she'd needed security. Now the weight of uncertainty about Ernie's remaining time bore down on her as his illness took its toll. Turning around, she saw Ellie and Harold making their way home, their footsteps echoing softly on the path. She supposed Harold stood out from the kids who roamed the areas around the "jewel streets" where all of the roads to the promenade were named after precious stones, yet poverty was observed through the clothes they wore. Although, Harold came from a respected family in the town. While she appreciated his good manners, she couldn't help but wonder if they were too young to be exposed to those grown-up things. Hmm… I'm not easily deceived! If only Ellie does as she's told, life will be much easier. She had to be stopped from making a fool of herself. Too young, far too young!

As she peeked through the hedge of the adjoining garden, Ellie's laughter rang out in the distance, and Agnes kept a close eye on them strolling up Diamond Street. Sammy tugged Ellie along, his legs marching in a brisk rhythm, eager to reach home. Accepting that her little girl had grown up seemed like an overwhelming task.

Agnes smiled. The clock was counting down, and she was only two minutes away from the deadline. Ellie had a tendency to be well behaved when it was convenient for her, but given her vulnerable age, it was crucial to keep her in check. Agnes deadheaded the roses and took in the perfume of the fresh blooms. She and Ernie couldn't allow immoral behaviour; it would be too much to bear in a neighbourhood like theirs, especially with Ernie's condition.

'Mam! You don't have to wait for me.'

Agnes looked up and pretended to be startled. 'Oh, er…hello, you two.'

'G'night then, El. See you next week, eh?' Harold winked at Ellie as he crossed the road. 'G'night, Mrs Brownlee.'

'See you soon, Harold. Call for me again – and thanks.'

'Nice boy, is Harold, but don't you be getting any ideas, young lady. You're too young to go courting.'

'Honestly, Mam, you know we're good friends, and anyway, what do you mean?'

Agnes recalled those exact words from her youth. 'Well, get in the house now, and you can make the cocoa.'

Twelve-year-old Tommy Brownlee raced out of the front door. 'Just going t' see Archie. He's got my Meccano truck we made last week. I want it back.'

Agnes grabbed him by the shirt. 'No, young man, you are not going over there again at this time of night. It's your bedtime now.'

Tommy argued, but Agnes swiped him over the shoulder.

'I said no, and I mean no! D'ye hear me, lad?'

'Ouch! That hurts, Mam.'

'It was meant to hurt. Now get inside the house and up to bed. Ellie will bring your drink upstairs.'

The following day, Agnes handed over a letter addressed to Ellie.

'Well, go on, open it,' she said, smiling and leaning over to look.

Ellie tore open the envelope.

'What does it say?'

With a nonchalant shrug of her shoulders, Ellie walked into the front room. The letterhead read "The Zetland Hotel", conjuring images of grandeur and luxury.

Dear Miss Brownlee,

Your application for the position of Chambermaid is now confirmed. Please attend this office at 6am on Monday 12 August 1936.

We look forward to receiving you.

Yours sincerely,

Beatrice Biggs (Mrs)

Head Housekeeper

'Damn it.' Ellie stormed into the kitchen, holding the letter. 'Six o'clock in the morning start. Up at five every day – oh bloody hell, I'll never be able to do that.'

'You'll have to do it, Ellie, you're a working girl. And don't swear, it's not ladylike. You've recently got into dreadful rough-and-ready talk, and I won't have it here. What would Reverend Woodford at our church say if he heard you talking like that?'

'Oh, Mam, don't be daft. I wouldn't talk like that in front of him. It's nothing to do with him anyway.'

'I jolly well hope you don't. We brought you up as a respectable young lady, your dad and me.'

Agnes folded her arms and felt her patience tested to the limit as Ellie gave her mother a brutal stare. She left the kitchen and passed Ernest a plate of Marmite sandwiches. He wasn't feeling too well that day, and Agnes had already decided she could do without Ellie's moaning.

'You two been arguing *again*?' he croaked.

'Well, you know how it is with that daughter of ours. She needs a firm hand, that one does.'

'Oh, come on, Agnes, she's not that bad. She's a bit rebellious, but you do go on at her. She's growing up now and needs to learn for herself. A good kid, really.'

Ernest gave a rasping cough. Aware of his illness's gravity,

Agnes prepared herself for the worst. She wondered how much Ellie and Tommy realised, too. It was best they didn't know too much, especially now. Tommy was too involved with his young friends. Ernie needed more medicines to help him overcome his constant coughing spasms, and now that Ellie was working, it would help with the expense of buying what he needed. She knew Ernest's black lung disease would never improve despite the sea air. 'He'll have to give up his job, Mrs Brownlee,' the doctor had said. 'Caring for the pit ponies at Lumpsey Iron Mine is better than going underground, but it's still too much for him. He has to rest more and get fresh air. Go home, now. There's not much more I can do.'

Now she lowered her voice. 'Ya know, Ern, when we first came to live here, I thought everything would be different.'

'You ought to be grateful it *is* different, Aggie.'

'Hush up, Ern,' she retorted. 'Don't mention *that* again, please.'

'It was *you* who mentioned it, love.' Ernest coughed again. 'Blasted chest. Get me some of that Vicks thingy, will ya? Have we got any hot water?'

Agnes did as he asked but hoped he'd return to reading his paper. He was a good man, but there would always be the nagging thoughts and the sorrow from the past and what was yet to come.

Chapter Three

Saturday morning. Ellie accompanied her mother into town. They visited Mr Dean's shop, where Harold stood behind the counter. As soon as he saw Ellie, he beamed.

'Oh, hello, Mrs Brownlee. Ellie.' He nodded a smile at Agnes.

Ellie hoped the formal greeting was a safety mask in the presence of her mother.

'How's the job going, Harold?' enquired Agnes.

'It's good, but I'm still getting used to these early mornings. I don't get a lot of time. I'm helping Pop today 'cause William's playing in the band this afternoon.'

'Lovely boy, is William. I hope he does well with his music. I heard him play his trombone last week at the charity concert. He's excellent,' said Agnes, smiling.

Harold noticed how Ellie went quiet. He thought he'd change the mood. 'I'm going to the matinee at the pictures to see that film, *Flying Down to Rio*. Would you like to come, El? It has Fred Astaire and Ginger Rogers in it. They say the dancing is fantastic. I really love dancing, so I go to the junior dances at The Spa – it's fun. Although I haven't been lately because of my school exams, but now they're over, I can go again soon. You can come with me sometime and learn to dance.'

Alarmed at Harold's boldness, Ellie looked at her mother and replied louder than usual, so everyone could hear. She was in *that* sort of mood. Her mother had been ranting at her again, telling her not to wear make-up. She'd only been trying out a Max Factor lipstick which Vicky had given her as a school leaving present. If her mother had asked about it, she would have said. Instead, she'd shouted at her.

'Can't afford it, sorry. Dad's ill.' Ellie knew her father had spent all last week in bed, and her mother had been going up and down the stairs with the vapour rub and hot water to help him breathe. Ellie had taken it upstairs too when her mother was out shopping; it was exhausting. Her dad was always calling for his newspaper, a cup of tea, or a clean towel. In that respect, she felt guilty about what she'd said, and regretted her words.

Harold frowned. 'It's okay, I understand…'

Agnes interrupted and tugged Ellie's arm to stop her from saying more. 'Ellie, whisht now.' She leaned her shopping bag on the counter and whipped her index finger over her lips. She didn't want to appear penniless in front of Mrs Wilson and Mrs Davison standing behind her. 'It's all right, Ellie. If Harold wants to take you, I'll pay.'

'Oh no, Mrs Brownlee, I earn my own money now, so I'll pay for Ellie. It's my treat.'

'Erm, well, I mean… Thank you, Harold.'

Alf Dean poked his head around the door of the adjoining storeroom. 'Hello, Mrs Brownlee. I'll be with you in a minute.'

Alf's homely demeanour gave Ellie comfort in the presence of the other customers. He was tall, slim, and wore a long white storekeeper's apron over a grey shirt. He was clean-shaven, and his thinning hair was combed over to hide his balding pate. He smiled, making Ellie wish her father could be more encouraging like Mr Dean. She realised now from where Harold had got his thoughtful nature. Mr Dean was always smiling, and Harold did that too. If Harold's father hadn't been in the shop, Ellie knew her mother would have been less agreeable. She'd learned that being one step ahead was to her advantage.

Agnes smiled. 'That's very good of you, Harold, but there's no need – you're a kind boy. Maybe I can treat you both to an ice cream.'

'That would be lovely, Mrs Brownlee. Thank you.'

Ellie's jaw dropped in astonishment. When her friends were around, she could always predict her mother's fake "yes" responses.

'Ellie, would you like to come here after the matinee, and we can play ludo with my brothers?' Harold smiled.

'Oh, Mam, can I? Do you mind?' Ellie looked at Mr Dean as he stood from stacking boxes. Excitedly, she didn't wait for her mother's answer. 'That'd be smashing. And they say Fred Astaire's a lovely dancer.'

Alf Dean smiled at Agnes, shrugged his shoulders, and gave a "Why not?" expression.

Harold pushed the conversation. 'I'll ask our ma to get some of her home-made ginger beer from the cellar, and we can all have a bit of a party.'

Agnes relented and looked at Ellie. 'Aw right, pet, that sounds a lovely idea. Why, yes, you can go.'

Ellie had got used to her mother's accent, which was more County Durham than Yorkshire. Her over-sweet tone was often a sign of what she thought was being posh, especially with Mr Dean behind the counter and two other women in the queue.

'I also need custard powder, Mr Dean, please,' said Agnes. 'And a bottle of Camp Coffee. Thank you.'

Alf reached for the coffee as Harold placed the Bird's custard powder box on the counter. Ellie noticed how he gave her a cheeky smile when her mother wasn't looking. She gazed at the boxes of KitKats and Mars bars and wanted to ask her mother if she could have one, but what was the point? She already knew the answer.

'From what I heard on the news, you'd better make the most of your groceries today,' Alf said. 'Supplies are short just now.' He changed the subject and turned to face Ellie. 'I hear you start work on Monday, love? Good luck – the hotel is marvellous, and you'll meet lots of interesting people.'

Ellie smiled. 'Thank you, Mr Dean, but I'll be busy cleaning and making beds. I doubt if I'll get time to talk to the visitors.'

Agnes tapped Ellie on the arm, not wanting her to get involved in the conversation. 'Goodbye, Mr Dean, Harold. Thank you.'

'Don't forget, Ellie,' Harold called out after them. 'Two o'clock matinee. See you in the queue. I'm helping Pop until just after twelve.'

As they strolled along the street, Ellie stepped into her own thoughts. Her mother had given her consent for her to go out with Harold. She ought to feel grateful. Still, her mother's characteristic gait showed reluctance as she walked stoutly, four steps ahead. Ellie thought her mother looked thinner recently – and she wore lipstick for church! Now she had her mother's consent to go out with Harold. Perhaps her mother wasn't that annoying after all.

Ellie arrived early and joined the line for the cinema, eagerly awaiting Harold's arrival. Uncertainties swirled through her mind like a dense fog. She didn't feel confident standing in line alone as a gust of North Sea breeze played with her hair. She smoothed her tweed skirt, another of Auntie Pat's cast-offs, and checked the top button on her cream cardigan. A girl in the queue turned around, and Ellie thought her long hairstyle suited her. Her mother's words returned to her thoughts: It's awfully low-class to wear lipstick at your age, Ellie. I see all that rude behaviour around town these days – no child of mine will be allowed to behave like that. Ellie couldn't make out the correlation between the two statements.

Her thoughts jerked as Harold joined her. He took her hand and squished it gently between his fingers.

'Hello, you,' he said. 'Glad you came.'

'I didn't want to be late.'

'The doors will open in a minute,' he assured her. 'You look really nice, El.'

'Thanks.' Ellie felt less shy, and ran her hand through her hair, but the sudden void in the conversation needed filling. She knew it was a silly question, but couldn't think of anything sensible. 'If there was one thing you'd like to do in this entire world, Harold, what would it be?'

He frowned, thinking hard. 'As you know, travel is on my mind,' he said. 'But I'd have to take you with me, El.'

'Aw, Harold, that's ever so nice.' She liked Harold's comforting and talkative nature. He had always been kind.

'Where would we go?' His eyes widened as he smiled.

'I fancy Paris,' she said, imagining the Eiffel Tower standing tall against the city skyline. The prospect of witnessing all those fashionable outfits, similar to the ones showcased in magazines, excited her.

'I was thinking of going somewhere even more exciting. America or Australia. They got kangaroos in Australia.'

'That's too far.' Ellie hoped he wouldn't go there. 'It seems everyone is going somewhere else these days, other than Vicky, and now that she's left school I don't know when I'll see her again. She's working at Woolworths in Redcar, gets the train every day, which surprises me because I always felt she was the arty type and preferred the outdoors.'

'Nothing's too far, Ellie. You have to be adventurous if you want to get on. That's what Pop keeps saying: "Do it while you can." He listens to the BBC and tells me what's happening in the world.'

She pinched her lips together. 'Hmm. I'm not sure. I wouldn't know, only what we learned in school,' she replied. 'I've never been that good at decisions. Our mam does it all for me.' She rolled her eyes.

Harold paid for the tickets and led the way to the back row of the auditorium. Ellie fumbled along the row to find her seat in the half-light, and almost fell over. Harold caught her as she stumbled, which made her feel foolish.

'Come on, El, it's okay. We can see it better here. It'll be too close to the screen if we sit at the front. Keep going. There you go.'

Ellie loved the excitement of sitting in a darkened cinema, surrounded by the smell of popcorn and the anticipation of the movie starting. With Harold's arm around her she felt a comforting warmth and a sense of anticipation.

Lights dimmed as the Pathé News reel came to a close. They waited for the supporting film to begin, and shared a bag of Smith's crisps. Ellie tipped the small blue salt bag into the crisps and shook it.

'Shhhh,' someone hissed from the seat in front. Ellie sunk low, realising what she'd done.

After a while, Harold held her hand and whispered in her ear. 'Can I kiss you?'

'Oh, er…'

'You're my girlfriend now, eh?'

'Oh yes, I suppose I am,' she replied, her voice tinged with a hint of uncertainty. In the cinema's darkness, she gave a playful and secretive smile. Harold's girlfriend? The thought had a beautiful ring to it.

Harold lifted his hand and steered her chin toward his lips. What's he doing? She froze for a moment and remained still in case she offended him. His puppy face had a few prickles here and there, and with the perfume of Pears soap wafting through her nostrils, she kissed him and felt her heart pound. Oh heck, real kissing.

Ellie exhaled. 'Oh, I see. *That* kissing,' she whispered as she gasped for air, glad no one was sitting beside her.

'What else did you think?' Harold mused.

She felt her cheeks flush and took two deep, calming breaths. She wanted to giggle, but thank goodness Harold spoke first.

'Was that nice, El?' he whispered in her ear.

'Mm, yes.' She nodded while watching the film, words failing her. She decided it *was* nice, warm and exciting. It also felt rebellious, but so what? She was doing what *she* wanted for a change – and in the dark, too. She bit down a smile; this could change everything.

They raised the house lights, and Harold left his seat to wander toward the usherette selling ice cream. 'I'll get you a tub, should I?'

Ellie nodded. 'Please.' She nibbled the end of her thumbnail, terrified that someone could have seen them kissing. Harold had been gone a while. Where was he? Then she craned her neck over the seated rows of heads and saw him.

'Here's your ice cream,' he said. 'Enjoying the film so far? The main one comes on next.' He caught her hand and gave it a gentle squeeze.

'Yeah, it's smashin'.'

With all the excitement, they finally settled to watch *Flying Down to Rio*. Ellie sang along softly with the chorus, almost kicking her legs with the girls performing on the aeroplane wings. The scenes sparked fresh energy in her thoughts. She loved Fred Astaire, and the story grabbed her by the hand to swing with the music. One day, she hoped Harold would take her to the dances, and she could also learn to dance like that.

'I wish I were an actress, but I don't have the confidence to do that sort of thing,' she whispered.

Harold smiled. 'I'm sure you could do it, Ellie, but you need a bit o' gumption to get up there and perform. I hope you'll get to do all those things you dream about one day.' He kissed her on the cheek.

Ellie sang the title tune in her head. The film left her excited and more determined to do something useful in her life. Ultimately, she couldn't stop smiling and longed to watch it again. Harold was so lovely; she wanted to feel like this forever.

The national anthem played as the clock on the wall read five-thirty, and Ellie adjusted her eyes to the bright sky outside.

'Were those girls really dancing on those aeroplane wings? It must have been terrifying. I felt dizzy watching them, mostly when that girl fell off her trapeze, you know – my heart was in my mouth. Tell me it wasn't real, Harold.'

'Oh yes, of course it was real. How else do you think they did it?' He laughed. 'No, just joking. It was trick photography – they wouldn't let them do that, and it's dangerous, anyway. At least they caught that girl before she fell into the sea. Maybe we can go to Rio, Ellie, when we take our adventure together.' He gave her an impish smile.

They arrived in Coral Street, taking the side door into his

parents' shop. She had never been inside the Dean household. On the mantelshelf in the sitting room stood pictures of the family. Good-looking William, who she knew from school, with his wavy blond hair and blue eyes. Peter, a cheeky ten-year-old, grinned from between his parents' sides. Harold's house seemed to have an atmosphere of calm and harmony.

'Come in, come in.' Mr Dean's hearty welcome made Ellie smile.

'Hi, Ma, Pop, we had a lovely time at the flicks.'

'Yes, it was absolutely wonderful!' Ellie exclaimed, her eyes sparkling with delight and a wide smile lighting up her face. With his impeccable style and graceful movements, Fred Astaire had left a lasting impression.

'I enjoy dancing too,' Harold said. 'We ought to do more of it. Maybe enter ballroom competitions at The Spa.' He sniffed the air. 'Hey, Ma! It smells like you've been baking cakes.'

'I have,' she said with enthusiasm in her voice.

Ellie noted how different Harold's mother was from hers. Betty Dean was short and rounded, a homely woman who wore a green-and-white flower-patterned pinafore. She always made everyone feel welcome at the shop. Her pink cheeks revealed her as an attractive woman in her mid-forties, and she was always smiling, like Harold.

'Come on, then, let's play a game. I'll call William and Peter and ask them if they want to play ludo,' said Mr Dean. 'Give me five minutes, and I'll join you.' He removed his spectacles from his nose and grabbed a handkerchief to clean them. Above the fireplace stood a pipe rack; a strong odour of sweet tobacco emanated from the mantelshelf.

Ellie turned her attention to Mrs Dean, who was bringing ginger beer, a plate of home-made biscuits on a tray, and a sponge cake with jam and buttercream.

'I hear you start work on Monday. I hope you enjoy it, Ellie.' She set the plates on a gateleg table draped with an embroidered cloth.

'Thank you, Mrs Dean.' Ellie watched as Harold opened the

game board and set out the coloured tokens. She spoke first. 'You didn't tell me much about your new job, Harold.'

'It's nothing too tricky. My boss discovered I'm good at figures, so he started me on wages on my first day. Since I was twelve, I've been helping Pop do all that stuff, right?' He glanced at his father.

Alf Dean pulled out a chair and nodded in agreement.

Harold continued. 'It wasn't hard, but I'm unsure how long I'll stay there. Perhaps, if I'm lucky, I'll get a promotion.'

Ellie placed the dice in the shaker. 'I wish I weren't doing this hotel job. There aren't a lot of choices for girls. I'm not clever enough to do anything else. At least, that's what our dad said.'

'Oh, Ellie, you're *brilliant*. Look at all those smashing stories you wrote – they were hilarious. You were very good at writing, and your teacher said how well you did in the exams.'

'I'm pretty good at doin' sums,' William remarked as he entered the room, leaving the door open. 'And swimmin' too.'

'Yes, Pop relies on you,' Harold said, smiling. 'You're good at lots of things, our kid.'

'Put wood in t' 'ole, lad. Keep the draught out of the room. You know how much the wind blows through from the shop,' Alf said.

'But, Harold, arithmetic isn't a job,' Ellie remarked as she watched William shut the door.

'Of course it is. That's what I do and why I got the job.'

'Promise you won't laugh at me, but…' Ellie caught Harold's gaze as he placed his counters on the board.

'Why should I laugh, El? Go on. What?'

'After seeing the film today, I'd love to sing, dance, or burst out of a cracker – do something exciting, like we did in the school plays. It made me feel…'

'You were Ginger Rogers?' Harold teased.

William cackled at his brother's remark.

'You'll be fine,' Alf piped in. 'You have a bright future, Ellie, and don't let anyone tell you otherwise. Although, unless you are famous, I don't think you'll earn much money acting. You must do your best to follow your dreams. You're a bonny lass, and I'm pleased you and Harold are friends. I'm sure you'll do well. Just enjoy it while you can. We never know what's around the corner these days, isn't that right, Ma?'

'That's what *I* told her,' Harold said.

Ellie smiled as Betty Dean rolled her eyes and poured two cups of tea into her best china cups.

'Our three boys are challenging, but we love them very much.' She looked at William.

Ellie wished her mother would say those kinds of things. She'd never thought of herself as "a bonny lass". God! What would Mam say if she knew we'd been kissing in the back row of the cinema? She reminded herself she mustn't say "God" that way; her mother had told her it was blasphemy, and Granny Brownlee had been worse. She'd told Ellie not to eat ice-cream cones 'in case a black man had handled it'. Ellie had never understood why; it made little sense and seemed unfair – what a strange family! The words "black man" scared her to death. She'd grown up thinking she didn't like ice cream or anyone with black skin, not that there were many of those in Saltburn. It didn't seem fair, but she couldn't explain it. She'd got over the fear but failed to appreciate the reason for her grandmother's words. Growing up with an overcritical parent had shattered her confidence. Why couldn't her mother be like Mrs Dean: kind and helpful?

Peter strode into the room and took his place at the table.

'Youngest goes first,' Harold said.

'Slow down, young man, you'll trip over yourself one day,' remarked Betty.

Peter shook the dice.

'Hey! You got a double, Pete. Have another go,' Harold declared.

Harold played footsie under the table with Ellie. She knew she mustn't giggle, and moved her foot back to the chair's stretcher, giving Harold a playful, hard stare. She noticed how he engaged with his dad, taking turns to shake the dice, and wished her parents would enjoy themselves like this.

After Peter threw a double two, he called out in a sing-song voice, 'I won, I won, ha ha!'

Harold smiled at his youngest brother. 'Yes, you won, Pete. Well done.'

Betty continued knitting, her needles clicking softly together.

'Ellie, it's a shame your mother doesn't believe you should have more freedom,' she remarked. 'Anyway, we're happy to have you to tea any time.'

Harold smiled at his mother's comment.

Ellie felt at home with the Deans, their warm smiles and inviting gestures making her instantly comfortable. Seeing them together, the easy smiles and shared glances, filled her heart with warmth, a testament to their deep bond. If only I could go to Rio with Harold. She smiled to herself, but sadly: time had beaten her, and she dared not be late home.

Chapter Four

Ellie yawned her way out of bed. It was five o'clock, and it seemed dawn had broken hours ago. She thought about the dark winter mornings. Perhaps, with time, she'd get used to rising early. She shivered, not sure if it was from the cold or her nerves.

After a last gulp of tea, she pushed her arms into the sleeves of her coat and gently closed the front door. She hoped not to wake her dad. The north wind bit her cheeks as she ran down the street; she mustn't be late. The tide had turned, and the aroma of seaweed chased her along the promenade. By the time she reached the empty and soulless road, the milkman and his horse-drawn float had delivered milk to the rows of Victorian terraces; he encouraged his horse to walk on. A woman shovelled horse manure behind them. Ellie ignored her and turned the corner to climb the hotel steps, finally untangling herself from the revolving doors. Breathless, she approached the reception desk and then realised the day staff were not due to start work until eight o'clock.

The doorman greeted her. 'Hello, young Ellie Brownlee. I heard you were coming today to work with us. I'll phone Bea and ask her to come down to fetch you. She's probably having a cuppa right now. Take a seat.'

Ellie sat in reception on a blue velvet armchair while the doorman phoned. She knew him, but where from? Ah yes: Arnie Gibbs. His mother used to own the newsagent's shop in the square.

As she sat, her thoughts turned to the day ahead. What would they ask her to do? How should she behave? The prospect of working in a grand hotel felt daunting. The aroma of freshly made coffee wafted from the restaurant.

A mature woman wearing a maroon overall descended the grand staircase. 'Miss Brownlee. I'm Beatrice, but please call me Bea – everyone else does.' Bea held out her hand.

'I'm Ellie,' Ellie returned.

Bea led the way upstairs to the domestic store and gave Ellie a well-laundered overall matching her own. 'Mr and Mrs Cornwell, room 5, are leaving today, so we need this one ready before the next guests arrive. Mrs Jameson, our boss, will provide you with a daily list of rooms to be serviced. Just tick the items off the list when you have completed them. The cleaning stuff for this floor is in that cupboard over there. I'll give you a key. Make sure you put the used sheets and towels in there.' She pointed to a white linen bag on the floor of the corridor.

Ellie sighed. Perhaps she had to get on with it. After all, it was earning her money. She nodded. 'Righto, I've got that, thanks.'

'I met your mum in town. I told her we needed help. She's not from around here, is she?'

'No, they moved from County Durham when Dad got sick, to escape the mines. Granny Brownlee lived in Saltburn, and they moved in when she died.'

'Ah yes, I remember old Mrs Brownlee. She was a nice lady. I met her a few times, many years ago. She used to go into The Station Café.'

Ellie didn't know her grandmother well, but remembered her face and what she said. Sometimes, they were not so wise words.

'I hope you'll enjoy your time with us here. We're a kind of *family*. You'll see when you meet the other staff members.' Bea smiled.

'Thank you.'

'I'll get one of the girls to come and show you what to do. Follow me,' Bea said.

Ellie briefly longed to be anywhere but here. Cleaning and meticulously following instructions seemed overwhelming. What was the point of spending the rest of her life as a domestic servant?

No way did she want that. Her initial goal was to become a hotel receptionist and be given a chance to prove to her father she wasn't as dumb as he'd once made out. She had to start somewhere, she thought. Being an actress was only a dream.

16 July 1938

Although Agnes's rigid nature created friction, Harold's kindness acted as a buffer, allowing their friendship to flourish. He vividly recalled every journey he'd taken with Ellie, from the vibrant streets to the peaceful and calming countryside. He loved her and nothing else mattered. Shopping and going to the pictures in Redcar were highlights. The trip to Whitby had been inspiring, travelling alongside the River Esk with the sound of the steam train, clackety-clack.

The image of Harold leaning out of the window, rubbing his eyes to remove the soot, replayed in Ellie's memory. They'd arrived at the station with his face covered in black blotches, and immediately gone to the chemist's shop to get an eyebath.

'I'll never leave you,' she whispered to Harold as she bathed his eyes, her voice filled with unwavering devotion. 'I hold on to the hope that one day we can spread our wings and fly away together, just like we used to talk about.' She knew without a doubt that their love was genuine, and her passion for him consumed her.

That day, being a Saturday, they arrived home after a bus ride from Staithes. Ellie loved the narrow streets, and the aroma of fish and chips in the village led them to a shop where a queue stood outside the door.

'It's my birthday next week,' Harold remarked. 'Our ma is putting on a bit of a do for me. Tea and cake, I think. You remember how she enjoys doing it? I know she expects us to be there.'

'Well... I want to come, but it's our mam. She put her foot down last week, saying that we're seeing too much of each other.' Ellie had spent the last few weeks not revealing anything about

Harold to her mother. She always froze when she mentioned him, so what was the point?

'Hang on, I'll get the fish and chips, you wait here on this seat,' Harold said.

Ellie agreed, and sat down with negative thoughts in her head. She hoped she could go to Harold's birthday. Now, it seemed, her father had stepped into the argument. He rarely got angry, and was often remote and within himself, but she knew that the slightest thing could upset him.

'I agree with your mother,' Ernest had said. 'You're far too young to be courting. You can see Harold every two weeks, but if you don't do as I say, you won't be able to see him at all. Don't you dare cross the line with me, young lady, do you hear?' He'd coughed and found it hard to breathe.

'But, Dad, I'm old enough to know what I want. We've known each other a long time. Please learn to trust me. I'm not a kid any more.'

'Look, El, I try not to interfere too much with your life. Your mother usually makes the rules around here, but it's a dangerous world out there, and by the time you're of age, you'll have learned a lot more. Your mam is worried about you, that's all. She cares about you.' His voice croaked, and his breathing had seemed more laboured than usual.

'Dad! Can't you say *something*?' Ellie recalled her frustration. 'Sorry, Dad, I know you're poorly. I didn't mean to be harsh.'

'Listen. It's not been easy for me. But you'll see, one day things will change, and you'll be glad we care about you.' Ernest had tried a smile and returned to reading, hiding each breath of pain behind his newspaper.

She'd had enough of all this. She didn't need to be treated like a child. She wasn't too young to go courting with Harold. Besides, Lottie Stafford from school had recently married in a hasty ceremony that excluded her school friends, leaving Ellie feeling disappointed. So why didn't her mother approve of Harold? What was it about him

36

she couldn't accept? It felt like a hopeless pursuit, with every effort met with defeat, leaving Ellie increasingly exasperated. If she hadn't been at work during the day, the empty streets and quiet atmosphere would have filled her with a deep sense of melancholy. All she desired was for someone to comprehend her and for her mother to relinquish her habit of keeping everything hidden. This was not who she wanted to be. It was like being in prison.

Harold returned with the fish and chips, and they sat with their thoughts, silently enjoying the flavour of the salt and vinegar mingled with the extra scraps of batter over the chips. She'd talk to Harold later about the birthday party. For now, she'd enjoy the sunshine and the delicious lunch.

Ellie's relationship with the Deans always made her feel welcome. With her curfew to return home needling her, she hoped Harold would continue to tolerate this ridiculous family turmoil and not give up on her.

When he'd visited the Brownlees, Ellie recalled, her mother had watched their every move. He'd told Ellie he'd felt uncomfortable when he'd tried to sit beside her at the table. Agnes had intervened, making sure they sat apart. He'd felt insulted and mistrusted. It was stupid – almost amusing. Ellie pushed it out of her thoughts. She was at the Deans' house now and in a happier atmosphere. Harold had been brave enough to go across to Ellie's mother and ask her if Ellie could attend his birthday tea. Yes, his mother had been right: if he smiled and showed politeness, she would surely say yes. And she did, but that stern look of hers had seemed so disapproving.

'Go on, Harold, love. Blow the candles out,' Betty enthused. 'I hope you enjoy the cake I made.'

'Nineteen today, eh?' Alf said. 'Get stuck in, lad. Your ma's cake is always delicious – you too, Ellie.'

'I wish I were nineteen,' Ellie remarked.

'Don't wish your life away, Ellie.' Betty smiled. 'You and Harold must enjoy your time together as much as possible. We understand –

we were young once, too.' She gave Alf a knowing smile.

'It's our mam, though. I just wish she understood about Harold and me.'

Ellie glanced at Harold. At last, her higher wage packet of an extra shilling a week had allowed her to buy new clothes, and she'd saved up for Harold's birthday present. She appreciated his compliment on her new dress. Perhaps she wasn't as stupid as her dad had made out. He didn't mean it, but his comment about her not being bright had stung her. It was also amazing that her motivation had finally caught the eye of her employers. Maybe it was time to show her capabilities.

'Maybe it's your dad's way of encouraging you to work harder,' Bea had said. 'People didn't take me seriously until I was older.'

Thinking about Bea's comment, it was time for Ellie to announce her promotion to the Deans. 'I meant to tell you, our head housekeeper is making an appointment with our manageress, Mrs Jameson, about my job.'

'Sounds good,' Harold said. 'I hope you get promoted.'

'I hope so, too. It could make a vast difference. I want to show Mam and Dad I can do this.'

'I'm sure you can, Ellie,' Alf said. 'The only person you need to prove it to is yourself.'

'Come on, El, it's a lovely evening. Let's sit in the yard in the sun.'

Harold carried Ellie's tea to the deckchairs. She sat down and placed her cup on the concrete floor of the yard. The changing glow of the evening reflected from the whitewashed brick wall. Her eyes caught the headlines of the folded newspaper which had fallen to the ground.

> The unsettling circumstances around the world make it
> even more possible that our men will have to go to war.

Ellie sucked in a breath and dared to ask the inevitable question. 'Do you think us girls will be called up as well, Harold?'

'I doubt it, El, but I have no choice but to go if ordered.' He furrowed his brow.

'I hope you don't have to – it all sounds dreadful.' Ellie grimaced.

'Anyway, it's the job of the men and we'll need your support at home. Nothing is set in stone right now. If we have to fight to keep the way we live, it has to be, but it'll only be for a couple of months. I suppose it's an opportunity to do things I wanted.'

'More tea?' Alf said, poking his head outside the yard door. He'd been listening.

Ellie saw him sigh deeply at the response, 'A couple of months.'

'I did all that stuff twenty years ago,' Alf retorted and went back inside the house.

Ellie had a sudden feeling of abandonment. 'Do you love me, Harold?' she whispered.

'What a daft question. Of course I do. I'll always love you.'

'It scares me, that's all. I don't want to lose you. Things are happening faster than I thought they would.' Ellie grimaced.

'We'll be fine, you'll see. It's such a pity that your ma doesn't accept our friendship. It would make it so much easier for everyone.'

'You've been so patient with our mam.' Ellie sighed. 'I have to go home soon. I promised I'd be back by eight.'

Friday morning. Ellie arrived at work and shrugged off today as being no different from any other day. There were beds to be made and sinks to be cleaned. Routine, routine – nothing ever changes. Only views of the picturesque scenery were a bonus. Nestling under Huntcliff stood The Ship Inn, once a place of smugglers, now graced by coachloads of families enjoying the seaside on weekends. As a child, she remembered sitting outside the pub with Tommy, drinking lemonade and eating a bag of crisps while her parents were inside. Sadly, they could no longer afford to do that. Perhaps she could do it again now that she was older, but this time with a glass of cider.

Ellie cast her mind to her appointment with Mrs J at ten-thirty that morning. She tidied her hair and smoothed her overall before descending the long, sweeping staircase to the reception. Clearing her throat, she paused and knocked on the door labelled "Mrs L Jameson".

'Good morning, Ellie – come in, sit.'

Ellie gazed at the noticeably tall woman in her forties standing by the filing cabinet wearing a fawn suit. A clip secured her dark hair at the back of her head, giving her an elegant appearance. Mrs Jameson always wore wiry gold spectacles that teetered on the end of her nose. She clutched Ellie's work record and held a green pencil, twirling it between her fingers.

Ellie gave a slight cough. 'I wanted to see if it will be possible for me to change jobs and do office work instead.' Her voice sounded timid, as if someone of such a low status as herself shouldn't be asking that kind of question.

Mrs J's spectacles finally slipped as she spoke. She used her index finger to push them back. 'No doubt you've heard on the grapevine that our receptionist, Pauline Cox, has handed in her notice. Given the current news about the possible war, she's got a job in London, which makes me wonder if her decision was wise.' She pursed her lips. 'I'll discuss this with Beatrice and explain. Perhaps it's time for you to do office training, learn to type and do the filing. After all, we need the help now, and we know your school and work records are excellent.'

Ellie's chest pounded at Mrs J's comment.

'In your application, it stated that you passed your exams at school. We need someone to handle the invoicing tasks and keep track of our stock levels. You will need to write the restaurant menus every day, and if you are unfamiliar with using a typewriter, our secretary, Eva, can assist you in learning how to do it. In addition, she'll guide you through the process of operating the Gestetner copying machine. Practice makes perfect, so be prepared to invest a significant amount of time and effort. With the way things are, you'll have to be an all-rounder. None of us knows where we'll be

40

from one day to the next, but in the meantime, we're happy for you to join us.'

Ellie took a breath and thanked Mrs Jameson for the interview.

'I'll tell you more after this weekend, my dear.'

Ellie's jaw dropped. She'd tell her father the news, and was curious to see his reaction.

Later that day, Ellie waited at the railway station for Harold. He greeted her with a kiss.

'This is lovely. Isn't your mother sneaking up behind us today?' He chuckled.

Ellie burst forth with all her news and ignored his comment. 'Guess what? I might have a new job. They're contacting me on Monday to ask me to work in reception. It's more wonderful than I'd ever imagined.'

'Wowee, El, that *is* wonderful. I hope you get it. Clever you, eh? Marvellous news, well done, love.' He kissed her again. 'Come on, let's go home. Today I thought about how far we've come since we left school. I'm very proud of you.' He reached for her hand.

'I'm proud of you too, Harold.' Ellie smiled at his comment, and again they kissed.

'One day, we can get married and have kids.'

'Oh heck,' Ellie replied. 'I don't think any of us can think that far ahead just now.'

'Oh, I do. Ma and Pop want me to do the right thing when you reach twenty-one.'

'Yeah, but, Harold, what if you're called up?' she asked, her voice filled with concern. 'The air has been filled with conversations about what if we went to war. I couldn't possibly get married soon. Mam and Dad would never give their permission with all this talk of war as well. None of it makes sense to me any more.'

Harold frowned. 'The war won't happen. I believe they learned from the last time, when Pop was a soldier. But last week, he told me to prepare for it – he's worried about me. He never talks about his time in the Great War. I've asked him, but he says, "My life in the army is all in the past, son, all in the past." He told me people at home had no idea what it was like, so what was the point? He hates the Germans because of what they did to him.'

'It must be terrible, having to go through all that.'

'Let's not think about it now, eh? We'll go home for tea and pikelets. Ma was making some today. Anyway, I'm so pleased they're considering you for the job.'

Ellie and Harold walked hand in hand, their footsteps echoing against the platform as they approached the great beast of the engine. In an instant, a thick cloud of steam burst forth, catching them off guard. Ellie laughed, then searched the old Victorian station platform, thinking that her mother could be spying on her.

'What's the matter, El?'

'I never know if our mam is watching me.'

'I'll speak to her soon, I promise. You know she's scared we do things – make whoopee and all that. She's only trying to protect you, I suppose.'

'Harold!' Ellie lengthened the "rold" part of his name, then gazed at the footpath for a moment, unsure if, with her following comment, he'd make fun of her. 'Don't you dare laugh at me, but only a couple of months ago, I saw a couple of dogs mating in the street, and I suddenly realised maybe that's what people do.'

He saw her seriousness, abandoning his laughter. 'Oh heck, don't you know *anything*, El?'

'No, it's like this. Mam always worries about me. She keeps mentioning that "babies are not wanted around here". She clams up and looks embarrassed every time the subject comes up. I didn't understand what she meant until I thought about it.'

'Oh Ellie. Didn't you learn the facts of life, the birds and the bees? Didn't anyone tell you? I can't believe you don't know. Oh dear. I thought something was off. Now I understand. It's me who's stupid, not you. I'm just trying to do the right thing for both of us.'

Ellie's eyes gazed at the pavement, and she blushed. 'Well, I do know, but…no, not everything. Our mam has made me scared about things like that.' She felt foolish admitting her inadequacies. 'I don't have anyone I can talk to about it, not even Bea at work, and Vicky's always so busy these days, I don't see her.'

'Oh, El, I'm sorry, I didn't realise. You ought to have told me. You know we can discuss those things, you and me.'

Ellie avoided Harold's gaze. He always sounded so matter-of-fact and helpful.

'My pop told me all about it just after my eleventh birthday. Look, El, love, after tea, I'll call for you with Sammy, and we'll take a stroll on the beach.'

'All right, then. That would be nice.'

He kissed her, and they parted.

What had she done, talking about all that stuff to Harold? The girls at school had always made fun of her. What would Harold say? She felt annoyed that she'd mentioned it.

It was Monday morning as Ellie stepped into her black skirt and buttoned her cotton blouse before starting work.

Bea called on her to chat during the tea break. 'Ellie, dear, I had Mrs J see me this morning. We've discussed this with our new manager, Mr Phelps, and you can do a trial period. We know how much you want to work in reception.'

'That's marvellous. When do I start?'

'Tomorrow.'

'Oh bloomin' 'eck, Bea! I didn't expect it to be so soon. Thanks ever so much.'

Bea tilted her head to one side and smiled. 'I got a new girl starting on holiday relief. She's doing room duties and may help us until we get someone to take your place. Mrs J wants you on the desk at eight o'clock.'

'You mean I can sleep an extra two hours in bed every day?' Ellie grinned.

'Well, I suppose you can, young lady, if you put it like that.' Bea gave her a kind smile. 'Off you pop, love,' she urged, giving her a gentle pat on the back.

Ellie had found Bea to be like a second mother, and loved working with her. At least she was still working at the hotel, and they would remain friends.

'Thanks, Bea. It's been great working with you. I've learned a lot, but we can still have our break together – I'm not going very far.'

The following day, Ellie sat in the hotel foyer waiting for Mrs J to arrive, but she couldn't help thinking about all those personal things Harold had explained on Friday night. It was hard to believe she hadn't connected animals with humans: why female dogs came into season, and…oh, how stupid she was. It seemed perfectly natural, if not awkward, that Harold had had to explain it. She now understood why people closed their doors in conversation about sex. Harold had said it was 'a bit of a closed subject, anyway'. 'It's sex that makes the world go around,' he'd said, but *we* mustn't ever do it until we get married, especially now with the war news, although…' She trusted him to say the right things, and he never made fun of her. They'd talked, and she'd felt relieved of her naivety. She had never really given it a thought before now. But what if he asked her to do it? Would she like it? His dad had told him everything, him being an ex-soldier. She'd had her period and her mother said it was something that happened to girls and she mustn't worry about it, it was normal at her age and part of her growing up to become a woman. God, I'm such an idiot! Her mother had let her down. Made a fool out of her by avoiding any sensible explanations.

She had never really thought about how babies ended up in your belly until now. According to the girls at school, filling the air with whispers and giggles, sitting on the lavatory was rumoured to lead to a surprise baby. For years, Ellie had believed them, resulting in her squatting above the seat instead of sitting on it. Stupid! What a fool. All this time with Harold and she pretended she knew what he was talking about for fear of appearing silly. But now her heart felt lighter and more assured, knowing she had found someone she could trust and rely on. 'Don't worry. It's part of life,' he'd explained. It was embarrassing and fascinating all at the same time. Perhaps her dad was right. She wasn't that bright after all.

The aroma of coffee and bread drifted from the restaurant, enticing Ellie. The housemaid moved gracefully along the hall, the loud drone of the vacuum cleaner accompanying her every step. She smiled, acknowledging Ellie.

'Ellie, good morning.' Mrs J came through the revolving door. 'Come with me and I'll show you your duties.'

Ellie jolted herself from the memories of Friday night to face the reality of Tuesday morning. Mrs J led the way and showed her how to greet the guests, file, and use the telephone.

During the morning, Ellie checked in the latest arrivals and provided the key to their room. Mrs J told her she had to smile and make them feel welcome no matter how she felt. The guests came first. Having watched the reception staff over the last few months, it all seemed natural to her. She belonged there.

The hours flew by. When Ellie glanced at the clock on the wall, it was almost the end of the working day. She handed the safe keys to the night porter as instructed, and by five o'clock it was time to leave.

'You did very well, Ellie,' said Mrs J. 'If you can take in all this information as quickly as you did today, you are certainly a fast learner. Well done, and thank you. So off you pop now – see you tomorrow, same time.'

Ellie hurried along the promenade. As she made her way home, she couldn't help but feel a new-found sense of growth and self-assurance. With Harold's love and support, she felt confident and ready to explore the possibilities of her future in her new job. It was time to tell her father. She'd kept it from him in case it didn't go well that day.

'Dad, I got the job in reception.'

Ernest, as usual, was reading the *Evening Gazette*. 'Oh yes, Ellie, that's nice. I hope you'll be able to do it,' he said.

'Of course I can do it! I told you I could. I'm not as daft as you think, you know.'

Ellie gave a deep sigh. Her father still took more of an interest in Tommy. She wished he had shown some sign of being happy for her, but she could tell by his appearance that he wasn't feeling well that day. Strands of his greying hair had become whiter, and his features were more drawn. As Ellie looked at him, she couldn't help but notice the tiredness etched into his face, with deep folds of skin under his eyes. He looked very sick indeed.

'Did you get a pay rise?' he asked, clearing his throat.

She decided not to tell him. 'I don't know yet. It's too early to say.'

'Didn't they tell you before you started? Oh well, that's good, then, Ellie, eh? It'll keep you out of trouble.' He returned to reading his newspaper.

Ellie went to her room. Her heart was with Harold now, and nothing else mattered. She'd make it on her own, be more robust and less like a child playing with her doll, being seen and not heard. The time for change was *now*. It was best to keep quiet and say nothing, but how could she succeed without support from her family? She had never wanted to be seen as a rebellious child. If only someone had sat down and explained everything. Why was being Ellie Brownlee so difficult?

Chapter Five

As autumn turned to winter, Ellie's new job helped build her self-belief. She loved meeting the guests, taking the time to greet each one warmly, and took genuine interest in their needs.

'Keep up the good work, Ellie,' Mr Phelps had praised her, a smile spreading across his face.

Mrs J's voice, soft yet firm, filled the office with warmth as she said, 'Yes, you're doing fine,' the words a soothing balm.

That evening, Harold invited her to a young people's dance. Agnes gave her permission, but, as always, there were conditions regarding what time Ellie must return home.

'Mam, I'm coming home an hour later than usual because that's when the dance finishes and Harold is teaching me.'

With deep reluctance, Agnes gave a frown and said nothing.

'Thanks.' Ellie smiled. 'Harold's an excellent dancer. He won a competition last month with his dance club partner, Kathy. '

'As long as you behave yourself, that's all I'm concerned about.'

'Of *course*. What else do you think I'll do?' Why did her mother have to spoil everything? Perhaps soon she will get her wishes, Ellie reflected. Harold might be called up, and then they really would be apart. She darted away from her thoughts; that idea was something she couldn't take right now.

On arrival at The Spa, Ellie ordered a lemonade. They met a couple of older school friends before Harold took her in his arms to teach her how to waltz.

'Follow me around the floor, forward, side, together,' he repeated.

Ellie danced until she caught the rhythm of the steps.

'One, two, three, that's it, on your toes. Well done.'

Ellie recalled she had gone to ballet and tap lessons for a year when she was eight, but then Agnes couldn't afford it any more, and she'd had to stop. She'd cried the next day: the only thing she really loved, and her mother had taken it away. She supposed it wasn't her fault.

'Right, here we go, on your toes, forward, side, together. Put your hand on my shoulder, that's it. Very good. There, see, I knew you could do it. Now follow me, and try not to tread on my toes.' Harold laughed.

Ellie watched the dancers, their feet a blur of motion across the polished floor, copying their every move with grace and finesse. She quickly became one with the scene, joining in the waltz with everyone else. If only she could make this a part of her everyday routine, relishing the bright lights, the rhythmic music, and the swirling dancers of the dance hall. Perhaps now was the right time to leave home and seek a different path in life. Despite being a lovely town, Saltburn seemed lifeless during the winter months. She couldn't live like this for much longer.

'Next time, I'll teach you the foxtrot,' Harold said.

As they walked home, Ellie felt the pain of her unfamiliar high heels, and Harold stopped in the alley to kiss her.

'One day, Ellie Brownlee, I *will* marry you.'

Ellie giggled. 'Honestly, Harold, I never know if you are serious when you say that.'

'I'm serious. Of course I'm serious. I want us to be together – always.'

Ellie smiled. Something beautiful she couldn't explain stirred within her, and she wished she could marry him at this very moment. 'I love you, Harold. You are the best thing to happen to me.'

'And you for me,' Harold assured with a kiss.

They walked on in the shadows of the back alley, and Ellie

stopped to fix her shoe. She cringed with pain at the blister on her heel. Harold helped her to stand and pressed himself against her. He knew he shouldn't, but couldn't resist.

'Are you feeling chilly?' she asked.

'No, I feel very…loving.' He held her closer.

In the dark, cold evening, the moon cast shadows from the walls, and there was only the sound of the occasional passer-by on the main road. A dog barked in someone's yard. Harold unbuttoned Ellie's coat, put his arm around her waist, and embraced her tenderly against the alley wall.

'Ellie, I love you. I love you so much.'

Ellie shivered. 'I'm cold, Hal. Keep hold of me.' His brother had called him Hal and Ellie liked it.

Harold looked into the clear night sky, where the stars twinkled and the moon shone on the rooftops and chimneys. He needed this. His conscience said no, but he'd harboured his emotions for too long. As they kissed, Ellie pulled in a sharp breath as Harold put his hand on hers to guide her to the right place.

'El, I love you. We're hoping to get married, and I want you to know how it is. Yeah?' he whispered in her ear. 'Understand?' He knew it would be unthinkable to make love to her just now. All he wanted was to feel her soft skin under his hands, a place he'd never touched before but something he'd longed to do. It had been a romantic evening, filled with whispered words and stolen glances. Ellie slid her hand to where it was warm and strange.

'Leave it there, love. It makes me feel so good.' He gave a deep sigh of extreme pleasure.

He slipped his hand down her blouse, and with a gush of deep emotion she allowed him to caress her. Of course, why not? She loves me, and I love her. He followed his feelings, breathing hard. It seemed so natural and beautiful. He wanted to shed tears as a sense of calm flowed through him. He moved his hands to the waist of her skirt and undid the buttons at the back. Then around the front to the mound below her belly, where he smoothed his hands across her.

'I don't want a baby, Hal. Please don't.'

'It's okay. You won't if we do this,' he whispered. 'I promise not to go the whole way with you. We'll save that for when we get married. I love you, El. I would never hurt you.'

A bark ripped through the quiet – the dog's sharp yap a stark contrast to the creeping suspense Harold was building – a sound that brought the nearness of houses into painfully sharp focus. But who cared?

'What did we do?' Ellie exhaled.

'It's…you know, what we spoke about.' Harold took out a clean handkerchief. 'It's okay, El – that's normal after I… I had the same feelings as you. I wanted to show you what love is all about, El, without us…well, you know. It's okay. It's my first time, too. I wanted to find out what it would be like to do it *with* you instead of…' He stopped for a breath.

'Oh, I love you, Harold Dean.' She wondered what he had done to make her feel like that. It made her want to cry tears of overwhelming happiness. She hoped no one had been listening.

Ellie saw him put away his handkerchief. As she buttoned her skirt, a subtle smile played on her lips, a silent acknowledgement of her ability to please him.

'I hope you enjoyed that, and you had your first one… Are you okay?' he whispered.

'My first what, Hal?'

'Orga…oh, never mind.' He furrowed his brow. 'It was lovely, eh?' He kissed her again, glad he hadn't gone too far with her. 'Love you lots.'

She fastened the buttons on her blouse and smoothed it down. 'What time is it? Oh flippin' 'eck, I'm half an hour late home. Mam will kill me. I'll have to tell her we forgot the time.'

'I suppose we did,' Harold said, his grin widening. 'Thanks, Ellie Bee, you were great. I shall never forget this moment.' He gazed into her eyes and wiped the tears of joy from her face. He put his arm around her shoulder. 'Come on,' he said. 'We ought to go home. Thanks, El, you're mine forever.'

Agnes waited by the front door. 'Where on earth have you been, young lady? You are late, your father is coughing his guts out, and I've been waiting here in the cold for almost an hour.'

'Sorry, Mrs Brownlee, but we forgot what time it was. We were having such a great dance, and now Ellie has a blister on her heel, so we ambled home.' Harold smiled at her, hoping he could calm the situation.

'I don't like it when you go down to The Spa – you two are still too young to mix with them sort of folks.'

Harold looked at Agnes and frowned. 'Sorry, I'll make sure it doesn't happen again. G'night, El. See you tomorrow.' He smiled at Ellie as he left the gate to walk through the back alley toward Coral Street and make his way home.

'I'll be having words with your mother, Harold, about this,' Agnes called after him.

'Harold's not a child, for goodness sake!'

'Get inside and don't be so impertinent,' Agnes retorted, shoving Ellie on the shoulder to push her into the hallway. 'I'm not letting you go down there again if you can't be trusted to return on time. All this lovey-dovey stuff. It's silly to get involved with Harold like this. I'm not blind, you know.'

'Ouch! It's not about "letting" me. I'm not a kid any more in case you hadn't noticed.'

Ellie had reached her breaking point. How dare her mother shove her around like that?

Anyway, what's wrong with being in love? Is it not a beautiful feeling that can make your heart flutter? Had her mother never felt the warmth of love's embrace? She had never witnessed her mother and father being affectionate with each other. Mr and Mrs Dean still had that warm, fuzzy feeling in their hearts. In an awkward moment, she had glimpsed Mr Dean tenderly kissing his wife in the kitchen. In Ellie's house, affectionate gestures like kisses were noticeably absent. Ellie patted her cheeks; they were still warm and rosy from kissing Harold.

'Get to your room!'

As she walked away, she could still hear the angry echo of Agnes's voice following her.

'And we shall see about you going out with Harold again this week,' her mother said sternly, her voice filled with disapproval.

'Mam, I wish you trusted me more!' Ellie paused at the top of the landing, refusing to be stirred by her mother's rants. She took a breath and went to her room. As she lay on her bed, her hands reached to where Harold had placed his. Oh, those feelings. She closed her eyes and peace and serenity overtook her thoughts. She had learned so much more about life since going out with him. Marriage could be her only way out of this horrible detention. He had been so gentle with her, and they hadn't "done it", only sort of so she need not worry.

Ellie shut her eyes, feeling the weight of exhaustion settle upon her. Sleep was the only thing on her mind, as she yearned for peaceful dreams to whisk her away.

As usual, Ellie walked to work. She wore her red muffler with matching gloves and quickened her step to escape the cold.

As the bitter November morning progressed, Ellie worked in the office until Bea asked her to come into the staffroom for an early tea break.

'I'm glad they agreed not to go to war. Harold won't have to join up after all. If he did, I dread to think what would happen to me. I'd die if I lost him.'

As Eva sat smoking her cigarette, she couldn't help but overhear snippets of the conversation. 'I wouldn't speak too soon about conscription, Ellie,' she cautioned, her voice filled with uncertainty. 'I bet Hitler isn't going to give up, you know.'

Bea sucked in her breath, realising Eva had spread doom and

gloom in the cosy staffroom. 'Let's not worry too much. We'll have to wait and see. Let's enjoy ourselves while we have time on our side. Neville Chamberlain told us some weeks ago to sleep soundly now.'

Ellie looked out the window and gazed dreamily at the sea views across the cliffs. She thought it was better to change the subject. 'I love our tea breaks. It gives us all the chance to have a natter.' She turned to Bea. 'You've taught me such a lot since I arrived here. I thought I'd hate this job, but, thanks to you, I don't. Hotel life has a family atmosphere. Remember Mrs Harcourt, who stayed here last week?'

'Yes, lovely woman,' Bea said. 'She told me the same thing because she comes to Saltburn twice a year from Newcastle. She told me the noise of the trains don't bother her and it's generally quiet here. She said she didn't want anything to change. I believe she's an artist and enjoys spending time in the Italian Gardens.'

Ellie also wanted nothing to change; only her mother, and sometimes her father. With all her heart, she wished they would accept Harold.

As Ellie went about her work, the thoughts in her head about Eva's comments made her anxious. She typed with a cover over the keys, as Eva had shown her how to touch-type. For an hour each day, Ellie practised on the home keys, A-S-D-F-G-F, space, using her thumb for the space bar, and, semi colon L-K-J-H-J, on the right hand, before making short words out of the letters without looking at the keyboard. Eva wouldn't allow her to move on until she had six lines, error free. Her mind often wandered to the lovely feelings after her evenings with Harold. She realised they had brought them closer than she could ever have imagined. Drat it! She'd made a typing error. Start again.

Chapter Six

July 1939, and all talk of war had increased tenfold. Listening to the radio became a daily ritual. As he sat on the train, thinking about his life, Harold regretted that Mrs Brownlee's wishes would probably come true. What if he and Ellie had to go their separate ways, and how could he possibly tell her he was leaving?

Harold arrived home to find his father looking pensive and stern in his armchair.

'Hi, Pop. What's up?'

'Harold, son, we need to talk, but have a cuppa tea first, lad.'

Harold knew that a cup of tea always put things right in their house. Had something happened to his mother? But then Betty walked in with a tray and a pot of tea for three and poured. Harold felt relieved that his mother was well, but the stern expression on both his parents' faces made him wonder what he'd done.

'Ma? Pop?'

'How's Ellie?' Betty asked.

'She's fine, and I wondered if we will marry before I join up.'

'Believe me, Harold, this is not the best time, dear. Our lives are about to change in a way you have never seen, which I know isn't easy. Marriage is the last thing you will think about.' Betty darted a glance at Alf supping his tea.

'You know all this talk of war? We heard today that the Germans invaded Poland,' Alf said.

'Yes, I saw the headlines too. Dreadful.' Harold shook his head in despair.

'You know what this means, son? It'll happen, with that government letter you got and all the warnings in the newspapers.

I think Hitler signed that agreement with crossed fingers behind him – all false hope.'

'I'm not keen to leave, of course, but we've been discussing what we'll do for the last few weeks, Ellie and me. You know, Pop, I'm prepared, and so is she. I think it's time I did something good for our country. I'm just upset to leave Ellie behind.'

Alf frowned. 'I'm not so sure, Harold, if this is *good*. You and Ellie are still very young. In the last war, what I saw was enough to ruin me for life – and what was it for? I'd reached a time where I wanted peace and to run my little shop without interference.'

Betty chimed in to change the mood. 'How do you feel about joining up?'

'I don't want to.' Harold shrugged his shoulders. 'But it'll be fine again when I return in a few weeks. I'll miss Ellie very much. It seems like we've been friends forever. Well, we have, I suppose.'

His father sighed. 'Harold, son, it could be months, years even, before you return. I heard there's a rumour about women volunteering as well, but I don't think it will happen. During the Great War, everyone thought it would be over by Christmas, and four years later – total carnage! Your lives will change – *you* will change. These are strange times. What you plan now won't be the same by next year. Let's not beat about the bush here, lad. It's a case of saying, "*If* you come back." I hate to sound pessimistic, but be prepared. Even you and Ellie may not be together.' Alf looked at Harold over the top of his spectacles. 'I'm no longer here to give advice, Harold. This is not a war of my generation. This is *your* war. It will determine your fate and that of our family. Be strong now. You will fight for Ellie to keep her safe, and everyone else around you, including us!'

Betty dug in her pocket for her handkerchief and turned away with tears in her eyes. She knew that Harold's world had fallen apart. Life without Harold and Ellie would be unthinkable. Betty felt an overwhelming sense of belonging as she embraced the strong bond she shared with Ellie, filling the void of never having had a daughter.

'We now have to defend our country from that dreadful German dictator. He's a menace.' Betty sniffed. 'I don't want you to go either, Harold. It's a mother's nightmare.'

Harold saw the tears in his mother's eyes.

'If we lose, we might all end up as Germans if we don't act now,' Alf said. 'None of us wants that! Naturally, it concerns me a lot, but you have to get out there and do what must be done. If Hitler can invade Poland, he'll do it to us too, with no warning! Your ma's right, Harold. He's a menace and has to be stopped. I disagree with the war, but there are things we must face and be brave.'

Harold felt he had matured – and all in the space of five minutes. His father's stern words and furrowed brow meant "Sit up and listen!" He imagined himself in army uniform, and closed his eyes briefly, but the longer he tried to shut it out, the more the vivid image refused to disappear. It was the uncertainties. His parents had rarely spoken to him that way; it unsettled him.

'They're announcing it on Sunday, so don't you go gallivantin' off somewhere. Instead, stay at home. The whole family can listen to the radiogram. Of course, Ellie is welcome, but she'll likely want to be with her family.' Betty sighed.

'I'll see her tonight. This couldn't have come at a worse time. I hope I'm not away for Christmas – it'll be a family tragedy. We've never spent it apart.'

Harold sat, staring into the burning embers of the fire in the hearth. At this moment, he wished he could be somewhere else, and gulped in a breath to stay focused. What would happen next? If he had to be the one to help save his family, then so be it.

That evening, Harold and Ellie bought tickets for the picture house. At the show's end, it was dark outside, and they took a path beside the railway track. When no one was around, they kissed. He wanted to love her, and felt torn between being here and his father telling him not to disgrace the family. Oh, how much he wanted to get closer to her. At this rate, they would never be this close again.

'Damn the bloody war! Why does it have to be like this?' Harold said.

'I don't know what to say. It's awful,' Ellie replied.

'It'll be all right. I promise to return to you, love. I'm strong, El, and I can look after myself, honestly.'

'Oh, Hal, I'm scared I won't see you again.' Ellie sniffed.

'Look, it hasn't happened yet. Let's not get so worried until we know for sure.' The thought made him feel sick, but when his thoughts had turned to travel, he'd felt this was the right time to do it – but not in a war zone! 'I'll always love you, El.' Harold kissed her again and then pulled away. 'No, I can't do this, El. I want you more than ever, but right now, it doesn't seem right. Let's go home. It's too tempting.'

Ellie gazed into his eyes and then hugged him. 'I'm really sad. It's so, so cruel, isn't it?'

They made their way home, holding hands and saying nothing. Harold only had one thing on his mind. Was this the end of an era? Bloody Hitler!

Part Two

The War Years

1939–1945

Chapter Seven

3 September 1939

Ernest shuffled in his slippers across the carpet to turn on the radio.

'Come on, Dad, cough it up.' Ellie patted him on the back and made a yucky face at the black sputum he'd coughed into the bowl. 'Take a deep breath. Sit down. You should've asked me to turn it on.' She helped him to his chair.

'Come on, Tommy, let's sit down and listen.' Ernest wiped his lips.

Tommy shuffled on a chair, biting his thumbnail.

'Sit still, Tommy,' Agnes commanded. 'Listen to the news. It's important.'

The voice of the announcer came over the air. *'At 11.15am Mr Chamberlain broadcast to the nation the following statement: "I am speaking to you from the Cabinet Room at 10 Downing Street. This morning the British Ambassador in Berlin handed the German government a final note stating that unless we heard from them by eleven o'clock that they were prepared at once to withdraw their troops from Poland, a state of war would exist between us. I have to tell you now that no such undertaking has been received, and that consequently this country is at war with Germany. You can imagine what a bitter blow it is to me that all my long struggle to win peace has failed. Yet I cannot believe that there is anything more, or anything different, that I could have done and that would have been more successful."'*

Agnes gazed at Ernest. The silence in the room became a frozen moment. Ellie held her breath. Visions of Harold in uniform made her want to collapse on the floor and cry floods of tears. Why did this have to happen when they had so many beautiful plans?

Tommy broke the silence. 'Will you have to go too, Dad?'

'Nah, not me, son. I'm no use to them at my age, and I'm not fit enough.' Ernest gave another rasping cough. 'I'll need you to help me, lad.'

'Hush, Tommy. Listen to the radio,' Agnes scolded.

Ellie waited to hear if they would mention anything about the call-up.

'"*You may be taking part in the fighting services or as a volunteer in one of the branches of civil defence. If so, you will report for duty in accordance with the instructions you have received. You may be engaged in work essential to the war for the maintenance of the life of the people – in factories, in transport, in public utility concerns or in the supply of other necessaries of life. If so, it is of vital importance that you should carry on with your jobs.*"'

'Will I have to go too, Dad?' asked Ellie.

'I doubt it, love. Women may be needed at home if all the men go to war.'

'They won't call up the women,' said Agnes. 'You'll have to stay at home for a while yet, until we hear more.'

Ellie stood, masking her tears, and made her way to the window. A jackdaw stood on the wall in the yard, and she watched it fly away. Wings would be useful at a time like this. She didn't want to stay home a moment longer than necessary.

Agnes gave a look of defiance. 'Bloomin' war, it's just like last time. Pointless.'

'No, Aggie, we have to do it. We must stand proud,' said Ernest. 'If she is needed, then so be it. You don't want that dreadful dictator to take over our country, 'cause the bugger will if we sit back and let him. I mean, he's already taken Czechoslovakia, and now it's Poland, then God knows it'll be the rest of us. No, I have to say, I favour this war. I wouldn't wish to be under the jurisdiction of the Germans. Let our lads do their job!'

Agnes shot him a withering glare before storming away, leaving behind an aura of frustration and sadness.

Ernest turned toward where Ellie stood gazing out of the window. 'El, how are you feeling, lass?'

Ellie furrowed her brow. 'I dunno. I feel as if someone has taken away everything I ever owned.'

'What's the matter with you?' asked Tommy.

Ernest piped in. 'She's upset. It's only natural. You'll have to help as well, Tommy. They'll need us all to chip in I suppose. We never got over the previous war, and now those bloody Germans are at it again.'

Dad's never going to manage the allotment, thought Ellie. Not in his state of health. She had a sudden thought of, what if he died? She shut out her morbid thoughts and wished Tommy would stop yakking on.

'Does that mean Harold is going to die?' asked Tommy.

'For God's sake, Tommy, shut up!' Ellie decided this was the last straw.

'No, it doesn't have to be like that, son. I mean, you wouldn't have been born if I hadn't made it back, d'ye see?'

By the look on Tommy's face, he didn't see. Ellie squeezed her eyelids together; she wouldn't cry in front of everyone. Why did they have to talk like that?

'What about Mr Dean? Is he too old as well?' asked Tommy.

'I expect so, and I believe he had a bad time in the last war, like the rest of us. I suspect, in any case, he'll be needed here to run the shop. We all have to eat, ya know.'

Ellie's face paled. She left the sitting room and ran upstairs, feeling lost and dumbfounded. What was she going to do without Harold?

'Hal, are you really going to join up?' asked Ellie.

They walked hand in hand along the clifftop, Sammy trotting beside them.

'I'll get the call-up papers soon, but I think I'll volunteer. It'll give me plenty of time to get used to it.'

'Volunteer?' Ellie's expression changed to one of deep sadness, and tears filled her eyes. Biting her trembling lip, she looked out to sea and tried to be brave, but the sound of distant herring gulls made her feel sad again.

'We have to do it, El. Every man who's fit enough must fight this Hitler bloke. Our pop says he's a bloody menace. He'll try to take over everything we ever owned, and we might have to speak German instead of English.'

Ellie's jaw dropped in horror. 'You can't mean that, surely?'

He stopped in mid-stride to wipe her tears. 'Well...we might.' Harold tried to smile. 'Pop tells me we have to expect anything now. I mean, our lives could change for the worse. There are people in Poland with no food, starving to death, and it could happen to us if Hitler invades here. Now do you see?'

Ellie knew how much Harold cared about other people, especially his family. 'When are you going, Hal?' She sniffed. 'I don't want you to go.'

'El, my love, I'll be back before you know it but I won't have any option.' He paused. 'It's on Thursday. After that, I have to report for duty the next day.'

'What? So soon?' Ellie widened her eyes. 'Oh no.'

'You'll need to be brave, love. I want to see you smiling in my head when I close my eyes at night. It's a decision made *for* me, not *by* me.'

'It's too quick.'

'When the boss says jump, you jump. That's what Pop told me. He said the army is a place for real men, and no, Ma and Pop don't want me to go either, but I've no choice. Be proud of me, love. I need to know you feel proud.' Harold turned toward her. 'Come here. Let me hold you.' He reached out to her. 'I'll write as much as I can.'

Ellie hated the finality and folded herself into his arms.

'When I get back, I promise to marry you and shower you with affection, making love to you like never before.' Mid-sentence, he paused and stole another kiss from her. 'Listen,' he pleaded, his voice filled with desperation. 'El, wait for me, please.'

'Of course I will, Hal. But if you don't come back, then what?'

Harold took in a sharp breath, his eyes avoiding hers. 'You must live your life to the full, enjoy what you have, and be brave. I will return to you. Yes, I will, but things will inevitably change. Promises, elusive as they may be, are not always within our grasp. I'm only going by what Pop told me.'

His words, laced with a heartbreaking sadness, confirmed her deepest fear: she might never see him again. Yet, how would she cope without him?

He smiled and kissed her again. 'Love you, El. Okay, let's make a plan. When I return, we'll get married and not wait a minute longer. That's a promise. No one knows what the future holds. But let's not go there. I'll do my best, but in the army, you're not in control, the army controls you.'

They walked silently. Harold seemed deep in thought, and Ellie held her breath to avoid the sobs.

'Hal... Hal, talk to me.' Ellie grimaced as the wind blew a chilling blast into her face. She saw the screwed-up look on Harold's face. He was almost mumbling to himself, cursing the cold. 'I'll be there for you, Hal – we'll write to each other daily.'

'Yes, we will. Pop said the mail doesn't reach the front line quickly, but it's like a birthday when it does. Your letters will keep you in my thoughts.'

'Where are you going first?' Ellie blew her nose.

'We must report to the Drill Hall in Redcar to enlist and begin our journey there. After that, I could be anywhere. I've no idea. Apparently, they don't tell you anything until the last moment.'

'Well, that's not very far away.'

'No, but we're not stopping there. I could be in Germany in a few days or some other country. Who knows? They're evacuating the children from the cities to places in the countryside. I saw it on the newsreel when I went to the flicks last night. Pop suggested I watch the latest newsreel to get an idea of what is to come. I knew your mother wanted you to look after your dad so there was no point in asking you to come as well. The youngest of those kids was only five years old – if you'd seen his face, it was heartbreaking. He looked so lost without his ma, so I must do something for the sake of those young 'uns. You should've seen them walking along the street, carrying Mickey Mouse gas masks and small suitcases. It shocked me. I have to do this for them, too. At least my brothers don't have to leave. Oh, bloody hell! I wish I didn't have to go either. It's distressing.'

Ellie knew all too well the crushing weight of abandonment. She would want someone to help her, too. Perhaps Harold was right. He must help those who couldn't help themselves. She mustn't be selfish, but… Yes, damn the bloody war!

A few days later, Ellie and Harold walked toward home for what seemed like the very last time. They'd part away from Ellie's mother. Harold didn't want Agnes spying – not today.

'Goodbye, my darling El. Please wait for me.'

'This has to be the saddest goodbye of my whole life. Come back to me safe and sound.' Ellie sobbed. 'Oh, Hal, this is awful. Why is this happening?'

He handed her his handkerchief. 'I'll do my very best. You'll see me sooner than you think. It'll all be over before we can say "jackrabbit", although…' Harold paused to think. 'I will get some leave,' he muttered, the thought of not knowing adding to his frustration.

As their lips met, they felt a rush of warmth and their fingers slowly separated.

'Bye, Ellie. Love you always.'

With a heavy heart, Harold stood and observed her graceful departure until she faded into the distance around the corner. It seemed as if a part of his very being had been left behind. He truly loved her; he'd never felt that way about any other girl. Now, just as he'd let his guard down and believed things were going well, the ground beneath him seemed to crumble, and his world was turning upside down. He could feel the weight of anticipation, and hoped this entire ordeal would soon end.

The following day, Ellie sat in the kitchen peeling onions; a good excuse to cry, she thought.

'Well, now that boy has gone away, you will look after your own family instead of spending time with *him*,' said Agnes.

'What is it with you, Mam? Can't you be nice for a change? I'll always love Harold, and no matter what you do, he'll return to me, I know he will.'

'Listen, young lady. There is a war on now. Anything could happen to Harold, and I think you ought to realise that life will not be a bed of roses. Your father isn't doing well these days. He needs a lot of care – you'll have to help look after him.'

'Yes, I realise.' Her mam was right. It couldn't have been easy for her.

'I need you to work hard. It's now a case of "put up and shut up". God knows what the government has in mind – we haven't even started. This won't end in a few weeks, you know. I went through the last war – it was terrible. You've no idea, have you?' Agnes sniffed and left the room, grumbling to herself.

Agnes had got her own way in the end. Ellie sighed and sensed a touch of irony. She scraped the potatoes her mother had left on the table. Her mother's paranoia was because of her overpowering anxiety about her father, and Ellie wished she would talk to her more about her worries. Harold had given her the strength to see life from a different perspective. She wanted her family to be like the Deans, easy-going and understanding. Would it ever happen? Oh heck. Life was very confusing. She'd try harder now to make peace with her mother.

Chapter Eight

It was a Tuesday morning when Ellie received her first letter from Harold. She smiled at his handwriting and slit the flimsy envelope with a letter opener.

Dorman's Hall
Middlesbrough
Private 4390597
Dean, Harold
28 September 1939
My darling Ellie,

Well, here we are, learning how to be soldiers! I have to finish this letter this afternoon, 'cause we're moving out of here.

First, I passed the interview in Redcar with the recruitment officer and the medical examination with all the blood tests. It was funny because a couple of the lads here fainted at the sight of their own blood. I shouldn't laugh, I know.

After signing up and receiving our uniform, we finally arrived at Dorman's Hall in Middlesbrough. Despite many unfounded complaints from some of the men, I can't deny that the food is delicious. Spark's Café is catering for us, and today I had a mouth-watering pork dinner that left me craving for more. They provided us with palliasses, which were just as comfortable as my feather bed back home. Our office, in the ladies' cloakroom, offers a cosy and warm atmosphere. I sleep well there by myself but I don't know how long we'll be here. We didn't get any time off in Redcar – otherwise, I'd have telephoned you at our shop. I wrote to Ma and Pop and now await a reply.

I'm sure I will say many things in my letters, but the main thing is I love you very much. A lot is happening here to keep us busy. I can't write any more as there is loads of work. The army isn't bad so far.

All my love,

Harold x

Ellie fingered the letter. She reread the words and hugged it close to her. He was safe for the time being. Thank the Lord! His sense of confidence strengthened her feelings.

The scent of freshly laundered clothes hung in the air as Ellie folded her last blouse; then, a firm knock startled her. She opened the front door.

'Hello, Mrs Dean. Mam is out now. Would you like to come in, and I'll make us a drink? Tea or coffee?'

Betty seemed to detect the sadness in Ellie's voice. 'Coffee, please. I haven't seen you since Harold left. How are you, Ellie?'

'I got news from Harold. He wants to know if you got his letter?'

'Yes, we did.' Betty smiled. 'We got it yesterday – I'm in the middle of replying. Harold's moved to Middlesbrough. Anyway, sorry I haven't been to see you, but how are you feeling, love?'

'As expected, Mrs Dean, thank you. Life won't be the same without him, will it? I wish he could have phoned, but he told me there wasn't any time.'

'Don't make it sound so final, Ellie. He'll be home soon, you know. We're all in this together.'

Betty kept giving Ellie a sympathetic smile while listening to her discuss her future. After a while, there wasn't a lot more to say.

Ellie lowered her voice. 'Our mam will return soon. Dad hasn't been well again. He's in bed upstairs, asleep. I'm looking after him while Mam is helping with the kids' gas masks at the WI. He was very poorly last week, but the weather has improved, and he seems brighter now.'

'Sorry to hear about your dad. I hope he'll get better. He's been so ill, hasn't he? We'll have to do without a lot of things soon. He'll need all the fresh food he can get. I'll speak with Alf and see what we can do. Have you heard what the prime minister said on the radio? We have to produce the greatest volume of food now. No plot is too small. I'm glad Harold is well fed. You know how he loves my Yorkshire puds.'

Ellie gave a polite smile. Her head was spinning, and she wasn't coping. All this chit-chat about the war would take time to get used to.

After a while, Betty stood to leave. 'Thanks, Ellie, for the coffee. It's been lovely talking to you. Perhaps you can come and see us soon. Take care of yourself, and don't worry. You can do nothing except support Harold the best way you know how, and I know you will. Bye, Ellie, love. See you soon.' She kissed Ellie on the cheek. 'Oh, and, Ellie, isn't it about time you called me Betty?'

Ellie gave her a hug. 'Bye. And thanks. You've been very kind to me, and I really appreciate it.'

Betty departed, and Ellie closed the door behind her. If only her mother were as easy-going.

A few days later, Ellie received a card from Harold. It was short, with a promise to reply soon.

> *I love and miss you, but I will write a longer letter when I've more time. It's hard work doing all this soldiering.*

She had already posted hers and couldn't wait to hear his next piece of news.

At the end of November, Harold wrote again. In her excitement, Ellie's fingers, clumsy and sticky with anticipation, fumbled as she tried to tear the envelope.

> *HQ Company*
> *4th Bn. The Green Howards*
> *Moreton-in-Marsh*
> *Gloucestershire*

My dearest El,

Thanks for your lovely letter. I haven't been able to write before this. We have been so busy training, and keeping in touch is hard. Sorry, love – I didn't mean for you to wait so long.

I miss you very much, and I'm trying not to think about the distance between us because I've moved south. As you can see, we're now in Moreton-in-Marsh for further training. It's in the Cotswolds, and all the houses have this lovely sandy-coloured stone. We arrived here after a long, weary ride, at three o'clock in the morning. I feel settled but tired and hope to get to bed early. We just arrived as a layer of snow fell. Winter is upon us once again. The countryside is marvellous, and the snow seems to enhance the scenery – it's like a Christmas card. Still, I sometimes despair at why I have to do this. Perhaps with time, I'll get used to it. When I said I wanted to travel, I didn't think of doing it as a soldier in the army.

Our ma sent me a pork pie, which I guzzled down, and now I'm just about to fry a pound of kidney and make a bowl of potato soup; it will make a delicious supper.

I've learned that being a soldier means doing lots of hard work, and I'm not sure how rewarding it is. I'm falling asleep standing up, with all that slog and lots of marching up and down. My muscles are sore, and I have blisters on my toes, but we know about blisters, don't we? Remember?

It won't be long before I can't tell you where I am or much about what I'm doing in the camps. Then my letters will not be so exciting as I won't be able to talk about army life, even to you. They won't even let me put kisses on the bottom of the letter in case it's a coded message. Everything is censored, but I'll mean it when I write to you and tell you I'm fine and you don't have to worry about me.

When I go to bed, I think about you. I have your photo in my pocket and kiss you every night. We must think of each other at the same time. Maybe ten o'clock every evening?

The 4ᵗʰ Battalion had our group photos taken today. It will be interesting to see if anyone can see me because I was shunted into the middle behind the officers.

Two days later – sorry!

It's a bit of a lost world down here. It's a village with a picture house which is too small for all us army lads. So, I haven't been out lately. We are billeted in a place that was once a school many years ago, and it has lovely fires in two rooms. I've bought cooking utensils, and we cook eggs and bacon for breakfast.

Life here is very different. We don't get up until seven each day. Since we have Wednesdays off every week, I find myself slipping back into laziness. I've made loads of new friends, and it's been amazing getting to know each of them. It's chilly here now, which means I'll have to ask our ma to send my other pullover as I forgot to pack it.

Each day, I hope to find a letter in my mailbox, but I'm left feeling let down when it doesn't materialise. It's likely that I'll start missing you and home a lot more than ever, but I suppose I'll figure out how to deal with it.

I bought tobacco and now smoke a pipe. It took a while, but now I have the knack, it looks good and suits me!

Keep smiling, my darling. Remember, part of you goes everywhere with me. I love you with all my heart, and we shall celebrate in style when I come home. Hope to see you soon.

Yours with love,

Harold

Ellie sat alone with her letter. It was great to hear how he was doing. During the next hour, she reread it four times, savouring every word. Smoking a pipe, eh? As she visualised him cooking bacon and eggs, the mouth-watering scents of sweet tobacco and sizzling bacon filled her imaginary senses. At least Harold has everything he wants – except me. With a sigh, she folded the delicate letter, tucking it carefully into the worn, wooden cash box. The small brass key clicked shut, sealing its secrets, before she slid it under the feather mattress away from prying eyes.

In the solitude of her room, Ellie immersed herself in the words of the letter, finding peace and connection. With her monotonous routine, there was hardly anything for her to write about in reply. Recalling the days when she had spent her time drinking tea, dunking a biscuit and chatting with Bea, they were not as comforting any more. And with the war, guests were fewer at the hotel. What would happen to her job? Most of all, what would happen to her? She might have to spend the rest of her days living with Mam and Dad. It was like being tied to the bedpost.

Harold's train finally arrived at the station after a gruelling journey through the snow. As the carriages slowed to a stop, the squeak of brakes filled the air as he caught sight of Ellie through the carriage window. His heart pounded with anticipation as he imagined being near her once more. Pushing through the crowd of passengers waiting to disembark from the train, he struggled to contain his eagerness. As he looked around, steam filled the station from the engine. Oh, there she is, he thought, spotting her in the mist. It felt good to be home.

To the amusement of the departing passengers, the couple ran with open arms toward each other. Ellie seemed to ignore the woman who said, 'Aw, isn't that lovely?', and the man who, on stepping down from the train, reminiscing about his time in the last war, called, 'Go get her, son. Make the most of it.'

'Hello, my darling. You look wonderful,' Harold said.

Ellie gave him a joyful smile. 'Wow, so do you. Your uniform makes you look very...very—'

His kiss filled her with such passion that she had to pause briefly to take a deep breath and collect herself.

Harold's arms folded around her. 'Ma and Pop didn't make it, then?'

'Your mam wanted me to meet you – she knows how important it is to us. We're having a celebration together at your house.'

'Oh, that's smashing. Let me look at you, El. Oh my, you look so pretty – it's your hair, I like the style. I've missed you so much. Merry Christmas, my darling – I know it's early, but I won't be here on Christmas Day.'

'Oh, that *is* disappointing,' she said.

They walked arm in arm.

'God, I've missed you, El.'

They made their way toward Dean's Grocers and the house at the rear of the shop. Harold looked up to see his mother's face framed in the windowpane, a gentle smile on her lips as she looked out – he gave an enthusiastic wave.

William dashed out of the door. 'Hiya, Hal. Welcome home.' He grinned.

'Hiya, brother – not so little now, eh? It'll be your turn soon.' Harold brushed William's hair with the palm of his hand. 'How old are you now?' he teased. 'Let me think… Almost seventeen, eh? I'm twenty-one next year.' He laughed. 'Where have the last few months gone? Time is so precious these days.'

'Your life is just beginning,' Alf said, a gentle hand resting on Harold's shoulder. 'Welcome home, son.'

Betty Dean emerged from the house with open arms and hugged him.

Harold pulled away from his mother and took in a deep breath after she'd kissed him on the cheek. 'It's great to be back home,' he said. 'It seems everyone wants to squeeze me to death today. Come on, let's go inside where it's warmer.'

'I'm joining the navy soon,' William interrupted. 'I'll be able to play in the band as well.'

Betty's eyes rolled in exasperation as she placed the kettle on the stove, a signal that Harold quickly deciphered.

'What, Ma?' William questioned.

'Okay, but don't sound so delighted about it. Enjoy your time at home while you can, love.'

The fire blazed in the hearth, and Ellie warmed her feet as Harold hung up his greatcoat.

Alf smiled. 'You look very grown-up, son. Gosh, how the army makes men out of you lads – I remember it well. So, what do you think of your handsome soldier boy, Ellie?' Alf spoke through his teeth as he puffed on his pipe.

Ellie grinned. 'He looks wonderful.'

'Tell me, what've you all been doing since I left?' Harold sat beside her, clasping his hands on his chest, his feet stretched before the blazing fire.

Betty provided all the latest gossip from the town. Everyone wanted to talk at once.

'Young Paula Thomas got married last week. You remember her from school, Harold?'

'And Pete's taking care of Sammy,' interrupted William.

With pride, Peter grinned from ear to ear as he embraced his extra responsibility as a dog-sitter.

As they enjoyed their sandwiches and cake, lively conversations filled the air. 'And don't forget that time when…and if you recollect…'

'I thought you said nothing happens in our town, Ma,' Harold said with a grin. 'I'd like to stroll along the beach when we've had our sandwiches. It's been a long train journey. I need the fresh air.' The odour of seaweed on the outgoing tide and the cry of gulls always made him feel homely. 'Come on, El,' he said. 'How about a quick run down the beach with the dog, as we used to do? Do you mind, Ma? We won't be long. Wrap up, love, and we'll brave the cold.'

'Can I come?' Peter asked.

Harold hesitated.

Betty wrinkled her nose. 'Peter, pet, I need you to help me clear away these things, please. Besides, Ellie and Harold have a lot to talk about.'

Alf agreed. 'Go on, then, you two. It'll do you good. We're looking forward to hearing about your experiences when you return.'

'Okay, let's do it,' Ellie replied, and grabbed her coat.

She watched as Harold buttoned his thick army greatcoat and stood in front of the long mirror in the hall. One thing the army had taught him was how to be neat.

'Your dad made all the blackout blinds and gave some of them to us,' Ellie said. 'He's been telling me how difficult it's been to get supplies for the shop.'

'Yes, we all have to expect a harder way of living. We still don't know what will happen if we leave England. It's all very confusing right now. A lot of talk and not a lot of action.' Harold shrugged. He caught Ellie's gaze. She'd left a big hole in his life, and it was so good to get her back, even if it was only for a short while. Nothing much had changed since he was home last.

'Leave England?' Ellie queried.

'Yes — overseas is where the war is,' he sighed, the weight of the conflict evident in his tone. 'Our next course of action depends entirely on the orders we receive. We might have to go to France or Belgium, or perhaps even venture off to a completely different country.' He knew exactly where he was going, but because of signing the Official Secrets Act, he couldn't disclose any information. And regardless, it was better for her to remain unaware.

Ellie said nothing and looked away.

They walked to the end of Diamond Street as Harold continued the conversation. It was essential to inform her of how uncertain the future could be. All that training and learning about army protocol had given him a different outlook. He needed her to see that things were not as easy as she thought.

'El, my darling?'

'Yep?' Ellie turned and met Harold's gaze.

'I'm not sure when I'll see you again. I'm not allowed to tell you where I'm going, and I suspect it could be the hardest part of being away from you. The not knowing, I mean.'

'I'm sad, especially at night, thinking about you.'

'Ohhh, don't say that. I want you to keep your chin up, love, because there's a high chance I may not see you for at least a couple of months. It could be a lot longer. You must be prepared.'

Ellie's eyes filled with tears. 'Oh, for God's sake, Hal, don't… You've been so close to me for such a long time. Saltburn is drearier these days, despite your mam's gossipy news. Most men have gone, except the older ones – it's a lot quieter than it used to be.'

'Look, love, it hasn't happened yet, so don't worry. If we're lucky, it'll all blow over by the time it's decided where our lads are going, and I'll be back sooner than you think.' He tried to reassure her, but he'd learned not to make any plans, nor to blab to anyone about his life in the army.

Sammy put his paws on Ellie's knee as if he knew her distress. She patted the dog then turned toward Harold, who folded her into his coat.

'El, love,' he said in a soft, affectionate tone, 'I'll keep writing. You're a strength to me. The lads are great, they keep up my morale, but I miss being home. I'm weary now. It's very draining, but I'm getting fitter. I'll show you my muscles later,' he jested, and raised an eyebrow. It seemed to make her smile.

They strolled hand in hand along the beach toward Huntcliff on the receding tide with the wind flapping their coats from behind.

'Remember the day when we watched the sun go down?' Ellie wiped the icy drip from the end of her nose.

'How can I forget? I keep that picture in my head as much as I can.' Harold smiled. 'We both have to be very brave. Life in the army is so very different from home. Everything is geared to a plan, which has to be done at the same time every day. No wonder it's called a regiment, because everything is so strict.'

'I want to get away from Saltburn, as far away as possible from my mother and from Dad's terrible coughing. Dr Marsdon says he needs to go to the hospital again for tests. He's getting worse since the winter set in. I don't know how our mam will afford it. I'm giving her extra money for his care, but it's never enough. He's really poorly now.'

Harold turned to Ellie. 'Come here, lass. Let me hold you.' He gazed into her eyes and kissed her. A gust of wind blew across their faces. 'I want to marry you when all this is over. I keep saying it, and I hope you won't get bored of me, but if I don't return soon, please remember I'll always love you.'

'Oh, Hal, please don't talk like that. It scares me.'

'You must understand. This is real. We're not playing games like we used to play ludo. Come on, love, it's getting colder. Sammy's all wet and shivering. I'll have to get him back home. It'll be dark soon.'

They walked back along the beach toward the road with only the occasional remark about the weather. Ellie's eyes filled with tears as she squeezed her lips together. Harold tried to cheer her but realised her nodding meant she wasn't listening. He couldn't tell her much – it would be too upsetting. They arrived back with the Deans in time for more tea. In two days, he would be gone again.

Ellie couldn't wait to open Harold's letter when the mail arrived.

3 January 1940

My darling Ellie,

I received your letter and a parcel from Ma and Pop. It's terrific how they think of the things I want. The soap came in time, and the cakes, as usual, were scrumptious. Happy New Year to you.

I'm now in Weston-super-Mare, and so far, so good, but not for much longer. I'll forward an address before we leave here (which seems due to happen very soon). You must imagine you got a letter if you haven't heard from me. You won't know where I am, so there's not much difference, whether it's thirty miles or three thousand miles, as I won't be able to get home very often. As long as you keep writing, it keeps me sane.

We've had a smashing time in Weston. The dances are great fun, and the local drama group put on a show for us. I love it here as it reminds me of home. The lads here are champing at the bit just now. All are ready for action at the drop of a hat. I can't imagine they understand what we're getting ourselves into. I want to think I do, but I sometimes wonder if I will ever see you again. (Sorry to sound so down, but I'm trying to be on top of myself – honest, I am.)

Despite the freezing temperatures, the charm of Weston makes me reluctant to depart. They have a pier like Saltburn, of a similar size too. I met a fellow soldier in my regiment, and we headed to the local pub for a pint. Remember that delicious ice cream we had? This chap lives in Stokesley, just a short walk from the ice cream parlour that sells it. Anyway, it's been a much-needed break, and I can honestly say it was terrific!

I've settled down once more. At first, I didn't mind admitting it was rotten having to leave you before Christmas, but now I'm back I'm happy and ready for action (well, sort of). We have our dates **CENSORED***.*

There isn't much more for me to write about, except to say, keep your chin up. Everyone is part of the war effort now.

Missing you, my darling.

All my love,

Hal

Chapter Nine

Harold met Bernie Dewhurst in a dimly lit bar in Weston-super-Mare, the air thick with the smell of stale beer and cigarette smoke. Bernie, a Green Howard in the same battalion as Harold, had dark hair and a moustache. He projected an image of dependability and connected immediately with Harold who felt a sense of ease and hoped their paths would cross again.

'My aunt lives here. I spent a lot of time on the beach as a kid,' Bernie said. 'She owns a guest house facing the sea, just up the road. There's always something to do, despite the winter. It's a fun place. It's great to be back in the old town. I love it here,' he remarked. 'I noticed the girl you were dancing with last night had her eyes on you.'

'Really?'

'Yes, really. The lass was all over you. What was her name? I've forgotten.'

'Carol? No, it was Caroline, I think... I can't remember. I was probably drunk and falling all over *her*, more like.' Harold grinned.

Bernie shook his head. 'There isn't a lot you can do about it now. We're moving on in three days. It won't be long before women are like gold. Say goodbye to whoopee land, eh?'

'I've enjoyed myself here. It's like being on holiday,' Harold replied.

'Yeah, but you only got three more days for a spot of...you-know-what, mate. It could be your last chance before the front line. There's this place I know—'

'I'm saving myself for Ellie,' Harold interrupted.

Bernie chuckled. 'If I'd had that chance last night, I would have taken it. We're training day and night, ready for the big push. We leave port on the twelfth, so get yourself out there, mate. Do something daring!'

Harold gave a sigh. Being in the army was daring enough. He felt torn between the anticipation of going abroad and missing Ellie and his family. Three more days. Then what? He rolled his eyes and dismissed Bernie's comment. Last night had been a bit of a riot on the dance floor, so many couples jostling for space. He wished Caroline had been Ellie.

20 January 1940

Ellie sat at the reception desk with the phone almost glued to her ear. There had been plenty of phone calls that day. 'Yes, sir, I'll write her a note for you.' She wrote on a pad, folded the message, and scribbled Bea's name on the back.

She hadn't heard from Harold in three weeks. Everywhere she stood bore constant reminders of their time together. Why hadn't he written? Betty had received a short letter and passed on Harold's words, but it wasn't the same coming from her.

The hotel porter strode toward the reception desk. 'I've been called up,' he burst forth with evident glee in his tone. 'Just heard about it.'

Ellie sighed. 'You sound pleased.'

'Yeah, it'll be great. I'll be in uniform soon, away from this boring place.'

Ellie heard the lounge door squeak, and hastily reached across the desk. 'Bea, I have a message for you. Please will you telephone this number?' She passed the folded sheet of paper to Bea.

'Thanks, Ellie. It'll be our Richard. He's coming home on leave.'

Ellie's gaze moved to the porter as she leaned an elbow on the desk. 'Dennis has news for us. He's been called up.'

Bea's grimace said it all. Ellie hoped Dennis hadn't seen her expression.

'Do your best, son. That's all any of us can do these days.'

Ellie saw the weak smile on Bea's face. The impending departure of Harold's brother, William, also resonated with Ellie's understanding of the Dean family's feelings. Their kinship was being torn apart, and she was sure it wouldn't be long before the war would influence her job too. The lack of guests left the hotel strangely quiet and the empty corridors echoed with an unnerving stillness. With rationing, there were days when she missed a good helping of bacon and eggs. Harold was absolutely correct in his assessment. What had once been their beautiful world had now transformed into a ghastly nightmare. It seemed the responsibility of completing the task fell on Neville Chamberlain and his team of politicians. She'd listened to the radio with her dad but the news was depressing. Where was Harold now? And was he thinking of her? How was she supposed to feel? She recalled her dad smiling at her across the room in a caring moment. For the first time, he appeared to understand her feelings. She'd smiled back, feeling close to him. He had been good to her and cared for her and Tommy, as a father should, but there was always that unexplained distance between them, which she'd tried hard to understand and never had the answer. She'd always respected him for who he was and how hard he'd worked in the mines to support the family. Now that Harold had joined the army, perhaps she needed her dad more than ever.

The following day, Harold packed his kit and headed to Southampton to board a ship with his fellow men. Before they embarked, His Majesty the King inspected the battalions on the dockside. Harold's orders were to keep his eyes straight ahead but he couldn't help but glance in awe when the King passed by. It was freezing cold, and his fingers were numb. He wasn't allowed to shiver. But the King! He felt a sense of pride as the monarch paused to wish him a safe journey. 'Thank you, Your Majesty,' Harold replied. He wanted to jump in the air and tell the world he'd spoken to *the King*.

When the formalities of the royal visit ended, Harold strode up to the gangway with his heavy kitbag. He'd never been on a large ship, and hoped he wouldn't feel queasy. It was snowing; no one was there to wave him goodbye. This was it, the war, and he hoped to survive.

Within hours, he'd arrived in France. A new perspective on his life swallowed him. The language, the people, the food and the scenery. Was this what he'd been waiting for when he'd said he wanted to travel? But it was cold, oh so cold! French people greeted him – *'Nous sommes très heureux que vous soyez venu. Dieu merci!'* – and he was of the opinion they were more than grateful for his arrival as he passed by, which made him feel it had been worth it.

Conditions in France had become a frozen nightmare. Every task took twice as long as the week before. With the intense snow and ice, it was hard to function. Even the radiators in the trucks froze while they were running.

With everything in order, Harold retreated to a secluded spot and penned a heartfelt message to Ellie.

29 January 1940
My dearest El,

How are you, my darling? I hope you had a good New Year. Sorry this letter is late, but we have been travelling. I'm in a village somewhere. We're having quite a to-do to translate the lingo. In a week or so, I will speak more **CENSORED**. *It's very icy here. I hope you are keeping cosy and warm.*

The ship's steady movement made the crossing exceptionally smooth, allowing us to relax and enjoy the journey. Even though the boat was packed with men, we could relax and doze off the entire time (fortunately, the ship was heated!).

The blackout here is not as strict as in England, and motor cars move along the road with headlamps blazing. I've not been paid yet, and I'm already broke and rely on army supplies to get me through. The money is confusing, but I'm getting used to it. Water has to be drawn from pumps, and we must be careful of typhoid and boil it first, although the weather is another story.

The water freezes so fast that the taps don't work. I've been cooking with snow today.

El, I miss you very much. I hope we won't be in this place too long and I'll be able to come home and see you. Events have unfolded with lightning speed, leaving me with little time to process anything. You know, being whisked away from Saltburn, and then on a ship – it was like a mystery tour and we didn't know where we'd end up. Bizarre!

Have you been to visit Ma and Pop? Please tell them I'll write soon. We're so busy preparing things. Can't tell you much more. Maybe you can give them this bit of news.

I've taken to smoking cigarettes now, although I indulge in a pipe, as you know. Cigarettes here are cheap but stronger, and English ones cost sevenpence.

Guess what? I saw the King. A movie camera operator took photos of us, so maybe you'll see me on the newsreel as I was in the front rank when he came along.

Well, my darling, I have a lot of letters and other things to catch up on. Please don't worry if I don't write regularly – it's not something I can do just now – but write to me and tell me your news. It helps me through the day. I promise to dream about you every night!

All my love and kisses,

Hal

It was time to get back on the job. Harold lifted his rifle over his shoulder. Training with the 4th Battalion had become less of a game and more about surviving the war in France. He was now in a place unlike anywhere he had ever been.

Harold's training had prepared him for the British Expeditionary Force in France. It wouldn't be long before they were on their way to war: a battle of wills, and too much uncertainty. Harold realised what his father had meant about not coming back. He didn't want to consider it, especially when he'd enjoyed himself so far, but this wasn't a holiday. He'd seen the headlines about a "phoney war".

Hitler had pulled back to allow troops "time to conquer all battles". It felt safer for now, but for how long?

As the days in France ticked by, the weight of keeping Ellie in his thoughts grew heavier, transforming letter writing into a tiresome chore. Time slipped through his fingers, as if it belonged to someone else. More bloody snow! He never got warm at the end of an extremely tiring day.

A parcel arrived, filling him with a mix of despondency and gratitude. It reminded him he hadn't made it home for Christmas. He'd moved on and was now billeted in a hut with a small stove that felt much more comfortable. He felt glad he wasn't starving to death, and the food was surprisingly good. At least, Bernie thought it was. Harold smiled; his friend was a good bloke and he was glad they had met up again in France.

A picture on the wall nudged his thoughts about Ellie joining the Auxiliary Territorial Service. He'd heard that women could now volunteer. Maybe joining them would offer the distance and fresh perspective she needed to plan a new life. It had certainly done that for him. But it was the memories of being with his family that saddened him. Still, he'd have to get on with it. He was here in France now and unable to tell anyone where he was or how he felt. So near and yet so far away.

Chapter Ten

Ellie finished work for the day and arrived home from the hotel with sad news. The Zetland was closing for the war effort. Bea was in tears when Mr Phelps made the announcement. Ellie stood to comfort her.

'It is with deep regret that we'll have to leave our jobs. With the war, we have a change of use for the hotel. Next week, this building will be in the hands of the armed forces,' he said. 'It is with sorrow that everything we do from now on will be completely beyond our sense of normality. We have no option but to do as we're told. I'm sorry about this. We've worked together for a long time. Now, I wish you all success and lots of luck. That's all I can say, except to add that we close on Friday. Thanks, everyone. I hope to see you after the war is over. We have to win.'

Ellie's hand shot up to cover her mouth, stifling a gasp. She scanned the faces of the staff, and their responses only validated her thoughts. With nothing to live on, what would become of them – and her? She was responsible for her parents; her dad had been poorly when she'd left for work that morning. The whole thing was a complete and utter disaster. At the weekend, her mother had run out of coal for the fire, and they'd had to take Tommy's old bogie handcart to the beach to find driftwood. With Tommy's help, they gathered a few sacks of sea coal washed up on the shore. The scent of old newspaper mingled with the earthy smell of the sea as Agnes kept Tommy busy rolling cones to feed the fire, making it burn longer. Days passed as the damp coal stubbornly resisted drying, its smoky breath choking the room. Ernest choked, and they ushered him outside into the cold, fresh air. It didn't seem to make a lot of difference and it took over an hour to make him feel relatively better again.

The following day, Ellie received a phone call. Mrs J answered it and passed the receiver to her.

'Miss Brownlee, this is Middlesbrough Hospital. It's about your father.'

Ellie swallowed hard as she grabbed the receiver. 'What? Oh no, it can't be.' She leaned on the reception desk and cried. She listened again. 'Oh heck. No, oh no! Well, thank you for letting me know,' she choked, and replaced the receiver.

'Bad news, Ellie?' Bea put her arm around Ellie's waist.

'It's my dad. He's…he's dying.' Ellie gave a sob as she spoke. 'He's unconscious. They don't expect him to last the night. He's got pneumonia. What should I do? We don't have a telephone at home. My mother and Tommy are at the hospital with him and it'll be dark in half an hour. How will I get there in the blackout? It's miles away.'

'Go home now, Ellie. Wait for news,' Mrs J said as she placed a caring hand on Ellie's arm.

'Thanks.' Ellie grabbed her coat and hurried her goodbyes.

She ran as the snow flurried and froze on her coat, and when she arrived home she pushed her key into the door and made her way to the kitchen. Without thinking, she attempted to fill the kettle, but then cursed: the bloody tap – frozen! What was to be done? How would she get to the hospital? Why did he have to die right now? She knew her thoughts were irrational, but it was a way of relieving her anger at the world. Tears welled as she sat at the dining table, gazing at the armchair where her father always sat. His newspaper was on the floor, its pages in disarray. Ellie took a deep breath. Could she get to the hospital before he passed away if she left now? Would it be too late? It was about twelve miles from here to the hospital. Time was against her, and the cancellation of the night trains only made the situation worse. Frustrated and overwhelmed, she cursed everything around her – the war, her job, the weather, and now this!

'Oh no, no, no, no!'

Knock-knock.

Ellie straightened her hair and wiped away her tears to answer the front door.

'Hello, El, how are you, dear? I popped in to see you earlier – I'd heard about the hotel – but there wasn't anyone at home. Is everything all right, love? Oh! You've been crying.' Betty placed her arm around Ellie. 'You'll find another job soon, I'm sure.'

'Oh, thank goodness you're here. No, Betty, it's my dad. He's in hospital.'

'Oh, Ellie, pet.' Betty hugged her tight. 'Come back to our house. It's getting dark. We have a telephone for the shop and can contact the hospital. I'm sorry, but we can't take the delivery van up there because of the blackout and the petrol ration, but a quick phone call will tell us what's happening. Anyway, we're expecting a lot more snow. It's dangerous to even think about going to the hospital tonight.'

Ellie grabbed her coat and scarf, and together she and Betty walked down the icy street. It was almost dark and eerily quiet. Ellie had nothing to say. Her mind was full of questions, with no one to answer them.

Betty hung on to her arm. 'Watch out, don't slip on this bit, pet. It's hard to see the ice.' They'd almost had to feel their way along the road. 'Thank goodness for the moon tonight. I just hope the Jerries don't decide to bomb us. It's light enough out here.'

They returned in time to find Alf looking for holes in the blackout curtains. 'Hello, El,' he said. 'What's going on, Betty?' He double-checked the pained looks on both of their faces.

'She's in shock, love.' Betty explained, and then made the phone call to the hospital.

Ellie took the receiver as the ward sister answered the call. She explained who she was. 'Sorry, I can't get to the hospital. Can I leave a message for my mother to call me at this number?' She replaced the receiver. 'No change, that's all they said,' she announced. 'I left your phone number, Alf. I hope that's okay.'

Alf nodded and gave Ellie a meaningful smile. Betty made tea and shared their rations with her.

A couple of hours later, the phone rang. Betty passed the receiver to Ellie.

'Hello, Mam, what's happened? How's Dad?'

Agnes replied in a way that Ellie knew was not her usual self. 'It's bad news,' she said softly. 'He's…he's died, Ellie. About an hour ago.'

Ellie heard the break in her mother's voice. 'Oh no, no, it can't be. What're we going to do? I can't believe it, Mam.'

'Wait till I get home, Ellie. We…we have to arrange a funeral. It's an enormous shock. I'm staying here until daylight – it'll be safer for Tommy and me, and if there's an air raid, we can go down the hospital shelters. Oh, what did we do to deserve all this? I'm not sure how we'll cope. Stay safe at home, El. I'll be back after midday tomorrow. Tell Betty, thanks for her help.'

Ellie heard another sob in her mother's voice and felt sadness for her for the first time in ages. Why did her father have to die? In her confusion, it all seemed inconvenient and frustrating. Overwhelmed by her father's passing and by losing her job, she felt a sense of numbness and helplessness. Overwhelmed with grief, she buried her face in her hands, desperately wishing Harold were there to soothe her. As soon as she could, she had to sit down and write him a letter. Each item on the to-do list felt like a mountain to climb, creating a sense of overwhelming dread.

Dearest Hal,

It's been two weeks since my father's passing. Our experience has been nothing short of disastrous. On top of everything, I find myself unemployed and with no prospects. The troops have confiscated the hotel, leaving us in a dire situation. Our mam is considering taking in lodgers, possibly soldiers, as the war progresses. They need billets for the forces. We already have soldiers around the town. As you know, Mam inherited the house from Granny Brownlee, and with Dad not having any decent money coming in, it was down to Tommy and me to help. Mam says the only thing to do is for me to volunteer with the ATS, and she'll rent out my room.

I miss you so much, and I hope you'll make it back to Saltburn soon. Life here is awful, and I wouldn't say I like every moment I'm alone without you, with only our memories to comfort me. I heard rumours about joining up. The army seems to do you good. I hope it will do the same for me.

I have little news for you under the circumstances. Not wishing to depress you with my tales of woe, I'll sign off and tell you I love and miss you. Where are we all going with this war?

All my love,

Ellie

Chapter Eleven

27 March 1940

Ellie called to see Betty. With a few days to mull it over, she'd come across a poster that had caught her attention. Betty nodded and listened with sympathy for Ellie's sadness.

'The poster said there's a lot I can learn in the ATS, so I enquired about it. Yesterday, I had an interview. My hotel and office experience could be interesting to them. It's all happening and it's exciting, but I'm petrified.' Ellie sighed. 'I'm not sure about it. It's like someone took over my life.' Tears were in her eyes as she drank tea in the shop's back room. 'Our mam seems miles away these days. She hardly talks to me. She keeps saying it's her nerves.'

Betty put her arm around Ellie's shoulder. 'Yes, it's dreadful, and who could blame her for feeling that way? Everyone's feeling jittery now, but your mother lost your dad, which makes it worse. Sometimes we have to do things we don't enjoy and learn from them. Your ma has to fend for herself now, but I'm sure the church will look out for her, and she has a sister-in-law in the Dales, doesn't she? I'll pop around and see Agnes soon. So, the ATS, eh? Well, may I say we're all very proud of you. Volunteering *is* the right decision. You'll have a good time there, too.'

Ellie smiled. 'Thanks, Betty. I'll be stationed at Catterick, I suppose.'

'Really? That's not too far, and near your aunt. You'll be able to come home easily.'

'Yes, but I doubt I'll get time for visiting and coming back here without Hal…it won't be the same, will it?'

'No, I suppose not.' Betty sighed through her words. 'But we're here for you too, Ellie, and don't forget your ma and Tommy.'

'We would've married by now if it weren't for the war and my age.'

'I know, dear, but you're still very young and have many things to learn. It could be months before we see Harold again. I only want to prepare you, El. If you need to talk, I'm here for you. Anyway, I'm sure joining up will be the best time ever, and it's not all doom and gloom.'

'Thanks, Betty. You've always been so kind to me.'

Ellie felt cheered that Betty had taken her under her wing. She'd become more of a mother to her than her own mam, but she didn't want to sound ungrateful. But the ATS? Now and then, fate intervened and things unfolded exactly as they were supposed to.

8 April 1940

Saying goodbye to Agnes, Tommy, and the remaining Dean family, Ellie couldn't shake the bittersweet feeling that filled the air. Betty's distressed expression didn't go unnoticed, and as usual, Agnes wasted no time in giving her stern advice.

'Just behave, and mind all those soldiers. Keep yourself to yourself and stay safe.' She did not kiss Ellie, but lingered a moment before hugging her. 'Bye, Ellie. Make sure you write to us.'

Tommy stood by the gate and waved. 'Bye, El. It'll be my turn next year. Can't wait to join up.'

'You're better off at home now, and I need you!' Agnes retorted.

Tommy caught Ellie's eye and grimaced at the thought of being told what to do by his mother.

Ellie stared at the upstairs window before turning back, imagining her father waving goodbye. She'd always wanted him to embrace her. *Bye, Ellie. Remember, you're a soldier now. Go make a difference for us all. I'm proud of you.* A few words would have been enough to know he loved her, but sadly, it was not to be. The lump in her throat made her want to cry. Once again, she was very much alone. With defiance in her gait, she quickened her step and set out through the subway to the station. There were no tears left to shed.

With an old brown leather suitcase that had once belonged to her grandmother, Ellie stepped aboard the train to Middlesbrough.

Along the rows of seats, she spotted her former classmate, Vicky Empsall. There was a spare seat, so she sat down beside her. Vicky's blue eyes and kind smile had always warmed Ellie; she had missed her a lot, having only met briefly in the town on a Saturday morning before Harold joined up. No longer a young lass in school uniform, Vicky wore a cream skirt and a navy-blue top with peg buttons down the front. Ellie had always wished she could look as stylish as Vicky, with her long curly hair and a navy bag slung over her shoulder. Her parents had money, and it made a difference.

'Hi, Vicky, fancy seeing you here! How are you? Going away, then?'

'I've volunteered for the ATS,' Vicky replied.

'Really? So have I. You mean you and I are off to Durham together to do our training?'

Vicky smiled and nodded. 'It seems that way. My Alan has joined up, so I felt it best to volunteer. We're one of the first lot of girls to do that.'

'Me too. I can't believe it. We'll be together again. I'm blubbering.' Ellie waved her hand across her face. 'You'll have to excuse me if I'm a bit of a weepy mess today. I'll get over it.'

'Yes, I know what you mean. I said my goodbyes last night. Anyway, let's make the most of a bad situation. You and I could have fun, with loads of new people to meet. All those soldiers in the camp. Isn't it amazing, eh? It's scary, too, but we'll manage. By the way, sorry to hear about your dad.'

Ellie nodded her thanks. She sat listening to Vicky talking about her family, her boyfriend Alan, and his joining the navy.

'How's Harold doing?' Vicky finally asked.

'He's with the Green Howards in the 4th Battalion.' Ellie looked behind her and lowered her voice. 'We think he's in France, but we're only guessing.'

'Oh, dear El. It's awful for us, but we've got each other now.' Vicky gave one of her beaming smiles and patted Ellie's hand. 'So glad to see you, love.'

'I've missed you too, with having to work and so on.'

The ATS bus idled patiently, its engine humming softly, ready to transport the girls to Durham. Both girls found a seat and squeezed into it.

'This bus is full now,' the conductor announced. 'They're sending another one in ten minutes, so hang on a bit longer, ladies.'

Ellie heard the girls outside making 'Aww' sounds. It had rained, and they were getting wet.

'We're almost there now, so hang on, and let's see what they got in store for us,' Vicky said. 'Exciting, eh?'

Ellie sighed at Vicky's remark. She remembered Vicky at school, always a happy-go-lucky girl, especially when they'd taken part in a couple of school plays and enjoyed the acting and singing. Perhaps she needed her right now to cheer things up.

Vicky smiled as the girls on the bus sang 'Ten Green Bottles', and everyone joined in. Ellie thought it best to do the same. It lifted her spirits. She enjoyed singing, music, and those films she and Harold had watched before the war broke out. Music from the radiogram always made her feel alive, especially on cold and blustery days, with sleet descending the windows as she listened to *Music While You Work*.

Upon arrival, they stood side by side, their luggage resting at their feet. An ATS officer in a khaki uniform awaited them.

'Welcome to Durham. Follow me, girls.'

Ellie walked in line as they had at school. It seemed right.

'Okay, please wait here,' said the officer. 'No doubt you are all starving hungry after your journey. Food is provided in the canteen. Go straight on, and you will get your refreshments at the end of the corridor.'

They stood patiently in the queue, waiting their turn to receive a steaming bowl of soup, a warm bun, and a comforting cup of tea.

'What a lovely old place this is,' Vicky announced. She placed her tray on the table. 'They don't give us much time to eat all this, do they?'

'I'm worn out already.' Ellie savoured the taste of her bun as she took a bite.

'Ladies! I hope you enjoyed your snack. You have precisely one hour, so please make your way to the recruitment office and wait in line. Thank you.' The ATS officer turned her back and marched smartly out of the hall.

In the queue, they each received their identical uniforms; a skirt, jacket, tie, underwear and toiletries were all a sign of what was yet to come. They signed the Official Secrets Act, had a medical check, and departed to their designated dormitories.

Vicky gave a jaw-dropped expression. 'Oh flippin' 'eck, El, these knickers are enormous! It's like being back at school again.'

'Love the colour,' Ellie said with sarcasm. 'It seems everything is khaki, even the stockings, and as for the shoes – great big clodhoppers!'

'Have you seen the pyjamas? Oh my God, we look like convicts.'

'Do we really have to wear all this stuff?' Ellie remarked.

Vicky doubled up with laughter. 'Well, not all at once. I suppose we have to try it on now.'

Ellie sighed. 'The shoes are okay, I suppose. They look comfortable enough, but I wouldn't wear them at home. Not exactly fashionable, are they?' She held up the pair of dark brown brogues.

'You're not at home now, El. This is for real. You're in the ATS.'

Ellie's thoughts homed in on her new surroundings. Was this the same routine that Harold had gone through last year? She tried on the shirt and fastened the tie. Her thoughts turned again to Harold. What if he hadn't realised they might not be together on leave? She panicked. What would happen if they never caught up with each other? She opened her suitcase and ensured she had put Harold's letter in a safe place inside her purse.

'Come on, El. Tell me what I look like, then.' Vicky stood in front of her in full uniform.

Ellie took a step back. 'Actually, Vicky, you look brilliant, but you must fix your tie. There's a gap between your shirt and the top button. What about me, then?'

'Bloody marvellous, El. If only Al and Harold could see us now, eh? I suppose this is it, then, and now we're ready to advance on Mr Hitler! Ha ha! We are British and don't give up that easily.' Vicky stood straight and saluted the King and Queen's picture on the wall. Under the picture hung a bold poster that read, "The test of a soldier is to keep his mouth shut when he would look big if he told what he knew." The image showed a soldier in a pub, surrounded by civilian well-wishers.

Ellie laughed. Vicky had taken her out of her sad mood. It was comforting to know that both were now in the same situation. Perhaps they would be an excellent source of support for each other in the coming months.

The sergeant and her entourage marched into the room. The girls stood to attention, as they had been shown.

'I have a detailed list of placements for your time at Catterick.' The sergeant read out the names, her voice filling the room with a sense of authority. 'Private Brownlee, typing pool. Private Empsall, library clerk…' And the list continued as placements were allocated for each girl. The word 'dismissed' hung in the air, its finality echoing through the room.

Vicky blew out her cheeks. How would she handle the suffocating grip of being controlled by another person?

May 1940

Ellie improved her typing speed and slept with the familiar sound of typewriter keys clicking in her head. She felt relieved they hadn't asked her to do anything too technical. At least it was what she was used to. After attending lectures on aircraft ammunition, she realised the importance of the complex study. The girls assembled for the weekly parade to learn how to march. All Ellie wanted to do was sleep, but there was far too much information going around in her head, and with all the physical training, she felt worn down. Harold's letter came to mind, and now Ellie understood his remarks too well, but he had kept her motivated.

Three weeks later, after many lectures and typing lessons, the two women boarded an army truck and headed to Catterick Camp.

'Bloody rain, again,' Vicky announced. 'I'm getting soaked.'

On arrival, both were in awe of the number of soldiers they saw on parade in the square.

'That's an awful lot of men out there, El,' Vicky remarked with a saucy look.

Ellie grinned. Vicky hadn't changed that much since leaving school. She was still cheeky and forward, but more grown-up than Ellie had remembered. If anyone was to keep up the morale, it would be Vicky. Thank God!

"D" Barracks was synonymous with a cosy and welcoming environment. Before calling it a night, they eagerly devoured their food parcel. Ellie sat on bed number 10, her eyes scanning the room to glimpse Vicky at bed number 15, positioned on the opposite side. Neatly stacked alongside basic toiletries were their sheets and pillows, ready for use. Amid the items, Ellie discovered an inventory list, alongside a sheet of paper containing meticulous instructions on bed-making and locker organisation. They were already familiar with these rules, having spent time in Durham. Inspections were to be held at random in the first weeks. Those who deviated from the rules would face the consequence of being burdened with extra duties.

'Attention!' the ATS sergeant bellowed as she entered the dormitory.

Ellie realised her new army life wouldn't be cosy. She stood to attention for inspection, and the sergeant walked along the line of girls in her dorm.

'Welcome to Catterick Garrison. This is a place of history and rules. You will get time off if you work hard, but you will be disciplined if you don't obey orders. Work is work, and play is play. Don't forget that! We take everything *very* seriously here. This war has to be won, and you are about to play an important role in restoring Britain to normality. You cannot afford to get involved with young men here. There will be sorrow and pain if you do, but we hope your time at Catterick will be enjoyable. Tomorrow you will be assigned to your new posts and rise from your beds at 0530 hours. Sleep is essential to a good day, so lights out early and blackout will commence at sundown. That's all for now. Dismissed.' As the sergeant marched out of the dormitory, the sharp click-clack of her brogues reverberated through the hallway.

'Oh heck!' Vicky exclaimed, blowing out her cheeks in frustration. She couldn't help but wonder if things would always be this way.

Ellie laughed. 'As you said, Vicks, we're in the army now.'

The camp's social life suited the girls and they were enjoying themselves. Vicky pointed to a poster about joining the camp concert party.

'Remember when we did the school concerts? They were fun, weren't they?'

Volunteers wanted for the concert-party comedy Christmas production of 'Cinderella'. Actors, artists, dancers.
If there is anything you can do to help, please get in touch.
Contact Sgt John Tindall.
(Go to reception for further details.)

'Let's join up, El. It could be fun. I can't sing or dance but I could help with the scenery. In school, I had a knack for art, if you recall?'

'I'd love to try acting, even though the thought of stepping onto a stage terrifies me. I don't suppose it's much different from when we were in school, though. I'm not sure if it's my thing, but I'm interested in going.' Ellie couldn't believe she'd let those words slip from her mouth.

'Come on, then. Let's see the person in charge,' Vicky encouraged. 'It'll help us socialise. What are you waiting for?'

They walked down a long corridor and knocked on the door at reception. Ellie giggled before entering and tried to put on a straight face as the person inside invited them in.

'Private Brownlee, sir!'

'Private Empsall, sir!'

They stood to attention and saluted.

'We'd like to join the concert party,' Vicky announced.

'Sergeant John Tindall. Get those hands down, ladies, and never call me "sir". I'm a sergeant. I work for a living! Did they not teach you anything in basic training? Anyway, I gather you're new here. I've not seen you before, although there are so many of us, you hardly meet the same person twice these days. For social events, we tend to be more relaxed.' A smile slowly formed on his lips as he realised that his introduction may have been a bit too harsh.

Ellie studied him; he had fair hair similar to Harold's and his accent sounded like he came from somewhere in the south of England. His green-blue eyes caught the glow of the office lights when he spoke. Vicky was correct. There were many good-looking men out there, for sure.

'We only arrived here at the start of the month. It's been hard work, but we're enjoying ourselves and want to socialise more,' Vicky said.

'Who can blame you?' he replied. 'We're relatively well established with our own concert party. Of course, we do have vacancies because people are being transferred elsewhere. Still, if possible, we try to stick together. With Christmas coming up, we're doing a pantomime. We need an ugly sister, and it's sort of a saucy version of *Cinderella*.'

'Well, don't count me in on that one. My brother would call me the ugly sister, but acting isn't something I'm good at. I can paint the scenery for you. I was good at art in school,' Vicky said.

'Oh, that's very useful, er...'

'I'm Vicky, this is Ellie.'

'And what about you, Ellie? Have you any acting experience?'

'Well, only at school, otherwise not. But I'd like to have a go.'

'Oh, good. Rehearsals are on Thursday evenings. Tell your CO you're with us. They're usually flexible about time off. Entertaining the troops is just as important as the war effort.' He gave the girls a tight-lipped but welcoming smile.

For a moment, Ellie realised she'd forgotten their reasons for being there. Of course, there was still a war somewhere but they could now enjoy army life while the bombs screamed in faraway places.

'We'd love to have a go,' Vicky said.

'How about this evening?'

'Okay, we'll come, won't we, Ellie?' Vicky nudged her friend.

They thanked Sergeant Tindall and left the office to walk back down the corridor.

'He seemed ever so nice. And very good-looking, eh?' A mischievous grin spread across Vicky's face.

'Don't forget you've still got Alan,' Ellie reminded her.

'Yeah, but I can look, eh?'

That day, another brief letter arrived from Harold. Anything was better than nothing. He was well and enjoying his new life. Ellie had smiled and felt proud when he'd mentioned in a previous letter that the King had passed by him on parade. What a thrill it must have been! She told Vicky about it when they went to the Navy, Army and Air Force Institute for their usual gossip over a cup of tea.

That morning, Ellie had started her first job in the typing pool. She related her news to Vicky, who supped her tea and listened intently.

Ellie mimicked the sergeant. '"You got to be a fast learner here, Private Brownlee. No time for shilly-shallying. Sit straight at your desk, or you'll get a bad back! The first rule of thumb is, 'Whatever goes on in this office, stays in this office', do you hear?"' Ellie gave a sigh. 'Oh my God, Vicky, it's like being back at home again with our mam breathing down my neck. "Are you up to sixty words a minute now, Brownlee?" she asked me.

'"Not quite," I told her, "but I did the test at fifty words last week and passed it."

'"Okay, you'll do," she said. "Just keep improving. The main thing is accuracy. You must check for spelling before the letters go to higher places for a signature." Honestly, Vicky, if I have to listen to the bloody *William Tell Overture* one more time, typing to the music, I'll go crazy. Then there's the exam soon. I'm not sure if I'll pass it.'

Vicky laughed. 'I told you you'd make a good actress. A comedy actress is somewhere within that demure look of yours, trying to get out. I'm glad we met up again, El.'

'Despite learning to type at the hotel, I've had to relearn, army style. My fingers are never in the right places.'

Vicky listened and nodded.

'… But typing is easy compared to Pitman shorthand with all those long and short vowels and "Pa, may we all go too?" stuff. It'll take me ages to get up to speed. And I can never read back what I wrote!' Ellie realised her life was about to take on a new meaning. At least there was the opportunity to get to know people from different backgrounds, similar to what she'd encountered at the hotel. All she needed was to be there and do the right thing, with the chance to be independent and confident. With Vicky by her side, what might turn up next would always be a surprise. 'So that was my day – how was yours?'

Vicky gave a cheery smile. 'Not as exciting as yours, for sure.'

Ellie's spirits lifted as she eagerly anticipated the excitement that awaited her. That evening, the girls rushed to the NAAFI, to be greeted by the sight of tables and chairs piled high on the stage. Ellie followed Vicky through the double swing doors, and they stood momentarily, staring at the room's vastness. A lectern poised for the next seminar was at the far end of the stage. Red velvet curtains hung against tall windows. It seemed they needed repair and cleaning after nicotine had turned them a darker shade of muddy red. A few people huddled together at the opposite end of the room; had they all gone to war?

A loud voice boomed from behind, which made Ellie jump. 'Can I help you, wee gerls?'

Ellie sighed with relief.

A tall, dark-haired man in uniform appeared, seemingly out of thin air, and wasted no time in introducing himself. 'I'm James Colgan, otherwise known as Scotty, for reasons that will become obvious.'

'I think we must be early,' Vicky said. 'Sergeant Tindall asked us to come here. We volunteered for the concert party.'

'Aye, dinna worry – the others will be here soon. We certainly need more women in the company. What would you like tae do?'

'Well, I don't do anything,' Ellie said. 'I have never tried acting except at school, but Vicky is very good at art and wants to help with the scenery. I said I would tag along.'

'Okay, sounds good. We'll ask you to do a reading and see how you get on.'

'I used to write stories at school and thought maybe I would write a book one day, but I doubt I'll get that far with the war and so on.'

'Why not keep a diary?' Scotty said.

'Never thought of that, but it's a good idea.'

Within minutes, the room filled with the hum of conversation. Ellie heard Vicky softly counting the people, her voice barely audible above the chatter of the crowd. Sergeant Tindall was the last to enter.

Ellie gazed around, smoothing her fingers over her lips. 'Oh, good, it seems like they're all here now.'

'Okay, gather round, find a pew, and stick your backsides on it.' Sergeant Tindall looked across at Ellie and Vicky and smiled at them. 'Glad you came. Just relax. You're not on parade here.' He grinned as he swung a chair and sat astride it, his arms leaning on the backrest.

The chatter died as Tindall spoke.

'As you know, we're putting on a pantomime at the end of this year. We have plenty of time to produce it, and then we can do something near Christmas if this ruddy war doesn't get in the way!'

One soldier spoke up, his voice filled with confidence. 'Don't worry, there's plenty of time.'

'Yes, I know, and I'm sure it can be done. First, let me introduce you to two new ATS recruits...' Tindall looked down at the sheet of paper in his hand. 'Private Empsall and Private Brownlee have volunteered to muck in, which seems normal around here.'

Vicky and Ellie both raised an arm in greeting.

'Now, I've made a list of parts for the play, and I want those people on the list to let me know if they can commit to the characters allocated.' Tindall turned toward Ellie and Vicky. 'Private Brownlee...erm... Ellie. I wonder if you would be prepared to do a reading for us with Alex over there?'

Alex raised his hand so Ellie could recognise him. Ellie smiled.

'I got Alex down as Prince Charming,' Tindall said. 'Phil Moxham is Dandini, and we have Sandy and Dave as the ugly sisters. Thanks, lads.'

The rest of the group tittered at the thought.

Vicky whispered, 'I think Alex will make a good Prince Charming, though he's very...sort of camp, isn't he? But isn't Prince Charming usually a girl?'

Ignoring Vicky's remark, Ellie hesitated and sucked in her breath. 'You want *me* to read?'

'Yes, you – go on, Ellie, do it. He doesn't bite.' Vicky dug her gently in the ribs with her elbow.

Tindall handed Ellie a script, and her heart pounded.

'Go on, El,' Vicky encouraged again.

Ellie took the script in her hand, thinking that her broad Yorkshire accent could make it sound funnier. Alex began to read his lines.

> *Prince Charming: And whoever the slipper fits shall be my bride.*
> *Cinders: Oh bloomin' 'eck, 'e's not asking for much, is 'e?*
> *[The Prince kneels down to fit the slipper. The back of his pants*
> *rip, and 'breaking wind' noises are heard.]*
> *Cinders: [Cups her hand around her ear to listen.] Pray, what*
> *is that noise? Who let those bombs go?*

Ellie looked around, doing her best to look serious.

As she progressed through the script, she became involved in the words and put her heart into the comedy innuendoes. She wanted to be funny, and the more she read, the more her confidence grew.

Prince Charming: Gather around, people of my kingdom.
[Forces the shoe onto Cinders' foot.]
Cinders: This shoe's only a size 4. [Looks at the audience with
despair.] I told props I'm a size 5.

When John stopped her, she was about to go to the next page, and the company clapped their encouragement.

'Ellie, that's marvellous. You're a natural.'

Ellie cleared her throat and whispered to Vicky. 'I never thought...'

'Honestly, El, it was brilliant. I didn't know you had it in you.'

Ellie laughed. 'Bloody hell, Vicky, neither did I.'

John took Ellie aside. 'Look, Ellie, I wonder if I can have you as Marlene's understudy until we know the situation with the company?'

'I'd love to.'

'And you, Vicky, can you come and see me afterwards? Maybe you can stay behind for our meeting with the backstage chaps in about half an hour?'

Vicky's delight was clear as she flashed a wide grin in response to John's request. Ellie couldn't believe her performance had been so impressive. Fun was precisely what she was seeking, and she'd found it in this experience. For the first time in her life, she felt a surge of importance coursing through her veins. She knew Harold would be filled with pride if he could see her now. Perhaps, after all this time, her life was about to take a new and exciting turn. Maybe the ATS wasn't all that bad after all.

Chapter Twelve

Ellie attended a quiz in the NAAFI the following evening, through an invitation from a fellow ATS girl, Margaret Boyes. They watched the Pathé News, and Ellie scrutinised the screen. Would she see Harold in the parade? No, impossible.

'Sit beside me, Vicky. Here's a chair for you.'

The three women sat at a table, pencils ready to answer the questions. Ellie noted that the girl on the adjacent table had fallen asleep. She shrugged her shoulders, sympathising with the girl's fatigue. All the marching up and down was tiring. Harold seemed to know about that too.

'Okay, are you ready? Question one. In which county is Tavistock?'

Ellie looked at Vicky and shrugged.

'Oh, I know that one,' said Margaret. 'Put Devon on your sheet,' she whispered. 'It's up the road from my aunt's house. We used to go for holidays near there.'

'Question two. Who built St Paul's Cathedral?'

The girl who'd been dozing hadn't listened to the question. Out of the blue, and half asleep, she put her hand up and shouted, 'St Paul, sir.'

Ellie saw the girl's horror when she realised what a stupid bloomer she'd made.

The room tittered with laughter, and Vicky spoke first. 'Sit down, Brummer, before you fall over.'

The buxom girl, flushed with embarrassment, sat low in her seat.

'Aww, she's tired out, poor lass,' Ellie said. 'We could all do with a day in bed!'

'What is the capital of Scotland?' the quizmaster called.

'Is that Edinburgh?' Vicky whispered.

'I thought it was Glasgow?' Ellie said.

'Don't confuse me, El,' Vicky laughed.

'She's right.' Margaret wrote "Edinburgh" on the quiz sheet.

The girls' comments and desire to provide the correct answers made them feel they could be the winning team.

'Okay, last question…'

As instructed, they passed their quiz sheet to the next table and waited for the answers. There were cheers from the opposing teams, and although Ellie's team didn't win, they came second, and everyone applauded.

'We did well, didn't we? By the way, El, it's drama night tomorrow. I've had a word with the lads. They want you onstage this time,' Vicky said. 'Sorry, I meant to tell you earlier.'

'Oh, really? I'm feeling very nervous. You'll have to come and watch us, Margaret.' Ellie squeezed her friend's arm to encourage her to come.

'I can't. Sorry. I have to attend that embarrassing meeting about sex and VD.'

Curiosity filled Ellie's voice. 'What's VD?' she asked.

'You mean you don't know?'

'Nope.'

'Oh dear, it's not nice.' Margaret whispered, 'It's an infectious disease you get from men. You know…when they've been…you know.' She nodded and faked a smile. 'The treatment is disgusting. I'm told they show some pretty awful photos. I hear some soldiers have left the hall and been physically sick or passed out when they saw the pictures.'

'Oh, right, I see.' Ellie's eyes widened. 'Yuck! It sounds awful.' She hoped she wouldn't have to watch the film. Anyway, they would be having their photos taken before the rehearsal tomorrow, so she wouldn't be going to that, thank goodness.

*

106

The following day, the ATS sergeant strode up and down the line of girls waiting to go on parade. 'Your tie isn't straight, Brummer. What's that dirty mark on your shoe, Empsall?'

'Sorry, sergeant, it must have been yesterday's rain.'

'Yesterday? Did you not clean your shoes this morning, Private Empsall?'

Vicky sucked in her breath; she hadn't noticed dirt on her shoes. Ellie checked while standing to attention. What's she talking about?

'I give you fair warning, Empsall. You have to do better than that.'

'Yes, sergeant.'

The sergeant moved down the line. 'How are you getting along, Brownlee?'

'Fine, sarge.'

'I hear you passed your typing speed – well done. I got my eye on you, so keep it up.'

Ellie felt some guilt. Vicky had been told off. Ellie knew her friend wasn't coping well with her job and wanted something more rewarding. It seemed Vicky was being picked on. It was unfair, like being back in school, except they had to work much harder. But what did the sergeant mean by 'I got my eye on you'? What had Ellie done wrong?

The girls were dismissed and allowed to take the rest of the day off.

Ellie and Vicky spent the afternoon sitting in Richmond's ATS-frequented tea room. Vicky ordered tea and scones, which Ellie thought were like rock cakes.

'I wish I didn't have to work in the cramped, stuffy typing pool. I'm glad we found the concert party, otherwise I'd be bored to tears. Scotty tells me they have a wonderful wardrobe mistress called Porky. Yes, it's one of the lads.' Ellie laughed. 'I'm told he's quite a character – he does all the sewing and glueing on the sequins. Apparently, his team made some fantastic costumes for their last production.'

'I'm good at sewing – perhaps I can help,' Vicky said.

'I'm a bit of a clown when it comes to sewing. I can darn socks, but give me a pattern and I'm useless. But I always wanted to learn. Betty Dean is very good at knitting. She can whip up a Fair Isle tank top in a couple of weeks if she's not too busy in the shop.'

Vicky took a sudden sharp breath. 'Oh yes, silly me, I forgot to tell you. I have news for you. There's talk of sending me on a course. I'm unsure what kind of course, but I think I'm in the wrong job. You can't say the library is exactly me, can you?' She sighed. 'I'm not very good at it. I'm more of a practical person. The sarge called me into her office this morning and asked me how I was getting on. I told her I wasn't, and she asked what I enjoy doing best.'

'I agree. It will be best if you're on munitions or something like that. You were always a "doing" person when we were at school, the outdoor type. Ah well, you'll find out soon enough. I hope they don't decide you have to leave Catterick, though. It will be a disaster for me.'

'Oh, you'd cope, Ellie, you always do. Of course, I want to stay here too. We're a team, you and me. Anyway, I don't know. I'll tell you when I have any news.'

'I wish I was doing something else too. The pressure to get things done is awful. My fingers and wrists are sore by the end of the day.'

'So, how are the Dean family doing? Have you heard?' Vicky cut her scone in half.

'I hear William has joined the navy, and young Peter is still at home with Betty and Alf,' Ellie said. 'What about your Alan? Do you know where he is?'

'The last letter I got was about a month ago, but he had nothing much to say. Only the boring stuff. I hope he's okay.'

'We'll have to be patient, I suppose,' said Ellie smiling.

Last week, when Vicky and Scotty had been deep in conversation, she couldn't help but notice an odd feeling that Alan was forgotten. It struck her that in recent days Vicky had cast him aside.

'How's your mam, Ellie?'

'Not heard a word from her recently. She sent me a postcard from Auntie Pat's which sounded cheery enough, but she is a strange one. I never felt wanted, and I don't know why she was overly controlling with Harold and me. I'm sad I lost my dad, but he had his ways too. I suppose I could return to Saltburn, but I've had much more fun here. If Harold gets leave, then I'll make it home for a few days if they let me.'

'Well, we got each other now and must make the most of it.' Vicky shrugged.

With Vicky at Catterick Garrison, Ellie felt a lot more secure. They'd give her a job close by, wouldn't they? She finished her tea, and Vicky poured her another.

Chapter Thirteen

After spending weeks in Amiens, Harold's battalion moved to Wavrin, where they received intensive weapons training in open warfare. His self-doubt caused him anxiety about what he was doing. Killing people was wrong, and nothing would make him think otherwise, but there was a job to be done and no going back. As the weeks crept by, he was meant to be preparing for war, but the fighting had temporarily ceased, leaving him in a strange state of limbo, the sounds of distant conflict replaced by an unnerving quiet. Hitler had pulled back for a while at least. The relaxed atmosphere felt more like a holiday, allowing him uninterrupted time to study. He waved his certificate for the communications test before Bernie. 'I've been dreaming in Morse code for six weeks,' he said. 'I passed the exam.'

'Radio operator, eh? Sounds good to me. Well done, Deano.' Bernie smiled and patted him on the shoulder.

'Not sure if I'll use it. I mean, when is this war going to start?'

'There's a football match this afternoon. We'll join in,' Bernie said.

'Yeah, I hear Alexis Thépot is playing for the French side. Seems unfair. He was Olympic champion, an international goalkeeper for the French in the '30s.'

'If we join the team, the French usually lay on a spread for us – cheese, wine and so on.' Bernie licked his lips. 'Yummy.'

'I have to tell you, Bern, I'm not a natural sportsman, you know.'

'Doesn't matter, you can dance – I can't. Do you realise it's been five months since we went through that terrible snowstorm? I can hardly believe it,' Bernie said. 'God, that was a long march! I thought I was dying. It was so cold.'

'I noticed we seem to do more training now instead of larking about.'

'I got a feeling about this,' remarked Bernie, a sense of anticipation in his voice. As he pondered, he quickly realised that it would be wise to keep his thoughts to himself. He'd been wrong before about these things.

The following morning, early, a message came through to attend an announcement.

'At 0630 hours today, the code word "Birch" was unscrambled. Germany has invaded the lines, and the battles of France, the Netherlands and Belgium have begun. You will gather up your weapons and hold on to the lines. We are to dig and hold positions at all costs. All I can say is, good luck, lads.'

Harold thought that if the end was nigh, this was it, the sky a bruised purple, mirroring the dread in his heart. His vow to Ellie and his parents to return home was as distant as the stars, a promise lost to circumstances beyond his reach.

A few hours later, the commanding officer's voice echoed through the air, ordering them to retreat. With their ammunition in hand, the men set out toward Dunkirk, the weight of their gear pressing against their shoulders.

'Too close for comfort, I'd say,' remarked Private Jonno Wilkinson, his voice carrying a weariness beyond his young age.

'Shut up, Jonno,' Harold said. 'I need to listen to this radio message.'

Harold's voice trembled as he relayed the grave warning of an intense battle awaiting them. The British Expeditionary Force was tantalisingly close, a mere fifty miles separating them from their destination. An even narrower corridor had closed down the route, allowing just enough access into Dunkirk. Harold powered down his comm unit, and with each agonising step, his feet throbbed and swelled, the dull ache a stark contrast to the comforting thought of making it home.

Surrounded by the enemy on three sides, they received orders to retreat. Harold marched on, closing his mind to the anguish he felt. With attacks from above and behind, the battalion got separated, firing with other companies. Harold was now in an enormous crisis, but told himself he was a Green Howard, standing proud. These tough Yorkshire lads would never tolerate German nonsense. Some were farmers' sons, steelworkers or miners, and hard graft came as second nature to them. He recalled the hymn from school: '*Fight the good fight with all of our might.*' Now, with the mindset of a real soldier, he would do just that, but it was all about survival and getting home. Knowing that there was only a narrow corridor, it was ironically reassuring to hear the other battalions keeping the enemy at bay. As they marched on, winning the war seemed a distant hope as they drew toward Dunkirk. Harold thought of Bernie; they'd got separated and lost sight of each other. He would only know his friend's fate for sure when he returned to camp in England. God, I hope he's all right.

Alert in readiness in case the Germans broke through, he took cover briefly to light a cigarette. All he needed now was to follow the line of men heading west toward Dunkirk. Checking left and right, he turned to look behind him: so far, so good. A bombed house still smoked in the distance as he sipped water from his canteen. He must conserve every drop. The memory of a woman's act of kindness, tossing them cheese and bread in the last village, was now overshadowed by the empty feeling in their stomachs since most of the food was now depleted. Only their emergency rations remained. They'd have to keep smoking cigarettes to stop the hunger pangs. Onward!

'Which way?' Private Eddie Agar, the youngest in the troop, was always the first to ask questions when panicked.

'Follow yer nose, the sea's in front of you,' Harold retorted. 'What else?' It seemed he was now in charge.

Harold hung on to his rifle and picked up the radio. Bang! The men took cover in a ditch by the side of the road. Bang! Bang! About half a mile away, a barn exploded in a fiery blast, sending debris raining down on them. A high-pitched ringing filled Harold's ears, threatening to shatter his eardrums, then slowly died away as he stood, leaving a stunned quiet.

'Come on, lads, *move!*' he shouted.

The men pressed on; the sound of their determined footsteps drowned out by more deafening explosions. Harold instinctively rubbed his ears. He dropped to the ground and hid in a ditch. Click. Click-click! The distinctive rattle of rifle bolts being rammed home confronted them. The enemy? Surely not. Harold raised his rifle, finger on the trigger, when the leading officer, picking himself up, challenged the remaining Green Howards to hold their fire. False alarm. Harold felt relief, realising they had met with a friendly battalion at a crossroads. For a moment, silence filled the air, as if the noise had vanished.

'Where ya moving to?' shouted the other battalion's CO.

'Going up to the beaches.' Harold identified the regiment with some relief.

The men lowered their rifles.

'777 HQ, eh?' Harold said.

'Yep, Royal Army Service Corps. I'm Lieutenant Ron Williams.' Ron reached out and shook Harold's hand. It was as if the noise of battle had stopped just for this moment.

'Harold Dean. What the hell are you guys doing here? Didn't you know there's a war on?' Harold's tone seemed good-humoured yet curious.

'Back there, we managed to load up the truck with all the supplies. Trouble is, we got lost. Our journey started smoothly, but our vehicle broke down. Now, a group of our team are working to repair it. It just needs to cool down. God knows what's in store at Dunkirk.' Ron shook his head. 'We're told there are no Germans ahead, unless there's been an infiltration through the lines.'

Harold seemed puzzled. 'You realise those buggers are

marauding up the road behind us and to each side of us? We can't afford to stop and chat. So why are you…?' He pointed to the small stack of ammunition behind the RASC company.

'It's bloody daft, really. We're here because…well, here is where we found ourselves! We're supposed to be drivers, clerks, cooks and batmen.' Ron indicated his Bren gun and shrugged his shoulders. 'We're damned well not supposed to be on the front line. Hope you make it,' he said with a look of despair. 'I'm the only one with proper training.'

'You chaps have little time.' Harold pointed toward his radio set. 'Best keep moving. Despite what you've been told, watch your backs, everyone, and keep yer 'eads down. I fear this could get really nasty.' Bang! Bang! 'Far worse than it already is!' Harold ducked down as he said it.

The weakened platoon of Green Howards parted. Harold gave Ron Williams a wry smile. 'Good luck, mate. Have a safe journey. Hope you get the truck fixed – at least you got transport. Hope to see you in Blighty.'

The road, after five hours of marching, became a cluttered mess of vehicles, from armoured cars to Bren carriers, stretching as far as the eye could see. The remaining men of the 4th Battalion finally caught up with their commanding officer, who took charge of the troops once again.

'Bloody hell. Look at all this lot,' said Private Agar.

Harold kept on marching. 'Yeah, I heard about it. Military police have stopped vehicles passing into Dunkirk. Only senior officers' vehicles are allowed. It seems they've piled up this far back.'

The CO, who had caught up with them, shouted down the line. 'Halt! We'll settle down here for a spot of shut-eye, lads. I didn't plan on stopping, but we must save energy for when we get to the beach. It'll be tough, so hang on to your weapons and watch your backs. Look, I don't want to keep saying this, but assess the situation and move on if anyone is injured. With or without the victim!

That's an order. No casualties that can't walk!'

That night, Harold took out his pencil from his top pocket and, before it got too dark, wrote a letter to Ellie. He could be dead in the morning, but he had to tell her he was fine.

If you find this letter, please send it to the person at the given address.

> *My dearest El,*
>
> *Sorry this is short. I wish I knew what had happened to you. It's been ages since I heard anything. I can't tell you what I'm doing, but I hope we'll be together soon. The last few months have been mixed, but please don't worry. I'm fine.*

What else should I say? Fine, I am not!

> *It's been hard not getting any letters. We have been busy marching here and there, but receiving your mail means much more to me than you realise. Damn the post and the war! This has to be the hardest thing I've been asked to do – ever!*
>
> *I just wanted to tell you I love you, and that I'm sure our parting will strengthen us both. I wish I could put kisses on this letter – you'll just have to imagine some. They say no news is good news. I hope that's right.*
>
> *So, nighty-night, my darling. I hope to post this in England.*
>
> *Lots of love,*
>
> *Harold*

After sealing the letter, he put it in his pocket. He prayed he wouldn't become a casualty, left behind on the beach only to become a prisoner of war in Germany.

The following morning, the CO gave the order. 'This is it, lads! The 5th Battalion is keeping the Jerries at bay. We're on our way home.'

The men cheered, and the CO raised his voice.

'However…'

The cheering fell silent.

'I don't have to tell you how dangerous our journey will be, but we have support from the RAF, the navy, and our defence forces. If it helps, you do a lot of praying from now on. Get going, lads. I wish you all the luck and hope to see you on the other side. The order has come through. It's each man for himself. That's it! Pack up your kit and let's get moving. Try not to get separated this time.'

Harold patted his pocket. The letter. This could be his last goodbye.

They tramped into Dunkirk with the sound of guns firing on the ground and above their heads. Death and cordite invaded Harold's nostrils, and the swirling, acrid smoke suffocated him as he staggered toward the strand. Footsore and weary, his grubby, war-torn face, etched with fear and fatigue, was streaked with grime and sweat. Along the route, the sight of abandoned tanks, burned-out cars and trucks, and a lifeless dog overwhelmed him, bringing back memories of Sammy in a negative light. With determination in their eyes, the RASC chaps and other platoons set about smashing up the vehicles, making sure that they were no longer an aid to the enemy. The sight that greeted Harold was a harrowing one – a British soldier's body lay on the ground in a foetal position, his head brutally wounded. Harold balked, his eyes widening in disbelief. Then came another line of foul-smelling and sorrowful-looking human bodies, but he looked away and concentrated on the steady thud of boots on the rugged terrain. Left, right, left, right. Keep going, don't stop.

A French woman ran toward him – '*S'il vous plaît. Ne pas nous laisser*' – and pulled on his sleeve. Giving up on translation, he offered a sorry smile and headed for the beach.

Twice, he had to take cover. The Germans were chasing them – bombs, artillery. Bang! It seemed they'd aimed everything they had toward Dunkirk. Must keep moving. If only he could find the rest of the battalion amid this dreadful turmoil. It seemed there was nowhere else to hide. He felt a hammering in his chest as he reached the line of soldiers looking for shelter. Thousands upon thousands of men lay wounded or hunkered down in the dunes. Finally, Harold made it to the areas the CO had chosen for his men. He flopped onto the soft sand, completely shattered.

After the dreadful destruction, more blood-spattered corpses lay broken on the beach. As soon as Harold set foot in this place, he was certain that he had entered the depths of hell. A voice shouted, 'Take cover!', and Harold's legs felt the vibration of a terrible shock wave that left him gagging and covered in sand. The gunfire that rumbled under his feet made him realise that this was the hell his father had gone through.

Someone cried out, 'Where the bloody hell's the navy?'

Harold crept forward to look at the sea. Where were the boats they'd been told would arrive to pick them up? There wasn't a boat or a ship to be seen. He hoped this trip wouldn't see him drowning in the English Channel or lying dead on a beach with the rest of the battalion. He'd got this far without injury, but how long could he hold out? Bang, boom! More gunfire whistled over the top of his head. He dived for cover as sand rained down on his helmet and stuck in his ears. Then he recovered and gazed along the shore. There must be around 200,000 men here, he guessed, and they didn't stop coming. What in God's name had brought them to *this*? A sea of helmets and blood.

Amid the chaos, the anguished voices of men separated from their units were heard pleading for help. Harold stayed in one place, following instructions. In the brief lull of artillery fire, he spotted Agar frantically digging into the ground, using only his bare hands, to conceal them from potential "overs". He dug down deep. Harold helped him, and then someone gave them a shovel. They turned to hear a loud screech of terror. A French soldier wandered naked, the result of the last explosion. The ripped clothes clinging to his back were evidence of the violent encounter, soaked in crimson. He screamed, *'Je ne veux pas mourir!'* before collapsing on the beach. Harold wanted to help, but the man had drawn his last breath, and there was no more to be done except wait. Harold closed his eyes to block out the living hell and, terrified of what lay ahead, had the sudden urge to fall into a deep sleep and never wake up.

The next day began quietly, but as Harold searched the blue sky, he watched a Hurricane fly low and drop a beribboned message.

Some men ran eagerly to catch it. Scribbled in pencil by the pilot, it read, 'Good luck, lads. We can do no more.' The message brought overwhelming emotions as one of the soldiers lay in the cold sand of the dunes, sobbing uncontrollably, the grains clinging to his damp cheeks until someone gently touched his shoulder.

Half an hour later, Harold recognised a familiar face. Someone threw packets of Woodbines toward the Green Howards.

'Is that you, Ron Williams? What the fuck do you think you're doin'? Get the hell down.'

'Got these from the store in Lille. Thought you will need them.'

'We bloody do, but there's no need to risk your bleedin' life for packets of fags, mate.'

Ron moved on. 'See ya on the other side,' he said, seemingly unperturbed, and continued chucking packets of Woodbines left and right.

Harold didn't have time to say goodbye before Ron disappeared into a muddle of death and destruction. He saw Ron hit the sand as a random explosion came close. A few seconds later, Harold watched a ghostly figure within the smoke struggling to pick up loose boxes of cigarettes from the beach, before carrying on moving down the line. For a moment, just one person had cared enough to bring packets of Woodbines into a war zone. Who would do that? Only this guy, Ron Williams. A hero. Harold wanted him to live forever. He gave an ironic smile and shook his head in amazement. Amid the deafening barrage of gunfire and the acrid smell of smoke, Ron vanished once more into the obscuring haze. There was no doubt of his courage – or was he just bloody stupid? No, courage was the answer. Ron was a survivor; perhaps there was a lesson to be learned from him.

The men scanned the shore as the sky burst with black smoke from a torpedoed ship. In the water, wounded men fought to stay afloat, their cries for help echoing across the empty shoreline. Some were fortunate enough to be rescued, but their luck ran out when their boat sank, leaving them in need of rescue once more. Where the bleeding hell was the "mighty" air force? Harold felt betrayed.

Someone screamed, 'They've left us on our own. They've forgotten about us! Jesus Christ! We're *all* going to die!'

By nine o'clock that evening, the battalion formed into groups of ten at the water's edge. They passed through a cordon into the shadow of an enormous setting sun and rolling waves of fire. The Germans were now aiming at the wooden pier, "The Mole". As Harold gazed across the darkening sea, the sound of crashing waves filled the air, reminding him of the courageous man who had swum the English Channel both ways. In the event of his ship being hit, what would be his course of action? He and his brother William were both adorned with medals for their swimming accomplishments. With each passing minute, his longing to get home grew stronger. The thin blue-grey line of the English coast cleared in the mist, and if only—

The sound of gunfire stopped his thoughts. Men were falling and clambering back onto The Mole, bleeding from their wounds. Queues of men waited for the boats to take them to England. Harold heard the splashes of screaming soldiers falling into the water. He cowered low as gunfire blasted the sand and exploded before him. Agonised screams from men lying in the open on makeshift stretchers broke his heart. For a moment, he wanted to die with them, but the picture of Ellie in his mind kept him awake. German gunfire once more strafed the beach before the remaining Green Howards. Bloody chaos! Harold awaited his turn to die. His stomach churned with a melding of hunger and dreadful angst, and he had drunk the last of his water. Agar suggested he get more from the town.

'No, don't go into town – everything's gone and you'll get yourself killed.'

'Well, let me get the canteens from those bodies.'

Before Harold could say anything more, Agar was gone. Five minutes later, he returned with two water canteens, and Harold patted him on the back for his bravery.

'God, it's crazy what you do when you have to do it. Well done.' Harold managed a smile.

*

Four nights later, the 5th Battalion had held firm at the front line. Harold remained cold and hungry, with nothing but relentless gunfire to keep his nerves on edge. He chanted, 'I love you, Ellie,' saying her name repeatedly, even though she couldn't hear him. It seemed to bring him closer to her.

The dead and dying littered the beach. Harold closed his eyes, not wanting to survey the scene but the sounds of shivering men moaning in pain still prevailed. No, please, no more! Get me out of here! Panic consumed him, causing his breathing to quicken and his mind to race. The longer he waited, the more likely he'd become one of them.

Despite the early summer months, the cold bit his hands and cheeks. He watched as the men, desperate to stay warm, took the coats and shoes from corpses and wrapped the clothing around their shoulders. He wanted to be sick, despite his empty stomach. With too many men to evacuate, he wondered how he would find his way back home. The situation had unfolded in a completely unforeseen manner. Heartbreaking! Yes, where the hell *was* the bloody navy?

He couldn't wait any longer; he needed dry clothes. An abandoned greatcoat lay in the dunes, and Harold wrapped it around him. Bodies were stripped of anything that might prove life-saving. But the stench... The indignity... He lay down in the dunes and again waited to die. This was it. Goodbye, Ma and Pop, Peter and William. Goodbye, my lovely Ellie. I love you all. I'm not dead yet, but I will soon be. Oh, God help us. God fucking help us!

The sound of gunfire quietened, and within an hour, Harold fell unconscious, exhausted, never believing he'd wake up again.

Hours later, there were excited voices. 'Hey, look...' A soldier pointed toward the sea. 'Look – look at all those small boats. Where the hell did they come from? They don't expect us to go home in those, do they? What the...? We'll be bloody sittin' ducks.'

An explosion threw sand into their faces, but they kept staring at the boats in disbelief. Harold saw an opportunity to escape. British boats! Had they risked their lives to pick up the stranded? A reverberating cheer rang out. With red, white and blue flags fluttering at their sterns, twenty small boats rode the waves just offshore.

Harold exclaimed, 'I'm getting out of here!'

Despite the hail of bullets, more boats arrived, their engines sputtering under the swell. The men raced toward the crashing waves, the salty spray hitting their faces as they waded into the surf to be hauled aboard a trawler, mimicking the motions of fishermen hauling in their catch. Amid the shelling, Harold pushed into the frigid, churning sea, the salty spray stinging his face as he waded toward the bobbing boats, his rifle held high. The sea seeped into his uniform, but he didn't care. Instead, he focused on the first boat he could find. Now a soldier among soldiers, all hoping God would save them, but then Harold recalled he'd stopped believing in God, especially now. A piece of shrapnel whistled past his head as the boat came alongside. It hit the man in front of him. Men floated in the sea with blood seeping from their uniforms; they were long gone, but Harold grabbed the wounded man's equipment straps before he drowned and held on to him. The man was still alive; he *must* save him. He checked the casualty's rank and realised he was from one of their lost platoons.

'Don't let me die! Get me home,' the man agonised. 'I need to see my wife and sons again.'

He passed out as Harold hung on to him in the cold sea, but the blood flowed, and Harold knew they might never survive to tell the tale. He'd been told not to save the wounded – but he had to rescue this chap. What if the same situation happened to him? The man was a comrade, and for him drowning wasn't an option. No going back now; it's too late. Without further thought, Harold disobeyed orders. They were on their way home; who would know anyway? He couldn't help the French soldier but would try to save this man. Those kids had a father who needed them. Harold drew a sharp breath and headed for the boat, dragging the wounded man behind him. Under fire in the small boat, they made it to the Royal Navy cruiser waiting offshore as two sailors stepped forward and turned the soldier's back toward them. They grabbed his straps.

'Go steady, lads, he's been hit in the shoulder,' Harold said.

The men grabbed the rescued soldier around the waist.

'Okay, you're next, mate,' the crewman bellowed above the artillery fire.

Exhausted, Harold slumped on the deck and lay beside his fallen colleague. He rolled over and tore the shirt from the soldier's back, packing the wound as shown in his first-aid training. It was a truly horrifying sight, something that he couldn't bear to look at, but Harold's determination to save this man kept his mind focused. He surveyed the scene as the Luftwaffe tried to break the defences, and each time they saw a German plane, it was coming down on the horizon. Harold watched as flotillas of small boats, shielded by the Royal Navy, sailed in the opposite direction to pick up more men from the beaches. Overcome with seasickness, his stomach churned as he realised he was standing in someone else's vomit. The vessel rolled, causing the waves to crash against its sides. More men were miserable and sick as the boat turned and made haste under fire. Harold reached over the rail and, at the sight of so much blood and the rolling sea, honked up a non-existent breakfast. As long as he kept his eyes on the horizon, and the ship sailed steadily in a straight line, his nausea subsided.

Harold tucked himself into the steps leading to the bridge. Then, numb with cold, hunger, and no more thoughts, the wind blew across him as they headed for good ol' Blighty. The wounded soldier moaned in dreadful pain, and Harold, shivering cold and soaking wet, moved his thoughts to a place he ought not to be. Seconds later – thud! Bang! More explosions. My God, that was close. Too close. The wounded man stirred again and shivered. Harold found an old sack to keep him warm.

'Come on, mate, stay with me, do you hear?' Harold encouraged. 'You're going home.' He was unsure if his promise would ever make good. But he had to believe it.

Once again, the sound of gunfire whistled overhead. Everyone ducked, but it seemed to fill the men with hope despite the incessant shelling and the smoke-thick sky. The land on the horizon was enough to push their determination to the limit. They *would* reach the shore. As the cruiser rocked in the swell, Harold kept talking to his "patient", which helped take his mind off the unrelenting malady overtaking his stomach. A sailor pushed his way toward him and glanced at the wounded soldier.

'I have to get him home to his family,' Harold said, pained with fatigue. 'He's got to get back home.' He felt he owned this soldier. This was *his* wounded chap, and Harold was responsible for saving a life. He thought about the man's parents, his wife and children on the other side, waiting for this battered and bruised man in his care.

A sailor passed by and smiled. 'Every turn of the screw brings me nearer to you. Hang in there, soldier. The lads below decks are sweating their guts to get you home, mate.'

Harold thought about what the sailor had said. Of course, he meant the ship's propeller. He'd remember that one for sure.

The sea calmed as they reached British waters, but there were only a few cheers; they weren't home yet. Harold looked down at the wounded soldier, whose blood had drained from his face.

'We're almost home. I'm Private Harold Dean, 4th Battalion. You stay with me, do you hear? Stay awake, soldier. I'll take care of you. What's your name?'

The soldier groaned and muttered, 'Tom Hinkley,' after which he passed out.

Harold knew he might never see him again.

As they entered the harbour, the distant sounds of cheering from the crowd reached their ears. Bloody hell, we're home. The exhausted men on deck, pale and unrecognisable, slowly regained their strength and readied themselves to disembark as the crew lowered the gangway. Harold noted their smiles and felt he must do the same, but he couldn't, not yet.

Finally, they disembarked to the deafening roar of the crowd – a cacophony of cheers, whistles and shouts that vibrated in their chests. Harold set foot on familiar ground, breathing in the earthy scent of his homeland, a comforting aroma he'd missed dearly. The cheering felt overwhelming, but he'd survived just as Pop had told him to. It was all that mattered.

The metallic clang of the lowered gangway echoed as lines of weary soldiers, their faces paled with hunger and exhaustion but attempting weak smiles, stumbled down. Ambulances lined the quay, ready to carry the wounded on stretchers to the hospital. Harold hoped he'd saved Tom Hinkley's life.

'Was I dreaming, or did we make it back home?' a voice came from behind him.

Harold smiled. 'No, you're not bloody dreaming, mate.'

'They've just driven off with your casualty.'

'I know, and I hope he makes it. He got hit in the shoulder – pretty bad, it was.' Harold puffed out his cheeks. 'That could have been me, but it missed.' He buried his head in his hands, overwhelmed by the need to cry with both joy and sorrow all at the same time. He didn't know how he felt; there was too much confusion.

As he stood in line, his body became increasingly cold and clammy, overwhelmed by a sudden rush of anxiety. He couldn't help but reflect on their incredible stroke of luck at being rescued. He let out a deep sigh, his shoulders slumping with the weight of emotion. The sights he had witnessed on those beaches were now etched into his memory, a haunting reminder of the pain and suffering he hoped never to experience again.

One of the ATS girls passed him a food parcel.

'Cor, jam sandwiches! Cuppa tea please. God, the relief.' Harold waited his turn for refreshments. 'I never realised jam sandwiches could taste this good.' He stuffed the bread into his mouth until he could hardly speak.

His immediate concern was to find a phone and reach out to his parents, ensuring them of his safe arrival. Nervously, he reached into his pocket to make sure the letter he had written to Ellie was still there. It was – however, soaking wet and unfit to be mailed.

'Here you are. I think these are your size.' The girl passed him a parcel of clothing.

Harold wanted to kiss her to say thanks, but didn't get the opportunity. He realised he'd probably overpowered her with his stink of seawater.

After changing into dry clothing, he felt secure and ready to go back to camp for the night. A symphony of steam and metal resonated through the station, announcing a much welcomed train. Enthusiastic cheers and shouts filled the air as Harold stepped into one of the carriages. Relief washed over him, and he wept as the memory of his actions lingered in his mind. He must try to forget, and return home after they relieved him of duty.

Harold gazed out of the carriage window. The green fields stretched before him, a peaceful scene, alive with flying birds and the occasional cars along the lanes; a world away from the haunted faces and terror he'd witnessed in France. There was not much sign of bomb damage here. He'd entered a world of calm where the war didn't seem to exist. Near the railway line there were delightful cottages with neat gardens, and Harold wondered if what he'd left on the other side had not been real. But it was real enough. The folks at home would never believe it, except for his father. He never talked about his war, and now Harold understood the reason. What was the point? The experience had been beyond anyone's belief. He closed his eyes and fell asleep to the rhythmic sound of wheels rolling over rails.

The next day, after arriving in Aldershot, he tried to make a phone call but couldn't get through. So, he wrote a postcard instead.

Dear Ma and Pop,
Arrived in England, coming home soon.
Love Harold

Chapter Fourteen

January 1941

The air crackled with unspoken farewells as Ellie felt it in her bones – her close circle of army associates was preparing to move on, leaving a void in her life. There had been a few changes within the camp. After three months and making her first debut, she'd finally got her chance to stand in for Marlene. The last few months had been a fantastic theatrical experience, but leave was never synchronised with Harold's visits to Saltburn. She found it hard to accept; it seemed most unfair. He couldn't even phone her.

'Honestly, El, you were terrific. You must do it again,' Vicky said.

Ellie clapped her hands with glee and vowed to write a letter to Harold to tell him all about it. 'I love being here. These people are all good friends.'

Vicky gave her a sharp reminder. 'These people are not friends. They're "forces acquaintances". You never know when or if they will return after the war. Be prepared,' she said. 'I'm your real friend because we went to school and grew up together. That's real friends, El.'

Private Leeman poked her head around the door. 'Sergeant wants a word, Brownlee.'

As Ellie walked toward the office of her commanding officer, she couldn't help but feel a sense of unease. She knocked nervously on the door.

A voice said, 'Enter.'

Ellie's mind shifted to the worst-case scenario. She marched into the office and saluted. 'Good morning, ma'am.'

'I came to watch the Christmas show, Brownlee. Well done,

you're a natural. I'm pleased to tell you that you passed your exam with flying colours.' Sergeant Coleman smiled.

'Yes, ma'am. Thank you.' But Ellie's sense of relief was short-lived.

'What I'm about to say may halt your acting for a while, which is a pity because I can see you're enjoying it. However, we're not here for full-time entertainment, so I have some interesting news. We only picked the best. The army is transferring you to a camp in Scotland to train for a special mission. Your posting will be classified. Therefore, you cannot speak about this, even to your best friend. Other ATS girls are being posted up there. As I say, we've picked the best and there'll be a promotion for you, once you've undertaken more clerical training. Again, I stress you will *not* be allowed to tell anyone where you are going. My words to you here will remain in this office. Do you understand, Brownlee?'

Ellie nodded, her eyes widening. 'Yes, ma'am.'

'Pack your personal things this evening and report to me at eight o'clock in the morning. You are now on the official payroll.'

Ellie's mind raced. Bloody hell, what the...? Oh no! 'For how long, ma'am?'

'Brownlee, there is a war on. Don't ask silly questions.'

Ellie's heart pounded. 'Yes, ma'am.'

She was leaving Yorkshire, but Vicky, Harold, her family, the Deans – everyone she'd ever known, she might not see for a long time. She left the office feeling overwhelmed and out of control. What would she do without Vicky? If this was what war did to you, she didn't like it one bit.

The following evening, Ellie left on an army truck heading for Scotland. She'd hoped to travel by train, but it wasn't an option; public transport was vulnerable to bombs along the east coast.

'Bye, Vicky. I'll miss you.'

'I'll miss you, El, and I wish I knew where you were going, but write to me soon, promise? We'll have the most wonderful party in Saltburn when the war is over. We'll get flamin', blazin' drunk!'

Ellie laughed through her tears at Vicky's remark.

Vicky waved farewell, a crumpled handkerchief clutched in her hand, amid a gaggle of chattering ATS girls also saying goodbye. The biting wind whipped around Ellie as she climbed into the rattling truck, her hands numb and frozen; she felt utterly alone. Abandoned. Why were they sending her away so quickly? She might never get the chance to act again. But the CO had said they'd picked the best, and Ellie reminded herself about the promotion. Perhaps she'd better believe it.

A young soldier sat next to Ellie in the truck with a rifle at his side. 'Hello, love. I'm Private Ellis. Stan to you.' He smiled.

A warmth spread through her as she realised someone cared.

'Chin up, gal. It's not the end o' world.'

'Hmm…the rate we're going, be careful what you say,' Ellie chirped.

Regardless, Stan persisted with the conversation, unwavering. 'We have to stay alert tonight. I could be in some foreign land by next week, but I won't let it get to me. We'll win this war by hook or crook, and I want to be proud to say I was part of it.'

Ellie was in awe of his unwavering optimism, which left her feeling humbled. In the last few weeks, Harold's letters had become scarce, arriving only every six or seven weeks instead of the usual weekly correspondence. It had nothing to do with his feelings; it was just how things worked. As the truck rolled north, a lonely, foggy darkness seemed to mirror Ellie's emotions, a fact that Stan couldn't help but notice.

'Hey, girl,' he said. 'I know, I know, it's hard. Who did you leave behind?'

'My boyfriend, Harold, and my best friend, Vicky. We all went to school together.'

Stan's cheeky smile and hopeful conversation comforted her. She felt safe sitting next to a soldier, knowing he'd look after her if the Germans came.

'What's your first name?'

'Ellie.'

'Where've ya come from?'

'Saltburn.' Ellie looked around at the girls on the truck.

'Oh, really? My family lives in Redcar. That's close enough.' Stan gave her a wink.

The other girls in the truck sang as they moved along the bumpy roads. '*This old man, he played one. He played knick-knack on my thumb—*'

The ATS sergeant complained. 'You can talk quietly, but don't sing. You don't know who's listening.'

Ellie mumbled to herself. 'Huh! That sergeant's paranoid. These trucks make enough noise by themselves.'

'I'm very privileged I got all you lovely young lasses to guard,' Stan announced with a grin.

The trucks stopped at a pub on a lonely moorland road. Stan jumped out, and the sergeant stood in front of them.

'Netty stop for you, girls. Watch out when you pull the chain, it doesn't always work first time. There's a cesspit next door with a toilet seat. The men can find a place behind a boulder. There's plenty around here.'

'Yes, sergeant.' Stan saluted.

'Well, go on, girls. Get on with it. There's that outhouse at the back of the pub. This is our only stop until we cross into Scotland. And hurry. We don't want to be a target, do we?'

The ATS corporal ushered Ellie forward. 'Come on, move along, girls. A quick one and out, do you hear?'

'There's no more newspaper to wipe your bum,' said one girl as she left the cubicle.

The sound of laughter echoed through the yard. With the continuing flush of the toilet chain and the time available, it stopped working.

'God, it stinks in there. I'm going to be sick.' Ellie balked. She held her nose, and when she finished, the flusher worked again, so she pulled hard on the chain, and water spilled on her head. 'Bloody toilet!' she swore, the lingering odour stinging her nostrils as she smoothed her dress, shaking the water from her dripping hair.

The sergeant waited. 'Your tie, private! Tuck it in. And keep your ruddy voices down.'

Ellie climbed back into the truck and, after further conversation with Stan, fell asleep.

A couple of hours later, someone tapped her arm. 'Come on, Ellie, wake up.'

She knew it wasn't Harold's voice, although the accent was familiar. Her eyes drifted sleepily toward the sound.

'We're stopping 'ere,' said Stan. 'It's time to get up.'

Ellie woke with a start. 'Oh flippin' 'eck, where are we?'

'Near Edinburgh,' said Stan. 'We have to be careful because of the recent bombing raids. We'll be camping until daylight because it's gettin' dark, then you girls will catch the train to Inverness at midday. You can stay here in the truck if you wish. It's probably warmer. We can't light a fire outside, but we can have tea and something to eat in the morning. We got Primus stoves in the trucks. In the meantime, we have hot drinks, soup and biscuits.'

He helped Ellie to her feet. The moment she stepped out into the forest, the eerie sound of barking foxes filled the air, their piercing cries sending shivers down her spine. Ellie hoped the snow wouldn't fall as she curled up tighter in her warm blanket. It was far too cold to be camping in the open.

The following morning Ellie climbed into the truck to collect her kitbag and Stan helped her. For a moment, she wished he were Harold.

'Go on, girl,' Stan encouraged. 'Enjoy your time in Scotland, and good luck. I'm going south again now. It's the last stop before we get orders for the front line. I've no idea where I'll be. They don't tell you until the last minute.' He smiled that cheeky grin that had kept her going these last few hours. 'Well, love, make the most of what you have here. I hope to see you again. Farewell, and look after yersel'.'

Ellie's heart sank. She wanted to ask Stan to look out for Harold, but what was the point? 'Thanks, Stan. You take care too. Come back safe.'

Upon arrival at Waverley Station, the ATS girls waited on the platform after gathering their kit. The train was late, but Ellie sighed in relief when they boarded.

'Inverness, here we come!' someone exclaimed.

Ellie hadn't a clue exactly where that was. She'd only heard of the Loch Ness Monster.

At first, Ellie couldn't take her eyes away from the breathtaking coastal scenery, green fields and snow-capped mountains. The previous night had deprived her of warm sleep, and it wasn't long before her eyelids drooped and she fell, exhausted, into a deep slumber.

After a delay because of an air raid over Glasgow, they made it to Strathpeffer. Ellie had no idea where that village was on a map or what they were doing there. She stepped from the train, dumping her heavy kitbag on the platform. The modest rural station entrance was awash with trucks and army personnel. Gazing up the hill at the grand Victorian buildings reminded her of home. She breathed clear and crisp mountain air and noted the mist lingering above the trees.

'Highland and Richmond Hotels!' shouted a soldier. 'Get on the truck, girls, I'll take you up there with your kit. We have to get your passes because it's a restricted zone.'

It wasn't only at the station where all the action took place. The army had taken over the entire village, and everywhere Ellie looked, someone was in uniform. Her eyes widened in awe as she gazed at The Highland Hotel, designed to resemble a majestic French chateau, complete with a long balcony and square turrets on each corner of the building. Was this the place the army had chosen as their accommodation? Surely not. Wow!

An officer greeted everyone with a warm, welcoming smile. 'This will be your home for a while, so make the most of it.'

Ellie's jaw dropped as she walked through the lobby. The oak-panelled walls, bay windows, deer antlers, tartan carpet, and beamed ceilings seemed so, so… Heck, this is Scotland. It's better than The Zetland. My God! It's amazing. She stood patiently in line, listening to the chatter of the other girls as they checked in. With each step up the elegant, sweeping staircase, she could almost hear the faint strains of a waltz and imagine herself dressed in a glamorous ball gown, twirling in Harold's arms. Perhaps it wouldn't be so bad in Strathpeffer after all. Her mood changed from one of disappointment to excitement and expectation. If only Vicky were here to share it.

Chapter Fifteen

March 1941

After a fortnight the slower pace of life in Strathpeffer had become familiar to Ellie, and she appreciated the quiet charm of the village. The anticipation of the mail brought about a new wave of anxiety. Had she lost sight of Harold with all the moving around? Would someone write to her, just anyone?! Despite finding a union with the Scottish girls, she missed Vicky. It wasn't the same without her; loneliness grabbed Ellie, like in Saltburn when everyone had left for the war. It was time to write more letters. If you didn't write, you wouldn't get anything back.

> *Dear Alf and Betty,*
>
> *I wanted to apologise for not writing to you. I also haven't heard from Harold in an age, and I hope he is okay.*
>
> *The evacuation from Dunkirk was a shock. I wish I knew where he is. I can't tell you much about where I am, either. All I can say is that they have moved me away from my usual place and I'm working somewhere with a lovely view. I know you'll understand. It's all been too much.*
>
> *If you've heard from Harold, please send me a letter with any updates on his safety. Although I'm happy enough, there's a void in my life without him. The ache in my chest grows stronger with each passing day as I long for his return, and I bet you do, too. The only correspondence I received was a brief letter informing me he had survived the ordeal at Dunkirk and a couple of brief messages apologising for the lack of mail.*

She let out a sigh of gratitude, silently thanking God that he'd made it home.

> *My mother hasn't written since her self-imposed "holiday"*

in the Dales, nor has Tommy. I am left with a deep feeling
of abandonment. Our source of information is the radiogram,
so we can only rely on what we hear to understand what's
happening outside. Although I am making progress toward a
promotion, I remind myself that it's still the early stages and
there is much more to be done.

Hope to hear from you soon. You know what the post is like.
With love,
Ellie

The following day, Ellie searched for more paper to write a letter home. The mail was either slow or lost in a bombing raid. She must try to contact her mother; it was the least she could do. She was halfway through her task when the loud, crackling announcement of a mail delivery startled her. She rushed downstairs, her footsteps dampened on the tartan carpet.

'Brownlee, one for you,' said the girl at reception.

As she opened the envelope, Ellie's heart sank when she realised the letter wasn't from Harold as she had been hoping, but from someone else. She recognised the handwriting. It was from her mother. She dashed back to her room to read it.

Dear Ellie,

How are you? Sorry I haven't been in touch, but I wrote a
couple of letters and when you didn't reply I realised you might
not have received them. Betty said she received your letter,
prompting me to try again. She said the post is dreadful.

I decided not to stay in Saltburn, so I wrote to Auntie Pat.
I planned to stay with her again in the Dales. The east coast has
been a target for the Luftwaffe, and Alf told me he is keeping
busy with the shop and watching the skies for German planes.
The army needs accommodation for billeting their soldiers, and
I can earn a reasonable income for Tommy and me. So, I think
I will let the house go to them and see what happens. It's early
days yet.

I think about you being in the army and hope you stay safe.

I wish I knew where you are. Everything is so very "up in the air" (sometimes for real!). I will write again as soon as I can. We miss you, Ellie. I hope our lives will change for the better soon. Things are changing for me as they are for you. I'll tell you more soon.

Love,

Mam

Ellie didn't know what to think. At least her mother had tried to write again when the other letters hadn't arrived. Ellie finished writing her original letter and changed a few words here and there. She mentioned that she couldn't write very often as her work kept her busy. Still, it was good to hear from her mother. She wondered what she'd meant by her "life change". Perhaps she felt more supported now that she was with Auntie Pat, and with Dad gone it hadn't been easy.

After her third week, Ellie received a communication from HQ and wished they had spelled her name correctly.

Dear Private Brownlea,

Please report to my office this Monday, 21 March 1941, where your role as secretary is confirmed. You will attend the conference room at 0900 hrs at The Highland Hotel, which we know will be convenient. Certain matters are connected to our project, and we feel you will be most suitable for the work we have in mind.

We're keen to improve your shorthand speed and require you to attend additional classes at The Ben Wyvis Hotel, but we can discuss this on Monday.

We wish you every success.

Yours sincerely,

Major Charles Darlington, DSO

Ellie had done nothing wrong. She must have more confidence in herself. They'd assessed her for typing ability, but her shorthand wasn't entirely up to speed.

The new ATS arrivals had made her feel less lonely, and as the week progressed, she longed to get back onstage. There was mediocre entertainment: movies, singalongs, and Scottish dance music at the Strathpeffer Pavilion, but Ellie wanted more. She needed to act again, but there didn't seem to be a group to join. It was all impromptu entertainment.

Saturday afternoon was Ellie's day off. She gazed through the bay window as new ATS girls marched from the station. Scottish companies at the camp were piped in by girl pipers to the tune of 'Scotland the Brave'. She recalled one girl explaining how they made their kilts.

'We were given loads of Sutherland Old Weathered tartan fabric and we're not supposed to wear kilts – it's not uniform. Anyway, our sergeant decided we'd try making our own. We had the material, so why not? I mean, we're Scots and entitled to wear a kilt, surely? Anyway, we borrowed a couple of old Singer sewing machines, pinned the tartan, and pressed the pleats under the mattresses of our beds. They looked so good we tried them out on parade. Just for fun, really. We knew we'd get into trouble.'

'But if it's not uniform, how is it you are allowed to wear them?' Ellie queried.

'Well, it's kind of amusing. We had a visiting general, and he said what a great job we'd done. He insisted we continue to wear them. You can imagine how thrilled we were. It was hard work sewing for the entire band, but we all mucked in, and the locals loaned us more sewing machines.'

Ellie smiled to herself. In certain instances, it was important to defy convention, to inject some joy into life.

While sitting in the hotel lobby reading her copy of *Woman & Home*, she felt someone creep up behind her, put their hands over her eyes, and whisper, 'Guess who?'

Ellie gasped. 'Hey! Stop it, what are you doing? No, I don't believe it. Vicky! Oh my God! What on earth are you doing here?' She grabbed hold of Vicky and hugged her as if her life depended on it. 'How did you know I was here?'

'Sergeant Somner told me. Well…she gave me a clue. She said I'd be reunited with an old friend. I was thrilled about it. It took a helluva long time to get here. We stopped because one girl got travel-sick and was very ill. We only made it on the train as far as Dundee, and then we had to cross the rest of the way with the truck. The train was too dangerous, so we left the sick girl behind. She'll join us in a couple of days, no doubt.'

'But…what are you doing up here in Scotland? I mean… Oh, you don't know how much I've missed you.' Ellie gave her friend a playful swat on the shoulder. 'It's been very lonely here, unable to communicate with the outside world.'

'I've missed you too, El. There are a few of us from Catterick here now, though. We've been training over the last weeks to ride a motorcycle. They want me to be the main dispatch rider. It's great fun.' Vicky beamed. 'You know how much I wanted to do more useful stuff. This is marvellous, although I don't relish the winter.'

'Really? *Really*? Clever you. And they sent you up here?' Ellie squeezed Vicky's arm. 'You're a tough old thing,' she reassured her. 'This job will suit you fine.'

'Well, Janet and me – that's the other girl on my course – we'll be the links between here and the Kyle of Lochalsh, wherever that is. We're doing relays. They don't want anyone to listen to messages, so they send the dispatch riders to deliver to the east and west coasts. It could be dangerous, but they trained us to hide the motorcycle and ourselves if we hear enemy aircraft approaching.'

'I can hardly believe you're here, Vicky. Have you heard from Al?'

'Yes, he's been involved with the Dunkirk evacuation. I've no idea where he is, except that he's somewhere in England, as far as I know. He was home on leave. It was great.'

Ellie wished she'd had that opportunity. 'Yes, Harold too, I suppose, but I can't be sure. She tried to change the subject. 'Look at you, eh? Riding a motorcycle!'

Vicky laughed. 'I know, it's incredible, isn't it? And I love it. I only fell off once when I let the clutch out too fast. So...what else has been happening? Where are you working, El?'

'Hmm...well. The situation here has unfolded so rapidly that I barely had time to react. I've been chosen to work on something essential for the war effort, and the army needs me. I've just started training. Even with you, I need to be cautious about what I say.' Ellie gave a deep sigh, wishing she'd been able to stay at Catterick. 'I hope to hear from Harold again soon, although I got a late postcard.' She held up the card.

> *Arrived in England, safe and sound. I'm not sure if we'll be on*
> *leave together. Sorry this is short. Missing you.*
>
> *Love,*
>
> *Harold*

Never before had a simple postcard meant so much to her, yet his words filled her with alarm. Was she able to meet him there? Yet again it seemed not.

'Who else have you brought with you?' she asked Vicky now.

'There's only two of us from our sleeping quarters and about six others from the other building. I'm glad we left Brummer behind. She drove us all mad, and I don't think she would have coped with Scotland.'

'Staying in this hotel is marvellous. So far, I haven't needed to share. I've got a small room to myself. The other girls often sleep four in one room. The special ATS girls get all the best rooms, and the food is wonderful. They don't want us idle-chatting to the other girls in our room. Well, that's what I think is the reason.'

'So, what happens next after this?'

'I'm about to do a further clerical course for the next three months.'

'Oh, you'll do it, El. You got determination and can turn nothing into something these days.'

'Thanks, Vicky. Maybe we can be a team again, eh? I admit I've felt rather lonely without my best friend.'

The two girls glanced out of the hotel window. As she looked around, Ellie couldn't help but notice the chaotic arrangement of trucks parked on both sides of the road. Women walked back and forth, their laughter only masked by the glass in the hotel windows. A girl strode confidently into town, leather briefcase tucked under her arm, three stripes on her sleeve. The camp housed around forty girls and 300 men, and there were still more arrivals expected. Ellie knew Vicky was "one for the men" and felt glad that her infatuation with Scotty hadn't come to more than admiration. Vicky wouldn't do anything stupid, for sure. She was better than that.

'I hope to get some leave, but our mam hasn't written much. Well, I think it's the slow post. God, I wish I understood her. Sometimes I feel she's hiding something from me – more so since she went to visit Auntie Pat. You instinctively know these things, don't you?'

'It's sad, I know. I never really knew your mam except to say hello at the Deans' shop when I stood behind her once. She rarely said hello back – she always seemed withdrawn. I didn't see her at any of the school concerts either.'

Ellie shook her head. 'Unless Harold is on leave, I doubt I'll get home – it's a long way and there's no one there now except Alf and Betty. I'll keep writing to them, but I'll spend my time off here and read.'

'What about the concert party?' asked Vicky. 'And are there any dances?'

'Concert party? No, it's all a bit impromptu, but there are a few dances. The Canadians are here. They got troops called Lumberjills here, too. They chop the wood in the forest. Amazing!'

'We shall have to see about the lack of entertainment. We could start our own, eh? Someone told me there's a hospital here. There must be some older people in this village who need cheering up,' Vicky said.

Ellie smiled. Vicky was back in her life and riding a motorcycle. Amazing! If anyone could inject some liveliness into this place, it would be her. But how long would it be before Ellie got a letter from Harold? Where is he? She supposed no one cared where she was because she'd moved camp. To say the least, the north of Scotland was remote, and Strathpeffer was hardly like Redcar or Middlesbrough. It was a small village. Nothing exciting really, except for the outstanding mountain views.

Monday morning, Ellie attended her appointment with Major Darlington with the usual salutes and formalities.

'Take a seat, Brownlee,' he said.

The major was a good-looking mature man with greying dark hair and a reassuring smile. Ellie assumed he'd gone through the Great War and was about to retire from the army. She liked him immediately but couldn't say why. Maybe it was his kindly face.

'I hear you did well at Catterick,' he said. 'Your CO was impressed by your acting skills.'

'Yes, sir, thank you,' Ellie said.

'We need service personnel here who can "act" by hiding a well-kept secret.' He raised an eyebrow.

Ellie thought about his words. She'd been acting out that part with her mother for years. 'I'm not *too* sure what you mean, sir?'

'When you work for me, you must adhere to the Official Secrets Act even more than you imagined. We run a classified operation up here, and you can't speak about it to anyone. What is said in this office, stays in this office. German U-boats have been spotted off the Scottish coast. We hoped you could become part of the special services protecting the north of Scotland from invasion. Other work is behind the scenes, and it's top secret. Your key role will be to assist me in carrying out this work. There's probably a promotion in it for you.'

'Yes, sir. I understand. Thank you.'

'It's all to do with mining. I must say, not very intriguing, but a vital part of the war effort.'

'Can I ask about leave, sir?'

'I know, you live in Yorkshire, don't you? We'll discuss that soon, although it's a long way to travel and the route isn't that safe any more.' He sidestepped the subject. 'Will you be able to entertain the troops here too? We could do with some shaking up in the entertainment department here in Strathpeffer.'

'Well, my old school friend is here, and between us we could probably muster up something once again, sir. We discussed this a few days ago.'

'Excellent cover. Enjoy outside entertainment while keeping your true activities secret,' the major slyly smiled.

Ellie took a deep breath.

'You'll be fine.' He tightened his lips in a smile.

'Yes, sir.' Ellie smiled back.

'So,' he said. 'I have a document I want you to sign, erm... I'm sorry we don't have time for you to think too hard about this. You'll have to get on with it and obey orders like the rest.' He scratched the side of his face. 'Don't worry, I'll keep you updated next week. Please sign this for your posting.'

Ellie checked the document and then signed it. 'Ah, understood, sir.'

'Now we have the formalities out of the way, I'll tell you more. You'll get leave, but we cannot take risks and allow you to mingle with the public too often. You understand that top secret means top secret, so going home will be very limited – we must keep contact to a minimum. You see, the thing is, if the Germans find out about our project, they will bomb the hotel and the camp, and all will be lost. So, you see, we have to be careful. High-quality glass is needed for periscope lenses and gun sights. If the Germans know where it comes from, they will want it for themselves because it's a precious commodity, and this is the best. A lot of the paperwork for this goes through here. So, we have to be careful.'

'Of course, sir. I appreciate the importance of maintaining secrecy.'

'Not a word to anyone, and I'll see you tomorrow at 0800 hours.'

'Yes, sir, thank you.'

After spending the last three weeks checking mail for censoring, she was glad to be working a vital job. She saluted smartly, a smile playing on her lips as she left the major's dimly lit office. He had made her feel valued.

The shrill message blared from the loudspeaker, making Ellie wince. A Scottish voice echoed across the room.

'The post has now arrived. Please come to the reception.'

Letters from home were a morale booster, and while she waited in line, she noted plenty of sad faces leaving the room. 'No mail, Suzie?'

'Sometimes, no news is good news. I lost my brother three months ago.'

'Oh dear. Sorry to hear that.' Ellie gave a sympathetic smile as Suzie walked out of the door empty-handed.

Suzie's words had an eerie effect, sending a shiver down her spine. While waiting for her turn, her anticipation built. The joy on her face was clear when she received not one, but two letters: one from Betty and the other from Harold. She opened Harold's letter first, postmarked Peterborough and delayed as usual.

My darling El,

Now, at last, I have time to write to you. I feel we've all been to hell and back.

Dunkirk was a nightmare, and I was afraid I wouldn't make it, but I felt proud when I got home. The experience was so traumatising I cannot bring myself to recall it, though I suspect I may have been instrumental in saving a man's life in the process. I was only doing what a good soldier would do, so I hope he makes it. As for me, war stinks! It was overwhelming and very scary. I'm just glad I survived.

The last letter I received from you was two months ago. I thought you'd forgotten me, and then I realised it was daft to feel that way. You joined the ATS, but I heard you'd moved camps after talking to Ma and Pop. So where are you now? No one will tell me your whereabouts, and I doubt I'll get to know because everything is so hush-hush these days. I pray you will receive this letter soon.

We're still moving around and debriefing after our recent fracas with "You Know Who" in a foreign country. I hope I never see myself in that situation again, but that's what being a soldier is all about.

When this war is over in TEN years (God, I hope not), perhaps we can start living again. I hope to go to Saltburn soon. I'll only get three days of leave. Will I see you?

Through his words, Ellie felt the sharp edges of frustration pressing against her with overwhelming sadness. She read on, homesick and with a touch of melancholy.

What is this war doing to us, El? I thought about you a lot while I was away. Your photo kept me sane. Unfortunately, the picture got wet during the rescue, and now I can hardly see you. I bet you have changed. Anyway, now you're in uniform, I need to see you wearing it! Please send me another photo if you can. Just one more thing: I was promoted with a pay rise. I'm now Corporal Dean.

Now, there's not much time to read or write. We're always on the move, but I hope we can catch up soon. I will always love you, El. Please wait for me.

Lots of love,
Harold

With a swipe of her hand, Ellie wiped the tears from her face, the rough fabric of her sleeve scratching against her skin. On the Pathé News she'd seen the boys' battered clothes and their haunted eyes, and knew what they'd been through. Not knowing if he'd see home again must have been a terrible weight on his shoulders, each passing moment stretching into an eternity of dread. Poor Harold.

The letter from Betty was full of local news, but nothing seemed important any more. Curious, Betty enquired about Ellie's whereabouts. Ellie realised she must write to her and Alf again when she had more time. All this secrecy was driving her potty, but she remembered Major Darlington's words and would be in deep trouble if she betrayed her country without thinking. It was an immense responsibility. But to the outside world she must appear to be just a lowly clerk toiling away in Major Darlington's office, nothing more. She had to play the role convincingly, suppressing any hint of her true mission.

Ellie replied to Harold that same afternoon, knowing she was too far away and unable to leave. She sent him a photo of herself in ATS uniform, taken at Catterick a few months before she'd set off for Scotland. On the back of the picture, she wrote, "To my darling Harold, with all my love, Ellie."

Twice during the next few months, Harold came home on leave, finding only the heavy stillness that spoke of Ellie's absence. Oh yes, the family were there, their laughter echoing in the familiar rooms, but without Ellie, the house felt something was missing.

Harold sat in the deckchair in the yard in the warmth of late summer as Betty swelled with pride listening to her son's articulate account of his life and friendships within the armed forces; a testament to his maturity.

'Got anything new to tell me?' asked Alf as he stood leaning against the back door eating a biscuit.

Betty stood from her stool. 'I must get on, pet. I have to chop the turnips ready for dinner.' She left for the kitchen.

'Well, I can't tell you everything. Dunkirk was a dreadful nightmare. I've learned Morse code and got promoted. That's all I can say, really. I could be up at the front line soon, but I'm only guessing until they give the orders. No sign of Ellie yet. I'm concerned I've had no letters.'

'Well, don't tell your mother about the front line, she'll worry herself to death, and I can't say I like it either, but there you go. Stay safe, that's all. Aye, lad, I remember it well. We're so glad you made it off those darned beaches. You're a survivor, son. Well done. We're very proud of you.'

Harold finished his breakfast and headed upstairs for a spot of thinking. Pop might be proud of him, but the things he'd seen still invaded his thoughts in bed at night, those dreadful days when he'd almost died. He needed more time to survive his life in the army. He needed his future with Ellie. An hour later, he returned downstairs wearing his coat.

'Where are you going?' Betty asked.

'Just taking a walk,' he replied, a slight smile playing on his lips. 'My head is so full of noise and I need to clear all the clutter.'

Betty smiled, a genuine smile that crinkled the corners of her eyes. 'Don't be too long, 'cause your dinner will be ready at half-past twelve.'

Harold walked along the track near the railway line where Ellie had made her hasty decision to do those things they ought not to do. The sweet scent of lilies and honeysuckle, a perfume reminiscent of her, wafted toward him, instantly bringing back a flood of memories, including her innocent smile. The war was now an affair of the soul. He felt his heart torn out by the bombing and army training. He recalled his father's words: this war could go on for years. Let there be no doubt: it was going in that direction. His time at Dunkirk had taken its toll, and he flinched at every bang and clatter that echoed through the town. As he stood there, a motorbike roared past, its engine backfiring loudly. Harold's body reacted instinctively, his legs buckling beneath him as he tumbled to the ground in a heap. His stride interrupted, he meticulously observed his surroundings, absorbing every detail to regain his sense of direction. Why on earth did that happen? He puffed out his cheeks feeling somewhat foolish.

He made his way home through the Riftswood, the place Agnes had mentioned when he'd first called on Ellie all those years ago. 'No going down the woods,' she'd said. Harold wondered why she needed to say that. The rhythmic click of his heels echoed as he walked the streets, prompting friendly calls of hello from the locals who recognised his uniform. His heart resided in the present, but his soul longed for his girl. The question of whether he would ever marry her lingered in the air.

He returned home to find Betty, Alf and Peter waiting with a meal on the table. Harold sat down and tucked into the Yorkshire pudding. It had never tasted so good.

'You'd think you'd never eaten, the way you polished that off,' Peter said.

Harold caught his dad's eye; their reminiscent glances said it all. He took a breath. 'Ma, you don't know how good that tastes. It could be my last pud for some time.' He took a gulp of water.

Betty ruffled her son's shorn hair in play. 'Thanks, pet.'

'To Harold and William, wherever they may go,' Alf said.

Betty glanced at Harold across the table. He knew that look only too well. Apparently, his mother was highly anxious about her boys – and who could blame her?

Chapter Sixteen

'Vicky, love? Let's rally some of our girls and ask the lads if they have any talent for acting onstage,' Ellie suggested. 'I've got a couple of days off. I can make posters and do what we did at Catterick. It won't be a huge event but we can make a difference in this small village, I suppose.'

Vicky looked up from the book she was reading. 'Yeah, why not? Good idea. Maybe you can do some organising. I'll look out the songs and use a few well-known ones, too. There are loads of things we can do. The local people here are very nice. I met some of them today and talked about entertainment.'

'Whoa there, Vicky! I've no idea how to get hold of the scripts we used to have.' Ellie thought for a moment. 'How about the library?'

'Or I could contact Scotty,' Vicky suggested coyly. 'Although I doubt if I can find him any more. They'll have stuff in the library. I can ask Sergeant Somner. She and I are more like friends than ranking colleagues.'

Ellie reminisced about Scotty and how he'd livened up an otherwise dull situation in Catterick. His wit had often had the girls in fits of laughter.

'*You* could write a play. I know you can – you were always good at that, El,' Vicky suggested.

'Heck no, that's a challenge too far, and I'm busy now at work.'

'Don't be daft. I can help you. It'll give us something to do on our days off. I won't be going home very often either, if at all. They need me here.'

'First things first. Let's get those posters out and see what happens. I mean, it's quiet here after the dreadful bombing in

Glasgow. It scares me that the Jerries will do it again. Those poor homeless people in the cities. Dreadful. It's been *too* quiet in the last couple of months. Does anyone know we're still here?'

'I hope they won't bomb here, El. We have to think on our feet these days. At least as a dispatch rider, I can go out to the countryside and get away from it all. It was terrifying at first, being among those mountains on my own – I just hoped they wouldn't send me out in the snow. If I see one of them eagle birds, I'll probably jump off my motorcycle and hide in a ditch, thinking it's a bomber. It's incredibly remote out there. I'd have to wait for rescue if I broke down. Could be days before they find me. I always carry a Mars bar or two.'

Ellie laughed at her comment but tried to see the serious side of Vicky's remark. She knew Vicky made regular sorties to Kyle of Lochalsh on the west coast. It seemed the perfect job, but there were always risks. If she set out early in the mornings, she could be back in time for tea if she was doing relays and didn't have to go all the way to Kyle. Her time was then her own. Ellie wished she could escape the camp on the back of Vicky's motorbike. Her description of the west coast sounded delightful, although Strathpeffer had mountains, too. Ben Wyvis was one of them.

It was the day that Ellie received notice of her promotion to corporal. She could hardly believe it. *Corporal* Brownlee, eh? Just like Harold.

Despite the unrest and distant sounds of conflict in southern Britain, both girls were grateful for their peaceful, rural refuge, far from the city's dangers. The grainy images flickered on the newsreel screen, shocking them both with their brutality. All those buildings were destroyed, leaving behind only rubble and dust.

In advertising for volunteers for the new concert party, Ellie and Vicky identified themselves as the Wyvis Players on the poster.

'I counted twenty-two replies – we'll need to audition them all,' Vicky said.

'At this rate, we'll need more help. It could quickly get out of hand if we're not careful,' Ellie said. 'I've almost finished writing the play. We'll need to use the Gestetner for copies of the script.'

'Honestly, El, you're marvellous,' Vicky replied. 'When we were at school, there was another girl named Ellie Brownlee. She wasn't like you. She was shy and afraid to open her mouth.'

Ellie laughed at Vicky's remark. 'Thanks, Vicks. It's nice of you to say so.'

Everything they'd learned about stage production in Catterick had taken off. The girls hugged each other in recognition of their first success.

'So what's next?' Vicky said.

'I expect we'll spend the next few months writing a new production!' Ellie replied. 'We'd better be getting on with it – we need to do it before Christmas. The next few months are certainly going to be challenging.'

As November drew near, six months having passed with Ellie working and Vicky travelling, a chill wind swept through the bare branches. As was usual at that time of year, the weather brought complications, with vehicles needing to be rescued from the heavy snowfall. There was a disruption in the delivery of food supplies. Vicky felt determined not to allow 'a bit of snow to get in the way'. But there were days when she couldn't ride to the west coast, and on one occasion she delivered a message in a relay, riding in the trucks. The snowstorm had them stranded for hours, and they had no choice but to dig their way out, and according to Vicky, their breath froze in the air.

'I wish I could be somewhere else,' said Vicky. Her hands were red raw with the cold.

With the rehearsals for the shows, their roles seemed well defined. Ellie directed, and Vicky designed the scenery. So, the ATS wasn't such a lousy job after all.

'Just bloody cold,' Vicky said.

'Thank God we're in remote Scotland,' Ellie replied after hearing further dreadful news about the Blitz. 'Those awful queues of displaced children, waiting for the trains with small suitcases and forlorn looks.' She recalled what Harold had told her. 'I can't imagine leaving home as young as they are. Harold was right, and it's so regrettable. I'm just relieved that we got away from those dreadful bombs.'

'When is it all going to stop?' Vicky remarked. 'I mean, are we safe to go home on leave? It's not all that safe here, is it?'

Ellie decided it was time to return to Saltburn and get answers from her mother. Perhaps she had already left for Auntie Pat's. 'I had been looking forward to catching up with Harold, but unfortunately, he won't be there. I wonder if we shall see each other again.'

A few days later, Ellie received the long-awaited letter. She knew who it was from before she opened it, and it wasn't from Harold.

Dear Ellie,

I know you haven't heard from me for a few weeks, but I wanted you to know, I'm no longer living in Diamond Street. With no other choice, I had to rent our house to the army. It was inevitable I suppose.

There is something else, and I hope you'll understand. Try not to be upset. I know it will come as a shock, but I'm about to get married again. Tommy is leaving for the army soon, and I'll be alone. I was visiting Durham after leaving Saltburn, and I met a lovely man who asked me to go dancing with him. He is with the Home Guard. We have been seeing each other for the last few months and going to tea dances. His name is George Watson. I don't want to be alone any more, and it's been a nightmare with the Blitz. I suppose living in the countryside will help me feel safer. Auntie Pat has been excellent. She understands, so I hope you will feel happy for me too. It won't be a lavish affair, just a case of signing the registry and having a drink in the local pub with a couple of friends and Auntie Pat.

I apologise for the lack of correspondence you've received. Things have been tough, with each day feeling like an uphill battle. I've been trying to untangle the messy threads of my life.

You will like George – his kindness shines through in everything he does. I hope the army is treating you well, with lots of new friends and support. You know I can't help but worry about you. I wish I knew where you are.

   Love,

   Mam xx

Ellie sat down in shock at her mother's words. The letter was very much to the point. She felt like ripping it into small pieces and throwing them all into the air. How could she do this? Her dad had only been gone just over a year, and there her mother was, gallivanting with some man she'd met and *getting married*? Unbelievable!

When Vicky returned to camp that evening, Ellie told her the news.

'To be honest, Ellie, I think she's done the right thing. I mean, being on her own and all that.' Vicky smiled. 'I can see you're bewildered by it. It's a big step.'

'I'm flabbergasted! It's most unlike her. I don't suppose I can even meet the man. I'll write her a letter. She's changed a lot since the beginning of the war. Mellowed, I think.' Ellie rolled her eyes.

'Come on, El, let's think about what we can do, eh? I won't see Alan for a while. Our leave doesn't line up. Why don't you and I go on holiday together and enjoy ourselves? Next spring, we could take our leave in the Highlands and explore the mountains. Do some walking and playwriting.'

Ellie let out a sigh. 'Yes, I suppose we should. I'm due to take loads of leave, but I don't want to take it in Yorkshire. It's too dangerous going down there, and Harold isn't there anyway.'

'Let's do it, then. I'll see if we can do bed and breakfast. I'll ask around,' Vicky said.

A wide, bright smile illuminated Ellie's face. No matter the problem, Vicky always found a way to make things right, her insightful solutions a testament to her warmth.

Chapter Seventeen

Somewhere in England!
Dear Ma and Pop

I received two aerographs, an airmail letter, some newspapers from you, and a very short letter from Peter, so I did well.

As you can see from my rank on the envelope, I've come down in the world, and I'm a private once again. Not only that, but I lost sixpence a day as well, just for staying out one hour late. It was a bit thick. It's no wonder the lads lose interest in the army when things like that happen. I'd been working ever so hard as well – it was my first time doing something wrong. I hadn't been out of the camp for weeks, but they didn't consider such things. Losing the stripe doesn't make much difference to me, but losing it for such a petty affair makes my blood boil. I hope the rest of the army is not like this; otherwise, the war will be lost. They treat us like kids, stopping our pocket money when we've been through hell. Last year, I saved a wounded man from drowning, doesn't that count? No doubt, no one cares about it. I didn't get a chance to tell anyone.

I haven't heard from Ellie for a while now. She told me she's started a drama group. They have been entertaining the troops and visiting local hospitals.

I am curious about how William is faring. There's a constant question lingering in my mind about whether you receive all the letters I send.

I'm afraid I won't be home this Christmas, and it looks like it'll be a long time before I can get back to Saltburn. Please don't send me anything, but save the money for when I return

*on leave. It's no longer a good idea to send stuff as parcels don't
arrive. So, both of you, no more for now.*

Love,

Harold

Harold sealed the letter. Life in the army was undoubtedly more challenging. He knew the next battle loomed, and the relentless sounds of weapons practice would fill the coming weeks as he prepared. Returning an hour late to camp and losing the rank of corporal had bruised him. Back home, if you made a minor mistake at work, people were prepared to forgive you. Not here. It was all black and white. Yes, sir, no, sir, three bags full, sir, et cetera, et cetera.

Shaken by his outburst, he knew he needed to actively help his army colleagues to earn their respect, and now the weight of his demotion pressed down on him as he moved among them. There was no point in bearing grudges. It only spilled over into the work. The horrors of Dunkirk, with its sights and sounds of chaos and destruction, had transformed him from a naive boy into a hardened soldier. He could never forget Dunkirk for as long as he lived. No matter how hard he tried, the visions of dead bodies and the wounded haunted him day after day. He wouldn't forget Tom Hinkley's face, or the men clambering and then falling from the structure of The Mole into the sea, bleeding from their wounds. Relentless visions of the French soldier burned all over his body, and the dreadful smell of rotting flesh – with all that in his head, how could he forget?

He supposed it was okay to bear grudges against the army now and again. Still, there were days when he wished he could grab Ellie by the hand, go away on holiday, and leave it all behind. Then again, his wish might come true faster than he envisaged. There were rumours.

Chapter Eighteen

'Oh, goody, a Christmas card.' Ellie looked at it several times before putting it away in her pocket. 'I can't believe the war has lasted this long. Let's hope Harold is safe.'

'I'm glad he still loves you,' Vicky said. 'He's been writing to you all this time, almost three years.

'But I feel my life's changing. We're changing. *Everything* is changing. I want to *see* him again.'

'Don't you think that's how I feel about Al?'

Ellie puffed out her cheeks. 'It's all so unfair, isn't it? But you have seen Al? I haven't seen Harold in many months.'

Vicky changed the subject. 'The old folks at the hospital really enjoyed the play, didn't they?'

'It was fun.' Ellie smiled knowing her conversation about Harold wasn't taking her anywhere. 'We have to get writing again – it keeps us going and blots out the horrid parts of what's going on in the world.'

Where was Harold now? Their bond felt it was weakening into simple memories. That darned word "when" cropped up too many times among the troops and Ellie was tired of hearing it.

Harold's journey by train took him to Liverpool docks to board the troopship RMS *Empress of Russia*. He stood in awe on the quayside. Gosh, she's enormous! The grey ocean of wartime stretched before her as she supported three weighty funnels, the odour of fuel oil sharp in the air. He waited in line to climb the gangway.

'Well, this is home for the next... God knows how long!' Harold gazed into the grey-and-green River Mersey and reflected on his time in Weston-super-Mare. There had been days when he'd put the war behind him and swept his experiences at Dunkirk under a carpet of hope for the future. Today was unlike any other; a day he never thought he'd see, filled with a strange mixture of hope and trepidation.

Across the quayside, a familiar face waited in line. Harold strode toward the figure waiting to board the ship.

'Bernie? It's me. Hello, pal,' he said cheerfully. 'I thought I'd lost you. Flippin' 'eck, you made it back. It's so good to see you. My God, I thought you'd… Amazing. We've been training. So glad you're on the same ship.'

The two men embraced. They talked briefly about the nightmare in Dunkirk, and Harold felt the emotion welling up inside him.

'Time to go. See you on board,' Bernie said.

Harold stood back, glad he had his friend as a source of support once again. It was a time of reflection, and both men hoped to make it home for next summer. Surely, the war would be over by then? This was now Harold's chance to fulfil a dream of seeing the world before returning to Ellie. He'd have a wealth of stories to tell her. Perhaps he would forget his time in France. That was the worst memory for all of them. But the past was over. He'd move on and let that be the end of it. He closed his eyes, savouring the thoughts of the warm sun and a gently rolling steamer.

But that day was not to be. The Bay of Biscay made him sick, the weather changed, and he spent most of the day hanging over the rail and toilets that couldn't cope with the congestion of continuous use. The day after, however, the sea's stormy grey hue gave way to a peaceful blue, casting a serene and idyllic aura over everything. As the ship sailed south at eighteen knots, he could feel the warmth of the day embracing him. His gaze fixed on the dolphins and the flying fish as they scattered through the wake, while the sirens on the lower decks added a discordant note, a constant reminder of the war. Time to write a letter home. He'd been told they were heading toward Freetown on the West African coast. He'd post it there.

Dear Ma and Pop,

We left Liverpool bound for a place far away. I'll let you know how I get on as the days go by. This ship is enormous, and we'll have a great time. The Canadian crew are marvellous, and we have the best of everything. Right now, I'm in the middle of the ocean. I haven't been seasick since a few days ago when the weather was rough, as the sea is like glass. They don't tell us much, except that we've been issued a different uniform, but I'll send you a photo once I get there.

One week later

Although I can't say which port we docked at, the natives came alongside us in canoes. They sold mangoes, bananas and pineapples. The tantalising aroma of fresh fruit filled the air, but our hopes of savouring it were crushed when they declared it contaminated and unfit for consumption. I couldn't believe it! However, I took the risk and ate loads without being ill. I wish we could have gone ashore, but it wasn't possible. It's scorching here and sweat is pouring from my forehead as I write. Our time afloat is far from empty. We're busy learning navigation and attending lectures on tactics and fieldcraft. It's great because there's a cinema on board and plenty of concerts to keep our minds occupied. The downside is that I have to do physical fitness daily in this hot weather. Still, our pace of life has slowed now to suit our time on the ship. I could get used to this.

Back at sea, a couple of days later
I didn't post this – sorry!

We crossed the line today: the Equator. Father Neptune came aboard with his queen and pirates – a real bloodthirsty lot, they were! (In reality, it was the crew dressed up.) We had to undergo a punishment read out to us by Neptune. A cruel prank unfolded as I felt shaving cream hitting my face, only to be followed by the bitter taste of oil and vinegar masquerading as whisky. After I swallowed it, they pushed me backwards in the chair and into a tank of water which we use as a saltwater swimming pool. No one escaped the punishment. It was a fantastic afternoon.

When you hear from Ellie, please let me know what she says and give her my news. I will write to her soon. Communication is tricky, as you know, and I fear we may never catch up with each other. I miss her a lot.

I'm going to the ship's cinema tonight to see William Powell in 'The Road to Singapore'. It's a 1930s picture, but I haven't seen it and I miss the flicks back home, so I'm sure I'll enjoy it.

How are William and Peter? I hope William is doing well in the navy now. He is such a bright lad and he will do them proud. I miss him too, and Pete.

I hope the sounds of sirens and explosions haven't become too familiar to you. Here, in this peaceful place, I had almost forgotten that such troubles exist.

In order to ensure I deliver this letter on time I will hold off on writing more until I reach the next port. I want to reassure you that there's no need to worry, I'm perfectly fine and thoroughly enjoying myself.

All my love,

Harold

Following a long and uneventful voyage, the ship sailed to Durban, passing around the scenic Cape of Good Hope. Harold posted his letter from Cape Town and felt a tinge of sadness as the ship passed by without stopping, only slowing down. A barge came alongside, following the pilot boat and bringing supplies. They took the outgoing mail, and the *Empress of Russia* continued her voyage around the Cape. Harold's jaw dropped as he gazed at Table Mountain, marvelling at its breathtaking beauty. Along the route,

HMS *Repulse* had trailed behind a group of other cruisers, diligently protecting the rear. The lazy, rolling days of life on board the ship were about to end. They'd had their orders, listened to speeches, and been told to expect the worst. The crew remarked that the *Empress of Asia* shadowed them but lagged en route to Cape Town, "damaged in the worst storm for sixty years".

13 December, Durban
Dearest Ellie,

Now I've only a short time to write to you before we reach our destination, and I'm so sorry I haven't written before now. It's been far too long. I went home on leave for a few days before we left. I hated going back and not finding you there. When this war is over, we can rejoice again.

I'm glad I missed the bombing of the junior school in Saltburn. It was an enormous shock to see our old classroom gone. While I was out walking, my jaw dropped at the sight of a colossal hole that had opened up in the middle of the street. A chilling reality in the town.

I have been in port again for a few days, and we've had a great time. The lights of the city and the neon signs were a spectacular sight to behold after the blackouts at home. It was like peacetime again. There were lots of stores, and Woolworths too! You would have enjoyed looking at the beautiful shops. There were skyscrapers like in America, an amusement park, and bags of dances! Also, the pubs don't close all day. It's very different from England. My mates and I went for a swim in the sea this morning, but it was dangerous for bathing as the breakers were very high, but that didn't stop us from having a good time. The lads had free bus rides, and the flicks were cheap. My best mate Bernie and I went where we liked. I made myself ill from overeating the fruit this time, I should have heeded the warning, but I won't go into that here! A lesson learned.

So, as you can see, I felt very sorry to leave. It was great to enjoy the freedom. I hope one day we can come back and see it together.

Although we still don't know where we're going, I don't think it'll be long before we get off the ship. It's like a mystery tour! I miss the mail, so I hope we get some soon.

Now it's getting hotter outside. I sleep on the deck at night, as my cabin is too stuffy. I went to the cinema on board today to see George Formby in 'Keep Your Seats, Please'. I've not seen it before, so I rather enjoyed it.

My beloved Ellie, I trust you are doing well and that thoughts of our time together linger in your mind. Please don't worry about me. I'm doing fine. Much love for my special girl. I miss you; it's been too long.

Hal

After more than two weeks at sea, the ship arrived in Port Tewfik and the troops disembarked from coal barges.

'I hear they're taking us all by bus through Suez and then to a place called El Qassasin. We're up for *more* training and preparation,' Harold remarked, rolling his eyes.

With each passing week, the grim reality of war settled upon him, forcing his carefully constructed life plans to be set aside. How could he keep a relationship alive when all this was happening around them? In France, the echoes of Ellie's loving words, a beacon in his despair, had fuelled his hope; but the future remained uncertain and yet he pledged to treasure her love always. He wondered how his brother William was faring amid the chaos of war, and silently prayed for its swift end before Peter reached the age to enlist.

Harold arrived in Port Tewfik wearing desert shorts, a shirt, and a pith helmet. He posed for a photograph with Bernie and his closest men, Snowy and Ian. Now, at last, he could show the family his army friends.

*

As the 4th Battalion prepared for their first Christmas in the desert, the soldiers could feel the scorching desert wind whipping through their tents. Regrettably, Harold came to the realisation that he wouldn't be able to make it back home for the festive season. The unusual frosty nights and scorching hot days had left him completely drained. With no relief in sight, they could only bear the sweltering midday heat by allowing sweat to pour down their faces.

The air was thick with swirling sand, much to Harold's annoyance. The fine sand covering everything felt like tiny knives piercing his skin. Food tasted of desert grit blown into the tent, and there was no Christmas mail. One soldier, depressed at the deep gloom, attempted to go to headquarters on foot, three miles away, to pick up the mail. Despite the battalion's pleas for him to stay put and not be a hero, he defied orders and vanished without a trace.

At Christmas dinner Harold took a mouthful of something he thought he recognised. 'Steak and kidney pudding,' he announced. 'Tastes okay.'

'Not as good as my mum's, but...' one man declared.

'What's for afters?'

'Steamed pudding and custard,' Bernie announced.

As Harold tucked into his second course, he tried to determine what flavour the pudding was supposed to be. It tasted vaguely jammy, but that was all he could taste. The custard was the best. Outside, the sandstorm blew harder. The chorus of 'Hark! The Herald Angels Sing' and 'O Come, All Ye Faithful' sounded soulful, long, and drawn-out. Men tried to have a sherry party inside the mess tent, but it became impossible because of the blowing sand.

Over the loudspeaker came the King's Christmas message to the troops. Harold listened.

'...the men who in every part of the world are serving the Empire and its cause with such valour and devotion, by sea, land, and in the air. I call upon the people to go into the coming year with courage, strength and good heart to overcome the perils ahead.'

The King's tone caused Harold to grimace. His Majesty's speech impediment was evident; each word was laboured, punctuated by long, heavy silences. Despite its infuriating delivery, the speech resonated deeply within him. Harold's proximity during the parade in England had given him a unique insight into the King's passion.

Christmas seemed shorter than at home, and the storms continued to blow. Harold's skin felt like sandpaper, and hurt like hell whenever he wanted to use his hands. The intensive training brought much fatigue, but he was finally on top of himself, except in minefield training, which he hated. Still, you didn't argue with the army. Instead, you did as you were told and tried not to consider the consequences.

Chapter Nineteen

That evening, Harold wrote another letter home.

27 December 1941

Dear Ma and Pop,

At last, I've got a letter from you, although you don't sound very newsy. Is there anything wrong? I'm concerned about you. Your message was dated 12 September, over three months late eh? It was good to get it, though.

No need to worry about me. You can see how futile it is to worry. We're well cared for here. We get papers sent, so you needn't post them. They may not arrive anyway. I hope you receive these letters from me. Everything is so slow. I'm in a place I've only read about in books. (I can't tell you where.)

Have there been air raids around your way again recently? I hope they're not making a habit of damaging Saltburn. I wonder if the bandstand can be repaired, although it wasn't much use anyway. Except for William – he enjoyed playing his music there. How is our lad? I hope he is doing fine. He doesn't write to me. Please tell him I need his news. And what about everyone in Saltburn?

The weather is much cooler up here (wherever that is!). It gets freezing at night, and I hate being cold. But I suppose my idea of cold will seem silly. I would hate to be in a snowstorm like we were in France.

We may soon move on to the next camp, and I'm hopeful for some time off, although I'm sceptical if it'll happen. We have a strict routine – bedtime is at nine, and we wake up promptly

at five in the morning. I may get healthier but not wealthier, as
the saying goes, but much wiser.

Well, Ma and Pop, no more for now. Keep writing. I'll get
your letters sometime soon.

Love to all,

Harold

'God, it's bloody hot out here – glad they gave us shorts!' Harold sat in the shade of his tent writing yet another letter home. He'd finally caught up with Bernie, and they sat together, trying to keep cool. They watched a couple of men larking about, cracking eggs on top of a tank.

'Mine's cooked,' shouted one of them. 'Yummy, makes a good scrambled egg.'

"I'd swap a hundred fags for a decent drink of clear, refreshing water. We're only allowed to shave every five days," Harold wrote in a letter home.

'I reckon this could be far less agreeable than France,' Bernie said. 'They say hot tea is good to keep you cool. You sweat, you see. We might have to share the water for washing.'

He turned to face the sound of arguing behind him. The soldier was pointing an aggressive finger at his mate. 'Yes, if we have to share stuff, that's how it is. Just shut up moaning, will yer?'

Harold shook his head in dismay. One minute there was harmony, and the next it was like a childish bun fight. It was to be expected, he supposed.

Ellie hadn't written, so in his last letter to his mother he'd asked her if she'd heard anything about Ellie through her letters. Betty had replied, "All she told me was that she wasn't near Catterick. I hear Cousin Archie is in hospital with yellow jaundice."

'I think I'd have liked a couple of weeks in a hospital to sleep in a decent bed,' he told Bernie now. And where was William in all of this? Harold thought he could have written, but he knew the situation too well and shrugged off his thoughts. Being at sea was more difficult for William, he supposed.

Bernie joined Harold for a bite to eat. His friend always seemed relaxed, and Harold wondered how he did that. So far, it was a lucky throw of the dice that the two men had sailed on the same ship.

'Hiya, mate. How're you doing? Food's gone downhill recently, but—'

Harold interrupted. 'I agree. It'd be great if the NAAFI could get more spuds. These biscuits are not helping my teeth. They give me toothache.'

'You're in luck, mate. Supplies got a delivery today. It's a real bugger when we live on one dollop of powdered egg and five chips! I don't mind the fried onions, but it's expensive at eightpence a go,' Bernie said.

Harold avoided repeating the adage, 'There's a war on, didn't you know?'

A few days later, Harold received a letter from his mother. She told him that Agnes Brownlee no longer lived on Diamond Street. By the time he received the letter, that was old news from the year before. This was another long-lost letter! If Ellie had been home on leave, she'd have been homeless. Betty wrote that she didn't know if Tommy was with Agnes; she presumed he was now old enough to join up. Harold replied, upset. His mother had nothing more to tell him. He scolded her for not writing two letters if there was no room in the aerogram. And why didn't Ellie write to him? Their relationship wasn't over; only the war kept them from each other. He'd asked his mother for William's address, but she never mentioned him, so what had happened at home?

He got out his photo of Ellie and felt cheered by her image. She looked terrific in her uniform, but wanting to see her again felt distressing. So, he put the photo back in his wallet.

That night, Harold wore two jumpers. The desert nights were

colder than he could have imagined. Sleep was almost impossible. Bloody trucks revving up their engines! He needed his rest.

February 1942

The act of writing gave Harold an outlet to express his turbulent emotions. The pen was a tool enabling him to sculpt his inner turmoil onto paper. Writing home became a therapeutic exercise.

> *Have you heard from Ellie again? I haven't, and I'm starting to wonder if she's deserted me.*
>
> *I cannot say I'm getting used to this way of life because my hands are now bandaged. Desert sores are nothing but a nuisance. It's a pity I don't get as much news from home as I used to. I rely so much on old news. Please send Germolene for my hands. There is nothing here to look at except sand and more sand. How I long to take a walk on the moors again! The heat is exhausting. I've lost weight, and water is an issue. The only thing that keeps me sane is thinking of you all sat by the fire, keeping warm. Right now, I could do with some cold air.*
>
> *I wish William would write to me. I've heard nothing about him except through you. It's unfair that I seem to do all the writing. Please tell William to write a longer letter next time now he's joined up. I need to read his news as much as he needs to read mine. I hope he's enjoying his life in the navy. I will write to him soon, but there isn't much time. He's probably in the same situation as me and his letters are not reaching me, so I understand.*
>
> *You wrote that Ma wasn't feeling well. I hope she's improved.*
> *Sending you lots of love,*
> *Harold*

'Okay, men. I have to inform you that General Auchinleck has launched Operation Crusader to end the occupation of Libya. Shortly, we will be undertaking manoeuvres, and the 4th Battalion will head toward the coast. It's going to be the hardest push we have done so far. I wish you all good luck.' The commanding officer stood to attention and saluted his brigade. 'Dismissed.'

Harold received orders outlining the difficult mission they were about to face. There came a moment when he realised he had nothing much to do or to contribute to the conversation. Despite everything, familiar tendrils of anxiety still haunted his mind. The moment of truth was approaching, and if he lived to tell the tale, it would be a miracle.

It was April 1942 when the 4th Battalion crossed the Libyan frontier. There had been more sandstorms. The men described it as a nightmare on wheels, blasting through the desert in trucks under these conditions.

Enemy patrols were now only twenty miles away as the column moved south-west. Harold received a radio message. *'Enemy spotted in your direction. Concentration of enemy transport ahead. Orders are to move forward and take them out.'*

A brilliant moon cast long shadows, illuminating the crisp, cold air. Harold and his fellow men advanced. He searched the skies and had never seen the stars twinkling so bright, with the Milky Way carpeting the sky. He whispered to Bernie, who lay beside him on his belly on the sand. 'God help us, Bern.' Distinct shadows of the enemy were plain to see over the horizon. Harold froze in the chilly night air, listening to his commanding officer's orders and communicating the enemy's position. Each step became more nerve-racking than the last. Was this the final straw? Would he make it? Here we go again. Please give me a chance to get home again. 'Good luck, Bern. You've been the best friend I've ever had.'

Bernie replied, 'Thanks, mate. We'll get out of this. I'll make sure we do.'

Chapter Twenty

The Strathpeffer Pavilion in the village centre hosted the production of *The Lady in the Office*. The comedy revolved around a witty ATS girl hailing from a noble family. Her fellow soldiers played a trick on her, but it quickly spiralled out of control. The plot took an unexpected turn when the girl cleverly outsmarted those who had deceived her.

Vicky praised Ellie. 'Well done, it was great fun, and considering we had little time to put it together, I think we did a smashing job. They all laughed at our jokes, which I wondered if they would.'

Ellie gave a deep sigh. She realised Harold was no longer writing to her. Since last October, only one letter had arrived, and she didn't know what to make of it. It was almost demanding that *she* write to *him*. But what was he thinking? She'd always written to him. Did he not receive her letters? Perhaps he was going through a hard time again. Was he ill? She'd heard about soldiers not coping with the war.

Ellie's mind wandered to another place as the concert party productions unfolded. With little time to write and no recent letters to respond to, she felt a pang of frustration. Had she wasted her time on the fleeting passion of youth? Could it be possible that her mother's words held some truth, and the war had left its mark on her? Despite her best efforts to push it away, the weight of reality finally settled, sinking deep into her thoughts. Perhaps now it was time to think differently about her promise to Harold. Damn the bloody war! She hoped he was safe, but the constant changes had derailed their plans. Maybe moving forward was the answer. With her loyal best friend by her side and the Wyvis Players productions to think about, all she could do was cling to the hope of Harold's presence in her future.

Ellie's time in Scotland gave her the life she'd often dreamed about. Despite the war, she and Vicky had turned a dreadful situation into something useful. The rewarding aspects of being an ATS girl, the closeness, the shared purpose, were sometimes overshadowed by the tragedies Ellie witnessed and the emotional toll it took. They had tried to focus on the good times. Many of their friends had lost loved ones, and tragedy seemed to come from all directions.

News spread rapidly as a massive fire engulfed one of the hotels, now used as a hospital, the acrid smell of smoke filling the air and the crackling of flames echoing through the streets. The girls looked out of their hotel window as smoke billowed from windows and fire engines surrounded the area. They watched as other ATS girls stood around, helping the fire brigade.

'Shall we go too?' Vicky said.

'I think they're okay. It looks like it's under control now. There's too many folks out there anyway.'

They were relieved to hear that all twenty-five patients had been rescued, but the hotel had suffered such extensive damage that it would need to be demolished.

'Oh heck,' Vicky said. 'We'll have to fundraise to help those people. It looks awful.'

This made Ellie think of how important it was to keep the concert party alive and maintain morale. It wouldn't be straightforward. Both girls were exhausted and needed support. They'd thrown all their spare time into show business by juggling between their duties of work and producing the concerts.

Ellie decided it was best not to go back to Saltburn. There were too many memories, good and bad. Two years was a long time to wait for Harold. Only now did she feel that the war would never end. So, what was the point in keeping up a wartime relationship? She scolded herself for thinking that way, but she hadn't stopped loving Harold, though it was hard to visualise how he looked now. It was one of those days when everything seemed to be off beam. It was time to take a break.

'At last, we get a holiday together,' Vicky said.

'This is lovely. The lady who owns this place, Mrs McLeish, said she will do sandwiches for us if we want to explore. She'll make a proper meal at night when we get back from our walk.' Ellie gave a deep sigh. 'It couldn't be better than this.'

'I love the view from this window,' Vicky said. 'It's very calming standing here.'

As the days went by, the occasional sound of gunfire and the roar of planes flying above served as a constant reminder of the tense atmosphere, yet nothing significant transpired. Ellie wrote in her diary, "If only every day could be like this." The sun warmed their faces as they hiked to the hills, the scent of pine filling the air, enjoying their Spam and egg sandwiches before settling down for hours of writing among the hills, and playfully acting out the parts. Harold barely crossed mind; his name a whisper in the recesses of her thoughts. Returning to the croft, they used the old typewriter Mrs McLeish had loaned them, the rhythmic tap-tap-tap of the keys filling the small space. Returning to camp, the script would only need minor edits, sparing Ellie a complete rewrite.

It wasn't until they arrived in Strathpeffer that both girls saw the mundane routine of army life and wished they were back at the old croft with dear Mrs McLeish. Unlike the croft, they had no control over what happened here. Vicky was still doing her sorties to the Kyle, often coming home frozen and exhausted after a 200-mile round trip. She'd mostly travel short distances, but she was the only messenger available to communicate to the west coast. She usually had Janet meet her halfway, but not always.

A few days later, Ellie and Vicky skipped around the dance floor at the Pavilion. The Canadians were at the camp, and Ellie danced in the arms of one of them. He introduced himself as Captain Jack Hatherley, and his charm impressed Ellie.

'How long you been here?' he asked. 'You dance well,' he complimented her above the loud music.

The waltz ended, and they walked toward the bar for a drink.

'Long enough,' Ellie replied. 'My boyfriend showed me how to dance.'

'Where is he now?' asked Jack.

'I don't know. It isn't easy at the moment. I'm promised to him – he's a childhood friend – and now I've no idea where he is. I've not heard from him in weeks. Actually, it's a few months now.'

'Oh, I see. So, what will you do?'

'Dunno, really. We've changed so much over the last few years. I worry it won't be the same. They say absence makes the heart grow fonder. I need good news, I suppose.'

'Ellie, there's a war going on, or haven't you noticed recently?' Jack smiled sympathetically.

'Oh no, not that again. Yes, I know, it's just me. I don't want to go back on my promise. Harold's a lovely person and has always been there for me. We didn't expect the war to last this long when we parted, and now I wonder if he's decided not to keep in touch any more.'

'I understand,' Jack said. 'Nobody expected it to be this long, and he probably isn't having a good time. It's different being a soldier on the front line. Anyway, you seem a sweet kinda gal, Ellie. I want to get to know you more. And who knows where this war will take us? We must enjoy ourselves while we can.'

'So, what did you do before you came over here?' Ellie tried to change the subject in case being a "sweet kinda gal" was something more than she bargained for.

'I'm a film producer – a small company, but we do okay. I was earning good money before I joined up.'

'Where are you from?' she asked, listening to his accent.

'A place called Trois-Rivières in Quebec. My mother was born there.'

'Oh, really? That's interesting. Sounds French.' Ellie raised her voice above the noise of the band.

Jack smiled, his eyes crinkling at the corners. 'I *am* French Canadian.' His dark hair was cropped short, and he wore the uniform of the Royal Canadian Corps of Signals. A sweet, soapy perfume emanated from his hair and wafted toward her as he spoke. She felt his charm.

'Oh yes, your accent sounds a bit French. So, what are you doing up here in Strathpeffer?' Ellie asked. She liked his blue eyes and handsome dark features, and how he smiled. She had to admit he was rather striking. His kindly manner gave her a feeling of warmth and generosity.

'I'm instructing at the training school. And you?'

'I'm…er… I'm a clerk for one of the majors, but I'm writing plays for the concert party in my spare time. I love doing it as I can escape the war, sit and write, and sometimes act. Ha! When I get the chance.' Ellie smiled. 'My friend Vicky – that's her over there.' Ellie gestured toward the stage, where the band played and below on the dance floor Vicky danced the jitterbug. 'She's the one with the blonde curly hair and lots of lipstick!' Ellie laughed. Vicky had recently dyed her hair, and used curlers every night before bed. 'Anyway, we spend much time together because we have no reason to go home any more.'

'You sound like you need cheering up, gal,' Jack prompted.

'Perhaps I do, but, as you said, there's a war raging, and we have to be careful. Our CO warned us about walking out with soldiers. She said there could be a lot of heartbreak, and severe punishments are not unheard of.'

Jack gave a pinched expression. 'May I walk you back to your unit?'

Ellie thought about it for a moment. 'Well, I don't think I should. It's not right.'

'You're not thinking of walking down that street alone, are you? All those eager men out there – it might not be safe.'

'I'll be all right, thank you.'

'No, I insist. I just want to do the honourable thing, that's all.'

Ellie paused to think. 'I'll just tell Vicky.'

She told herself it was fine and accepting Jack's escort back to the hotel wasn't doing any harm, though a nervous flutter remained in her chest. She left him at the bar and interrupted Vicky's dancing; her partner didn't seem to mind.

'Sorry, Vicky, darling, but Jack wants to walk me back to The Highland. I'll tell you about it later.'

'Ellie! Be careful. I sometimes feel like a mother to you instead of a friend.'

'Jack seems nice, and guess what? He was a film producer. I expect he only wants to ensure I'm safe going down the main street, and it's getting dark outside now. I told him all about our plays. He's very keen to talk to me about it. Maybe this is a chance to learn more.'

Vicky laughed. 'Honestly, Ellie, there's no stopping you these days, is there? I'm glad for you, but there's a war raging—'

'Yes, yes, yes, Vicky. I've heard it all before, and I'll probably scream if anyone says that again. Look, must dash, love. Come and see me tomorrow and I can tell you all about it. Jack is waiting for me. Bye.' Ellie turned toward the exit.

Vicky grabbed her arm. 'And behave yourself, do you hear?'

'Don't be daft. I've still got Harold waiting in the wings.' Ellie turned her back on Vicky, a coy smile playing on her lips. She knew the nickname for the ATS girls. The letter "T" stood for "tarts". She didn't want to get a poor reputation. While she intended to maintain her composure, the weight of Vicky's comment lingered in the back of her mind, causing her to question her loyalty to Harold. But having a chat with Jack about films could provide valuable insights and information. With a polite nod, he stood at the door, his cap tucked under his arm.

Chapter Twenty-One

On 26 May 1942, Rommel launched an offensive, bypassing the Gazala line and striking the British armoured reserves at its rear. Although he defeated the British tanks, he was without supplies, and logistics convoys couldn't penetrate the enemy line. The 4th Battalion lined the desert plains. Harold crouched low, gun poised, ready to fire.

The CO shouted, 'Get down, lads!'

Boom! As Harold crawled on his belly, the desert vibrated with the rumble of approaching tanks, and the crunch of their treads on the sand. Boom! The sharp sound of the explosion pierced the air, catching everyone nearby off guard. The acrid smell of smoke filled their nostrils, signalling the impending danger ahead. Boom! The sound filled the air, bouncing off the dunes and leaving their ears ringing and their hearts pounding.

'We're completely exposed, defenceless!' a voice exclaimed, with a fear in his tone.

The terrifying sound of bombs filled the air, their explosions sending bodies soaring through the sky before crashing onto the scorching sand. Harold kept moving forward; he would get those bastards and strangle them to death with his bare hands! If only.

In his last radio message to HQ that morning, Harold's words sent a chill down their spines: 'Enemy straight ahead.' The advancing forces had eventually overpowered the 150th Brigade before the 4th Battalion Green Howards were also surrounded. They pressed forward, led by the enemy under Rommel's direct leadership. Harold's spirits plummeted as he picked up on the change in language, a sure sign of impending doom and defeat.

'Droppa your weapons and surrender.' The voice of an Italian soldier gave the order.

'I'm still here, mate, but this is it, Deano. We're in the shit. Goodbye, my friend.'

Recognising Bernie's voice, Harold shouted, 'Not if I can fuckin' help it.'

'Shut up. You will not speak. Stand up! You will not move, understand?'

Visions of his parents, William, Peter, Ellie, and Sammy, played like a movie in Harold's head. For some stupid reason, there then came a mental picture of The Ship Inn, where he'd had a pint before he left for the call-up. The voice came back at him in broken English. They had smacked into the Italians, and Harold knew his worst nightmare was about to begin.

'Bernie, do as he says, mate.'

As Harold approached, he noticed the men discarding their weapons and forming a single-file line. With no other options, he assumed he had to do the same as everyone else. The battalion had surrendered, and the weariness etched on their war-torn faces told the complete story. Prisoners of war. It had all been far too easy for those bastards! Who would do this to them? Had they sent the Green Howards up to the front line to test their proximity to the enemy? This wasn't just bad luck, surely? These lads were outstanding soldiers; they knew what they were doing, but orders were orders. Smack-bang into the enemy's hands. Shit! Who gave this order? He removed his radio unit and dumped it with the rest of the equipment and ammunition. With reluctance, the weaponry mounted as each soldier laid down his arms. With the all-too-sudden change of state, Harold gazed at the long line of prisoners standing behind and in front of him as far as the eye could see. A soldier pointed a rifle, and Harold flinched. This was it. He waited for the gun to fire, but the soldier holding the gun pushed him to one side.

'No talking, or you die!' He gestured aggressively to show the men where he wanted them to place their hands.

Harold lifted his arms high above his head and interlocked his fingers at the back of his neck. With a heavy heart, he relinquished his resistance.

Tired and hungry, they marched in the searing heat, sometimes begging for water but not getting any. Two of the men in the battalion passed out. The guard shot them where they lay; an example to the others. Harold drew a breath and saw the bodies writhe in pain and then die. Shit! Not again: Dunkirk was enough. Oh no, no, no!

All night and the following morning, they marched toward Tobruk without food and with very little water. Harold despaired at the relentless line of soldiers. Yes, he was still alive, but perhaps not for much longer. But remember Dunkirk, Harold Dean – you're a survivor. He'd heard stories of starving men and Jews in the German prisoner-of-war camps. The fear of his own mortality gripped him tightly, making him desperate to hold on to life. He repeated to himself, 'Gotta keep going,' as his legs ached and his breath grew heavy. 'Gotta keep…'

After a gruelling march through the heat of the desert, the convoy finally reached the coast. Harold, amazed he was still breathing, staggered with a thirst like no other, relentlessly putting one foot in front of the other until he collapsed on the ground.

'Get up, get up. They'll kill you. Stand up, man, stand up!' Someone helped him, and he was on his way again.

His mouth had dried out. If only they would give him a drink, he'd be all right again. Where were they taking him? Was this his last resting place? 'Water, water,' he begged.

An Italian guard seemed to catch his desperation, and gave him a bottle.

Harold replied in the only Italian he'd learned to show his gratitude. '*Molto grazie.*'

The guard smiled, so Harold knew that somewhere within he had a kind heart, and maybe a girlfriend back home, just like him.

Harold nodded again. '*Grazie,*' he repeated. The soldier seemed sympathetic, and Harold wondered how much he could trust him. Was the water laced with poison?

The Italian guard smiled again. 'You will be well with us. We are not like the Germans,' he whispered. 'My brother is in England. He may have freedom and go to dances.' The guard cautiously glanced around to make sure no one was listening, then silently walked away.

Harold found it hard to trust the Italian soldiers, who spoke in hushed tones and exchanged secretive glances. Having seen two of his men shot, how could he believe this guard? He was a prisoner now, and the thought terrified him.

While awaiting his fate, he fell into a twilight sleep through sheer exhaustion and dehydration. No sooner had he closed his eyes than the soldier beside him gave him a hard nudge.

'Time to go, Deano. We're moving on again.'

Unable to focus, Harold could hardly see his hands before him. His lips hurt and cracked as he tried to speak, so he gave up trying.

In the heat of the day, Harold boarded a truck with his fellow men and, not seeing where they were heading, they arrived on the dockside in Tripoli. His mind felt numb with anxiety in a world he could no longer comprehend. He'd been a good soldier, so what had gone wrong? The searing pain of betrayal was once again the worst feeling in the world; a familiar agony from when he was let down on the beaches in France, except there would be no one to rescue him here.

An Italian steamer moored to the quay waited to take them to Naples. More trucks arrived that evening, their engines rumbling and their headlights cutting through the darkness. Harold sat shoulder to shoulder with others on the deck, the weight of his sadness and despair obvious in the suffocating air. The ship had just left port when four men jumped overboard and attempted to escape. As the guards raised their rifles, the deafening sound of gunfire filled the air. Harold closed his eyes to avoid seeing the dead bodies of his comrades floating in the water. He'd trained in the "what ifs" of being captured and knew it could be challenging, but this…

As they left the harbour, he scanned his surroundings, taking in the sights of screaming seagulls and colourful boats. As the ship rolled out to sea, the tropical breeze brushed against their skin. Oh, for some trees and greenery! He closed his eyes and tried to think about the North Yorkshire Moors and their purple heather. He'd never complain about the rain again.

Oh God! Where was Bernie? They'd boarded together. Surely *he* didn't jump in the water? Ah, there you are! Bernie was relieving himself over the ship's side. Harold tried to smile. Pissing on the enemy was probably a good idea.

'Not much coming out there,' Bernie jested, 'but I needed that.'

Harold lay on the deck in the shade as the ship left the harbour. He felt himself shaking in fear, and curled his hands into tight fists. He'd do anything to go home. The mocking laughter of his captors still echoed in his ears, adding to the inferno of his anger. The whole thing was a bloody shambles. He slept on deck to the sound of the ship's engines throbbing and the deep blue Mediterranean beneath him. As the sun set, the evening breeze cleared his thoughts.

Chapter Twenty-Two

Ellie skipped breakfast that morning. She called by the reception and picked up a letter with a Saltburn postmark. These days, it was rare for her to receive mail from home, but she instantly recognised the familiar handwriting. Opening a letter these days often proved mentally taxing. With a swift motion, she tore open the envelope and eagerly scanned Betty's news.

Dear Ellie,

I hope this letter finds you well. I realise you are not receiving my letters as much as I wished, but I hope this reaches you soon.

I haven't been feeling well recently because Alf and I had some horrible news. It's about William. We think he's been lost at sea on HMS Penelope. There were survivors but no news of William. We are in the deepest gloom. I wanted to tell you this because today we received another letter from the War Office. Harold is listed as going missing on 4 June 1942 in the Middle East. We are dreadfully sad, and as I write this to you, I am very tearful, but I know you will understand my feelings. Although Harold's disappearance was reported, the absence of any obvious signs of injury was not reported. We only hope that he is being held as a POW in Germany, and that no further harm befalls him. As of now, we're still in the dark and eagerly awaiting any news. It's best we don't tell Harold about William just yet. It will be some time before we can write to him. We'll do that as soon as it is appropriate.

Alf is trying to stay busy with the shop to help take his mind off everything. Unfortunately, I can't do that. The anxiety of it all is just too much until I know more. I cannot bear to lose

William in this way. I am very sorry to bring this sadness to your life, and let's hope this war can end soon. We have to keep faith. May God help us.

All our love to you, and please write soon.

Love,

Betty and Alf

Ellie didn't know where to look as she folded the letter and slumped in her chair.

Vicky turned to her. 'What's the matter, El?'

'I've just had a letter from home. It's Harold and William. Terrible news. The one thing Harold always dreaded. He's been captured, we think. This is awful. Won't someone stop this bloody war? I'm scared for him. The worst news is they think William has been lost at sea. His ship, HMS *Penelope*, went down with more than half the crew lost. Ellie leaned forward at the table, resting her forehead on her hand while glancing to observe Vicky's reaction. There were tears in her eyes.

'Oh, El. I'm so sorry.' Vicky placed her hand on Ellie's. 'What will you do?'

'There's nothing I can do, is there? And poor William. Poor Harold. The Deans are having a dreadful time.' Ellie sobbed.

'Come on, El. We'll get through this, and so will Harold – it's hard on both of us, right?'

Ellie's stomach growled as she headed to the office, the dull ache a constant reminder of her skipped breakfast. On arrival, the major was meticulously searching through a filing cabinet, flipping through papers and folders.

'Brownlee, is everything okay?' he enquired, his tone filled with concern.

'Just had some awful news, sir.' She told him about Harold being reported as missing.

'Well, if he was captured in North Africa and the Italians have taken him, I'm told they are pretty good at looking after their POWs,' he assured her. 'Let's hope he isn't in Germany.'

'His mother will let me know more information when she has it. The worst thing is, his brother William has been lost at sea too.'

'Oh heavens, that's too bad. Look, there isn't much to do today. Take it easy, and I'll make us a cup of tea.'

Ellie thought it was ironically amusing, the major making tea. That was her job. She smiled through her tears. 'I'll do it, sir.'

'No, I insist,' he said with a smile.

Here was a man who knew how she felt. He'd been there and done it all, thought Ellie. 'That's very kind, thank you.'

The rest of the day continued as usual, but Ellie couldn't concentrate. Harold's life seemed so remote from her own. The major suggested she finish earlier than usual.

The following week, Ellie met with Jack. He walked close to her after leaving the dance, and when he offered his arm, she took it to walk up the road to the hotel. They had met up after the last dance, and Jack had been cosy with her. Ellie decided that male company was what she needed. There were plenty of men here, but Jack seemed different from the rest, and that night she needed someone to lean on.

'I got sad news. My Harold and his brother are missing,' Ellie said.

'Oh dear, I hadn't expected that, Ellie. Both of them? Jeez!'

'Neither did I, but I ought to have done. It's been at the back of my mind for several months. Being stuck here, I feel utterly helpless.'

Jack was about to say something more when Ellie changed the subject. The tide of sympathy from her friends was too much; she couldn't handle it. To distract herself from the devastating tragedy, she abruptly changed the subject.

'So, you worked in films? Have you met anyone famous, Jack?'

'Er, yes, er... I only had a *small* film company. We weren't exactly MGM, but people like Gloria Swanson occasionally popped in to work with us. She was very nice, but that was for something special we were doing at the time. We did more in the way of public information films. You must begin at the bottom and work up to stardom when you produce films.' He gave a warm smile.

'Oh, really? Still, it all sounds interesting.'

Jack shrugged. 'It's part of the job.' He brightened for a moment. 'Perhaps you will allow me to read your work sometime?'

He wants to read our plays? Wow! She smiled. 'Er, yes, why not? So far, we've had some excellent reviews from the locals and the army. We put on other plays, too. Although Shakespeare will prove a bit of a challenge.'

'Ah, Shakespeare, eh?' Jack turned to face her and stopped walking. 'Wait,' he said, taking off his cap before kneeling.

Ellie stood back. What the…? What was he doing?

Hang there, my verse, in witness of my love;
And thou, thrice-crowned Queen of Night, survey
With thy chaste eye, from thy pale sphere above,
Thy huntress' name that my full life doth sway.
O, Rosalind! These trees shall be my books,
And in their barks my thoughts I'll character,
That every eye which in this forest looks
Shall see thy virtue witness'd everywhere.

Ellie giggled, remembered the last line from her schooldays, and recited it with him.

Run, run, Orlando; carve on every tree
The fair, the chaste, and unexpressive she.

'Oh, my goodness, I didn't expect that!' She laughed. 'You were amazing. Were you in that play?'

'Nope. I learned it at school.' Jack smiled.

'So did I! But it's the way you recited it. You sent shivers down my spine.'

'Do I pass the audition?' asked Jack.

'I didn't think of it as an audition, but perhaps you could join us. Of course, I must explain all this to Vicky tomorrow.' Ellie gave a small laugh.

'Let's not waste time. Can we do this again? How about Friday?'

'Yes, that would be nice, thank you.' Ellie's thoughts jerked. She mustn't forget about Harold. Jack's kindness was overwhelming, but she didn't want to feel obligated to him.

'Thank *you*, fair lady. I wish you well. See you on Friday.' He replaced his cap and paused as Ellie turned to face him.

'Goodnight, Jack, and thanks for the entertainment. Okay, Friday.'

Their eyes locked, and a silent understanding passed between them. The desire in his gaze was unmistakable, and he almost kissed her, but Ellie's mind conjured up Vicky's cautionary words about the complications of getting involved with men, and she stood back.

With a graceful flick of her wrist, she waved her hand saying, 'Thanks for walking me back and goodnight. See you soon,' her voice light and cheerful, promising a quick reunion. It felt good that someone in films had shown interest in her plays. She must tell Vicky. How exciting!

Ellie went to her room, thinking that Jack had been charming and polite. His Shakespeare recital had lightened her mood, after all; he'd made her laugh. She hoped she hadn't given him the wrong impression. Harold must be suffering and she couldn't wait to hear further news from Betty. She hoped he was still alive – her poor darling Harold. What if he never came back? Where was he? Would he write to her? Did he still love her, or had it all been a dream? Her mind filled with "what ifs". She shuffled across her room in her slippers and opened the bathroom door. The bath looked tempting, so she turned on the taps. As she undressed, she checked her reflection in the mirror. Oh, Harold, where are you? she thought. If only she knew. Darn the bloody war!

Late on Friday afternoon, Ellie worked throughout the day, the clock ticking relentlessly in the background. The morning air was crisp as she hurried between hotels, the weight of the major's files heavy in her bag. That evening she dressed smartly, her hair neat under her cap. Even in uniform, the faint scent of her perfume and the subtle gleam in her eyes let her femininity shine through. Exhaustion weighed heavily on her, but the thought of the dance spurred her to put on a brave face. You have to keep up morale; otherwise, you fall apart, she thought.

'Are you ready, Vicky? I hope you like Jack. It's fantastic that he's offered to read our plays and do a spot of producing for us. What do you think?'

'Sounds interesting. Let me know if you find out anything else. Invite Jack to the show. Come on, let's paint the town red. You look brilliant, El.' It seemed apparent that Vicky was keen to get there.

'Thanks. I don't feel it, but so do you.'

Ellie and the other girls entered the dance hall, but she couldn't find Jack. Then she glanced toward the bar, where she spotted him chatting with another girl, and their eyes met as he walked toward her.

'Well, hello, my lovely friend, how are you?'

'Busy day today... And this is my friend, Vicky Empsall. She's a dispatch rider.'

'Nice to meet you, Vicky.'

They shook hands.

'Likewise,' Vicky replied. 'Look, El, I've just seen that chap I danced with the other night. Do you mind if I go over and say hello?' She gave a cheeky grin and whispered, 'You don't want me playing piggy in the middle. Back soon, love.'

'No, you go. I'm sure Jack will keep me company.' Ellie turned toward him for assurance.

'Sure will, honey, and may I have the first dance?'

Ellie spent the next half-hour dancing until her feet hurt. Jack bought her a dandelion and burdock.

'I don't drink alcohol. I have to keep awake for my job. I've been warned not to drink.' Ellie shrugged.

Jack smiled at her comment.

It wasn't long before Ellie got into an in-depth conversation about the concert party and invited Jack to see the new show.

'We got an excellent review. I saw it in the newspaper,' she said. 'Can't wait to come and see you.'

The night moved on, and despite enjoying more dancing, Ellie felt she would make her excuses and explain her fatigue. 'Jack, do you mind if I leave you? I'm so tired, and I have to get my beauty sleep. There's been too much going on at work and I need to stay alert. I mustn't let the major down.'

They left the dance hall.

'Here, Ellie, take my arm.'

'Thanks, Jack, that's very sweet of you.'

'Pleasure,' he said.

They walked in step and made small talk before turning toward the hotel. He mentioned ways to help her improve attendance at the concerts, and asked her what they were doing about advertising. 'I think I can help you on that score,' he said.

Delighted, Ellie smiled, a fleeting expression that didn't quite reach her eyes, her mind already elsewhere.

'I think I need the company right now. Vicky is great, but sometimes I feel very lonely, and then I think about Harold, and it isn't easy when he hasn't been in touch with me for such a long time. I know it's not his fault, but you can't help thinking the wrong things. Anything could have happened to him.'

'He's thinking about you, but perhaps not as much as I'm thinking about you, Ellie. You are a lovely lady.'

Ellie felt herself blush. What was she supposed to say? Jack turned to kiss her goodnight. She pushed her cheek toward him, but he took her in his arms, and the kiss on the cheek turned into a lips-to-lips kiss.

'There, how's that?' Jack raised an eyebrow. 'Better?'

Ellie didn't know what to say. It was the first time she'd kissed someone in that way since Harold went to war.

'Come on, babe, don't look so worried – it's fine. We may as well enjoy ourselves while we can.'

'But, Jack, I'm supposed to be saving myself for Harold.'

'Harold has probably been doing the same before he…ya know. That's something soldiers do when they are away from home. With me, it's different. I do it because I like you a lot.'

Ellie blew out her cheeks. 'You took me by surprise. I know nothing about you.'

'Give it time,' said Jack. 'I really would like to get to know you more. We like the same things, don't we?'

'I suppose we do, but that doesn't—'

He lifted her chin and came close. Ellie didn't know what to do. She felt she had to be polite, like when Harold had kissed her for the first time. Jack looked very handsome in his uniform, and once again, he made her feel special. He seemed a well-practised romantic, which made Ellie feel guilty. She couldn't help comparing him with Harold.

'Perhaps we could—'

Ellie interrupted. 'Look, Jack, you have been more than kind.'

'So, does that mean we can walk out again soon?'

Ellie found it hard to say no.

'When I see you next time, I'll bring you silk stockings.'

'Oh, there's no need.'

'Yes, there is. Of course I want the best for any girl of mine.'

'But… I'm…' Ellie tried to say that she was *not* his girl. Well, not yet – or ever!

He kissed her again. 'Now, don't tell me you didn't enjoy that, Corporal Brownlee.'

Ellie smiled and gave a small laugh.

'Can I see you tomorrow? We can talk about this further and see how you feel. I really do like you, Ellie. And anyway, I would like to get back into film-making after the war. I don't really want to go into farming. My brother can do all that stuff without me. Perhaps Britain is the place to start, after all those bombings and terrible things that happened in London and Coventry. I could report on the newsreels or something like that. Maybe I need to find a top-notch camera team and establish a film company here – the scenery

185

is perfect for cinematic shots. You could be part of that.' Then Jack suddenly developed a coughing fit. 'It's okay. I've had a cold recently. I'm fine, honest.' He seemed short of breath.

Ellie froze. She knew very well that coughing could signify something more serious. She told herself not to be so silly. Jack was fine. 'You sure?' she asked. She couldn't believe her luck. She had only recently met him, and he seemed keen to help with her plays. Was he right about Harold? She'd seen the other soldiers with some of the ATS girls. It was understandable, given the circumstances, but it wasn't like Harold to be as forward as Jack. She wished Harold could write one more letter to confirm that he was well. It had been four months.

'Goodnight, sweet girl. I'll come to the hotel and pick you up tomorrow night. We can have a quiet drink together.'

When Vicky returned, Ellie discovered that both girls had been doing similar things that evening. Vicky was living it up with Mike, an American soldier. They compared notes, and Ellie confessed to Vicky that although she liked Jack, she felt guilty about her relationship with him. But perhaps he could make her into a film star. She giggled at the prospect, but didn't want Vicky to think that maybe it was a bit more than just "liking him", because it wasn't. Was it?

That night she slept with a guilt-ridden mind. Jack seemed kind and very confident, but it didn't feel right. She tossed in her bed and then fell into an uneasy sleep.

Chapter Twenty-Three

Two days later, Harold arrived in Italy. Heavy hearts burdened the captives as the enemy marched them to a tightly guarded camp; the air hung thick with the smells of fear, dust, and body odour. The moment they arrived, a vibrant wave of excitement surged through the prisoners behind the wire, who expressed their elation with a chorus of whistles and cheers that filled the air. For some inexplicable reason, Harold felt an urge to wave back, but was restrained by the harsh grip of reality. They'd been instructed back home: 'Don't tell them anything, whatever the cost.'

Bernie wished his pal a quiet 'Good luck', and they were on the move again.

The guards shoved each soldier into a hot, stuffy, darkened room with no windows, and demanded them to give their names, ranks and numbers. The humiliation of it all. Harold kept silent. He wouldn't tell them anything.

With a gun pointed at his head, an Italian soldier spoke. 'You tell us your name, rank and number, or you die! Understand? Understand?' He pushed the gun into Harold's cheek.

Harold said nothing. His brain no longer kicked into survival mode. He stared at the floor beneath his feet. From the journey, agonising pain consumed him.

'Have it your way, soldier.'

With a cold glint in his eyes, the Italian raised the gun, the metallic click echoing in the silence, and Harold waited to die, his breath catching in his throat. On second thought, he couldn't bear to think of Ellie's reaction. With a heavy sigh and the weight of the world on his shoulders, he finally gave in, his body slumping. What would his comrades say? He had committed the ultimate act of betrayal against his country. As the guard moved away, Harold let out a sigh of relief and quietly muttered the words they were waiting for. He braced himself for whatever challenges they would throw his way. As the day wore on, he couldn't help but notice the dark cloud of misfortune that seemed to follow him everywhere.

A week later, Harold had permission to write a short message home.

I survived! In a transit camp in Italy. Letters to follow.

He could write no more. No love and kisses – nothing. It was also a message to reflect his mood. He knew they would understand.

Deeply humiliated, the prisoners were escorted by guards to the train station and put on a train to Rome. After a long and arduous journey, they reached their destination: Campo 78 in Fonte d'Amore, Sulmona, where the remnants of the former prison camp from the Great War still stood. Harold thought about his parents. A cold dread washed over him as he hoped they hadn't believed he was dead; the thought sent shivers down his spine. Thank goodness he'd let them know.

Harold and Bernie made every effort to stay together. They arrived at the camp to hear men cheering a football match. Harold kept looking over his shoulder to see if Bernie was still there. If he could see him, it would make him feel more secure. But, yes, Bernie was still behind him, thank God! A wave of melancholy washed over Harold as he took in the sight of the few men sitting on the steps of their huts, their expressions vacant and lost. He gazed at the towering mountains, their majestic peaks reaching toward the sky. They made the North Yorkshire Moors look like molehills. The scenery was a striking mix of green hues, although a layer of dust covered everything, reminding him of the desert.

Upon arrival, the prisoners immediately locked their eyes on the men confined within the enclosure. The prisoners' faces turned toward the wire fence, their cheers leaving Harold utterly bewildered. What were they doing? The intention behind it all was to welcome the new arrivals but also make the Italian guards an object of humiliation. The men looked gaunt, their hollow cheeks and tired eyes speaking of hunger and hardship. Bloody thousands of them, Harold thought, mostly British and Australian by the look of their uniforms. The reality of Campo 78 was now realised. He was a prisoner of war; he didn't have to fight any more. How would he survive on mediocre food rations, and in the face of beatings by the guards? Oh no, not this. He recalled the voice of his captor while in the desert. Perhaps they didn't do that here, he hoped.

The guards corralled them to rows of huts with bunks along each wall. The British prisoners had impressively organised each area, carefully designating spaces for the various ranks to ensure order. Bloody typical, Harold thought, the sight bringing a wave of both irritation and relief.

A familiar figure showed her face at A. Dean & Sons, Grocers.

'Hello, Betty, how are you?'

Betty turned. Agnes Brownlee stood there looking slimmer and wearing make-up, her hair tied in a roll at the back of her head. She wore blue clip-on earrings and a smart suit, giving Betty a big smile.

'Agnes, what are *you* doing here? I thought you were…'

'I've just come back to check our house isn't falling down.'

'How's Ellie? We haven't heard from her in ages.'

'Hmm…' Agnes retorted. 'Neither have I.'

'Really?'

'I know there's a war on, but she knows where to find me. Anyway, I have some exciting news I want to tell you. I got married.'

'*Married?*'

Agnes smiled at Betty's reaction.

'Congratulations, Agnes. I hadn't realised…'

'George and me, we're happy now. And what about young Harold? How's he doing?'

'It's been an emotional time for all of us.' Betty expressed delight at the card they'd received from Harold.

Agnes wanted to ask about William too, but Betty spoke first.

'Regarding William—'

Agnes interrupted her. 'Yes, I heard about William and want to say how sorry I am. It must be dreadful for you, not knowing.'

'Alf and me, we feel as if God has deserted us. I'm also concerned about you not hearing from Ellie. Perhaps you could write to the War Office and ask about her, or Catterick? Maybe someone there will tell you where she is.'

'The last I heard, Ellie was working on a classified army base. Maybe that's why she doesn't write. Who can say these days?' said Agnes.

'But it's not like her. She's such a lovely girl. I hope one day she and Harold will meet again. It's been a dreadful time, and this letter from Harold was only a few words long. He's now officially a POW in Italy. I'll tell you, it was a gift from heaven. I hope he can hold out long enough to come home safely.'

'I'm both saddened and pleased for you, Betty.' Agnes gave a sympathetic smile, then searched in her bag for a pencil. 'I'll leave you my new address in County Durham. We're living on George's farm just outside of Consett now. It's much safer there, and some evacuees are staying with us. If you hear from Ellie, let me know.'

Agnes wrote down her address and said her goodbyes. She thought how strange it was that Ellie hadn't been in touch with either of them. Working on a secret army base would keep her busy. Surely just one letter to say she's faring well.

Betty gave a half-hearted smile. 'I hope you hear from Ellie soon. Be sure to let me know when you do.'

'I will. Good luck, and let's hope a miracle brings your boys home safe.'

Betty thanked her, and as soon as Agnes had left the shop, Betty took out her handkerchief and wiped her eyes.

Chapter Twenty-Four

Harold wrote his first letter home after being in Campo 78 for three weeks and suffering from bedbugs and fleas. The small print on the left-hand side of the postcard gave a stern warning not to write on the right-hand side, or the card would be withdrawn.

Dear Ma and Pop

Sorry have not been able to write before now, but can only write when we get these forms. So, don't expect to hear from me very often.

I hope you got my last letter. Longing to hear from you, as I still have no kit. Please send towels and as much to eat as possible.

The Red Cross will tell you all you wish to know.

I will write a longer letter next time. I wish it were all over.

Love,

Harold

He posted the letter that afternoon, but after that, despair took hold. His stomach pained him. When captured, dressed in desert clothing, he'd had to pull his belt to a tighter notch to stop his shorts from falling down. Still, it didn't matter too much about the clothes. It was food he needed. As of September, the weather was still warm. It was the months ahead that worried him. He'd need jumpers and trousers. His shorts would never do. His underpants had a hole where urine had rotted the fabric. Although he washed them every few days, he often went without them under his shorts to ensure they were clean and dry again. A mother of one of the Green Howards sent him some new underpants, and the soldier gave Harold a pair.

'Remember, you owe me a pair of knickers when you leave here! I'm only doing this 'cause you stink, Deano.' He patted Harold on the back and gave a hearty laugh. 'The hazard of being a POW, I'm afraid. Don't worry about it. We're all getting used to it now, old boy.'

Harold felt some shame. Heck, I stink now, do I? However, a pair of underpants was the best gift anyone could give him right now. If only he could escape the relentless torment of the bedbugs invading his living space.

It was a warm October afternoon, and there were still no letters from Harold's parents. He felt unbearable desperation. He'd always discussed these things with Bernie, who was adept at keeping himself positive. But these days, Bernie wasn't always there for a conversation. Instead, they had both discovered a path to escape their hardships. It was all about self-belief, and the promise of hope.

The local peasants, their faces etched with empathy, offered words of comfort and secretly shared their own struggles in broken English. They pushed blocks of cheese and bread through the wire fence, but after a week, there was a noticeable improvement. Despite its reputation, the camp food was surprisingly palatable and the guards conveniently ignored the exchange of food between the locals and the prisoners. Harold wrote another letter home, hoping more mail would arrive soon. He phrased it as if things weren't too bad, hoping it would ease some of the emotional burden on his parents.

Dear Ma and Pop,

I hope you got all the previous mail from me. I'm settled now for the duration and in a good camp where, at last, we have most things we need. They even have a dance band. Yesterday, they found me a new battledress and overcoat, and at last I sleep in a bed with sheets. However, having been here quite a few weeks, I realise there are still a lot more things I need. Could you send me pyjamas and some shoes or slippers?

In addition, I need a cardigan and some needles, as well as shaving soap and hankies.

I met Stan Barker yesterday. He has moved to Campo 19. Can you let his mother know he is doing fine? You know where she lives. Remember me to everyone, and don't forget to tell me how they are all doing, otherwise I shall think myself one of the forgotten men! I miss dancing at The Spa. I'm afraid my dancing days have been cut off by the hose tops, and I no longer have much inclination for it.

Sorry if this sounds like a shopping list, but I have a lot to catch up on here. I miss you all very much.

Much love,

Harold

'I hear it could be December before we get any kit,' Bernie said.

'December? Oh hell, you're a bundle of joy this morning. Don't you think we've been through enough without all this? Dunkirk was a bloody nightmare, and now I don't know if I'll survive the soddin' war – none of us lads does. It's become a do-or-die situation.'

Bernie felt the panic in Harold's tone. 'Well, I heard some of the lads saying it was a while before they got their Red Cross parcels, and many chaps have been here much longer than us. Just hang in there.'

'I must write to Ellie. She'll wonder what I've been doing, neglecting her like this. I find it hard to know what day it is as I've lost all sense of time.'

Bernie frowned. 'It's not your fault, Deano. I hope for your sake she's still there, mate. Just write and tell her how it is.' He walked away, not wishing to further the conversation; it was all too much.

There was nothing much Harold could do but hang around and watch the lads kick a ball on the field, so he sat in the afternoon sun with a pencil and paper and wrote to Ellie. Perhaps Bernie was right. He must allow her to see things from his point of view. It wouldn't be easy.

My darling Ellie,

I know this is short, but I wanted you to know I'm safe.

I'm in a prisoner-of-war camp in Italy and want all this to end. I have no idea if or when we'll see each other again. My heart is very down, but I want you to know that you must consider where we are today and tomorrow with our friendship. I want you to enjoy yourself. It will be best to not feel alone, waiting in hope. Hope is all we have left now, but it doesn't look good, does it? Try not to worry, my heart is always there for you, but you certainly don't want what I have here. It could be a very long time before I see you again. This is all so unfair.

Please write to me soon. Sorry. You will always be in my thoughts.

Love,

Harold

With a heavy heart, he put the letter in the postbox. He didn't want to give up on her, but their promises in 1939 now seemed futile. His dad had been right. The hope was lost for sure; he could be here for years – if he survived that long. It was unfair to ask her to wait. He wished she would write to him and tell him how she felt. His requirements had ballooned into a complex and overwhelming list of necessities. Clothes, shaving soap, warm socks, food, chocolate – yes, chocolate would be lovely. He must stop thinking about Ellie, but all those beautiful memories – how could he forget? He was stuck in a stupid prison camp somewhere in Italy, unlikely to see home for God knows how long. He gazed at the sky, where two eagles soared on the thermals above the mountain. If only he could fly like that, but the Germans and the Italians were everywhere, and even if he could fly, there would be no chance of escape, not now.

A voice startled him. 'Hi, Deano. Someone told me you were here.'

'Good heavens, is it? Is it you mate? How you doin', Dekkers?' Corporal Derek Taylor had served in Dunkirk with Harold. He'd met him a few times in a bar in France. 'My God, how long have *you* been here – and you survived the beaches?'

'Four months, three weeks, two days, and a few hours,' Dekkers said, looking up at the sun. 'Yes, I survived, with a few minor injuries. I was lucky. I got a lift home. You just got here, then? It's great to see you. I wish it were under better circumstances. You look a bit down, Deano. How about you come to one of our concerts this evening? We'll cheer you up.'

'My Red Cross parcel hasn't come. I'm so disappointed. No one seems to know where I am, that's what's depressing me.'

'Yes, it's slow, but you'll think it's Christmas when the parcel comes.' Dekkers patted Harold on the shoulder. 'Come on, mate, let's cheer you up.'

Harold smiled for the first time in days. His tanned legs were turning cold at night inside the hut. He only possessed one thin blanket and slept in a pair of borrowed socks, which he'd tried to wash in twice-used water to freshen up. 'I bloody well hope so,' he said.

'Say you'll come. It'll be good for you, honest it will.'

'All right, I'll be there.' Harold smiled. He knew he sounded like Moaning Minnie, and it wasn't like him to feel like this. Dekkers was right: entertainment was a good thing. He wasn't his usual self at all. There were plenty of other chaps in the same situation as him. He must try harder. Harold saw that Dekker's legs, exposed by his shorts, were covered in wet lesions. 'Gosh, that looks bad. I've got some Germolene. I used it for my desert sores and these damned bites. Do you want some?'

'Oh, please, mate – it's got worse.'

Harold handed him the tin. 'Looking forward to seeing you at the concert.'

'Righto, seven o'clock – we can chat more later. I've got to rally up more of an audience. See you, and thanks for this – I think it'll help. Glad I stopped by.'

Harold felt more hopeful now that he'd seen Dekkers. He was a chap who would know everything about the camp's movements and what was happening there.

*

As the evening progressed, Harold eagerly made his way to watch the show. The event took place in the mess hall, with a makeshift stage set up for the occasion. Ensuring the best view, only the Italian guards were permitted to sit in the coveted front-row seats; each chair a testament to their privileged position. Though their smiles seemed friendly, a palpable tension hung in the air, and Harold couldn't shake the feeling of unease that prickled his skin.

When the show opened, the sound of cheering and whistling seemed distant. He felt he had gone deaf recently. They opened the concert with 'Keep Your Sunny Side Up'. It was the rest of the lyrics that caught his feelings.

> *There's one thing to think of when you're blue,*
> *There are others around much worse off than you!*
> *If a load of troubles should arrive,*
> *Laugh and say, 'It's great to be alive!'*

It was an old song, but Harold thought the lyrics described his situation perfectly. He really was lucky to be alive.

Later, one chap led the singing on an old piano they'd rescued and repaired. It still sounded tinny and out of tune, but it didn't matter. Everyone sang at the top of their voice, drowning out the music. In the sketches, men dressed as women wearing lipstick which someone had managed to acquire. It seemed like anything was possible if you knew someone. The concert amused the Italians, who joined in wholeheartedly with the wolf whistles and the cheering. These men seemed calmer and more relaxed about the running of the camp. Perhaps Harold ought to relax too. Later, one of the British lads, who sang tenor, gave a heartfelt recital from the opera *Tosca*. Harold had never heard it before, but Bernie told him the Italians were softies, and it was supposed to make them feel homesick. They seemed to fall for it. Bernie grinned at Harold as they watched one of the guards wipe away a tear.

Dekkers was right. The concert had cheered him up; it was just a matter of time before a letter would arrive. He must be patient. A

196

worse camp existed, they had learned, where other soldiers were held in conditions so grim that even the thought of it sent shivers down Harold's spine.

November loomed, a grey, overcast sky mirroring Harold's gloomy mood as he anticipated a winter of endless rain, snow and dreariness. He must learn to keep up his morale by reading books and writing letters, especially to William, and also send Peter the card a friend had drawn. Anything to keep his mind occupied, whether it was reading a book or solving a puzzle. He would do a small amount of laundry if they had enough water. Some lads who'd recently received parcels felt sorry for him and shared their food with him. There was still no letter from his parents or from Ellie. He must keep writing to ensure that they got his messages. And even if they didn't get through, it was a way of letting off steam. He wrote home and told them about the camp entertainment.

> I went to the camp play 'The Middle Watch' last week. It was hilarious how the chaps produced such a show out of practically nothing, with 'girls' who were almost girls. Ha ha! I really enjoyed it.
>
> Hope you are all well. We are doing our best here to stay on top of ourselves. Hope to hear from you soon.
>
> Love,
>
> Harold

The mail arrived, and Harold expected nothing. He'd given up looking for letters but decided that being in a prison camp was not as bad as he'd expected, although bad enough.

But that morning, Bernie burst into the hut, his face flushed with excitement, shouting good news. 'Hey, Deano! You got loads o' mail. I've seen your pile.'

At Bernie's remark, a hearty laugh escaped Harold. 'Really?' He dashed off to look.

The weight of the bundle in his arms was reassuring, and, humming a happy tune, he returned to the hut. He spent the whole day immersed in news from home, the paper rustling between his fingers as he read. Agnes Brownlee got married again? Good God! But where the heck is Ellie? His mother couldn't understand it. Harold didn't understand either, but there was much not to understand in wartime. He gave a deep sigh. He'd never understood Agnes either, and perhaps he didn't have to any more.

Harold noticed there was no mention of William, although Peter was doing fine. His mother said very little about his brother's progress in the navy, and Harold had a hunch that something could have happened to him. In his next letter he would ask her to explain about William – it had been too long; without a word. What was she thinking? Something was amiss and he'd felt that way for some time. Did she forget? Surely not. His mother knew something and she was keeping it from him. He must ask her for cigarettes too, when the Red Cross parcels got through. Perhaps one day soon he would take them all on holiday and paint the town red, white and blue. He was pleased to hear about Sammy. His faithful dog was still strong and "sends his love".

But there was still no news about Ellie. What was the point of keeping the poor lass waiting? He knew he would never see her now. Would he see anyone from home ever again? Forget the holiday! If only she would write. It had been three years and two months since he'd joined up. Had she given up on him? Was this a sign of the end of their relationship? Perhaps he had to think differently now. There was so much news, and yet there was still no Red Cross parcel.

With the pale sun sinking, casting shadows across the mountains, Harold mused that despite being imprisoned, it had been a surprisingly lovely day.

Chapter Twenty-Five

Ellie received two letters four weeks after the date Harold had written them. The first one explained his capture, the second was not what she expected. With a heavy heart, she opened the letter, her thoughts burdened with guilt. It was clear from the second letter that everything had changed. Her eyes scanned Harold's sad words, and a single tear rolled down her cheek. His sudden change of heart felt like a sharp jab.

> *I've thought this over after my last letter, and I don't know if or when we'll see each other again. I would hate you to feel imprisoned like me. I hope you'll forgive me; I only have your interests at heart. If you want to enjoy yourself, I am happy for you to be free. Perhaps it's me feeling sorry for myself, but when I think about it, it's the sensible thing to do. It's unfair of me to expect you to hang on to memories. I think this is the best way. The man your heart remembers is now not the person you used to know. I've had a less-than-easy time. It's been an enormous struggle. I've changed and I expect you have too.*
>
> *Please treasure the memories we made together. Maybe we can pick up the pieces one day. It could be another ten years, who knows? There is no sign of it ending soon: I cannot escape from here, so do you really think it's fair for me to expect you to hang on all that time? I know I shall regret saying this, but your life must go on. This is not the plan we had in mind. War does that to us all. I may not survive, and you'll have waited a very long time for nothing. You have freedom, you must take it by the hand and let it guide you. I'll understand if you have*

met someone else. I cannot expect you to love a photograph of me forever. Let me know how you feel. I need to know, Ellie.

As always, lots of love,

Harold

Ellie's heart pounded and the words stabbed her. Did he really mean it? She acknowledged that he was right. But all those promises they'd made... It now felt so wrong. Wait another ten years? She must be sensible and go with whatever life threw at her. This was wartime; she'd learned to expect nothing from it and to enjoy what she had while it was hers. Jack had also tried to show her that waiting was not a good idea. Perhaps fate was taking a hand in this. Was Harold trying to let her down gently? No, he'd said it plainly enough and it seemed he was only being his usual kind self. A visible sadness clouded Ellie's face, her shoulders drooping and a sigh escaping her lips. She'd seen films of prisoners and how dreadful they looked. Poor, poor Harold.

Later that day, she wrote her reply, wiping her tears from the paper. She didn't want to give him up. It would feel like a betrayal. What should she do?

Dear Harold,

I'm so sorry you were captured, and appreciate your honesty about if or when we will see each other again. I suppose we have to put our memories behind us. We grew up together and had wonderful times, but I don't have a clue where I will be tomorrow. You are right. We can't make plans any more.

I rarely get mail. My mother seems happier now, and possibly changed for the better since she remarried. I don't know where Tommy is, and everything has become complicated. If you get this letter – and I say IF – please don't think I've deserted you. We must put our hopes and aspirations on hold for a long time, and who knows what that'll bring?

I'll always love you, Harold, but if freedom won't happen now, then we must make changes. I will never forget our beautiful days, strolling hand in hand along the seashore. Oh, *how I wish I could turn back the clock, but I agree: we must be realistic. Please get on with your life as I will with mine. I hope we shall meet again in the future. I haven't given up on you, but please understand I won't write again for a while; it's too upsetting and challenging for both of us with the post as it is. Sorry! I still love you, but life is keeping us apart. If you want this, my heart is with you, and I'll do as you ask but if anything changes, who knows, perhaps we can meet again. It's a hard decision for anyone to make now. Three years can feel like an incredibly long time to wait for someone.*

I'm working very hard and have no time to think about anything. My job is one of those for which I have to be on my toes with discipline. I'm writing plays with Vicky Empsall (yes, the same one as at school), and we're entertaining the troops. We've been to some great dances recently. If that's what you call enjoying myself, then it's what I have to do.

I'm sorry if this is not the letter you wanted to read at this challenging time. It hurts me to think that you are experiencing prison camp life, but keep yourself fit, and I hope you receive this soon. My thoughts flow with you.

All my love,

Ellie

With a sense of finality, she sealed the envelope and carefully inserted it into the postbox at reception. Climbing the stairs felt like trudging up an endless mountain. With a heavy heart, she took out a handkerchief and blew her nose, keeping her eyes low on each tread, and trying to contain her emotions.

Later that day, Ellie caught up with Jack, and they passed by Vicky who was on her way to the NAAFI. Ellie felt distant, but Jack asked her to take a stroll toward the village later that afternoon. She knew it was the right thing to do, releasing Harold from the burden of waiting for her. She still wanted him to write – just one more letter to tell her how he was doing. It was silly to assume they would see each other again. This war had made her wiser, and with Jack by her side, she knew she was better off living for the moment and not for the past. Jack wasn't a serious affair; she'd have to wait and see. It would be a difficult process to let Harold go, and the war's devastation had fractured their once-deep friendship beyond easy repair; understanding the extent of the damage would take time. Why did it have to be like this? Still, there was hope, always hope.

'Ellie,' Jack began, a thoughtful frown creasing his brow. 'I'd like to get to know you more. I mean, we're walking out now, laughing and enjoying each other's company. What do you think?' He smiled.

'How do you mean?'

'I know we've only been friends a short while, but I more than *like* you, Ellie.'

This news jarred Ellie's thoughts. He seemed far too impulsive. She had only that morning dropped her letter to Harold in the mailbox; the weight of her words now felt heavy in her chest. Their relationship was complicated, to say the least. They weren't officially a couple, yet there was clearly something between them. Her voice, a hesitant whisper barely audible above the hum of NAFFI clientele, replied, 'But…we hardly know each other'. Ellie sighed softly at her own remark, but it was true, they didn't.

'I'm sure we will soon, Ellie, and I think you are a good person.'

Ellie smiled. Jack had been very kind and thoughtful. She loved his passionate ideas for the Wyvis Players – more advertising, more charity concerts – but the thrill of being in love was a different kind of excitement altogether. Her heart felt heavy with guilt and the weight of uncertainty. The letter she'd written to Harold would bring closure to their teenage pact, and she should now be able to nurture her career as an actress. Harold undoubtedly would have approved of her actions.

'So, what do you think?'

'Let's take a walk outside.' It was time for Ellie to make a confession. 'I got a letter from Harold.'

Jack's eyes narrowed. 'And?'

'He's written to me from a POW camp in Italy.'

'Oh, I'm sorry to hear it.' Jack hesitated. 'Do you still love him?'

'I wish you hadn't asked me that. It's a tough question for me right now. I can't forget our relationship, if that's what you mean. But Harold's not here, and it's unlikely we'll meet up again. I have to be sensible. He will always be special to me, no matter what happens. I replied to his letter.'

'Tell me more.' Jack leaned forward, and his fingers formed a steeple around his lips.

'I agreed that we must move on with our lives. Harold wants me to enjoy myself, which I suppose is what I'm doing with you. He realises he could be in the prison camp for a very long time. I know he's trying to be fair and only has my welfare at heart – he always had. Harold's like that. How would you feel if you were in those circumstances, Jack?'

'I do not know, and I hope it never happens, but he sounds sensible.' He gave a curt nod.

'Anyway, in answer to your question, give it time. I need to be sure I'm doing the right thing, that's all. I don't want to feel I've let Harold down.'

'Okay. So…?'

'I just want us to enjoy what we have while we can. I mean, it could be that you'll also be posted somewhere else. Who knows? And me too, and the whole waiting game will start all over again. Both our lives are a mess. It's not our fault – we control nothing that we do. We belong to the army and no one else. It's important to be sensible.'

'I hear what you're saying, but does that mean we can still, you know…court?' Jack cleared his throat with a slight cough.

Ellie smiled. 'Well, yes, if *courting* is what we do. I mean, I like you and—'

'You only *like* me? Nothing more?'

'As I said, I need time, Jack. Okay? Too many uncertainties. Let's keep enjoying ourselves, eh?'

Jack hugged her. 'Okay. That's my girl,' he said, and kissed her cheek.

As they walked through the park, Jack spied a bed of roses. He cut a flower with his penknife. 'For you, my darling.'

Ellie squeezed his hand. 'Thanks for being so understanding, Jack. My job is critical right now. The major relies on me to keep communications going. I can't tell you about it, but sometimes I'm typing my socks off. So, you'll have to excuse me if I get tired easily.'

'I understand,' he said. 'Let's go back to the hotel now, huh?'

Chapter Twenty-Six

1 December 1942

Harold made his way toward the mess hut and took his seat at the camp concert to see *Pygmalion*. A great production, he'd been told. After all, there was nothing much else to do.

He still hadn't heard from Ellie, but that was nothing new. Lost in a sea of swirling thoughts, he sat, the cacophony of conversation around him a distant, confusing hum. At least this year, Christmas will be better than last year, in that terrible sandstorm. Ah well, let's hope the Christmas parcel arrives soon. All of these thoughts made him wish for comfort, where everything was clean, tidy and sweet-smelling.

Bernie settled onto the wooden bench beside Harold, positioned in the fourth row back from the intimate stage. The air filled with the lingering aroma of tobacco as soldiers puffed on their cigarettes. Harold joined in and lit up the last one in his pocket. He grimaced when the man on the other side of him coughed up phlegm, revolted as he watched him casually spit it onto the sawdust-strewn floor.

A wave of laughter and whistles washed over the stage as the play began, and Harold's voice, strong and clear, joined in. For a couple of hours, a lightness settled over him, a temporary reprieve from the despair that had been clinging to him.

The next day he wrote to his parents, relating his time at the concert. His thoughts were also on William being at sea.

Hey Ma, you didn't tell me again what William is doing?
I know something is wrong! Why doesn't he write to me?

A previous thought struck him. What if his brother really had been in conflict and wounded? He told himself not to be so stupid.

They would have said so plainly. He wrote on, asking for food, blankets, chocolate and underwear. But what about William? Was he all right? That thought got stuck in his head, so annoying! He now felt sure that something was "off". Very odd.

A few days later, he sent his family a Christmas greeting. He was late posting it and didn't seem to care any more as long as they got it...whenever!

Merry Christmas, and a happier New Year.
Always thinking of you,
Harold

15 December 1942

Dekkers paid a visit to Harold at the hut. There was a smell of cooking as he walked through the door. One of the men had made macaroni cheese, from a recipe given to him by his mother. He'd been given pasta and a lump of cheese by an Italian woman who'd pushed them through the wire fence. She always left a parcel for whoever was lucky enough to get there first. It wasn't right, being stuck here for Christmas. Each day, the bland watery soup and stale bread roll was a reminder of what Harold was missing, his mother's delicious home baking. He'd put another notch in his belt in a negative direction.

His bunk became a gathering spot as Private Freddie Higgins settled down for a chat, their voices mingling with the sounds of camaraderie.

'Hiya, mate, how're ya doin'? I've got good news and not-so-good news. Unfortunately, our Red Cross parcels won't arrive until after Christmas, but we *will* receive them before New Year. As usual, there has—'

Harold chimed in. '—been a delay, I know. It's always the bloody same around here.' He puffed on his cigarette. 'I suppose patience is a virtue, as they say. I'm trying to stay cheerful. It's so cold now, and I hate being outside in the snow because I have nothing warm to wear. I'm sick and tired of wearing that stinky blanket. If only I could wash it. Perhaps I'll put it out in the snow and clean it that way.'

'So…the good news is that the Red Cross Christmas parcel should have cake and Christmas pudding. It's the snowy weather that's caused the delay. Food's getting short here.'

'You're right. We'll have to be patient. We'd be a lot skinnier if it weren't for those kind Italian women outside the camp leaving us food.' Harold managed a smile. 'Looking forward to it. The food, I mean, not the being skinny part. Anyway, I feel sorry for our lads fighting in the mountains. This weather is getting worse. At least here we have shelter and a fire.'

'I wondered,' Dekkers said, 'if you'd give us a hand with the Christmas decorations? We need volunteers to make paper chains.'

'Oh, okay, now there's something I *can* do.' Harold rolled his eyes. 'Maybe it'll cheer me up.' He scolded himself for being so petty. He didn't mean it.

Dekkers laughed. 'We got some English tea to drink as well. The good stuff. I'll make a fresh pot for you, and it's Monday, so we got fresh Typhoo today. Jim Pargeter's mother sent him some, and he's promised to share it in our hut. By the way, thanks for the Germolene. My legs have cleared up now. I'd suffered many weeks with that. Much appreciated.' He pulled the tin out of his pocket.

'Oh, good, glad it worked. I'll be there. We'll have a party! Thanks.' Harold grinned, with some sarcasm in his tone.

'See you, mate. It's going to be all right, you'll see,' said Dekkers.

Harold had written the letter urging Ellie not to wait for him, and the ink had been barely dry when a wave of regret had washed over him. He imagined her in tears. She would understand, surely? He felt he'd abandoned her. Perhaps he should have been stronger, but this was his way of being strong, and giving her a chance to live again. Writing the letter had broken his heart, but it was the sensible thing to do. He would look for her again if he ever got out of this godforsaken hole!

*

Two days later, Harold got a letter from the army.

Dear Pte Dean,

> *Please find enclosed a letter from a comrade. We're passing this on to you, and hope it will boost your morale in light of your current situation. The letter is from a soldier whom you rescued at Dunkirk, and who wishes to thank you personally. We hope it reaches you safely.*
>
> *Many thanks.*
>
> *Yours sincerely,*
>
> *Sgt Philip Foreboys*

'Hey, Bern?' Harold stood reading, mouth agape. 'It's a letter from that chap whose life was almost cut short as we left Dunkirk. You remember, the one I told you I rescued from the sea?'

Dear Pte Dean,

> *It's been a while, but I wanted to tell you how utterly grateful I am that you saved my life at Dunkirk. My wife suggested I send you this letter, and I hope it reaches you, wherever you may be.*
>
> *I was admitted to a hospital in Aldershot and recuperated there. I hope you will come and see me when this war is over, and we can breathe in the sweet scent of freedom together. I now live in Gloucestershire, surrounded by rolling hills and quaint English countryside. We recently moved to this area, for reasons I cannot disclose.*
>
> *Thank you for everything you did for me. Your kindness will always be remembered. Please keep in touch. I have two sons, and it's been fantastic to have the opportunity to spend time with my family, and this is because of you. I shall always be in your debt, and hope this dreadful situation will soon end, wherever you are.*
>
> *The very best wishes, and good luck.*
>
> *Tom Hinkley*

'How amazing. I must write back – I'm glad he's okay.'

Bernie smiled. 'You're a good bloke, Harold Dean. I'm pleased he's well again. It's sad about you and Ellie, but this war has damaged relationships – I expect it'll make us stronger when we get home. All is not lost yet.'

January 1943

Harold's Christmas didn't happen. He did his best to join in the celebration even without Christmas pudding and cake. He wrote to his parents that a lot was missing from his day. Despite the camp inmates attempting to recreate the feel of Christmas, it was a failure, and the forlorn looks on the men's faces said it all. The Brits had done their best with the decorations and making paper chains, but it wasn't good enough. Everyone's sadness was apparent to Harold and the weather outside was the coldest ever! All he wanted to do was fall asleep in his blanket. His health was robust, but he'd caught a cold, making him feel worse. No bloody letters again! He divided his time between reading, watching films, and attending concerts.

Finally, with Christmas and New Year behind him, he received his Red Cross parcel.

'Hell, this is like winning the football pools,' Harold jested.

Bernie smiled. 'It's good to see it's cheered you up. Let's see what you got.'

Among all of the things he needed, the Christmas pudding was the first delightful discovery inside Harold's parcel. As the weeks had gone by, the stream of parcels had brought a renewed sense of purpose and joy to the POWs' lives. Red Cross parcel day was always the most important day of the month. He was grateful for being relatively safe in the mountains, where eagles soared and a few planes flew overhead. Of course, there were distant bombing raids and the crack of rifles in the town, but surely the Allies knew there was a prison camp on Sulmona's outskirts? Perhaps it was the snow that held things up. The Maiella mountains dominated the skyline in the distance and it seemed the Germans were everywhere outside the camp, leaving a fugitive with no place to hide. He knew all about the escape tunnels underneath the toilet block, but the right moment never came. All that spooning of the earth was not for him. At least here, on the wintry nights he had a fire. If he escaped, there'd be little hope of survival in this weather, and many gave up. Harold had learned to live with the trials of life as a prisoner of war. Perhaps, he thought, it won't be long before our lads break through the lines, and we'll be rescued.

The following day, Harold slipped a letter into his pocket and retreated to his bunk.

Dear Harold,

I'm sorry I haven't written to you about William. I hope you can sit somewhere quiet and read this letter. We haven't mentioned anything about him so far because we know nothing. We have tried to get further information, but there has been no contact.

His ship went down in the Mediterranean, and most lives were lost. This doesn't mean we have lost our brave William to the sea: we live in hope.

Harold sucked in a breath and closed his eyes. Oh no! he thought. No, no, it can't be. He read on.

Because of your circumstances, we did our best to keep it from you because we knew what a dreadful time you must have been having. It wasn't until you were settled as well as you could be that we decided it was time you knew about it. I realise you wondered anyway. I'm sorry for not telling you sooner.

This is one reason why I've taken over the writing from your ma. It was difficult for us, and then we got the news that you were missing too. That was more than we could take, and although we did our best to keep our letters positive, underneath that were two unfortunate parents. I'm sorry to tell you all this, but you must know.

Please ensure you stay healthy. We love you very much, and I hope this war will end soon. It's gone on too long already. Peter is doing fine at the naval base in Portsmouth. He hurt his leg in an accident, so they gave him a role in the hospital for a few months. A sailor with a broken ankle isn't much use to anyone, thank goodness! We hope he's biding his time until the war's end.

Please pray for William, because we fear the worst now. It's been too long.

Love,

Ma and Pop **CENSORED**

Stupid army! Despite the censored writing, Harold knew what lay hidden underneath.

Harold bowed his head. This was terrible news. Poor William.

Bernie came into the room to find him in tears. 'Hey, what is it, mate?'

'My younger brother, William. Lost at sea, they think.'

Bernie rushed out of the room with the words, 'Don't go anywhere. I'll be back in a few minutes. Hang in there, okay?'

He went to find the padre, and when they returned to Harold, they settled down into a couple of chairs. Harold told them the story in the letter. Father Michael said a prayer that made Harold feel slightly better knowing someone cared, but it didn't last long. Father Michael's presence was not really needed. It had made Harold feel more sad, but he didn't wish to appear ungrateful. What was the point of it all? Only one thing that he'd said resonated. Never give up!

After a cloudy week, Ellie's letter arrived. On reading it, Harold's morale took another step back. It had all been too much, and he lay in his bunk with a pillow over his head.

Bernie sat reading a book, and saw his dilemma. 'Come on, Deano, up you get, old boy. You aren't alone.'

Harold wished to die alongside William, consumed by regret over abandoning Ellie. He didn't know what to do. He was stuck in this soddin' camp, and no one cared. His thoughts pounded deep inside his head, begging him to let go and cry.

Bernie slipped out of the hut and returned with Dekkers.

'Hey, Deano,' said Dekkers. 'What's happened to you?'

'He's had word from home about his girl. I think they've decided the war has broken them up.' Bernie put his hand on Harold's shoulder. 'Come on, mate, we'll get you through this.'

Dekkers turned to everyone present. 'Look – us lot, we're all good mates,' he encouraged. 'We care about you. I'm so sorry to hear about your brother – my condolences.'

Harold attempted a smile, but the ache in his chest remained, a dull throb that no outward expression could mask.

Dekkers made tea with lots of sugar and gave it to Harold. 'We're here if you want us,' he said. 'I'll come back later and see how you're doing.'

Harold's gratitude for the compassion shown by his fellow men lessened his anguish.

That night, Harold needed to hang on to his sanity. In the camp there was no chance of sex, although at night he'd often heard men breathing more deeply than usual in their beds, muffling groans in their pleasure. When that happened it excited others too and produced a domino effect, but Harold had always wanted to keep his dignity. But he'd been saving himself for Ellie, and now he'd let her go, what more was there to save himself for? It didn't seem to matter now, and so, without further thought, he aroused himself with an imaginary woman. The following day, he was grateful that no one mentioned it.

Chapter Twenty-Seven

Lost in a magazine review of a production of Oscar Wilde's *The Importance of Being Earnest*, Ellie sat, the faint smell of coffee lingering in the air. She closed the magazine and reflected on her time with Jack and their latest concert. It seemed he'd enjoyed helping with the production of their own plays. Ellie had asked Vicky to act, explaining that her talents were more than just those of a backstage girl. She was good at learning lines and made the audience laugh.

With every show, the troops packed the seats, especially for the Christmas production of *Cinderella*, which Ellie had adapted from Scotty's version. As the pantomime progressed, everyone laughed and hooted – it was a time of reflection and an opportunity to get away from war talk for a few hours.

'But I got no clothes to wear for the ball.' Ellie, playing Cinderella, was "surprised" by a flash of light when an older woman appeared. 'Why, who are you?' Cinders asked. Ellie was dressed in rags, holding the iconic sweeping brush.

'Your fairy godmother!' replied Ronnie, a male member of the cast wearing an elegant gown and holding a magic wand. 'I produce fine clothes from t' market down t' road in Strathpeffer.'

As many came from the Midlands and Yorkshire, the audience laughed and appreciated the dialogue.

'From t' market?' asked Cinders. 'Do they sell 'ose tops down there as well?' She turned toward the audience with the back of her hand across her cheek. 'Our producer needs a new pair.'

'Nah, they don't do 'ose tops, but I can get you a pair of silk stockings on the cheap.'

'But I don't have a ball gown to wear!' said Cinders.

213

There was another flash. Ellie moved to stage left, and the lights lowered briefly. Ellie left the stage to change into her ball gown, but Vicky came floating by wearing a wig and a copy of Ellie's gown. She hid her face behind a fan to allow the audience to think it was Ellie who had appeared in the flash of light. The stagehands pulled a pair of giant cardboard mice across the footlights. Then, Bang! Flash! there entered the pantomime horses with the glittering coach that Vicky had designed, with help from the backstage boys. The audience gasped. Vicky got into the carriage and rode away to the ball. As soon as she left the stage, she passed her wig to Ellie, and the curtain lowered to prepare for the palace scene. Cinderella tried on the famous glass slipper that fitted her perfectly. Finally, the prince had found his bride.

The cast took their curtain call, and Ellie held hands with Vicky and Jack as they took a bow. Success! thought Ellie. They'd done it. The cheering and flowers at the curtain call showed them they could do it again soon.

'You were wonderful, darling,' Jack said. 'When the war ends, we'll try to get you a few dates in the local theatres. If you want to be an actress, this is the way forward.'

'Thanks, Jack, I appreciate your compliments, but please don't keep saying "when the war is over". It's a habit everyone's got into,' Ellie teased.

Backstage, away from prying eyes, Jack kissed Ellie. She put her arms around him and gave him a coy smile.

'I'd like to think we could get married,' he said.

'What? But, Jack, I don't want to risk being left a widow with a kid in my arms. You know the rules here – friendliness, but no special relationships. We can't possibly do this while we're part of the army. I don't want to get into trouble, especially with our jobs.'

'Oh, Ellie, it won't be like that.'

'Oh yes it will – it's far too risky. Look, Jack, to be honest, this is moving much faster than I'd imagined.'

Ellie had yet to decide about Jack. She was still trying to get over losing Harold to the Italians. It was too soon. She must get to know him better. Based on what he'd told her, his family seemed fine, but he could be dead tomorrow, and then what? She couldn't let the major down; he'd been very kind to her, and she'd worked hard to ensure the project was kept secret. Oh, Harold, why did this have to happen to us? She recalled how Queen Victoria had mourned Prince Albert for the rest of her life. Ellie didn't want to be like that. This was Harold being cruel to be kind. It wasn't his fault. What should she do?

Vicky knocked on Ellie's door, and Ellie couldn't wait to tell her the news.

'Jack's asked me to marry him after the war. But…but… I don't feel right.'

Vicky realised Ellie's revelation didn't seem full of joy. 'What? You can't. You hardly know him, and rules are rules here.'

'Yes, you're right, but hold on, Vicky. Let me finish. I told him we can continue courting, but marriage is out of the question unless the war ends. I mean, the army won't let a wedding happen anyway, and I'm still trying to get my head around losing Harold. At the moment, Jack is more than a good friend, but that's it. It's all so unfair. They're scrutinising anyone who wants to get married, and while we're in this dreadful situation, it's too complicated. You must fill out all these forms, granting permission can take a year, blah blah blah. No, I'm not doing it! We've been courting for a few months, so I know him…*reasonably* well.'

'I know all that, but, Ellie, do you *really* know him? I've seen him with you, and he's very overconfident. This is where I don't think I can help you, love. The decision has to be yours.'

'Canadians are like that, Vicky. Do you like him?'

'He's not my type. I mean, he seems smart, sophisticated and charming, but the thing is, I'm not sure about him, and don't take this the wrong way, Ellie, but it's the way he forces ideas on us. He likes to have it his way and doesn't listen to my suggestions. I would worry about it, especially in a relationship.'

'Yes, I know. I agree with you,' Ellie said. 'But…'

Vicky pushed further. 'There are a few girls here who got married before the war and, now their men are abroad, some are already widows. To me, it sounds stupid. The war habitually takes our men and doesn't give them back. We're still young. My grandmother married when she was thirty and had a wonderful life. "You don't have to get married so young, you know." That's what she always told me.'

'Honestly, you sound more like my mother every day.' Ellie laughed. She stood to straighten her uniform. She'd always considered Vicky a good-time girl, but she had a caring side, and often seemed old-fashioned, like Ellie herself. Perhaps that was why they got on so well.

Vicky smiled and pointed to Ellie's skirt. 'Charlie's dead,' she said. 'Your slip's showing.'

Ellie lifted her slip so it didn't show below her skirt, and stood in front of the mirror. 'Thanks,' she said. Vicky certainly seemed like her mother at times, but she always seized the moment to enjoy herself. 'I'm not sure what to do about Jack. I fear I've let Harold down.'

'Ahh, so that's it, eh? If I were you, I would enjoy Jack's company and not get pregnant. You told me Harold understands.'

Ellie smiled. 'I haven't got that far yet, but it's not for want of him asking me.' She joined Vicky, who sat on the edge of the bed.

Vicky smiled from the corner of her mouth. 'Just you be careful. You don't want him leaving you with a young 'un, do you? It's easy for him to go sloping off back to Canada.'

Ellie looked horrified at the thought. All that bickering with her mother, but perhaps she'd been right – no, she mustn't think that way. Her mother's announcement about marrying again seemed shocking enough. Good luck to her! With Ellie's poor dad hardly resting in his grave, Agnes couldn't wait to jump into bed with the first bloke who'd offered it to her. She shook her head and grimaced. It was all very yucky! Or perhaps it wasn't like that at all, but it felt that way. Ellie hadn't been home, and worse still, she hadn't met her new stepfather. Would she like him? Well, as long as the marriage made her mother happy, then it wasn't for anyone to criticise. 'You're right,' she said eventually. 'I'll do my best not to get too involved. I'll consider Jack's offer, and if the war lasts two more years, we'll get married.'

'Heck, love. You won't make him wait *that* long, will you? I mean, he's a man who wants his you-know-what.'

'Oh, Vicky, I don't know. It's hard to decide, isn't it?'

'Didn't you and Harold do it? I mean, you can tell me.'

Ellie sighed. 'Well, we tried, but things got in the way. The war, for example, and my mother.'

'Can you honestly say you love Jack like you loved Harold?'

Ellie didn't answer for a moment. 'He's been very good to me.'

'Ellie, darling. Be sure. As far as you are concerned, Jack's a good-looking bloke with all the right army credentials, but you must ask yourself if you have the same feelings for him as you had with Harold.'

Ellie understood what Vicky meant. She promised herself she would take care and not lead Jack further in their relationship. She had to be sure. But she had just one concern. Vicky was right, but would Jack wait for her?

'You're going to have to decide soon. Just two words of advice from me. Be careful! If he loves you, he'll wait. And whatever happens, you make sure he's wearing a rubber johnny. You remember those films we saw about VD – enough to put you off rumpy-pumpy for the rest of your life.'

All this talk made Ellie feel overwhelmed and she turned toward the window to think. 'What about you, Vicky? What's happened to Alan? Have you heard?'

'Oh, he's fine. I also don't believe in letting him wait for me. We must enjoy ourselves, otherwise the war will take it away. I'm sure we'll meet again. You and I are in the same boat, El.'

Vicky's words rang true. Wasn't that more or less what Harold had said? Ellie changed the subject. She wasn't in the mood to contemplate relationships. 'Oh yes, Vicky, I meant to ask you – all things aside, did you check on the progress of those costumes for next week?'

'Yep, and Jack's organised a Friday dress rehearsal for next week. Darling, I'm going to bed now. I'm tired, so I'll see you soon,' Vicky said.

'Where are you going tomorrow?'

'They rarely tell me until I get into work. I hope to be back around six o'clock tomorrow night.'

Ellie stood to open the door for her friend. She hugged her, and they parted. The conversation had been tense but well advised. Thank goodness for Vicky Empsall. Ellie smiled as she watched her friend walk down the corridor. Without Vicky, her life would be very lonely. 'Night-night,' she called.

Chapter Twenty-Eight

February 1943

The glorious snowy afternoon in the Italian mountains gave Harold a brief spell of sunshine. He wrote a postcard home, asking his mother not to worry about him. He admitted that times were tough, but added that each day seemed to improve on the last one. The horrible news from home was still in his thoughts. He wrote, "Please send more chocolate and underwear," and thanked his mother for the parcel he'd already received. Was there any more news about William?

A few days later, his mother dealt him another blow. "A bit of bad news: we put Sammy to sleep because he had a stroke." Everything and everyone seemed as if they were falling apart. He couldn't wait to get out of the camp to make his parents' lives happy again. His sadness at the news of Sammy made him think of Ellie again. Had he really given up hope of escape from this dark place, the despair clinging to him like a shroud? The sounds of 2,000 men filled the camp; amid the chaos, he was just another face in the crowd.

Easter came and went with the same boring routine. Harold heard on the grapevine about an Australian guy who'd suffered a deep melancholy. He'd tried to escape, but a guard had shot him in the leg. It was only after some time had passed that they'd amputated the soldier's leg. Escaping wasn't worth the effort. Harold wrote a pleading letter to his father: "Come and get me out of here, it's really boring! I haven't learned the art of patience, I'm afraid."

He admitted he had little to say as the weeks and months progressed. With no more mail from Ellie, he realised he could do nothing about it. "Oh, for a fireside chair and a radiogram," he wrote.

Locked behind a wire fence, he still couldn't be constrained from saying, 'It won't be long now.' Those words were a mantra for everyone. When the time came, he knew he would burst forth with every ounce of joy in his heart. Each day in Campo 78 seemed to bring a fresh wave of disappointment, making him believe that leaving would never be possible.

It was now summer of 1943 and there were whispers about Mussolini being voted out of power; the mood in the camp changed. The prisoners heard about the peace talks with the Allies and how the new Italian government had accepted the terms.

One Friday afternoon in July, Dekkers arrived at the hut with news. 'Have you heard?' he said. 'Mussolini's been thrown out of office. The Italian government surrendered and agreed to join the Allies. They've carted him off to some island or another. There's no longer an Italian army.'

'Really?' Harold said, wide-eyed. 'Oh, you know what that means, of course?'

'The problem is that they're making it fuckin' difficult for us to get rescued. The bloody Jerries are relentless. I predict there'll be hell over the next few days. I hope we're not in the middle of it all.' Dekkers shook his head.

Following two bombing raids by American aircraft and the Italian capitulation, the morning of Sunday 12 September 1943 dawned with the sounds of a crazed Irish soldier yelling and running through the camp, his arms flailing. 'Pack your stuff – we're heading out this instant,' he exclaimed.

They heard shouts of triumph coming from the Italian guards. To Harold's amazement, they were destroying their furniture. Crashes echoed through the air as tables and chairs were mercilessly set on fire. Joyful cries and exuberant Italian shouts left no doubt that this was the sweet taste of freedom.

Harold looked at Bernie. 'What?!' they exclaimed together.

'But the Germans have occupied all the towns and villages in the Abruzzo valleys. They're everywhere. Let's hope our lads get through,' Bernie said with despair in his voice.

The Italians ran around the compound, barking instructions. 'You go now, bye-bye. We're on your side. *Non-avete paura*, you'll soon be free.'

The camp commander gave orders to open the gates. A joyous roar, a wave of sound, crashed over the camp as the news spread – freedom! The guards, already fleeing to their homes in the countryside, were no longer a threat.

'What the hell do we do?' asked Harold. He looked around him as thousands of bewildered men stood in the compound.

'Dunno, but it feels good. Let's just get out of here,' replied Bernie.

Some men were unsure if they would be better off staying in the camp or escaping into the mountain slopes of the forest. The only sensible things to do were stay if you were unfit to travel or leave if you weren't. Their line of escape was outside those gates, and they would have a long, dangerous walk south to reach the Allies. There would be Germans around the foothills and in every town.

'We need a plan,' Harold said.

'Did you say a plane?' jested Bernie.

Harold shook his head. How could Bernie make jokes at a time like this?

At first, both men were cautious. A loud cheer echoed through the camp – they were free, but with thousands of men trying to escape and wanting food, getting to the camp kitchen would be a battle. Making a dash from the hut, they stealthily entered the barracks and looted as many supplies as possible. Somehow, they'd fared well, pushing and shoving the other men aside.

They crammed what little remained of the Red Cross food parcels – mostly biscuits and powdered milk – into a couple of rough hessian sacks, the meagre contents spilling out as they fought over the scraps. Harold discovered a spare sack, its coarse fabric rough against his hands as he tightly packed it with a few tins of olives and several plump bread rolls. Bernie had a fight with a French soldier over a piece of cheese as Harold snatched a pair of damp, still-slightly-stiff socks and a woollen blanket from a washing line.

'Not too much. We'll never carry it all,' shouted Bernie as he recovered from a bruised chin. 'Hurry up, Deano, come on, let's go. Out the way, son, we're leaving,' Bernie said. He almost got a black eye from someone doing the same thing. 'Quick, grab some food and water. We're getting out of here. Hurry, Deano.'

Harold seemed concerned. 'How do we get around the bloody Jerries?'

'Take that knife. We're gonna need it. No, take two of those kitchen knives.'

Some men remained to take the consequences rather than wander the countryside. 'Good luck, soldier. We're staying here and going to…wherever.'

Bernie dismissed their comment. 'Huh! I'm out of here.'

'I've got my compass. I always keep it in my pocket,' Harold said. 'Hurry up, Bern, before they change their bloody minds. My God, we're free. No more Red Cross parcels!' Harold shouted. He wanted to tell the world, I'm on my way home, but he wasn't free yet. His father always said, 'You can't put food in your mouth unless you grow it first.' Where would he and Bernie get more food if the Germans still lurked in the valley? What if they starved to death? There were cows and sheep in the mountains, and they would survive if they planned a strategy and lived off the land.

They couldn't find Dekkers, but then, they didn't look for him. They had to do something now – and be sharp about it. Two men would survive better than three, and they knew Dekkers would have done the same. The question now was *how* to do it. Which way should they go?

With the enemy patrolling the roads, they made haste up the mountainside and heard shots from the valley below.

Bernie patted Harold's shoulder. 'Which way?'

'Straight up that bloody mountain and we won't stop until we reach the top. We can keep low and hide in the forest. I feel this will be the hardest thing we've ever done. But it's the simplest option. We've got to make it to the Gustav Line and find a way through. The valley is too fiery for us just now. The higher we go, the better. Come on. *Move*,' Harold urged.

In the glow of the setting sun, they walked in the shadow of the mountainside. With Harold's compass to guide them, it wasn't long before they saw the faint line of the coast. They climbed higher to where sheep grazed and cows chewed the cud. It took all their energy and strength to keep walking, often stumbling over rocks, checking the landscape for anyone who might give them away. How did strangers know whose side they were on? The abrupt shift in their circumstances exposed them to significant peril.

As night fell, Bernie suggested they seek somewhere to sleep in the safety of the forest. They found a large tree split into a hollow amid sycamore and mountain ash. Crawling in, they huddled side by side, covered only by their blanket. From below in the valley, the sharp cracks of gunfire reverberated through the air. Harold felt a wrench in his stomach for fellow soldiers who may not have made it. Eventually, it was eerily quiet, but then they heard the faint sound of wolves howling.

'Hell, we need to watch our step,' Bernie said. 'Listen to that lot – they sound menacing.'

A warm feeling of comradeship had brought them closer together, but the intense fear, mixed with horrible suspense, left their minds blank and their bodies utterly exhausted.

The following morning, they awoke before sunrise, shivering in the pre-dawn chill, the air biting at their exposed skin. As the sun rose, casting long shadows across the mountainside, Harold gazed upon the orange glow on the peaks illuminating the scree and jagged rocks as it journeyed higher. Bernie checked his watch. Six o'clock. He mustn't ever forget to wind it.

'We must be sure not to get complacent. Every step we take today will be dangerous,' Bernie said. 'Freedom has its drawbacks, I'm afraid. Just take a deep breath of that clear mountain air. You might never pass this way again.'

'No need to tell *me* that, Bern. We need a better plan, mate. Shhh, listen…'

They heard distant voices speaking English and realised they weren't the only ones who had taken this path. Harold smiled. There was no point in joining them.

'We'll keep climbing. The Germans won't come looking this high up,' Bernie whispered.

They packed up the last of their provisions and searched for water. After walking another thousand feet, Harold pointed to a shepherd's hut and cautiously approached. He stood by the door, ready to turn on anyone who tried to pounce on him. He had his knife. Bernie went into the hut first while Harold stayed outside. He found a small stove where a chimney poked through the roof. A table stood with two bottles of wine and an old corkscrew. Whoever had left them there wasn't far away, or perhaps it was a gift to wandering shepherds? Bernie poked his head out of the door, gesturing to indicate that the coast was clear.

They were about to take the wine for themselves when they heard a voice. A shepherd gathered his small flock of sheep and gestured for his dog to lie down. Harold and Bernie couldn't escape, so they listened and waited. The dog kept barking, which drew attention to the two men.

The same voice called out, '*So che ci sei dentro, non aver paura, sono tuo amico.*'

Bernie gave a wry smile. 'It's okay, Deano. He wants to befriend us.'

'You sure?'

'He told us not to be afraid, I think.'

'You *think*?' whispered Harold.

The man came closer and opened the door of the hut. He spoke English. 'Is okay. You a good friend of Italia. I food you.'

Cristo, a shepherd from the valley preparing to move his sheep for winter, welcomed them. He held out his hand. With an enormous sense of relief, Harold took it and introduced himself. It was the first time he had shaken the hand of an Italian.

Bernie spoke in his acquired basic Italian to tell Cristo how grateful they were for his friendship. He asked how to get over the mountain, and the best road to the south.

'No, *troppo pericoloso*,' Cristo replied, and raised his hands in despair.

He offered them a bowl of lamb stew, and they took it, thinking this could be their last meal for a while. Harold knew their supplies wouldn't last long as winter wasn't far away. And while Cristo had warned them about the dangers, they must take their chances. The three men sat drinking wine. Heavenly! Harold knew he needed to be careful, as he hadn't consumed this much alcohol in a long time.

'You go see Bruno Galante,' said Cristo. He drew a map with a stick on the earthen floor of the hut. 'Big house, many *mucche*.' He made a noise like a cow and pouted his weathered lips as he spoke. 'Bruno is friend.'

Bernie asked him how far it was to Bruno's farm. Harold furrowed his brow, trying to comprehend.

'*Quattro ore*.' Cristo raised his hands to reveal four fingers.

'Let's do it, Bern. Four hours isn't too long. What have we got to lose, eh?'

'As long as we got our boots and food, we'll be fine.' Bernie stood by the door and watched the clouds skirting the tops of the highest peaks.

Cristo gave warnings of the terrible things he'd had to endure. 'You must be one step before yourselves. Germans all over Italy.' He showed Harold where to find water and gave them a few supplies.

'Oh! Bread and cheese – all this for us?' Harold felt deep gratitude.

They patted the shepherd's back before going along the well-trodden path.

'*Grazie. Arrivederci.* Thank the Lord for Cristo,' Bernie said as they left.

After wandering for many hours with the setting sun on their shoulders, they still hadn't found Bruno Galante. A German plane flew overhead, and they hid in the forest. They were sure they were in the right area, and wandered up a long, lonely path toward a farmyard in the half-light. It was unnervingly quiet, and Bernie hoped they wouldn't disturb 'some overzealous sheepdog'. The old barn offered little comfort, but they bedded down for the night amid the sweet smell of hay and the sounds of scuttling rats.

The next morning, a young girl, appearing to be in her early teens, with smooth brown skin and deep, captivating eyes, entered the barn. Her words became a chaotic jumble of sounds and accusations, a furious storm that left Bernie struggling to understand. He attempted to calm her, his words pouring out in a desperate plea, begging her not to give them up to the Germans. He tipped his hand to his lips, signalling the need for a refreshing sip of water.

'*Sulmona, prigione, Inglese,*' Bernie said to indicate that they were English prisoners. '*Abbiamo bisogno di aiuto.*'

Harold looked quizzically at Bernie, wishing he'd taken the trouble to learn more Italian.

'I told her we needed help.'

Upon realising they were English escapees from the Sulmona camp, the girl's anxiety subsided. '*Uno momento, per favore,*' she replied. Holding up her hands in a "wait" gesture, she quickly instructed the men to stop and dashed into the house.

Bernie checked Harold's expression. What if she wasn't on their side and told her father to contact the Jerries? Should they make a run for it now? No, wait, remember what Cristo had said – most people were on their side.

Too late. The farmer came out. 'Welcome, welcome,' he said in

English. 'I heard about the desertion of the guards on the radiogram. I didn't know if it was true, but now I do. Come inside and meet the family. We have little to eat until our friend brings the donkey cart from the valley tomorrow. Maybe if you stay here a few more days, we can find a way to get you back to England.'

Harold and Bernie stood there with gaping mouths. Bruno spoke excellent English. Should they run now? Did they trust him?

'Come – come inside and sit. We'll talk now about what you must do. You are safe here. Everything has changed. We're on your side now, but I have to say, I was always on your side. This is my wife, Agata, I'm Bruno Galante, and this is my daughter, Maria.' Agata gave a nervous smile.

Bernie gasped. They had found the man they were looking for.

The tension that had gripped Harold finally eased, replaced by a blissful sense of relief.

Bruno gave them a glass of wine, and as he finished pouring, his wife returned with the cart. He explained the situation and ushered her to provide a bowl of beef stew and polenta.

'Our farm is large, but we manage well with just the three of us. Our son is in the army and is a prisoner of war in England, but who knows what will happen to him? We know he is treated well, and I must do the same for you.'

Ravenous, they ate the stew and washed it down with the wine. It was the best food they'd eaten in two years.

'Well, this is an interesting state of affairs, isn't it?' Bernie laughed, and Harold thanked Bruno for his understanding.

'Of course, this does not mean you are safe,' said Bruno. 'The Germans will hear of this soon and come looking for you. I must find a place for you to hide. If they find you, you will be shot or sent to a labour camp, but we want to help you. Maria is good at outwitting the Germans.' He smiled at his daughter, who gazed in awe at Harold and Bernie. 'We must be careful because my family is also in danger. The Germans have dropped leaflets. Anyone found harbouring a prisoner of war will be shot. They are already arresting young boys over the age of sixteen. It's a blatant violation of our laws. *Questi bastardi non hanno pietà*. These *bastardi*…no mercy,' he translated. 'They jump from their trucks, seize our young men, then speed away. Some are as young as twelve years old.'

They couldn't let Bruno take the risk, but he was very persuasive and it was challenging to say no.

'We must make a hiding place for you if the Germans come this way. We have a place under the hay barn we can use. It is cold and damp in the winter, but you will hide. We'll take care of you.'

'Thank you, Bruno, but we'll be gone in the morning. It's too dangerous for you all, and we miss our families too, and we've had enough of being locked up for so long,' said Harold.

Bruno smiled. 'No, no, listen to me. The British are good people and we should never have been at war with your country. Our son tells me they live in good conditions and eat very well. He said it's like a holiday because they can go to the town and help on the land. He's an excellent farmer. The Germans are terrible – they treat their prisoners as slaves and pieces of meat. I don't want you to get caught.'

'And we don't want you to be found out, Bruno. Your life and those of your family are at stake. I can see they mean a lot to you. I heard from the shepherd, Cristo, about a family who lost everything because they harboured English soldiers. The Germans set their house on fire.'

Agata removed the bowls and scrubbed them clean in a rustic stone sink. Harold couldn't help but notice the way she glanced at Bruno, silently urging him to release them. Even though she couldn't communicate in English, Bernie and Harold grasped her meaning. Her anxious demeanour seemed clear as she chattered away to Bruno in the Sulmonese dialect. Suspicion filled her gaze as she looked at Harold and Bernie. Once again, Bruno insisted it was too dangerous for them to move on and they must wait a while longer.

Whenever it was safe, they chopped wood for the fire and helped the family draw water from the well. All tasks were carried out under cover of darkness. All the while, they made plans for their journey to the coast. Bruno had a map which they carefully perused each evening.

Every time they made to leave, Bruno advised otherwise. 'I don't think you will make this journey. It's still too dangerous, and the weather is not in your favour. You will die in these mountains. You are safer here – we can wait until we get good news. I'm sure it won't be many weeks before the Americans arrive, so please don't leave yet – we can take care of you.'

Bernie looked at Harold and shrugged his shoulders in a gesture of helplessness. 'What do you think, Deano?'

'Well, anything's better than what we've been through, but if Bruno gets caught it'll be the end of this lovely family, and us too! Cristo warned us not to stay long in the house of an Italian family. Maybe we'll do this for a few days and see how it goes.'

'I hear we're not alone. There are others in hiding close to here, in caves and huts,' remarked Bruno. 'It won't be long now before you are free.' He gave a broad smile, showing elderly teeth.

Harold had often temporarily given up hope, but when he did, he'd learned how to pick himself up and decide that to give up was to die. Dunkirk had taught him that, and losing William too. He must see everyone back home again. To think about William now seemed too depressing. Bruno had been kind, and Maria had learned more English in just the few weeks since they'd arrived at the house. Bernie remarked to Harold that she was a beautiful young girl, and if only she were a few years older… He'd been too long without female company.

Over the following weeks, Bruno heard that the Germans had offered two thousand lira, or about twenty pounds, for information leading to the prisoners' capture. This was a lot of money and a terrible temptation for the locals, but he knew none of his friends would ever betray him. They were loyal now to the Allies, and anyone suspected of Fascist sympathies would be lynched.

The men took great pains to stay hidden, and spent their time in the barn during the day. They wore peasant clothes and those of Bruno's son, Antonio. Bruno provided a hiding place underneath the stable. The trapdoor was concealed with a loaded hay cart, and Bruno burned their prisoner of war clothing after first cutting off the buttons as a souvenir, which he then buried near the olive tree in the courtyard. So far, it seemed to work well: the winding mountain path offered a clear view for at least two kilometres, making it easy to spot anyone approaching. The Germans would have to climb steeply up the track, and motorised vehicles wouldn't make it up the narrow mountain pass. Bruno told the fugitives he'd set a trap along the trail so that they would hear the approach of any intruders. A cable was fastened to the main gate, and when the gate was opened you could hear the ting-a-ling of a small bell at the stable door from five hundred yards. Harold didn't think the tactic was reliable – the wire cable was far too long to be of use – but Villa Maria, named after Bruno's mother, had become a welcome place of refuge and they couldn't ask for anything better.

Bruno had an arrangement with his friend Vincente, who once a week brought food and wine to the mountain farm to exchange for vegetables and milk. The peasants in the valley worked together as a resistance against the Germans. Life had changed for the Galante family with Harold and Bernie as unexpected yet dangerously vulnerable guests. At least the sheepdog barked, and the hens clucked when spooked, which gave them fair warning of intruders. The soldiers hated hiding, but it was better to be part of a family than to suffer the unhealthy atmosphere of a prison camp. Finally, however, Harold decided that something had to be done. A weight had settled heavily on his shoulders. They couldn't stay much longer – that much was clear – but the encroaching winter and the inviting shelter of the place made a longer stay inevitable. It seemed they had fallen into the trap Cristo had warned them about.

Chapter Twenty-Nine

Dressed in their festive attire, Ellie and Vicky anxiously awaited the curtain call marking the end of the much-acclaimed charity Christmas concert. The girls took a bow onstage, and Jack followed. Amid the joyful sound of whistles and cheers, they were presented with flowers and humbly took another bow.

The months between the autumn and winter of 1943 had passed without incident. Despite the war, the soldiers and locals loved the concerts, and Ellie soon realised how much they enjoyed themselves. As it was Christmas, Jack had wanted to do something special: carols, songs, dancing – anything to help relieve the daily routine. They took their show to the local hospital, where Private Janie Walters opened the programme by singing Judy Garland's 'Over the Rainbow'.

Vicky decided that she and Ellie would do a sketch together. They devised a way of getting everyone to laugh.

'You only need to say something rude and saucy, and the audience thinks it's funny,' Ellie remarked. 'They're easily pleased. Bless the lot of them.'

Jack knew a chap called Frank Collins with a lovely singing voice, and invited him to perform. The show ended with Janie and Frank singing a duet. The girls sang 'Knees Up Mother Brown', and by the end of the evening they'd raised £100 to help the Red Cross send more parcels to the troops.

Ellie said goodnight and returned to her hotel room with Jack holding her hand.

'Darling, you were wonderful tonight,' said Jack. 'I'm glad we're both on Christmas leave together. Is there anything we can do outside the camp? I mean, will you go home to Saltburn? I promise to find an agent for you when we get out of here.'

'Why do you ask?' Ellie said with an ounce of curiosity.

'Neither of us has been away from here since we met. Can we take a trip somewhere?'

'I've nothing to go home for,' Ellie said sadly.

'You got me now. How about if we spend the weekend together?'

Ellie tightened her belly. 'Jack, I recognise your eagerness for me to devote myself to you, but I request your patience.'

She kissed Jack on the cheek, then he turned to her lips and kissed her full on. Alone in her room, he held her tight in his arms and placed his hands on her neck, sliding them down to her bosoms.

'Jack, please don't...you must understand. I've told you how I feel and you're not making it easy.' But what if we don't make it through the war? She was afraid of making the biggest mistake of her life, and realised Jack's irritation, but as Vicky had said, he would wait if he loved her.

'I just wanted a feel, that's all,' he teased, and removed his hands. 'I'm sorry if I offended you, but I have needs, too.'

'We will continue as friends and make the most of our current situation. You know, with the concert party.'

'Okay, honey. You've made your point. You will tell me when you're ready, though? I think I've fallen for you in a big way, and I'd hate to lose you now.' He caressed her cheeks. 'Sorry.'

'Aw, Jack, that's sweet, love, but I assure you, you'll know when the time is right, yes?'

Jack sighed heavily and sat by the window, making Ellie wonder why he felt this urgent need to get married while they were in this unwelcome predicament. Did physical intimacy hold more significance than genuine commitment? He's a typical man, she thought, her eyes rolling as she stifled a sigh, the weight of his words heavy in the air. A nagging doubt made her ask what did he see in her? There was something about him that seemed too good to be true. She recalled the day she'd wanted Harold to make love to her. God!

The bitter taste of regret filled her mouth; despite her foolishness, her love for him had been profound and true. Jack was different. Harold was always so sensible and thoughtful in his actions. Jack wasn't like Harold, with whom she'd felt safe. He'd understood her more than anyone. But she must stop comparing Jack with Harold. This war had put her in an awkward situation. She'd lost her dad, her family hardly ever wrote, and decisions about Jack would never be one of her good points.

'Goodnight, Jack. I'll see you tomorrow, darling. We'll go somewhere, perhaps on a day trip to Inverness, catch a train, find a pub with a welcoming fire, and have lunch there.'

'Sounds good to me, but, *ma chérie*, please don't keep me waiting too long, will you? I feel sure the war will end soon.'

'Hmm, we've been hoping for too long.' Ellie smiled and let go of his hand.

'I love you, Ellie.' His smile told her he meant it.

'I love you too, Jack. But marriage is a serious step. I'm pleased you understand.' Somehow, Ellie knew those words were not ringing as pure as she'd felt they had with Harold, but she had to get used to it. What she needed right now was a whole lot of care. Who else but Jack gave her that kind of attention? In wartime, you had to go with the flow.

Chapter Thirty

February 1944

Harold lay on his straw bunk under the barn. Fleas from the cat had bitten him from top to toe, and his nights were hardly restful as he scratched his legs until they bled. It was like the prison camp, but at least here Agata dressed them with a bandage and poultice to relieve the itching. He felt a wave of comfort wash over him as her motherly touch enveloped him. It was then that the thought of William, sharp and sudden, pierced his mind. The poor lad had probably had it worse than he had. His brother was a strong swimmer, capable of handling rough waters, so there was a chance, wasn't there? Harold had mentioned William's disappearance to Bruno, who had patted him on the shoulder and offered words of sympathy.

As evening settled, the rhythmic clip-clop of a donkey cart announced Agata's friend's arrival. 'The Germans are coming!' she called out, letting them know that they were just a short distance away in the valley. 'I heard the gunfire from the valley. I fear English soldiers are dead. I tell you they are coming.' She huffed and puffed her words. 'I rode up here on the donkey to tell you. We trotted all the way, and the poor beast is exhausted.'

The two men wondered what they should do.

'Did I understand that right?' Bernie said. 'We're in the shit again.'

The floor under the barn was a secure hideout, and as soon as the messenger left, Bruno suggested they rest there for a while. 'It is soon time for you to move on. They will not make it up the mountain for the next four hours, if they are walking. You should rest before your journey. You will head to the border where your men await your arrival. It will be best if you make your way south to

Campobasso. May God be with you, my friends. There are shepherds in the mountains – you can trust them. They'll provide you with the food you need for your journey. I will give you the map.'

On colder nights Bruno had taken risks and allowed them to sleep in the house. They made sure they left no trace of their presence, and religiously washed their pots and cutlery as Agata had shown them. It was a quiet night, and they'd become used to living with the cows as they kept the stable warm. Bernie kept reminding Harold that the barn's odour was a healthy pong and wouldn't harm them.

A deafening banging noise echoed through the stillness of the night, rousing everyone from their slumber at one o'clock in the morning. Someone arrived at the farm door. No one ever came this way at night, especially in deep snow.

Maria shouted, '*Papà, Papà, vieni subito!*'

A German officer stood at the door. Bruno pretended he didn't understand any German or English.

The officer snapped, '*Wie viele Menschen leben hier?*'

Harold and Bernie knew this was it. Time to go – and quick. In silence, Bernie pointed to the blankets, which Harold grabbed along with the map and torch. They'd practised sleeping in their boots for the last few weeks, and they were ready. One after the other, they squeezed through a narrow window in the cellar – no time to cover up all traces of their presence. Bernie threw the emergency kit to Harold, who caught it, and they scrambled into the safety of the forest, running for their lives. Bernie stumbled, and Harold ran back to help him up from his knees. Breathless, they ran up the mountainside, knowing they might never see Bruno and his family again.

Back at the house, Bruno shrugged his shoulders, pretending not to understand. In broken Italian, the German officer tried again and became impatient. The men accompanying him pushed past Bruno and ransacked everything in their path. The house was suddenly full of raging Germans. They opened cupboards, checked under the beds, and tried to kick the dog but missed. They wanted to look into everything, and Agata stood there terrified. The soldiers found nothing: no clues, no trace. Bruno tried to look innocent. Then a soldier stood with Maria and asked her questions. She pretended she didn't understand, and the soldier pushed her toward her mother. He tried speaking in English with her, but she looked blank. He got angry when he discovered they weren't getting anywhere.

'*Siamo venuti per i prigionieri di guerra Inglesi,*' said the soldier who'd searched Bruno and Agata's bedroom.

Bruno replied, '*Quali prigionieri di guerra?*' He denied everything. It was easier now to say they weren't hiding anyone in the house because Harold and Bernie were no longer sleeping inside the house.

The soldier pointed a gun at him. Maria cried out and held her mother tight. The women cowered in the corner of the room. Bruno could see how scared they were, and wanted to avoid further confrontation. He must distract the Germans' attention by taking them outside to the disused pigsty on the other side of the yard. That would allow Harold and Bernie to hear their voices and escape from the back of the cow barn as they'd practised.

It was pitch dark, the moonlight hiding behind the clouds. The officer had a torch, but its batteries only provided a flicker of light. Bruno knew they would leave him alone if he at least appeared to be cooperating. That would mean more time for Harold and Bernie to escape. He kept the Germans talking.

Another officer tried again, in English this time. 'Now we go to the barn where you have the cows, yes?'

Bruno furrowed his brow looking as if he was attempting to understand. '*Ah, sì, sì, il fienile.*' He nodded and led the Germans toward the barn with only the fading torchlight to guide them. Once there he took his time lighting a lamp, then sneezed, which blew out the flame. He kept the wick low when he'd finally lit it a second time.

In the darkness, the well-hidden trapdoor remained unnoticed. Bruno made sure the Germans were distracted, then he tripped over a leather strap lying on the floor. It took him a few more seconds to stand up. With his arthritis, he struggled to maintain his balance. In pain, he let out a cry and muttered to himself in Italian. Unsure of the fate of Harold and Bernie, he clasped his hands tightly together and sent out a silent prayer, yearning for their safe escape and journey to freedom. His heart raced, a rapid drumbeat of fear and anticipation. The odds of surviving this seemed slim, miraculous.

The officers climbed the ladder into the loft. They poked their bayonets into hay bales in case anyone was hiding there. 'We thank you for your cooperation. There is no sign of prisoners here. We will leave you to your bed. *Gute Nacht.*' They left the farm arguing in German among themselves.

Bruno knew they were annoyed at having come all this way for nothing. As soon as they were gone, he returned to the barn, put his hand on his chest, and smiled. 'They made it! Godspeed, Harold and Bernie, and may you return when the war ends.'

Exhausted from the steep, moonlit climb, the two British soldiers sat heavily in a ditch in the dark forest, the cold seeping into their bones.

'God, that was close,' Harold gasped. 'I hope the Galantes are safe. It's bloody freezing out here.'

They took a drink from the icy stream.

'I reckon someone told them about us,' Bernie said. 'They must've walked a good few hours to Bruno's place. Who'd bother to climb that high if someone hadn't tipped them off?' He shook his head and wiped his mouth with his hand. 'What shall we do, Deano?'

'Keep walking,' Harold said, patting his chest pocket. 'I've got Bruno's map. We'll study it and move on as soon as it's light. There could be another shepherd's hut like Cristo's if we're lucky. The Italian people have been so courageous and kind, it's astonishing.'

His heart beat faster as he spoke. 'It's the Fascists we have to worry about.'

The two men crept through the forest, feeling the give of snow under their boots as they walked ever higher. There were strange noises in the darkness. Close by, Bernie heard a wolf howl.

'Shh, listen – there it is again,' he said.

Harold shivered and patted him on the shoulder. 'Come on, keep moving.'

Each tree they passed had a personality of its own. In the moonlight the branches seemed like arms draped in long sleeves. Harold walked into a spiderweb and brushed the silky strands from his lips and hair, spitting them out while he stumbled over rocks. The thin air made them breathless, and the ends of their fingers numbed with cold. Each step became more tiring than the last. They decided it was better to descend to keep warm than to go higher. Walking south meant drawing nearer to the enemy but closer to the border where British troops had invaded through Sicily. Harold turned a phrase he'd heard at Dunkirk into something more in the moment: 'Every step that I take makes my back ache.'

They stopped for a rest.

'I reckon that's Villavallelonga, the village ahead of us. It's very flat land down there and we would be too easily seen,' Harold said.

As they hid behind a rock, Harold studied the map. 'We're still dressed as peasants, so we can risk finding food. Maybe we can get away with your Italian if I pretend to understand. I know enough words to make a conversation – Maria taught me.'

'I don't know.' Bernie shrugged. 'But we've come this far.'

The moonlight clearly defined the shapes of the trees. Ahead lay immense peaks as they continued walking under the girdles of stars stretching across the sky. A wind blew across the mountaintop, dragging soft blankets of newly fallen snow and delicate glistening diamonds in the frozen air. The majesty of the scene filled them with awe, a hushed silence settling as the silvery new moon illuminated their path, its light a gentle guide. Below, there were lights in the valley. It was as if they were dreaming, but it was cold, and their fingers and toes were numb. They must keep moving.

Another three hours until dawn and, with sore feet, and drunk with fatigue, they stopped and fell into a place they thought safe: a deep hollow about a kilometre from the roadside. As they looked out, they could see the constant movement of German convoys, reinforcing the fact that they would need to fight for their freedom. Their ears were met with repetitive gunfire coming from three British planes soaring above, and the faint response of machine guns firing below. As they sat, the sounds of war gradually died, leaving them in peaceful stillness once more. Both men needed a plan to get across the valley unseen. They'd have to travel at night, following the trail that Bruno had suggested. They had to make it – no turning back now.

Harold fell asleep in the hollow, exhausted, cold and hungry. Bernie followed.

After a few hours, Harold prodded Bernie. 'Shit!'

They heard voices. How many were there? Harold couldn't see, but it sounded like there were three Germans. Harold and Bernie had no weapons. Nothing was going to protect them now. They were dead in the hole where they hid. A ready-made grave. They stayed as low as they could and waited another agonising minute.

'*Hande hoch!*'

'Shit. Here we go again,' Harold whispered to himself.

'Come with us and keep your hands up.'

Bernie spoke in Italian.

'You foolish man.' The officer laughed. 'We *know* you are English.'

Harold wanted to kill him.

As they marched down the valley, the sound of guns being cocked sent shivers down their spines.

Bernie looked at Harold in utter despair. 'Do we have to go through all this fucking nonsense again?' he said.

*

The sound of a heavy engine grew louder as a truck approached. They spent an hour idling by a tree, their hands bound, before being escorted to a quaint building in a nearby village. Despite the Germans' persistence, Harold and Bernie remained silent, offering no valuable insights.

They questioned Harold first. 'Where have you been hiding?'

'In the mountains. We lived off the sheep and cows.'

Behind him stood a German officer with a gun. Harold felt desperate to do something stupid and escape. But no – that wouldn't be very intelligent. It was as if he had become a character in a film he had seen, the experience now feeling even more real and overpowering. The German officer scoffed at his reply.

They interrogated Bernie, who told them the Italian guards had let them out of the prison camp, and they'd had no reason to stay. He was good at stating the obvious and getting away with acting stupid, though he was far from it. The Germans gave up on questioning him, and the officer lost his patience and gestured for Bernie to be escorted to a waiting truck, where Harold waited under guard.

Three hours later, amid the clamour of Pescara Railway Station, they wearily marched toward a cattle truck, and were told to get on board.

'Take your boots off,' the guard snapped.

They found over thirty men in one wagon, warming their feet with their hands, and hardly any room to sit down. Heads hung and eyes glanced at the newcomers. They seemed too dejected to make conversation. There had been very little to eat or drink since leaving the farmhouse. Harold and Bernie's stomachs pained them with lack of food. They could only grab a couple of food parcels which someone threw into the truck when the train stopped at the next station. They devoured the food, stuffing their faces until crumbs littered their clothes, and even then, they eagerly scooped up every last crumb from their laps. A British officer, his voice cutting through the men's disgruntled muttering, commanded them to share their dwindling provisions.

'Fat chance we have of escaping now,' Bernie said. 'My feet are like blocks of ice.'

Harold scanned the miserable faces around them. Some lads he recognised from Campo 78. But he couldn't believe who he saw in a corner of the truck. 'Dekkers?'

Bernie saw him too, and they squeezed their way toward each other with arms open for a manly hug.

'We're so glad to see you. We're sorry we had to leave you behind, mate,' said Bernie.

'It didn't exactly do us much good. We're being sent into Germany via Klagenfurt in Austria.' Being the man who always knew what was going on, Dekkers reported that they faced more than a ten-hour journey on the first day. 'We've got a lot to tell the folks back home, eh?' He sighed. His face had a cut on it, and blood had congealed on his cheek.

'Where've you been, mate? We wanted to find you, but...' Bernie took a deep, pained breath and closed his eyes.

'Now is not the right time to ask me that,' Dekkers said, frustration clear in his voice. 'It's a long story – too long and too destructive to tell. Let's focus on making it through this journey alive, shall we?'

The men spent the next hour discussing what to do. Could they escape from the train, and if so, where should they do it? No guards were in the truck; if the train stopped, they could run away. But what good would that do? Surrounded by hostile territory, they'd face the daunting challenge of surviving with no provisions, or even a pair of boots to protect their feet. They would be shot. The bitter cold would surely inflict frostbite upon them, forever robbing them of their ability to walk. Perhaps they were better off staying put. At least they'd be fed, though Bernie wasn't so sure about that. Dekkers suggested they go with whatever was coming their way. Despite their best efforts, they were unable to do anything more.

Once again, the three men huddled together, the damp chill

seeping into their bones. Harold wondered how much longer they could endure this misery without succumbing to illness. It was now daylight. The snow fell, and Harold's fingers froze as the train trundled to the Austrian border. Despite their cold and hunger, their voices, thin but determined, sang 'Chattanooga Choo Choo', matching the rhythmic clang of the train on the tracks; a brief, fragile moment of camaraderie before despair returned. What was the point? Harold had no spirit left to fight. Instead, he closed his eyes and slept on the floor as the singing died.

Throughout the day the train continued its journey, and finally, as darkness descended, it came to a stop at the Austrian border, its wheels screeching on the tracks. Battling exhaustion, Bernie jolted awake when someone tossed food parcels into the wagon. Without warning, ten men leaped from the train. They stole the food, opened the doors as the train was leaving the station, and disappeared into the darkness to the sound of shots being fired. Harold decided he couldn't go through with it. In the middle of occupied Austria, escaping now would be suicide. They needed to stick together. Besides, this war couldn't last much longer. There had been many rumours, though it was impossible to know the truth. Would they ever be rescued?

As the sun arose, Harold opened a gap in the door to see the Karawanken Mountains of Yugoslavia in the distance. The train stopped again in the city and then moved on to Graz, and the German guards ordered the men to disembark. Harold couldn't wait to arrive; he felt ill and could hardly keep his eyes open. All he wanted was for this to stop. It was a nightmare. If only he could wake up in his bedroom in Saltburn.

After another hour, they reached the transit camp, which was the same as any other camp: routine, stinking urine, and boiled cabbage. Except this time, German soldiers barked orders at the prisoners – and at each other.

After hours of interrogation, the three men left the camp on another train. They travelled into Germany to Stalag XI-A near Berlin. There was nothing to see or read, so they slept. The doors were closed, and it was almost pitch black inside the wagon.

'Another hellish journey,' Bernie announced, and creased a corner of his mouth in sheer defeat.

North-west of Dörnitz, the prison camp at Altengrabow stood as a grim reminder of the war's atrocities. As the prisoners formed a line, the sound of shuffling feet filled the air, creating a sombre atmosphere. Harold's bewilderment grew as he took in the sight of the countless prisoners, packed together, their shoulders touching, along the perimeter fence. Their weary faces told a story of hardship and struggle, confirming to him that this was the harsh reality they faced. He couldn't help but feel frustrated at the Allies' failure to make it. At least the camp in Sulmona had been relatively civilised. This looked like hell.

He checked the men's uniforms and discovered many nationalities standing by the fence. French, British, Belgian, Serb, Russian, Italian, American, Dutch, Slovak and Polish prisoners of war. Everywhere he looked, Harold saw men in ragged khaki, hardly able to move around without bumping into one another. Only at Dunkirk had he seen such chaos. A familiar odour came from behind the wire, a whiff of memories from his days in Sulmona which added to the stench of sick bodies and death. Harold gagged at the thought of having to go through it all again. He placed his hand over his mouth, wishing to fall asleep and never wake up.

Separated from his companions, he was left alone to find his way around. He discovered a longing to care about the man in the next bed, or the soldier suffering battle fatigue who constantly stared at the ceiling. He would keep himself mindful of how much worse it could be.

They gave him a job at the hospital, cleaning the wards, and he narrowly escaped having to remove a dead body from a bed. By the time he arrived, someone else had done it. The corpse, stark and still, was wheeled away on a trolley. He watched, then squeezed his eyes shut, the metallic tang of blood still heavy in the air. He must preserve his sanity.

On 3 April, Harold sent a postcard home.

> *I'm sorry I haven't written in a long time. It is an endless story, but I've been desperately wandering around the countryside in the freezing cold, trying to get home.*
>
> *It's been a bitter, bitter disappointment. I have nothing, once again, except the clothing I stand up in. I left everything behind when I escaped. Don't worry about sending parcels; I won't receive them. I will let you know soon.*
>
> *I'm getting plenty to eat at the moment. I'm very anxious to hear from you again. By now, I have learned the art of patience – or giving up, more likely, but I'll try not to give up.*
>
> *Love,*
> *Harold*

It was two weeks before Harold caught up with Bernie and Dekkers. The relentless smashing of rocks in a quarry left their muscles throbbing with pain, each movement becoming an agonising effort. Bernie, usually the one to comfort Harold's broken heart over Ellie, now appeared gaunt and distant. He hardly said a word.

In the mess hut, Harold put up a notice. Perhaps someone knew what had happened to William. He knew it was a long shot, but he had to try.

Lost at Sea
Does anyone here know what happened to HMS Penelope?
Are there survivors here at the camp? Looking for Bugler
William Dean from Yorkshire.
All information to Pte Harold Dean, Hut 128.

Harold's job at the hospital dragged him into further despair. It wasn't long before he almost became a patient and not an orderly.

All he could do now was wait and see if anyone would answer his question. There was nothing to occupy his mind except dead bodies and men crying out in pain.

'How…how…how're you doing?' Harold stammered.

'It's always so cold,' said Dekkers. 'I'm looking forward to warmer days again,' he added dreamily.

'I… I got my food parcel yesterday.'

'Hey, Deano, are you okay?' asked Bernie.

'What do you mean?'

'Your voice.'

'My nerves are getting to me. I'm struggling to think about what I want to say.'

'POW shock – I've heard of this before. You take care and rest, okay?'

Harold promised he would, yet as the week progressed there were days when words didn't work for him. He was grateful that Bernie did his best to get him out of the doldrums, but he couldn't speak; words refused to come. His mind was in other places, wishing someone from home was there to comfort him. Instead, he kept staring into the void, unable to answer questions and gazing without expression. Had they heard about William yet? How were they coping at the shop? Were his parents still living there? So many questions, and the few frustrating answers were driving him nuts. He awoke in a sweat, paralysed – no one wanted to listen. The situation continued night after night.

Finally, on 19 April, he wrote a letter home, the only way of spilling out his emotions. He told his parents he had nothing to say: whatever had happened last year and the year before, he'd say the same things this year, and anyway, he could only send one letter every two weeks. His morale was now lower than ever; it was the second most challenging letter he'd written so far, the first being that one to Ellie over a year ago.

With the warmer weather, Harold's fate was sealed as he learned he could be transferred to a labour-intensive camp. "Don't worry, I'll be fine," he wrote. He wondered if he'd ever see his parents again.

The hard graft strangled him. He was not up to working in a quarry, nor did he want to talk to anyone. Consumed by grief and exhaustion, he tried to fit in with the others. As the days went by, he realised his stammer had worsened until his words took too long to express, and he gave up talking. The memory of his own complaints about the King's droning, monotonous speech surfaced; now, the halting words of his own voice was a stark reminder.

The air crackled with a palpable sense of fear and dread as Christmas, only a week away, loomed like a dark storm cloud. Bernie and Dekkers had transferred to the same camp as Harold. Harold met a fellow soldier who said he was from Middlesbrough, and they immediately bonded. With a hint of curiosity, the soldier enquired about Harold's surname. The name 'Harold Dean, Green Howards, 4th Battalion' was like a mantra to Harold, and one of the few phrases he could say without stuttering.

'Maybe I'm mixing you up with someone. Do you have a brother in the forces?'

'I got t-two brothers – well, I-I-I had two, but one of them d-died.' It was the first time Harold had spoken about this with anyone other than Dekkers and Bernie.

'Do you know of a chap called Billy Dean?'

Harold said, 'No, sorry.' Then he quickly realised…perhaps… no, it couldn't be… William?

'There's a young British sailor here who comes from Yorkshire. He tells me he was on a ship in the Med which took a devastating hit, and he had to swim for it.'

Harold's thoughts raced through every word his dad had ever told him. In his heart, he desperately wished for a world in which everything would be okay once more. Suddenly, his ability to speak clearly returned, and he blurted out, 'William?'

'I'll find out,' the soldier said, his voice filled with unwavering determination. 'This young lad is in quite a predicament, so don't get your hopes up, mate, but it sounds right, doesn't it?'

'It's a common name,' replied Harold. 'I d-daren't hope.'

In the silence of his bunk, Harold's mind raced with worries about William's fate. All afternoon, he waited anxiously with a knot tightening in his belly. Finally, around five in the evening, he saw a blond-haired young man being pushed by his friend in a makeshift wheelchair. Harold gazed in horror at the figure wrapped in bandages.

'Hiya, brother,' croaked William, looking sorry for himself. 'Am I glad to see you.'

With a sudden burst of energy, Harold rose to his feet and drew in a sharp breath. A wave of gratitude washed over him like an overwhelming tide. Despite his scepticism, he couldn't shake the feeling that a divine presence was by his side, leading him over every hurdle. It was unbelievable, but there he was: William, sitting before him against all odds. 'Bloody hell!' he exclaimed under his breath, unable to contain his astonishment. 'It, it really *is* you.' His knees buckled, and he stooped to the floor to be at the same level as his brother. Suddenly, all that suffering seemed much more bearable. Harold carefully embraced William. They gazed at each other, then embraced again in disbelief. 'Where, where the hell have you been, you little bugger?' Tears fell onto Harold's cheeks, and his bottom lip trembled. William looked dreadfully older. His face bore scars from being in the sun too long – or were they burns?

Quick, shallow breaths punctuated William's responses, showing his exhaustion. 'Hospital. I nearly drowned. I burned my hands and almost lost my leg. I must have fallen unconscious, and when I woke, I didn't know who I was. Neither did anyone else. This fisherman and his family found me on the beach in Italy. The rest is history. I've just arrived here after a very long train journey – it was awful. I need dressings on my leg, which is healing nicely, and I might need operations on my hands. I've been in so much pain, you couldn't imagine it. They moved me to a German field hospital. I was there for a long time and in a coma for about a month. It was the pain. I couldn't write. I couldn't speak. I almost died.' William cried in Harold's arms. 'Hal, I love you. I really love you.'

'No need to fret, young 'un,' Harold's gentle voice soothed. 'I'm here now.' Was he dreaming again? 'Oh, W-William, I've missed you so much. I'm surprised I didn't see you in the hospital. T-t-tell me more,' he begged, closing his eyes briefly.

William passionately recounted the harrowing tale of his ship being torpedoed, vividly describing the deafening explosion and the searing heat of the water. 'Despite the pain, I swam ashore. I lived with this fisherman, Solo, for several weeks. My injuries got infected, and they had to carry me to a local hospital, where I collapsed. Over the next few months, I couldn't do anything except sit in a chair. I was too weak to stand or speak to anyone – traumatised! Bloody hell! I feel so much better for seeing you, though, Harold.'

Harold wiped William's tears with his hands. His once-lovely blond hair was now a scorched mess, with patches of baldness and healing scars marring one side. 'Do Ma and P-Pop know about this?'

'Not yet,' replied William, 'but they'll know when they get my letter. Someone wrote it for me a couple of weeks ago, but you know how long it takes to deliver mail. I'm sure the authorities will contact them as I haven't been here very long.'

'Don't worry. They will know because someone will have told them by now. They'll be thrilled. Pop thinks you are...y-y-you know...lost forever!'

'What's happened to you? I can hear a slight stutter in your speech. Did you realise?' William noted.

'Yes – I've been through so much in the last year, it's hard to think straight and get m-m-my words out.'

William stared at his bandaged hands. 'We need a good rest when we get home.' Then he changed the subject. 'Have you heard from Ellie?' he said, recovering from his emotional outburst.

'I wish you hadn't asked me that,' Harold whispered, his voice filled with sadness. 'Not sure if I'll see her again. I wish I could tell you more, but I know nothing about her and...oh, why does it have to go on this long? When I heard about D-Day, I didn't think it would take all this time to get through to us.'

'Now that you're here, we must take care of each other,' said William. 'At least we're both alive. I've missed you all so much. Oh, Hal, I meant to say, you're the best brother in the world.'

William smiled and wiped away a tear with the back of his arm. His pained face made Harold want to wrap him in a blanket and nurse him better.

'I'll introduce you to two of my friends.' Harold appreciated the world again, and almost everything within it felt weirdly good.

The following morning, Harold got permission to be with William and introduced his brother to Bernie and Dekkers.

'What an incredible story,' Bernie said.

A wide, bright smile stretched across Dekkers' face, crinkling the corners of his eyes. 'It's truly remarkable.'

Chapter Thirty-One

Harold's spirits soared. Despite his emaciated appearance, William's resolve to take care of himself kept him going, even when he felt the pangs of hunger. Harold came to the realisation that his stammer hadn't improved, but nor had it worsened. William hoped it wouldn't be long before they were home, although they agreed that being here with Dekkers and Bernie gave them a sense of familiarity and warmth, like being with family.

Harold rarely left William's side. They read books together, did crosswords, played ludo and snakes and ladders – anything trivial to take their minds away from where they were. There were many rumours, but there were also days when hopes seemed dashed. At least the four men had each other to lean on. They attended the camp concert parties and the cinema, and didn't mind watching the same films for the fourth time.

Today was just another day of relentless boredom. Dekkers enjoyed keeping William's mind off his injuries, and Bernie kept him occupied playing draughts. He kept telling William he'd come to babysit Deano's little brother. Now there were two Deanos, it would be confusing. Bernie stuck to calling William 'young Billy', and William shook his head; the thought made him smile.

January 1945

Dear Ma and Pop,

Yet another bloomin' year stuck here, and it's so flippin' cold. I've stopped speculating about when the war will end. Sorry I didn't write, and I know this is short.

I expect you are dancing in the aisles about William. He's doing fine, and we're keeping each other company. Sorry, there's not much more to tell you.

Love,
Harold & William

Chapter Thirty-Two

April 1945

It was the end of April, and an air of change filled the camp. The men listened as loud explosions broke the mood.

Bernie sat on the worn wooden tabletop, the cigarette smoke curling around his face as his crossed legs swayed rhythmically, a desperate attempt to calm his racing mind. 'I hope those buggers of ours don't hit the wrong targets,' he said. 'It's gotta be any day now. They can't allow us to suffer this stinking hellhole any more.'

At dawn on 2 May 1945, they heard rumblings of wheels and cheering. Thousands of prisoners stood in the compound, their hands pressed against the wire fence. They watched as trucks loaded with rations lined up outside the gates – the American troops had arrived.

'Oh my flamin' goodness!' Bernie felt his bottom lip tremble as he watched the rescue teams arrive, accompanied by ambulances carrying doctors and nurses dressed in their crisp official uniforms.

The crowd erupted into deafening cheers, filling the air with an overwhelming roar.

Dekkers, who wasn't that tall, eagerly hopped up and down, trying to catch a glimpse over the heads of his fellow men. 'I can't see a damn thing!' he shouted in frustration.

'I'd give you a leg up, but there isn't room,' Bernie said, laughing through his tears. 'We're going home, Deano.' Then he bent down to William. 'We made it, lad,' he said. 'We're going home – going home at last, young 'un.'

The joy brought tears to many eyes, and the two brothers embraced again. 'We're going back to Ma and Pop,' said William. 'Hoo-bloody-ray!' He sobbed.

The men waved enthusiastically, their joyous shouts echoing over the rumble of countless trucks, which filled the air with the smell of diesel and dust. Overwhelmed with relief, others sank to their knees, sobbing and gasping for breath.

The chaotic welcome that ensued saw pushing and shoving to get to the front of the queue. The Americans kept order, and wounded prisoners could go first. Harold asked to stay with his brother, as he'd been promised he could. He told the Americans he'd been working in a hospital. The medical team said they would allow him to travel on the truck with the other casualties. Six long years of hell, he thought. He and William must now learn to live again. Harold stood by William in his wheelchair. Bernie pretended to shake his wounded hand.

'Bye, you two,' Bernie said, and with a grin he turned to Harold. 'See you on Civvy Street. I'll miss you, mate. Try to get in touch. You know where my aunt lives? Come over as soon as possible, or try to find me at my parents' house. You got the address up north.'

'Bye,' said Dekkers. 'I'll not forget you. If I'm up in Saltburn, I'll find you. Dean's Grocers? Okay, that'll do. Good luck to you both. Get well soon, Billy.'

A sense of urgency filled the air, punctuated by shouts and the pounding of feet as the men scrambled to safety. Twice daily, the army shuttled prisoners to freedom, their hearts filled with hope to finally make it home. The determination in their eyes was clear as Harold and William pressed on, never glancing back. As they looked ahead, they could see a daunting path, but their unwavering determination to reach home pushed them forward.

On 8 May 1945, the war officially ended, leaving a lasting impression. Following the reported suicide of Adolf Hitler, the Allies accepted Germany's surrender, marking a pivotal moment in history.

Harold's ship docked in England and he temporarily parted from William to return to barracks for medical checks. A few days later he went to the hospital, where he and William finally met again. 'They've let me go – drafted out,' Harold said.

'Yes, me too,' said William. 'I got the all-clear to leave.'

'I never want to talk about this again, do you?' Harold murmured.

William nodded. 'We just have to be thankful we both made it home. The rest, I'm not so sure. I'm not at all certain where to start. I mean, will I ever play my trombone again?'

Harold gave a deep sigh. 'If we hadn't been in that camp, God knows what would have happened to us. Your mate who told me you were there probably saved our sanity. Yes, you'll be fine. I'm sure someone at the hospital back home will give you lots of treatment for your hands.'

A few days later they left the army to make their way homeward.

As the train rolled on, a heavy silence settled between the two men. They barely exchanged a word. Lost in his thoughts, Harold pondered if anyone would truly comprehend his inner turmoil. He hoped he'd never go to war again, but felt nervous about returning to Saltburn. Would it be the same? It would take him a long time to get over his experiences. Nearly three years banged up behind a wire fence – too long. Ellie, his parents, Peter, and everyone he knew would have changed. He missed Bruno, Agata and Maria. They'd saved his life, but the capture had been the final straw and had cracked him as quickly as one of Maria's chickens' eggs. In his heart, he held a secret hope that Ellie was back in Saltburn and he'd get the opportunity to see her and finally provide her with an explanation for his confusing letters. But what was there to tell? The sights, sounds and smells all blended together in a chaotic symphony. It was wartime, and millions of people had gone to hell and back. His story was one of many. He mustn't complain. He closed his eyes for a minute or two and slept away the rest of the long journey to Darlington.

William's voice rang in his ear as he shook Harold's arm. 'We're here, Harold. Come on, get up, lad. Give us a hand with the baggage.'

Chapter Thirty-Three

Jack arrived to give Ellie the news. 'They've surrendered – isn't it wonderful?'

Cheers rang out through the camp.

'We're going home.'

Ellie wasn't sure where "home" was any more. She'd promised herself to Jack, and there was no point in going back to Saltburn. Harold probably wouldn't be there, and it would unsettle her. What if he'd died and never made it home? She didn't want to think about it. If she went back, he might not want to see her. She felt confused and unsure about what would happen next.

'Honey, once this is over, we should look for work. I have savings in the bank now. So we can go to Canada soon to meet my family.' Jack gave her a warm smile.

'I'd like that, but I want to do a play too. What about that chap you met while you were away in February? He gave you his card, didn't he? Wasn't he a theatrical agent before the war?'

'Once the celebrations are over, I'll call him, but there's no reason I can't be your agent, is there? There's bound to be professional rep companies all over the country. If anything, he's probably the right man to contact. He'll know the best shows, which might be very helpful to us. We should look in that theatrical newspaper, *The Stage*. You'll have to audition, which isn't something you've been used to, and I'll have to take a temporary job once the army doesn't need me any more.'

Ellie grimaced for a moment. She was going to miss all this army life. The shows, the laughs, the audiences. Could she trust Jack to get her a place in show business? She must stop doubting herself –

and him. Of course she could do it. Why not? She'd proven herself in the army and she could do it again.

'Let's go celebrate,' Jack said.

On leaving the hotel, they took a deep breath and were immediately greeted by the sound of trumpets, bagpipes and cheering. It was as if the whole of Britain had exploded with joy.

'I shall miss you,' Vicky said. 'You were a rock for me. I wish you and Jack every success. I'm leaving in a few days, I might not see you, but I'll try to say goodbye, Jack. See you later, Ellie.'

Ellie paused as Jack walked on and Ellie grabbed Vicky's sleeve. 'Do one thing for me when you get back to Saltburn. See Harold. If he made it home, tell him I'm sorry, and I'll always love him, but the war made it impossible, and it's hard to see a way forward in these circumstances. I'll try and write to you soon.'

'It's not too late to change your mind, Ellie…but yes, I'll see him.'

'Thanks, but I doubt our paths will cross again if I'm going to live in Canada with Jack. I'll be staying down in London for the time being. Jack's got me a couple of auditions.'

Vicky sighed. 'I hope it turns out okay. I'm unsure it's the right way to go, but I'm not your guardian. So you have to do what your heart tells you.'

'Oh yes, it will be the right thing. Jack wouldn't say all those things unless he meant them. You know what he's like, but one thing I'll say, Vicky – you've always been my guardian angel. Thank you.'

'Good luck. Friends for life, eh?' Vicky said. 'Write soon.'

'I hope so.' Ellie kissed her on the cheek.

They hugged, then caught up with Jack and walked along the road with everyone singing, dancing and rejoicing to the sound of the church bells and pipers playing 'Twa Recruitin' Sergeants' and 'Mairi's Wedding'. The girl pipers, their homemade kilts swaying rhythmically with each note, filled the air with lively, traditional Scottish music, their steps a counterpoint to the melodies. Today had to be the best day of their lives.

Part Three

After the Break of Dawn

1945–1948

Chapter Thirty-Four

December 1945

'Harold! There's someone to see you,' Alf called upstairs.

Leaning over the banister, Harold craned his neck to glimpse who stood in the hall. 'Oh my goodness! It's…wait, no, it's…oh, hello!'

Vicky Empsall stood there, radiating an air of maturity.

'Vicky? Oh gosh, it…it…it…really is you,' Harold said, descending the stairs.

'I wanted to talk to you. Is there somewhere we can sit on our own?' Vicky seemed out of breath.

'W-w-w-we can s-sit in the front room if you like.'

Vicky could hardly believe it. Was this the same person who had left Saltburn in 1939? He'd lost much of his hair, he was skinny, and he had a stammer.

'I was with Ellie throughout the war and we did everything together. Her mission was top secret, and getting away from the camp was tough. It wasn't a camp as you might think, but a requisitioned hotel.' Her voice sounded like she was making excuses for having stayed in a luxurious place during the war. She wanted to say it was very comfortable, but that would be inappropriate. While Harold had been enduring goodness knows what, she and Ellie had experienced the time of their lives. 'When did you last hear from Ellie?'

'It's been three years since we wrote to each other, and she agreed it was better not to wait. It's too painful to even think about it. So I wrote to her and we both decided it was a s-s-sensible thing to do. We both grew up, but I still live in hope.'

'Yes, I know. Although, I'm sure she still has a soft spot for you,

Harold.' Vicky smiled. 'You've been through a dreadful time, and even Strathpeffer was filled with uncertainties despite the good times we had there, but we're so proud of you and William and how you persevered. I suppose you knew she has a new man in her life. She also said she'll always love and remember you and the good times you had together. Anyway, sadly she's not coming back to Saltburn and she asked me to tell you that she's looking for acting work.' Vicky hesitated.

Harold looked down at his hands. 'Yes, I would have liked to have heard it from her. So, who's the lucky fella?'

'A Canadian officer she met ages ago. She saved herself for you for a long time and then gave up after you wrote to her, and that's when Jack came on the scene, although...' Vicky stopped in mid-sentence. 'He seemed to take over her life. I'm not one for gossip, Harold, but honestly, I worry about her. Jack's rather...er...well, I don't know, but I'm not sure if he's using her for his own gain. You know how naive she used to be. I don't think she's the same person you once knew. She's become very outgoing and loves acting, but there are still things she isn't very good at.' Vicky laughed. 'I think decision-making is one of them. She's easily persuaded.'

'Do y-you know where she is now?'

'That's the sad part, because she's gone away with Jack and, although she promised to write, I haven't heard a word from her. But it's early days. I know they were looking for work before she went to Canada. She got your letter and was dreadfully upset to hear what had happened to you. We worked hard. I was riding through the mountains on my motorcycle. Ellie was so busy being the major's secretary that we had little time. We wrote plays and performed together in our spare time, which was great fun, but she lost faith in ever being in love again, and I suppose we both gave up. We were there for the experience, having fun with the troops and winning the war. I gave up on Alan. Do you remember him? It was just something we all did. I know you'll forgive her. You never know what's around the corner, but, like Al and me, he's back on leave and we hope to get married in the future. We just had to accept that the war wasn't going to bring us together, but all that has now changed. I feel a nice girl will come along and love you, Harold. It's all so sad, isn't it?'

'Thanks, Vicky, for your honesty. I'm glad you came to see me.'

'Are you keeping well?' asked Vicky.

'No, not really,' he replied with a shrug. 'I'm barely coping, I suppose. I miss my mate Bernie, and there's nothing to do around here. Boredom was the most dreadful thing in the prison camp, until William arrived and brought a spark of excitement. That helped me a lot. It's been the same old routine since I came back – a never-ending cycle of boredom that feels unchanging. The townsfolk here still seem to wear the same clothes and go about their routines just as they did six years ago. I thought we were fighting for a better world, but nothing's changed.'

'I know what you mean. Alan tells me the same thing,' Vicky said. 'You probably need a holiday.'

'Thanks. If you hear from Ellie, tell her there's still a place in my heart for her. It's not the same without her. The memories are still strong. She's everywhere I look. Her photo kept me going when I was in the prison camp, but I lost it when we escaped. I took that as a sign I'd never see her again. I vowed we'd marry, but now that can't happen. We've lost her, you and me, haven't we?'

Vicky gave an ironic smile. 'Maybe not, but only time will tell. We have to move on now, Harold. Well, I must let your family get on with their Christmas. I bet you're looking forward to your mam's Christmas pud, right?'

'Oh, absolutely. Bye, Vicky. Thanks for coming round, and Merry Christmas!' Harold gave her a hug and a kiss on the cheek. Her perfume smelled divine.

Vicky left the house, and after their conversation, Harold wished Ellie was back home. They had once suited each other, but now it could never happen between them. Life in Saltburn was like a wet Sunday afternoon every single day.

March 1946

Harold enquired about his old office job, but his position was no longer available. With his head in his hands, he despaired. The nightmares refused to stop, and pleasant dreams were a distant memory. There were days when he felt no reason to carry on. He had no routine left – all had been destroyed by the sound of guns and visions of corpses on the beach. It had to stop, but he didn't know how to make it do so.

The phone rang at the shop. Alf answered it.

'For you, son.'

'Who is it?'

'Not sure. It's a man's voice.'

'Hello, Harold Dean here.'

'Hiya, Deano, it's me, Bernie.'

Harold's face lit up. 'Hi, Bernie, mate! What a lovely surprise. It's been ages. I thought you'd forgotten me. How did you find me?'

'I miss you, old boy. You said Dean's Grocers, so I checked and got the right number.'

The two men swapped news.

'It hasn't been good here. I'm finding it hard to cope with civilian life. I feel some days like I'm bursting out of a cracker that doesn't go bang! It's all a bit of a let-down. Where are you?' Harold said.

'At home in Weston. Mum and Dad moved down here a few weeks ago, so we're no longer in Yorkshire.'

'Weston?'

'Yeah, Weston. My aunt, you remember? The old girl passed away, so we sorted out her old house. At least it wasn't bomb-damaged. I'm looking for a job, but it's difficult.'

'Sorry to hear it. I know what you mean.'

Bernie made a suggestion. 'You sound really down, old chap. Why don't you get a train and come to the West Country? You can stay with us for a few weeks if you wish. We can go to dances and meet those girls we never spent time with when we were last here – remember? It's lively down here just now.'

Harold's demeanour brightened. 'Are you sure, Bern? Will I get in the way of your h-h-house-moving?'

'Don't be soft. We're mates, yeah? Anyway, we both deserve a break.'

Harold smiled at Bernie's chatty conversation. 'I'll talk it over with my parents. I'd love to come. If you let me have your phone number, I'll call you back tomorrow. What happened to Dekkers? Did he make it home okay? Where is he?'

'He lives… Hampshire? Yeah, he was in the regiment down there. It might be some time before he gets in touch as he wasn't due to be demobbed until later in the year. He was a great support for us all,' Bernie said.

Harold jotted down Bernie's phone number. 'Okay, you'll hear from me tomorrow. Thanks so much, Bern. Bye.'

As William reassured him of his hands' recovery, a sense of relief flooded Harold, the lightness enhanced by Peter's return and their shared laughter. The family members all nodded in unison. It had never been a better time to change things.

'Yes, go on, Harold, take a trip. You got savings in the bank, and now you can enjoy yourself. You certainly deserve it, and we can take care of William,' Alf said. 'Just do it.'

Harold returned Bernie's call, and they agreed to meet up. In the days before the trip, he awoke many times in the night, and often distracted himself from his dreams by strolling through the empty streets and along the promenade in Saltburn. Despite his plan to visit Bernie, his anxiety seemed to grip him by the throat, and he doubted it would ever improve.

He returned home in the dark via the back alley where he and Ellie had had their first passionate encounter. As he leaned against the wall, smoking a cigarette, he took in the salty air of an incoming tide. The image of Ellie, her skin flushed and hair tangled, making love to him, sent a wave of longing, a cruel reminder of his deprivation in the cold, damp prison camp. Overwhelmed, he broke down, his sobs shaking his chest with agonising intensity. It was okay that everyone commended him for being a brave soldier. The relentless pangs of hunger and thirst, combined with the crushing weight of family separation, led some to consider suicide – a despair few could truly grasp. He'd also lost the person he loved most to someone else. Sulmona had not been as bad as Altengrabow, but at least at Altengrabow he'd found William, and he was eternally grateful for that. Then his mind turned to Bruno, and he couldn't stop churning out the sorrow; a pain like a horror movie he had seen too many times, and which refused to stop playing. He hoped that Bruno, Agata and Maria had survived. He must return to Italy one day and tell them he was sorry for all the trouble he and Bernie had caused them. Oh, the guilt. When would it stop? It might have been his fault, and how could he live with that thought? Oh God! What if they *hadn't* survived? What if…? How could he find out?

Harold wore his brown double-breasted demob suit and carried an old leather suitcase he'd found in the loft. Betty watched him depart at the station, the platform echoing with the clang of the steam engine. On departure, he waved and waved from the carriage window until she was nothing more than a distant figure. There was a fragility to his mother's movements; a sort of stillness that told the depth of her recent emotions. The war had left its mark on everyone, etched in the lines on their faces and the weariness of their movements – a palpable sense of loss hung in the air. It was time to move on, and a few days of rest and relaxation with Bernie seemed like just the thing Harold needed.

He'd wanted to appear fashionable, and had bought a trilby hat to keep his head warm and hide his thinning hair. This had to be the day when things changed for him. He thought about the fun he'd missed and how much he looked forward to dancing again. All he wanted was to be healthy and accepted back into society. Perhaps a holiday with Bernie would be a fresh start and a chance to look for someone new who wouldn't break his heart. Good old Bernie – what would Harold have done without him?

The train departed for Bristol from Darlington. One more train change at Temple Meads, and he was on his way to Weston-super-Mare. A young woman with long dark hair and brown eyes entered the carriage. She smiled at Harold, and he asked her where she was going.

'Weston. I've got a job there. It's not much, but it's better than stopping at home with Mum and Dad. They're lovely people, but I'm sure you know how it is.'

'What kind of work?' Harold enquired.

'Hotel receptionist.'

Harold smiled and almost laughed out loud. 'I had a girlfriend who did that kind of work before the war, and she really enjoyed it. Were you in the forces?' he asked.

'I was in the ATS.'

Harold couldn't help himself, and wanted to know more about her. He'd vowed not to talk about Ellie, but today he felt relaxed, and his stammer wasn't as bad as in previous weeks. He told the girl he'd been in a prison camp and was trying to get over it by having a holiday in Weston with a friend.

The girl introduced herself as Jenny Fortune. 'That must've been the worst experience,' she said. 'It'll do you good going to Weston – it's a great town, I'm told.'

'What a lovely name,' Harold said, changing the subject. 'I bet everyone tells you that. I hope you bring me better luck. Which hotel are you working at?'

'The Royal.'

'Sounds like a grand place.'

Jenny put her hand inside her bag and produced a brochure for the hotel.

Before the train pulled into Weston station, Harold had poured his heart out to her, and it seemed she found him equally fascinating.

'We were worlds apart,' she empathised.

'Yes, you're right. Maybe I'll see you soon – that place looks good. My friend and I could come over for afternoon tea. After my experiences, sandwiches are much appreciated these days, believe me.'

After the journey, he felt ready for anything. Jenny had listened to him, understood his sadness, and now she would leave him, but wasn't that just typical of his bad luck? He hoped to see her again. Afternoon tea was a great idea; an excuse to meet her again.

Bernie stood at the gate on the station platform, and Harold showed his ticket.

'Oh, my goodness, look at you,' Bernie said. 'Great hat.'

The two men shook hands. Bernie patted his friend on the shoulder. Harold wanted to embrace him, but thought better of it since they were in public. Now that they were no longer prisoners, the forced camaraderie was replaced by a more natural friendship.

Jenny stood behind Harold in the queue. He turned around to find her.

'Thanks for the conversation. I wish you every success with the new job. Bye.'

Bernie smiled as they walked away. 'You just couldn't wait, could you? You haven't got one of those for me in your suitcase, have you?'

Harold shrugged. 'Well…anything's possible.'

The two men walked from the station to Bernie's parents' house.

'Mum,' Bernie said as he introduced Harold, 'this is my best mate, Harold Dean. We went through the mire together, didn't we?'

Harold nodded. 'We sure did, and I wouldn't want to do that again. I feel most fortunate to be alive. Good to meet you, Mrs Dewhurst, Mr Dewhurst.'

'I'm Alice, and this is my husband, Philip.'

They shook hands.

'It's very good of you to invite me to stay.' Harold gave a nervous smile.

'We're in a mess, as you can see, but we should have everything straight again within two weeks.'

If she'd seen the mess he and Bernie had had to put up with, she'd know that this was paradise in comparison.

Harold gave a brief smile. 'Maybe I can give you a hand. Just ask if you need help.'

'I will, Harold, thank you,' Alice agreed. 'It's getting late, so you'll need your rest. Bernard tells me you've come from Saltburn. We know it well, of course. I'll bring you a pot of tea. Bernard, dear, show Harold up to his room.'

They climbed the stairs, and Bernie opened the bedroom door. 'This room is for you, mate. Better than what we've been used to, eh?'

Harold shook his head at the distant sea view of the Bristol Channel. 'No wonder your parents came down here.' He turned to Bernie. 'I-I-I'm finding it hard to deal with all the shit we endured. Do you feel the same?'

'Yeah, for sure, and I've spent the last few weeks trying to make sense of it all – it's hard going. It's the nightmares I keep having, and they don't go away.' Bernie changed the subject. 'By the way, how is young Billy doin'?'

'He's managing fine, but he's younger than me and probably found it a bit of a daring adventure, being on the ship – he's like that. However, the poor kid has been through a lot of pain. His fingers had fused together with the burns – they wrapped his hands up in one big bandage, and it didn't do the healing process any good. So the hospital operated on his hands, which means he still can't feed himself properly, but he's learning fast. At least he can walk better now.'

'He's a good kid. I enjoyed his company. Perhaps he's still in denial about it all. I would keep an eye on him if you can, because it might just dawn on him soon what really happened. And look for signs of melancholy getting the better of him.'

'He'll be okay. Our pop was a POW in the Great War, so if anyone can help William, he can.' Harold smiled.

'We'll go into town tomorrow afternoon and visit a tea shop I know. They bake wonderful cakes,' Bernie said.

'Is there any chance we can go to The Royal Hotel? The girl I met on the train told me she'd got a job there. It'd be good to call in and say hello.'

'The *Royal*? Okay, if you want, but it's very posh in there. Perhaps we can treat ourselves?'

'They do delicious sandwiches, I'm told.' Harold agreed at the mention of the word 'treat'.

The following day, Harold and Bernie walked through the hotel doors and toward the reception desk.

Jenny Fortune's eyes widened in disbelief. 'Why, hello – I didn't expect to see you again so soon.'

Harold introduced Bernie, who told her they were treating themselves to afternoon tea after all the problems of the last six years.

'Your friend told me what you've been through,' Jenny empathised. 'That's an excellent idea. I'll ask if we can get a table for you.'

Harold caught Jenny's arm. 'I wanted to thank you again for your company. It was so good to talk to a stranger.'

'No problem.' Jenny smiled. 'It was a pleasure, and time is a good healer.'

She guided them into the restaurant, where several people sat at tables overlooking the promenade and the pier. Harold felt conspicuous in his demob suit, and if it wasn't for Jenny, he might have turned around and returned the way he'd come in.

'If you need anything, just ask Carlos here, and I hope to see you before you go.'

Harold smiled. Jenny's a lovely girl, he thought. And Carlos? Was he a POW in England?

After ordering their sandwiches, Bernie wanted to decide what they should do to cheer themselves up.

Jenny came to their table with brochures advertising shows and events in Weston. 'I thought these might be useful for you.'

'How kind,' Bernie said as he took them from her and gave her one of his warm, cheeky smiles. 'Thanks. What would you like to do, Deano?'

'I used to go dancing a lot, but I gave up on it ages ago. So let's go to a dance – why not? By the way, Bern, is there any chance you can call me Hal now that we've left the army? I don't want to be reminded, that's all.'

'Okay, *Hal*,' Bernie teased.

Jenny returned, and Harold thought to include her in the conversation.

'Bernie and me, we were just chatting about dances. I wondered if you would like to join us tomorrow night?'

'Oh, that's so kind of you both, but I'm on a late shift for the next few nights. That's such a shame. Come in again soon, though, and maybe we can make another arrangement. Sorry, chaps.'

Harold shrugged and kept a smile on his face.

'You're looking better this morning, Harold. Don't rush to go back home. You can stay longer if you wish,' said Philip.

Alice explained that having two extra men to help move the furniture was most helpful. There was laughter and joking between them all, and for the first time since his demob, Harold felt normal again.

He phoned home. 'Bernie's parents have invited me to stay longer. I just thought I'd let you know.'

'Go for it,' Alf said. 'You deserve to have a good time. Please send us a postcard.'

Chapter Thirty-Five

In their London digs, Ellie scoured the pages of the latest issue of *The Stage*. Finally, Jack had contacted his colleague for a list of local theatres to which Ellie could travel for auditions. He was her agent now, but Ellie wasn't sure if she liked that idea.

Ellie's landlady had laid down rules. In the solitude of her own room she penned a letter to Harold, her guilt weighing heavily on her heart, while later, she crafted a response to Vicky. Hoping for Harold's continued good health, she hurriedly wrote of her intentions, mindful of the possibility of Jack asking to come into her room and asking questions. Writing a letter allowed her to release her pent-up emotions, even if she never intended to send it. Nevertheless, since the war, it wasn't right to shun Harold, especially after everything Vicky had mentioned in her letter. Also, Betty and Alf had been the kindest to Ellie when her dad had died, and so she must write to them soon too.

> *Dear Harold,*
>
> *I know this letter may come as a surprise. A belated apology for my silence, but I've given this a lot of thought. As you now know, it wasn't always my fault.*
>
> *I've often wondered how you are doing after being away. I'm so glad you made it back home. It wasn't easy for any of us. As far as my family is concerned, I don't have anyone. Mam remarried, and I've no idea where Tommy is. My life fell apart, and I got very down about it. Vicky Empsall and I were in Scotland together, which you know anyway. Throughout my acting tour across the country, I've immersed myself in the sights*

and sounds of different theatres. I'm auditioning with a large repertoire company, but I'm not signed up yet.

Our relationship back in Saltburn was special, but I've changed a lot, and I bet you have too. I'm guessing Vicky has informed you about every detail that's been happening with me, from the latest gossip to my plans for the future. I know you appreciated her visit. Yes, okay, we promised each other we would wait, but need I say more? We grew up, didn't we? Although I was distraught when you wrote, we had to do something sensible, and I valued your honesty. I wish you every success, and I will always consider you my first love. I'm so sorry, Hal. Everything changed, and so did I.

Stay well, good luck in the future, and take care of yourself. Give your mam and dad my love.

Lots of love,

Ellie

In a moment of hesitation, she held the letter delicately, contemplating its contents, before relinquishing it to the gaping mouth of the postbox across the road from her digs.

She and Jack were in theatrical digs: Ellie had her room, and Jack had his. The landlady made sure they did. She seemed to be always watching them. Jack was working temporarily at the BBC, and got up early each day to catch a train.

Confident in her sensible decision about Harold, Ellie decided she would now focus on building a life with Jack and envisioning their future together.

Chapter Thirty-Six

'I hear the old market building is open now. It's been converted into the Playhouse,' Bernie said. 'You know how much we enjoyed those plays in the camp.'

'I'm game if you are, Bern,' Harold said. 'What's on, d'ye know?'

'Let's go see *A Bill of Divorcement*. I'm told it's by the playwright, Clemence Dane. This is real theatre, none of that stuff with men dressed as women.'

Harold laughed. 'I've no idea who Clemence Dane is but it's about time we had some fun. We deserve it.'

They made their way up Market Street and bought tickets. The matinee started at two o'clock. Harold focused on the decor. The theatre walls, draped in rough hessian, created a warm contrast to the ornate, gilded ceiling above, which they couldn't help but admire. It looked pristine and magnificent.

Harold bought a penny programme, took his seat for the start of the play, and read the cast list. He'd never heard of any of the actors. 'God! We're so behind the times.'

The audience clapped as the curtain opened. At last, he could sit and enjoy himself with no more bombs. All he needed now was a lovely girl by his side instead of Bernie. He thought of Jenny. Perhaps they should have asked her to come along, but she was probably working again. He must go back and see her.

At the close of the play, the two men took a short walk to the nearest pub.

'Enjoy it?' Bernie said. 'Bit of an odd family, eh?'

'Yeah, we should do this again soon. Maybe go to the cinema as well.'

*

That night, Harold awoke at a quarter to three in the morning and couldn't get back to sleep because of the sound of two cats fighting in the street. He dressed and walked by the seashore, as he often did in Saltburn. The aroma of salt air from the Bristol Channel filled his nostrils with memories. He had been far away from the sea in Italy and Germany. At least here, there were no recent memories of Ellie to fill his thoughts, only the mewing of herring gulls as dawn broke across the eastern sky. The Blitz had ravaged parts of the town, particularly the Boulevard, High Street, and Grove Park areas, leaving behind a landscape of rubble and destruction; however, the morning was filled only with the gentle shushing sound of waves along the shore, as if the world was holding its breath.

His mind filled with questions. What should he do with his life? Without a job, he couldn't see the future and it seemed life would never be the same. He stopped to light a cigarette, spitting a strand of tobacco from his lips as he gazed across the sea. With every passing moment, he wanted the stillness of the dawn to go on forever.

The sound of the breaking waves fizzing across the sand filled his ears, instantly transporting him back to a time when he was a different person. Now that he and Ellie were no longer together, he questioned if that dreamlike scenario could still happen. The twinkling lights of South Wales on the horizon transformed the twilight into a scene straight out of a fairy tale. Think again! He had to do something with his life. Perhaps he and Bernie should go into business together. But what would they do? He hadn't a clue. The army had stripped away his confidence, leaving him feeling vulnerable and uncertain about surviving in civilian life. Every time he tried to form independent thoughts, he faced a challenging battle. A job and a girl like Jenny would be the key to restoring his life's value, as they would bring not only financial stability but also the joy and comfort of companionship. There was a disconnect between his heart and his head. He wanted to cry – yes, *cry*! A sob entered his throat.

'Oh God, what am I supposed to do now?' he murmured. He must stop thinking like this; it was destructive.

Despite some anxious moments, Bernie and Harold were enjoying their week as they wandered again through The Colonial pub's swing doors. According to Bernie, this was a popular hangout for actors from both theatres, giving it a lively feel. It was a cosy place to drink – a large room with a smoky atmosphere and filled with laughter. Harold hung up his coat on the peg by the door. The two men ordered a pint, then a second, and then a third. Harold felt light-headed, but not enough to be reeling. He knew better than to get drunk after Bernie's mother had been so kind. The wind on the promenade sucked in the pub doors with a loud bang. Instinctively, both men hunched over and jumped, their leg muscles tightened, ready to run.

'Oh shit.' Bernie blurted out. 'I spilled my beer.' He placed a hand on his chest and blew out his cheeks.

'We may laugh, but trust me, I'm still a nervous wreck,' Harold said, his tone balancing between humour and genuine worry.

Their eyes met the barman's across the dimly lit room; a sympathetic look passed between them.

Harold took a breath and composed his thoughts. 'That nice girl I met – you know, Jenny – I'm thinking of inviting her for a bite to eat,' he remarked.

'Now you're talking, Deano – I mean Hal. Make sure she's got a friend for me.'

Harold expressed his amusement and pushed Bernie's shoulder playfully. 'I'll ask her for you.' Then from across the crowded room he saw a girl wearing a pale blue suit. She had long blonde hair. He only caught a glimpse of her from the side, but she reminded him of someone, and he couldn't place her. 'Who was that girl sitting there? Haven't we seen her somewhere recently?'

'I think she was one of the actresses in the play we saw.' Bernie couldn't shake off the shock of the pub door slamming shut, and his mind was still racing to make sense of his reaction.

'I thought I'd seen her,' Harold said. 'They all look so different when you see them closer.' He turned his attention to the sign for the toilet. 'Must go to the bog,' he announced.

At that moment, the actress returned, and Harold noted how she stood as she talked to a man in a light-coloured suit. Harold could tell from his accent that he was American. He walked behind the actress, careful not to bump into anyone as the theatre group occupied most of the space in the narrow passageway.

'Excuse me.' Harold squeezed through the small crowd, opened the toilet door, and unbuttoned his trousers. Phew, that's better. All this beer, I'm not used to it.

After leaving the gents, Harold returned to his seat. He put his hand in his pocket and found the programme he'd bought for the play. 'So, which one is she?' he asked Bernie.

'I think she was the one who...'

'Ah, yes. According to this photo, the actress's name is Carrie Leigh.'

'Nope – never heard of her,' Bernie replied. 'You're not thinking of asking her out as well as Jenny?'

Harold gave a titter at Bernie's remark. 'No, that one's for you.'

The two men made their way home, and despite Harold having told himself not to drink too much, it seemed they were taking one step forward and three back. Finally, they arrived home after midnight and crept upstairs to their beds.

Chapter Thirty-Seven

Harold knew his holiday was almost over; the dwindling days hung heavy in the air. He didn't wish to outstay his welcome, though their time together had been filled with fun and laughter. He'd enjoyed himself with Bernie, but the late hour reminded him that all good things must come to an end. There was one more task on his mental to-do list first, though: see Jenny and find out if she's available for a date. However, he kept putting it off, as Bernie always had other plans.

She wasn't on duty when he arrived at the hotel, and he didn't want to leave a message, so he left.

Both men returned to the pub that night.

'Good to see you lads again,' the barman remarked. 'Always like giving something back to our army lads. Here, have a free beer.'

'It was tough,' Harold said, noticing Bernie's tired eyes.

'You okay, mate?' Bernie smiled at Harold.

'I just need to reflect for a while, maybe take a walk along the prom. You know how it is.' Harold wiped his fingers over his lips.

'Okay. Look, Hal, I'll see you back at the house.' Bernie yawned. 'I hope you don't mind. Will you be okay?'

'Yeah, fine.' Harold nodded.

Bernie took a sip of his beer and wiped his finger across his moustache. 'I'm feeling exhausted these days. I think that bloody camp in Germany almost saw me off.' He didn't finish his drink and decided he'd had enough. 'Are you coming back or staying here?' Bernie asked.

'I'll have one more.'

Bernie left and Harold turned toward the bar. 'Just the one pint.' It felt good to be on his own.

A woman had her eye on the two men at the bar. Ellie had caught the train the previous day to arrive in Weston for an audition. Harold didn't notice, but she was sure it was him as soon as she heard his voice. And then she remembered that, in one of his letters written before Dunkirk, he'd mentioned a chap he knew whose aunt owned a guest house here. Could it be...? Styled with Brylcreem, his short golden hair had thinned. He seemed taller than she remembered. But six years was a long time; people had changed. Harold ordered another drink while chatting to the barman, and as the conversation progressed, she heard him speak and knew it was him. It had to be, but how could she approach him with Jack close by? She held her breath. How on earth...? No, surely not. Impossible! Yes, it is him. It is. She must find a way of attracting his attention. But Jack might get jealous, and then there could be trouble. He was like that, despite his kindness to her. Was this really Harold, or was she being silly? He received the letter telling him she was marrying Jack. He'd understand. After all, it had been his idea to end it, and she'd reluctantly agreed. Her mind echoed with the past and the present, but what of the future? But here in Weston?

Ellie sat around a table with Jack and his friends, Jack's back to the bar. As Harold left the pub, Ellie made her excuses to visit the ladies' room and followed him. Why was she doing this? It couldn't be right: she was engaged to someone else, but what if she had made a mistake? Marrying Jack was the right thing to do. She hesitated, but almost felt like tiptoeing up behind Harold and saying, "Guess who?" It had to be him. Or was she about to make a fool of herself?

Harold left the bar and Ellie followed him outside.

'Harold Dean?' she called softly. If it wasn't him, she could apologise, say it was a mistake. But what if he made a fuss? She had little time to say hello. Perhaps the whole idea of chasing rainbows was ridiculous. She almost turned away. Her keen mind, however, said do it, and she couldn't hold back any longer.

Harold didn't seem to hear her; the wind blew her voice across the sea, so she tried again as she got closer. But no, it wasn't him; this man was taller and thinner. Harold stopped, captivated by the twinkling lights dancing on the sea and the joyful, lingering melody of the band from the Grand Pier; Ellie waited a short distance behind him. She almost turned around to leave. Then… Yes, it *is* him. It really *is* him, she thought. Oh my God! She rushed to catch up.

'Hello, Harold. I thought it was you.'

Harold turned, looking puzzled. His eyes opened wider.

'Did you get my last letter – the one from a couple of weeks ago?' Ellie said.

Harold furrowed his brow. 'What? Oh heck. Ellie? Ellie?' He held out his arms to hug her, but she didn't respond. 'What letter? I've been here for two weeks,' he said.

'Look, er… Jack is waiting for me. Can we meet at the stage door tomorrow? Come to my dressing room at the theatre. I have a second audition for *A Bill of Divorcement*, and if I get the part, I must sign the contract on Thursday. So, I'll explain around nine-thirty tomorrow night. Please don't follow me back to the pub. I'm with the actors, and…well…it's awkward. I'm staying at The Royal for a few nights until we can get digs – sorry. I wanted you to know I'm here, that's all.'

The curiosity inside Harold seemed strong, and it looked as if he had a thousand questions ready to burst out of him. 'Ellie? Oh my God…it can't be…'

'Must go, okay? I'll tell you tomorrow. Please, please say you will come.' Ellie quickened to join her friends, leaving Harold wide-eyed on the promenade.

'But, Ellie…' Too late. She was already walking through the pub door where everyone could see her.

Ellie pretended to come out of the ladies to join Jack in the bar.

'You seem out of breath, darling,' he said.

'I went outside for a spot of fresh air. All the cigarette smoke here makes my eyes water, and I need a clear throat for my big day tomorrow.'

Meanwhile, outside Harold stood, staring back at the pub door.

The following morning, at breakfast, Harold told Bernie what had happened. Ellie had meant so much to him, but now he wondered what she wanted. There was anger and curiosity all at the same time. 'What do I do?' Harold felt his world falling apart again.

'It's been over six years,' Bernie said.

'That's exactly it – I don't know! She's got an audition for that play we saw the other night. She's even more gorgeous than I remember her. I mean, is this really happening?'

'You *do* know, mate. You harped on about missing her so often while we were in hell. It would be a pity to ignore her invitation – stupid, even.'

'Yeah, but she's with someone else now.' Harold thought about his conversation with Vicky. She had had doubts about Ellie's relationship with Jack. But was that just female gossip? He hoped Ellie's audition went well and she would get the part. He jerked his brain into hopeful thoughts. Why did she want to see him behind this other chap's back? Perhaps it was innocent enough, and she only wanted to catch up. She belonged to someone else, which made Harold angry that the war had messed up his future with the only girl he'd truly loved. Perhaps she only wanted to say goodbye. He had to know. Why had she rushed off like that, her dress flapping in the wind, her face filled with worry? Did Jack intimidate her? She had indeed changed, her sophisticated and elegant dress a stark contrast to how Harold remembered her. What should he do?

Harold waited all day with a knot in his stomach. He churned around the whole scenario like the washing in his mother's poss tub. He passed by the theatre three times: the first to find out where the stage door was, the second to be sure, and the third to feel confident. He'd had enough of walking alone. The memories kept flooding back with every step. For an hour, he sat on a bench and watched people passing; it was a long day without Bernie. He should have invited him, but they'd been inseparable, and this was a rare opportunity for some solitude.

At seven o'clock, with over two hours to wait, Harold returned to the pub. Maybe Ellie was hiding in there once more, but if she was with Jack, there would be no opportunity to have a conversation with her. A heavy sigh escaped Harold's lips as he reluctantly, but respectfully, obliged her wishes. Was it simply chance that had brought them together in this meeting? If she had desired to, it was an opportunity to let go of their past friendship and move on. She and Jack were a couple, but it seemed clear which one of them held all the power, and Harold didn't think it was Ellie.

He entered the pub; the landlord caught his eye. 'The usual, sir?'

'Please,' Harold said, and he paid for the drink with half a crown and held his hand out for the change. He supped it slowly, but even so it didn't last very long. He mustn't get intoxicated.

At a quarter past nine, he stood at the edge of the road, ready to cross and make his way toward Market Street. As he knocked on the stage door, the sound echoed through the empty hallway. When the door opened, a commissionaire adorned with gold-braided epaulettes stood before him.

'Yes, sir?'

'I have an appointment with Miss Ellie Brownlee.'

'No one here by that name,' the commissionaire said.

He was about to shut the door when Harold heard a voice from the stairs.

'Fred, it's okay. He wants to talk to me. We're old friends. Louise Chambers is my stage name.'

'Oh, I see,' he relented. 'Sorry.'

'Come on up, Harold, but we have to be quick. I'm leaving soon.'

Fred looked at Harold and, in a flat tone, replied, 'Don't be too long – I shut these doors at eleven. Some of us 'ave to sleep, you know.'

In disbelief, Harold glanced up the stairs. Ellie stood at the top, a vision of beauty with her hair tied elegantly at the back of her head in a snood. She wore a vibrant red suit, the three buttons down the front adding a touch of sophistication, while a grey silk scarf wrapped snugly around her neck provided a contrast. As she kicked off her high-heeled shoes, Harold couldn't take his eyes off the way she had changed as he followed her to the dressing room.

'So glad you made it through the war,' Ellie said, a shaky smile playing on her lips as she looked at him.

'Yep, but it was bloody hard. I don't want to talk about it, really.'

'I thought about you a lot, Harold and held back for you for over two years, but then everything went wrong. Did you really not get my letter the other week?'

'Nope, I've been down here with my mate Bernie, as I mentioned. His parents have just moved down here and we've been helping them.'

'Oh, I see.' She looked concerned.

'What was in the letter?'

'Oh, a lot of things,' she said vaguely. 'I wanted you to know more about Jack and me. We're hoping to go to Canada soon.'

'So…why *am* I here?' Harold asked.

'It was purely by chance that I saw you, and I was in complete disbelief. So, I felt it was best to catch up and explain everything that's happened.'

He wanted to say, "Is that all?", but thought better of it. Hearing about Jack made him wonder why he had bothered to come here. 'Will I meet Jack? Vicky told me about him.'

'It had been too long, so I was happy to hear from her when she called. But, no, I'd rather you didn't.' She hesitated, her mind racing to come up with the right words to describe him. 'He's…it's better you don't.'

'I see.' Harold paused, the weight of his words hanging heavy in the silent air. He realised her relationship with this Jack person was possibly more serious than he had initially thought. 'Are you going to marry him?'

Ellie hesitated. 'Yes,' she said. 'I am. We're getting married in Canada in two months. I wanted to do it here, but Jack can be very persuasive. He's been good to me during our time in Scotland.'

'I was once good to you until bloody Adolf Hitler took you away from me.'

Ellie gave a half-smile. 'Look, Harold,' she said, her voice tinged with desperation, 'I tried my best to save myself for you.'

'Then don't marry Jack. We can finish what we started. True to my word, I've come back for you.' Harold attempted to smile, but his lips remained still and unresponsive. He wanted to tell her he needed her, to feel her hand in his, and to promise to love her forever.

Ellie took a deep breath. 'It's too late,' she said. 'I *am* getting married, Harold. It's the right thing to do. Life changes us.'

'But are you sure that's what you want?'

Ellie hesitated. 'I'm promised to Jack.'

'Do you love him as much as you used to love me?'

Ellie gazed at the floor. 'I'll write to you and let you know how I get on. Jack will be back for me in half an hour. Would you like a quick cup of tea?'

'No, thanks. I'm staying at this address but will be going home in a few days.' Harold found a pen in his pocket, and wrote Bernie's address on the back of the theatre programme he'd left in his pocket and gave it to her. 'Best be getting back.' He turned to the door of the dressing room. 'Listen, Ellie—'

'Harold—'

Their conversation collided.

Ellie spoke again. 'I didn't mean for all this to happen, but there's no turning back now.'

'Just one last kiss, eh?'

Ellie smiled. 'Oh, I don't know…'

Gently, she guided him onto the landing, but he pulled her close, the warmth of his body against hers, and kissed her softly on the cheek, respecting Ellie's boundaries. As the stage door crashed open, he instinctively pulled away from her, his heart pounding with anticipation of who would emerge.

'Jack?'

'Who the hell are you?' Jack snapped, as he ran up the stairs, breathless.

'My name is Harold Dean. Pleased to meet you.' Harold held out his hand, but Jack didn't respond.

'Why are you here? I know perfectly well who *you* are.'

'Ellie and I, er…we accidentally bumped into each other the other night.'

'You never told me,' Jack said to Ellie. Then, to Harold, 'Get out of here, soldier. This is not the place for you. Ellie and I are getting married soon.' He showed Harold the open door.

'How d-d-dare you say that? I only came to say goodbye and wish you luck.' Harold realised he was under stress: his stammer was returning.

Jack lurched forward and grabbed Harold by the arm to push him toward the stairs. 'And don't you dare come back, do you hear?'

'Don't do it, Jack,' Ellie pleaded, her voice filled with desperation. 'He's only come to say goodbye.' Her eyes brimmed with tears. 'What's got into you? Leave him alone. He doesn't mean any harm.'

Harold grabbed Jack by the throat, but then slipped and fell down the first four steps. He grabbed the metal banister. 'I fought a war for the likes of you,' he shouted. 'Unlike you, in your cosy office on some Scottish army camp, I was a real soldier. I suffered at the hands of Adolf Hitler while you were swanning about picking up women.'

This made Jack even angrier, and Harold punched him in the stomach.

'Fucking well go back to Canada, and I hope Ellie can tolerate you,' Harold shouted. Then he saw Ellie's face; she was close to tears.

'Come back with me. Don't let this thug bully you into marrying him.'

'I'm fine, Harold – please go. Sorry.'

Harold left Ellie in tears, and, slamming the door behind him, he vowed never to contact her again. She'd made her mind up, and that was the end. He walked back to Bernie's house, distraught and bruised, wiping away the tears from his eyes. It was not like him to break down, but soon he realised that all the dreadful things he'd experienced were coming to the fore. He must man up; it was never all right to cry.

Ellie returned to the dressing room.

'For God's sake, Ellie, what do you think you were doing?'

Her thoughts turned to everything she had missed while in the ATS. The letters from Harold, the family she didn't know any more. The memorable walks along the promenade. She jolted herself back to reality as Jack pulled her toward him.

'I'll ask you again. What the hell do you think you were *doin*'?'

'It was all innocent,' she tried to explain. 'I didn't tell you about it because I wanted to close a book on a relationship I had a long time ago. That's what! I was only saying goodbye before our trip to Canada. So, it wasn't as relevant to you as it was to me.'

Jack turned his back. He looked like a sergeant major with his hands clasped behind his back, carrying a big stick. 'Why did he turn up here? You must've known he was coming.'

Ellie thought it was better to keep quiet and let his temper cool. They would talk about it in the morning. 'I'm going back to the hotel,' she explained. 'You coming? We mustn't argue like this.'

Jack stood sour-faced. 'Are you sorry for what you did tonight – kissing *him*?' He pointed to the place where Harold had stood. 'I saw you, you bitch. Why?'

'Me? Sorry? Don't you dare – don't you bloody *dare* call me a bitch. What's got into you, eh?'

Ellie gathered up her bags and stormed out of the theatre. When she arrived at the hotel, her heart raced, thinking about what had happened. Was Jack always going to be like this? She stared at the wall in her room. What would she do? Jack had his good points, but what if he wouldn't make her happy for the rest of her life? Was this as example of what was yet to come? Harold had never spoken to her like that – ever! Their short reunion had been nothing short of upsetting. He was thinner now and didn't seem as confident. Vicky had told her he'd been through dreadful pain and anguish. Poor Harold. Her helplessness made Ellie realise she didn't have to endure all this sorrow: she could help Harold instead. What was it to be? Leave Jack and return to the familiar comfort of Saltburn, surrounded by friendly faces, or brave the daunting uncertainty of a new life in Canada? The thought of arriving there only to be trapped, unable to return, filled her with a sense of impending doom, a cold dread that clung like an evening mist. She alarmed herself with her thoughts, provoking fear. Jack had scared her recently with his jealousy whenever she talked to other men: 'Who's that? What did he want with you?' He had yet to return from the theatre. Her suitcase remained packed, a silent symbol of her uncertainty. If she left him, how would she find the courage to tell him? There would be many things to resolve. She couldn't do it.

In a burst of fury and a slam of the door, Jack filled her room with the raw, potent smell of his anger. The way he looked at her – a piercing stare filled with a silent threat – made her feel dreadfully intimidated.

'Jack, it's okay, calm down.'

He left the room and made his way to the hotel bar, his agitation growing stronger. With each sip of whisky, his senses dulled until he returned to the room and lay on the bed, lost in a drunken slumber.

The following day, after what seemed like a short night, Harold packed his clothes to return to Saltburn. He thanked Bernie, Alice and Philip for everything. 'Maybe we'll return to Italy to visit Bruno, Agata and young Maria one day,' Harold said looking at Bernie.

Bernie smiled. 'Yes, she was a lovely girl, wasn't she? That family risked so much for us. Do you remember when Agata showed us how to knead dough? It was plastered all over us, and Bruno returned from town asking where the snowmen came from.'

'They were a proper family, like mine.' Harold gazed at the floor. 'I hope they survived. We ought to find out. I've found it hard to live with myself since we left. Bernie, what if they…? We don't know if they are still alive, do we?'

'We should go back, but, as you say, what if? I'll call you soon. Are you ready for the station? At least the train journey will give you time to rest. Sorry to hear about Ellie, but I suppose all good things must end.' Bernie squeezed Harold's arm. 'Maybe we'll go back to Sulmona one day. We never really saw the town, and they say it's a pretty place.'

An expected ring of the shrill front doorbell shattered the quiet of the house.

'That'll be your taxi,' Bernie said. He answered the porch door and a brief conversation was heard. 'Come in, come in. Welcome.' His grin was almost as wide as the open door.

Harold looked into the hallway to see Ellie standing there with her suitcase.

'I'm coming with you,' she called. 'There's no excuse for what happened last night. No excuse! I prayed I wasn't too late.'

'You mean…?'

'I've walked out of Jack's life forever.'

'What? Are you sure?'

'Enough is enough!'

'Oh, Bernie, Alice, this is the love of my life, Ellie.'

'I gathered that,' Bernie said, still smiling. 'Good to meet you at last.'

Alice stood there with a smile on her face. 'Hello, Ellie.'

Harold took Ellie in his arms and greeted her with a kiss on the cheek. 'I can hardly believe this. But what about the play?'

'You're more precious to me than any bloody play, Harold Dean.'

Alice was still smiling.

'Let's go home,' Harold said.

'Does this mean I can take Jenny Fortune out for dinner?' Bernie gave a deliberate silly grin and fluttered his eyelashes.

'Why not? You don't need my permission.' Harold mused. 'Good luck. Give her my best regards. She's a lovely girl. I'll miss you, mate.'

'I'll miss you too, Hal. Come back soon.' Bernie covered his lips with the back of his hand so Ellie didn't hear him and whispered, 'Good luck. Ellie's gorgeous.'

'Bye, Harold. God bless,' said Alice. 'We enjoyed having you. Come back soon, and next time, bring Ellie with you.'

Bernie hugged his best friend. 'See you on the other side?' he reminisced.

'I'll write to you soon,' Harold said. 'Come on, El. We have a train to catch. Taxi's waiting.'

Chapter Thirty-Eight

'Why is it always raining here?' asked Ellie.

Upon arriving in Saltburn, the train's wheels screeched to a halt, the sound echoing through the station. Hand in hand, they made their way to the Deans' corner shop. Ellie felt overwhelmed by the town's run-down appearance, filled with the sound of hammers and the sight of ladders as builders worked tirelessly. Momentarily, memories of London's glamorous scenery made her regret her decision to leave. Even Weston had been much better, and had more things to do. She hoped one day Saltburn would once again become the seaside resort it had been.

They walked through the subway as in bygone times, but, in her heart, Ellie felt detached from the old place. She would have been in Canada, far away from anyone familiar. Was Harold still the same man she had left behind, with his kind eyes and gentle smile? Jack's pushy nature had kept her constantly on edge, desperately trying to please him, while Harold she hoped had remained unchanged despite the hardships of war and his emaciated appearance. She longed to nurture him and cocoon him in a cosy blanket. No matter what, she was determined to stand by his side. He was her brave soldier, and his courage and sacrifice would always be remembered.

As usual, Betty Dean fussed around the shop, rearranging the merchandise and adjusting the displays. She worked diligently to stack the shelves, ensuring that each item was placed in its designated spot. It was disappointing having to wait so long for normality to return but they knew they had to be patient as rationing would not be lifted for some time.

Harold strode through the door as Ellie hid around the corner.

'Oh, hello, dear. How was the holiday? It's good to have you back.' Betty set her eyes on Harold's beaming face and embraced him.

'Ma, I have a wonderful surprise for you.'

Betty searched his face for clues. 'What now?'

As he wrapped his hand around the doorknob, he felt excitement as he guided Ellie inside.

Betty's hand flew to her chest. 'Oh, oh! Ellie! How wonderful to see you,' she gasped. 'Oh my, just look at you – so radiant and glamorous. It's so amazing – how did you two…?'

'Long story, Ma. I'll tell you when we get a chance. Where's Pop?'

'It's been a long journey home,' Ellie said.

'He's doing a delivery in the old van. He'll be back soon. Come on, let's make a pot of tea,' said Betty. 'It's wonderful to see you.' Her face, though etched with the passage of time, still held the same youthful spark. Even with the dignified air of maturity about her, the homely sweetness and inherent kindness in her nature shone through; a comforting presence.

William heard the commotion and came to see what was going on.

'Hiya, kiddo,' Harold said. 'Look who I found in Weston-super-Mare.'

Ellie's shock at seeing William limping and wearing cotton gloves made her suck in a breath. During the train journey Harold had talked about his injuries, but she hadn't expected to see William looking so pained. Guilt weighed heavily on her heart for losing sight of Harold during the war. The Deans had endured the unbearable uncertainty of not knowing if their sons were alive or dead; a harrowing experience for such a kind and beautiful couple. Ellie fingered the small necklace she wore. She sat with William, and they exchanged information about their wartime experiences. Harold had claimed William possessed more courage than anyone else in their group. Ellie smiled at them both. As Harold lit a cigarette, she couldn't help but feel William's pain. A delicious smell of warm biscuits filled the air as the Dean boys anticipated their mother's arrival with a tea tray. Nothing had changed in that aspect, except now there was a glimmer of hope in what lay ahead.

'I miss playing my music,' said William. 'I hope my hands won't hurt so much by next year, and I'll be able to play in the band again.'

'That would be wonderful if you could,' Ellie said.

She listened to their stories. This family had gone through so much, but it was like starting over. Ellie couldn't help but notice how Harold consistently brushed off the subject of the camp in Germany whenever Betty brought it up, making light of it with his jokes.

On Alf's return, overcome by Ellie's presence, he wiped his eyes and complimented her on how she had grown up to be a lovely young lady. 'You look wonderful.'

Then Harold made an announcement. 'Pop, Ma, William, we have something to tell you. Ellie has accepted my proposal and we're going to get married as soon as possible. I want you, William, to be my best man.'

Betty hugged them both. 'Wonderful news.'

'Fantastic,' William replied.

Alf congratulated his son. 'It is wonderful news indeed. Congratulations.'

The following morning, Ellie and Harold walked toward her Diamond Street house, the sounds of the town – a faint mixture of car horns and distant chatter – barely reaching them. She didn't think that anyone still lived there, and used her key to let herself in through the front door hoping her mother hadn't changed the locks. To her shock, she found much of the furniture ruined. Cigarette stubs were not in ashtrays but in jam jars on the floor, and the wallpaper and ceiling were stained with nicotine. Using an iron, someone had destroyed her mother's best table with burn marks. All the knick-knacks were missing from the shelves, and when Ellie went to her old room, the carpet had tea stains and cigarette burns on it. She sat down and cried. Five years of neglect had left their mark; a gritty layer of dust clung to everything, especially the shelves.

'This is shameful. We ought to complain. These guys are the scum of the earth,' Harold said. 'We were never allowed to behave like this, even in Italy. We had to keep things in army-style order, otherwise, we might not have survived.'

The first thing Ellie did was search for a bar of strong-smelling, pungent pink carbolic soap from the cupboard under the stairs, the scent instantly familiar from her childhood. Thank goodness it was still there where she recalled her mother used to store it. Harold wrestled with the dripping tap, his knuckles white as he struggled to replace the washer. The rhythmic drip, drip, drip echoed in the otherwise silent kitchen. Harold helped her move furniture, and in the hall, Ellie found a pile of unread letters that had been delivered to the house three years before. As she sorted through them, she found letters from Harold. Abandoning her chores, she read the first one from the Sulmona Campo 78, in which he described how starvation felt, in the days he'd relied on donated food. Ellie felt overwhelmed that she hadn't received this letter. Things could have been very different if she'd known all this. In Italy, Harold had tirelessly written letter after letter, refusing to give up on her even when it seemed he would never return home. Then, finally, he'd made a decision for both of them. Ellie covered her mouth with her hand as she read. He'd only let her go because he loved her. Oh, if only he'd known how much she'd missed him!

Harold came through the hallway and found her sitting on the stairs, tears dripping down her cheeks.

'Look what I found.'

'Oh hell, where did you find those?'

'Them buggers never delivered them! They sent them here instead when they couldn't find us.' The ATS had hardened Ellie's words; her language now had a blunt, direct force. She didn't have her mother breathing down her neck any more.

Harold gave a deep sigh. 'I thought life would get easier when we returned from Dunkirk,' he explained. 'I've since found out I was wrong, Ellie, my darling. We have to move forward with our lives. Once we're married, we can enjoy our time together. None of this was our fault. Perhaps one day we can go back to Weston and let our kids play on the beach.' He gave a laugh. 'One other thing I'd love is to return to Italy to visit the Galante family. They saved our lives, Bernie and me. I'd love you to meet them.'

While Harold put his arm around her shoulder, Ellie remained absorbed in the letters. As he gently lifted her chin with his finger, their eyes locked in a moment of connection.

'You've made me incredibly happy!' he exclaimed, his chest swelling with emotion. 'The hardships I endured were pale compared to the joy of seeing you once more.'

As she turned to him, he gently brushed away her tears, comforting her and kissing her on the lips.

'I'm sorry, Hal,' she whispered, her voice filled with remorse.

'You have nothing to be guilty about. We didn't know how long I would be away. I let you go – as I said, none of this was our fault. I was so depressed in that prison camp, it was awful, but now we have a future. Come, let's move on, shall we?'

With Harold's remark, Ellie left her sadness behind. 'Rest more,' she said. 'We must get you over this and start afresh. I shall read your other letters later, then maybe I'll understand how it was for you. Sorry I was so engrossed in other things. I suppose it was my way of surviving the war too.'

Harold kissed her deeply. 'It's me who loves you now, Ellie Bee.'

Over the weeks that followed, Ellie and Betty planned the wedding. On a Thursday morning, Alf received a phone call at the shop.

'Oh, hello. Yes, you can speak to her yourself. Ellie, it's your mother.' He handed her the receiver.

'What? Never! Hello, Mam? How did you know I was here?'

Agnes's voice was barely audible. She whispered, 'I didn't.

I phoned Alf, hoping to hear news of you. I was worried as I had absolutely no clue where you might be.'

'Worried? Didn't you get my letter saying that I was in London?'

'Well, no, I didn't. I've moved to the farm now. Of course I was worried. Have you been home? I'm told the army has left.'

'Oh yes, they've left all right! And what a terrible mess it was. Hal and I have been cleaning the house from top to bottom. We're getting married and we decided that, as you aren't there, we'll live in it after the wedding, if you don't mind.'

'Hm, married, eh? Well, thanks for taking care of the house.'

'Well, if it's good enough for you, Mam, then it's good enough for me.'

A brief silence ensued.

'I may as well tell you, Ellie. I won't be coming back to Yorkshire. It's great being with George. He has a grand house, and we plan to stay here, so if you want to live in the Saltburn house, you have my blessing. We'll fix it with the solicitor and maybe give you the house as a wedding present, and then you can pass it to Tommy to rent if you want to leave it. You see, I met George before I met your dad – they were friends. I suppose I have to say that Harold is right for you too. I'm happy for you.'

'Well, that's very kind of you.'

Ellie's sharp sarcasm made Alf look up from his newspaper, and he left the sitting room, realising he shouldn't be there.

'What's happened to Tommy?' asked Ellie.

'Oh, he's still in the forces – gets demobbed in '47.'

'Is he all right?'

'He's currently in Aldershot, but there's a possibility that he might make his way back up north soon. He writes to me now and again. Yes, he's grand.'

'What about the wedding, Mam?'

'Don't worry about me.'

'I'll send you an invitation.'

'No, don't bother, Ellie. There's no point, really.'

'This is your daughter getting married – don't you care?'

'Yes, of course I care, but…'

'I would like you to come.'

'I'm unsure if it would be appropriate – you know, because of my circumstances here. What I mean is… I mean, you and me, we, er…'

'I don't understand. What's the problem? You mean we don't get on?' Ellie snapped. 'I suppose, knowing you, that's to be expected. But look, Mam, I'd better ring off as Alf uses the phone for the shop. Call me again soon, Mam, and thanks a lot for the offer of the house – we'll need it. Give me your number and I'll call back soon. I do wish you'd come to the wedding, though.' She found a pencil and scribbled down the number. 'Okay, I'll ring you soon. Cheerio, Mam.'

'But, Ellie, wait – I might be able—'

'Bye.'

Ellie clenched her jaw. Was it just another convenience for her mother to give her the house as a wedding present? No, she mustn't think like that. She'd always felt her mother was hiding something. Perhaps she would never know. But the house was a very generous gift. Maybe things *had* changed. Now that the war was over, she must develop a greater capacity to accept her mother's emotional distance. She eagerly anticipated their upcoming conversation, hoping for a change of heart. The change that was desperately needed could only be achieved through the coming months.

Chapter Thirty-Nine

'Ellie, love, shall we go for a walk on the beach?' Harold felt it would be good to catch up on the past. His life felt like a puzzle with many missing pieces. Poor Sammy. His absence left a void in Harold's heart, a constant reminder of what was lost. With the wedding to plan there was no time to think about his faithful pet, yet the house felt eerily quiet and devoid of life without little Sammy.

Ellie agreed and removed the overall that Betty had given her; she'd been cleaning the kitchen. She brushed her hair, swiped lipstick over her lips, and pushed her arms through the sleeves of her coat.

When they arrived at the beach, it was like old times: walking hand in hand, with no bombs to fear, only friendly people doing the same as they always did.

'El, I wanted to ask you something. Did you and Jack…you know…? No, that's a silly question.'

'What? You mean, did we do it?' Ellie grinned.

'Yes, that's what I meant.' He gazed into the distance.

'I'm still "intact", if that's what you mean.' Ellie locked her palms together and gave Harold a coy smile.

'Really? Oh my, I should've known better than to ask you that question. Sorry.' This was unlike the Ellie he once knew: to be so bold in how she spoke. 'I'm sorry. Since we're getting married, do you want to wait until we're wed? It's just… I've not, you know, done anything, and I'm longing for you. I'm not sure if I know how any more.' He laughed.

Ellie smiled. She wanted her time with Harold to be extraordinary. 'It worked fine because I didn't want to get pregnant, so there were no complications.'

Harold smiled at her comment. Maybe she really had waited for him to return, well…maybe. She'd got her sparkle back and was undoubtedly wiser and more confident than she'd been on their last walk along the seashore. As he anxiously awaited her reaction, he hoped his appearance wouldn't put her off. She was certainly more lovely than ever.

In the days leading up to the wedding, Ellie's anxiety mounted as she tried repeatedly to contact her mother, whose only response was a card, declining the invite. Ellie was furious, but soon got over her mother's reaction.

Several days later, Vicky and Ellie met in Saltburn. The salty sea air and cheerful sounds from The Ship Inn calmed her instantly as she happily greeted her friend. Finally, everything fell into place, a feeling of perfect completion.

Ellie met Harold's gaze as they stood at the altar. Not once did Harold stammer as he recited his vows, and with confidence, Ellie said, 'I will.' After signing the register, they walked hand in hand down the aisle to the sound of church bells above them and made their way to the reception.

It seemed fitting to have the wedding reception at The Zetland Hotel, with a honeymoon in Scarborough to follow. Ellie wore a plain cream summer dress and a broad hat with artificial flowers around the brim.

'You look gorgeous, my love,' remarked Harold with a smile. He squeezed her hand as they walked through the hotel doors, confetti strewn in their hair.

Ellie grinned. 'Your mam and dad did you proud with that suit. You look so handsome. Husband and wife, eh?' she whispered. 'It's very romantic.'

They kissed. Bernie walked down the steps in the churchyard and Harold's throat tightened into a knot as they caught each other's eyes. Each seemed to know what the other was thinking: happier times are ahead now. Don't look back. Bernie came toward Harold and shook his hand.

'Congratulations, mate. Do come down to Weston as soon as you can. I miss your company.'

With tickets in hand, Ellie and Harold settled into their seats on the train, excited for their trip to Scarborough. At the hotel that night, Harold quietly observed Ellie as she undressed before slipping into bed beside him. With a tender touch, he brushed her hair, the scent of her shampoo filling the air. Between them, there was a profound silence; the air itself seemed to hold its breath, a shared understanding that needed no words to bridge the gulf between them. Finally, with the utmost tenderness, he laid her down on the plush eiderdown, his touch sending shivers of passion through her.

'Yes. Oh my,' she gasped, her eyes widening in amazement.

In the last moments he breathed heavily with a sense of euphoria, burying his face in the pillow. 'I'll always love you, Ellie. I promise.'

Ellie's passion overwhelmed her, and tears ran down her heated cheeks. Then, out of breath, she whispered in Harold's ear, 'If that's how it's supposed to be, it was worth waiting for. I love you too,' Ellie replied.

Chapter Forty

January 1947

Harold relayed the dreary details he had gleaned from the pages of the local newspaper. 'There are severe snowdrifts on the moors. The trains have stopped running, and now there's a coal shortage. I'm bloody freezing. Here, you have this blanket, Ellie. My God, this is almost as bad as Italy in winter.' He chopped up a chair and burned the wood. 'What about that old bureau?'

'No, better not, that was my dad's,' Ellie said.

Instead, they axed Ellie's old wardrobe in the spare room. With some beaches covered in a thick blanket of snow, even sea coal was hard to collect. They walked around their rooms bundled in coats and blankets against the cold.

'You can't go job hunting in this weather,' she warned, pointing to the thick snow covering the ground.

The only thing Harold could do was sit at home fidgeting and help Ellie when she asked him, which made him feel useless. To keep warm, they fed the open fire with unwanted items, the acrid smell of burning wood and varnish filling the air, a smoky haze hanging above them. A few salvaged logs were dropped off by Alf, though they were soon reduced to ashes. The wheelbarrow proved a stubborn beast to control along the meagrely cleared trail, the uneven icy surface making steering a laborious task.

Harold tried to sleep, but the bed was a battlefield of tangled limbs and muttered frustrations each night as he tossed and turned. How were they going to sustain themselves? Their wartime savings were dwindling, and everything inside the house was cold, miserable and frozen. It became difficult to focus on household tasks. A sense of apathy ensued. Ellie did her best to focus on Harold's needs, but each day it became harder to think about how best to keep the house warm.

Harold's memories of prison camp life kept returning. He felt he'd let everyone down by being stuck there for so long, and cursed the officer who'd ordered them on patrol in the desert. On the day of his capture, he'd almost died. It was challenging to come to terms with being alive when his colleagues had died. He'd heard that Snowy and Ian had lost their battle against the harsh weather and the lack of food. How could everyone here know how that felt? They were all complaining about the snow. What did they know? Yet Harold's life was back to everything he'd wanted, except for the bloody weather. Why couldn't he shake off these feelings?

On those days, his stammer returned, and although he could see Ellie wanted to help, it was hard to put his feelings into words.

'Do you want to talk, darling?' She put her arm around his shoulder.

'Nope, not really.'

'Hal, you must talk to me. Keeping everything bottled up isn't good for you.'

'I'm not keeping it bottled up. I like to think, that's all.'

'Think about what?'

'They didn't tell us it would be like *this* when we got home. I thought I'd seen enough deep snow to last a lifetime,' Harold recalled.

'I bet it was worse than this in Italy in those mountains. Would you have joined up if you'd known how dreadful it all would be? None of us knew – we were *told* to join up. You had no option! We just went in there and did it, and we won the damned war because of you and the other lads out there. We'll win again once summer comes. It's going to be fine. We're fighting our own personal battle just now, and like the war, we'll win! Try not to worry, love.'

'Wise words, El, but the trouble is, I *do* worry. But you're right. We'll get through this. We've done it before, we can do it again, but this time, together.' He managed a smile.

Ellie sighed at the crumpled and unwashed clothes in the basket on the chair. She couldn't face washing in lukewarm water in the poss tub *again* – the clothes wouldn't be clean, and her hands were already sore from the cold. Frustrated, she gathered sticks and twigs, attempting to light a fire under the tub in the washhouse. They'd have to wear the clothes they stood in until the snow cleared, and when she got coal, she could do a better job of it. Putting them outside froze all the sheets and towels board-solid, and they never got their clothes dry in time to wear them again. The sight of laundry strewn about the kitchen reminded her of a Chinese laundry, and the smell of damp lingered, making the walls mouldy. The windows were so frozen that she couldn't see out of them, no matter how hard she tried.

'Oh God! This is worse than the prison camp,' Harold remarked as he observed the mayhem surrounding him. 'At least there we had fuel in the winter. There were lots of trees.'

Ellie was trying to cope with her feelings about this dreadful crisis, and missing her acting career. Despite her love for Harold, she realised that their arguments were becoming more frequent, and they'd only been married a few months. There was no mail for weeks, and when the postman *could* turn up in the snow, he brought only bills. Their whole world had broken down. Harold switched on the radiogram.

They listened to the news: *'This is the coldest winter in 300 years.'*

'Depressing, isn't it?' she said. 'But we'll get through it, you'll see.'

'Anyway, it can't go on forever, but it feels like it.'

'It's hard to see the summer ahead when we have frozen windows in our bedroom and this leaky hot water bottle to keep us warm at night – if we're lucky!' She poured the cold water from the rubber bottle down the sink.

'We've got each other, Ellie, and that's important.' He stubbed out his cigarette.

'*Tomorrow will bring more snow, but within a few days it will become warmer. Floods are forecast in the...*'

When the weather finally broke, Ellie was at her lowest ebb. The washing piled up, and Harold did nothing but complain. She was so distraught that she threw one of her mother's best plates at him, which smashed against the door. She sank to the floor in tears. Harold stormed out into melting snow, slamming the door behind him, showing no empathy for her feelings. Left by herself, Ellie broke down. She knew it wasn't Harold's fault, but the weather seemed to bite her every time she tried to make things right. The washing made the house damp, with sheets and towels hung everywhere. This was far worse than the exhaustion she'd felt in Strathpeffer. Was being married always going to be like this? And what about her ambition to be an actress? It certainly wasn't her plan to live in squalor.

On that same afternoon, Betty and Alf called to see how they were getting along.

'Come on, Ellie, I'll help you tidy up, love,' said Betty.

Ellie felt ashamed; the house was in a dreadful mess. Her mother had always kept it neat and sweet-smelling. All she needed was space and for the snow to stop. If only Harold could get a job, then things would be different. Instead, his mind seemed filled with despair and endless grievances. The Harold she once knew seemed like a distant memory. She reminded herself that she could have been in Canada by now, but recalled that Jack had once told her the snow there could be as high as the house.

Betty used to believe a warm pot of tea could soothe any trouble, but the war had made even simple tasks feel like a burden, the weight of rationing heavy on their shoulders, each cuppa a reminder of loss. She put the kettle on the gas stove, and Ellie stood there thinking of the money they hadn't got to pay the gas bill. She broke down in tears.

301

'I'm sorry, Betty, it's too much for us. I don't know how you cope with it all.'

Betty placed her hand on Ellie's arm. 'Certain things in life seem to go on forever, but you get used to the terrible disappointments. Accept them as being part of life. It usually turns out fine in the end, believe me. I've noticed Harold's been very irritable recently. But, of course, I shouldn't be surprised after all he's been through, but it's tough for you, I can see.'

'He spends so much time within himself, and barely talks to me.'

Alf poked his head around the kitchen door, having heard the conversation. 'Give him time, Ellie. He's been to hell and back. We're having the same problems with William. I remember it well. They only need a loving wife or mam and dad to guide them. We'll help you, and you must take a holiday as soon as this weather changes.'

'A holiday? We can't afford to cross the bloomin' road to your shop right now.' Ellie sniffed back her tears.

Alf gave a sigh. 'I've been thinking. We want to buy you something, Betty and me. We have money in the bank and want you both to search for jobs. What if we paid for you to go on holiday? You could try the Lake District, or Wales. There are many hotels in those places, and you could look for work there.'

Ellie wanted to say, 'Yes, how lovely', but it was not her place to do so. 'I don't know, it's a lovely thought, but I'm not sure Harold will accept it.'

'I insist!' Betty declared, her eyes widening. 'Don't be silly. They say the floods will die down at the end of this month. Spring is here and you must go job hunting. This could be the only chance you'll get. You could rent out this house and live on the proceeds. It'll give you both something to look forward to.'

Ellie wondered why she hadn't thought of it before. How stupid she was! Of course they needed houses for those who'd married after the war. Arrangements were being made so that they could own their own home. Ellie still thought it was a peace offering from her mother, but was glad she'd done it. She must thank her again in her next letter.

'Oh, hello, you two.' Harold arrived home from his walk. 'Nice to see we have visitors. Excuse the mess, it's been awful.'

'They say the weather is improving, and about time too,' Alf said.

Ellie's eyes averted from Harold's.

Betty chipped in. 'Listen, son,' she said, leaning in close, 'your pop and I have a brilliant idea.'

'Oh, for God's sake, Ma, don't start again! I tried all last year. There's nothing for a down-and-out ex-prisoner of war in Saltburn. No one cares any more about us soldiers.'

'*We* care, and we've decided we're paying for you two to take a holiday so you can look for work. Being in this house is depressing. We understand, you know. When we thought we'd lost William, it was dreadful for me. I thought I'd never take a step forward again. I know what that feels like.'

Ellie butted in before Harold had time to think about it. 'Can we, Harold? Your parents came up with the idea that we should rent this house out. I'm sure our mam would agree, now she's got this George chap to take care of her.'

'Let me think about it,' Harold said.

'Well, don't think too long. It's an offer you can't refuse. We'll look after the house here for you – all you need to do is pack a suitcase and take a train,' Alf said in no uncertain terms.

Ellie's face brightened at the thought. She willed Harold to say he'd do it. This could be her chance to get back on the stage, and then if Harold got a job, it would be okay again.

Chapter Forty-One

The following morning, Ellie paid a visit to Vicky, who'd told her on the phone that Alan was finally coming home and they were getting married.

'I've got news for you, Vicky. Can I come in? Oh, hello, Mrs Empsall. How are you?'

'Yes, yes. Come in,' Vicky and her mother chorused.

Ellie explained about her in-laws' holiday offer, and the house.

'Are you going back to Weston?'

'I think so, but it's difficult at the moment. Hal finds it hard to accept his parents' generosity. He'll let me know this afternoon.'

'When?'

'May or June, not sure.'

'So, you'll make our wedding, then?'

'I jolly well hope so, Vicky. I'll mention it to Harold and see if it works for him.'

'This was the worst winter ever,' Vicky said. 'It wasn't even this bad in Scotland.'

'Yes, I know. We've had nothing but terrible news and bad things happening to us all for the last seven years. We need to have fun now. Hey, I just had this thought – I'd feel better if you and Alan wanted to rent the house from us. Mam's sorted out the legal stuff for me, and we've signed the contracts. We might sell it one day, but you could live there for reasonable rent. What do you say?'

'Really, El? Wow, that's a wonderful offer.' Vicky gazed at her mother. 'What do you think, Mam? Should I ask Al about it?'

'It sounds a good idea,' replied Mrs Empsall. 'Not that I want rid of you, Victoria, but you deserve your own place.'

'Let me confirm with Harold first, and I'll let you know.'

The girls savoured Mrs Empsall's jam sponge cake with a cup of tea in their hands.

'How's Harold doing? He didn't look well when I saw him before all that dreadful snow,' asked Mrs Empsall.

'This is the reason we're thinking of moving away. Harold needs a job and won't find one here.' Ellie felt she shouldn't leave Harold on his own for too long. She fidgeted in the armchair. 'Sorry, this is short, Vicky, but I must go home. There's a lot to talk about.'

'We understand,' said her mother.

As Ellie waved goodbye, the sun came out, and the sound of melting water running down the gutter gave her hope that change was on its way. Daffodil buds had formed on the plants in the gardens.

When she arrived home, Harold seemed happy for a change. He whistled a random tune. Ellie smiled, and then he kissed her.

'I really love you with all my heart, Ellie Bee. Sorry for being so grumpy.'

'I'm Eleanor D now,' she reminded him. 'Dean!'

Harold chuckled and brought her a cup of tea and a biscuit. 'Would you mind if we returned to Weston-super-Mare? I'd like to see Bernie, and perhaps we could stay at his parents' guest house. It used to belong to his aunt, if you remember, it's a delightful place, and they have a lovely garden.'

'Hmm…despite the memories, I don't mind returning to Weston for the summer. It would be a great place to look for work for both of us.' She kissed him. 'Before I forget, Harold, I've an idea. You know that Vicky's getting married?'

Harold nodded.

'Well, she and Alan are looking for a place to live. Granny Brownlee wanted to keep this house in the family. So, it would still be our house but rented.'

'Yes, fine, of course. After all, it is yours now.'

'Well…remember there's a clause in the agreement that if we sell, half goes to Tommy. By then, we should have recovered with a house of our own. It'll bring in an income for us.'

Ellie's life had taken a sudden turn for the better. There was a new life out there somewhere – she must believe it.

That evening, Harold made love to Ellie in a way she knew meant they had finally settled their differences. The war had been testing enough, and then suffering the snow and the cold. She hoped things would soon return to normal – whatever "normal" was these days.

Chapter Forty-Two

May 1947

The glow of the morning sun crept down the garden wall. Ellie dressed in her eggshell-blue dress as maid of honour for Vicky's wedding. She wore a straw hat and high heels.

'Come on, darling, I'm ready to go,' she called.

As Vicky stood at the altar, Ellie felt the weight of the vows, the dying whispers of the guests, and the solemnity of the occasion; a stark reminder that every marriage faces trials. However, she knew that Vicky, her grounded and genuine best friend, would have a successful marriage. That, too, was a necessity for her.

'You once told me that real friends are for life. You were right. I shall miss you a lot,' Ellie said.

The girls hugged each other and said their goodbyes.

Ellie left a list of instructions for the house. With help from Betty and Alf, they spring-cleaned everything, and the perfume of lavender wax polish filled the house. Happy for Vicky, Ellie hoped they would see each other again soon. It felt as if they had all been walking in circles, and now they were back to where they'd started.

Later that day, the newlyweds were chauffeured to the station in Alan's father's car for their honeymoon. His father waved goodbye and wished them luck.

Ellie and Harold, still buzzing from the weekend, paid a visit to the Deans. Peter was home on leave, enjoying the comfort of the familiar surroundings. In the shop, Alf made sure William was always busy, the satisfying clink of coins in his pocket as payment for his efforts.

'See, Pop, I can carry those boxes – it doesn't hurt so much any more.'

'I hear you're playing your trombone again. It's marvellous. Well done, lad. By the way, I like your new girlfriend – is it Joan?'

William smiled. 'Yeah, Joan.'

'Your ma likes her too. Best get to know her more, eh? I can't take all these weddings just now.' Alf laughed.

'We can't thank you both enough for giving us this wonderful opportunity,' Ellie said.

'You are family, Ellie, you always have been, and we believe in helping you succeed. But, yes, we have a little nest egg in the bank, and we'd rather spend some of it on you two,' Alf said. 'We can't take it with us when we go. Peter and William are in charge of the shop now, but I won't be retiring for a while yet. Their turn will come one day soon.'

'Well, it's time we were off. Goodbye, little brother,' Harold said to Peter. He gave him a hug. 'Good luck, and don't let your ship sink!'

'I told him that too,' said William, rolling his eyes, hoping Peter would never have to endure the trauma he had. He turned to Harold. 'I'll miss you, our kid. We went through a lot together, didn't we? At least I won't be going back to sea.'

'Sure did, and maybe we can talk about it one day without feeling bad.' Harold wrinkled his nose and smiled. 'If I can't find work, I'll be back soon. Hope you'll come and see us.'

The family walked to the station together. As Ellie and Harold departed, all the Deans waved goodbye and watched the train as it steamed off on its way to Darlington.

Chapter Forty-Three

Bernie stood at Weston station with a young woman by his side. Harold recognised her immediately.

'Hello, Harold,' she said. 'So glad you came back to Weston. Hello, Ellie. It's wonderful to have you back here.'

'Jenny! Look at you two. I'm so glad you both got together,' Harold said. 'You survived the dreadful winter, then? Hey, meet Ellie.'

They returned to the guest house and Alice made dinner. At home Harold had dinner at twelve-thirty, but things were different at Bernie's house. It was all about evening meals now. The chicken stew was yummy, he thought.

'I've booked tickets for a show tomorrow night,' Bernie said. 'It'll be like old times, eh? Then perhaps we can go to a dance at the Winter Gardens.'

'Old times? I sometimes feel really old these days. I gather you mean before we were deployed to France?'

'Yeah, something like that. Come on, let's enjoy ourselves.'

Six weeks later Harold returned from town.

'I got the job! I'm at the council offices in their accounts department.'

'Wow, that's wonderful. Now we can put a deposit on the flat we liked. Well done, love, and when do you start?'

'Monday. The pay is good, and maybe we can finally afford to buy the things we could never have.'

Monday evening soon came around.

'How was it, darling?' Ellie asked.

'Yes, yes, terrific, friendly bunch of people. They welcomed me with tea and biscuits and showed me around the building. More bomb damage, mind you, but they seem very nice.'

'I'm so proud of you, Hal. We have been through a dreadful time together, haven't we?' Then Ellie thought that perhaps her remark was insensitive. It was Harold who'd suffered most, but he now looked happier for the first time in months. This was the right moment to discuss her own news. She recounted the contents of the audition letter she'd received that morning, unsure of how he'd take it.

'Yes, do it, Ellie. I'm sure you'll love it. It'll help with our income. Good luck.'

Ellie smiled with relief.

The following morning, Ellie took a bus into Weston. She stared at her empty hands, recalling how she had parted from Jack. They would never see each other again. What a funny old world this is.

Dressed in her favourite red suit, she walked confidently into the audition to wait her turn in a queue of ten other actors.

'Miss Chambers, please.'

With an air of experience, she stood onstage before a producer, a director and a choreographer.

'Good afternoon, Miss Chambers. Can you tell us more about yourself and your acting experience?'

Ellie informed them of how she'd produced and acted in many plays during the war. She explained about writing her plays and how much money they'd raised for the war effort. She mentioned Jack and how she'd learned a lot from him.

The director smiled. 'Thank you. It seems you enjoyed the hard work.'

'Yes, it was a wonderful time, and now I'd like to move up the ladder of success and do more.'

'Can you dance?' asked the choreographer.

'Well, I'm not trained, but yes, I did a lot of dance routines for our productions in Scotland.'

'Would you mind doing a reading for us?'

'Not at all,' replied Ellie with enthusiasm.

The director nodded. 'Here's the script – away you go.'

Ellie glanced at the part she hoped to play. She read through the first few lines and then performed her role.

After two minutes, the director said, 'Stop. Thank you, Miss Chambers. We'll let you know within a few days.'

Ellie was glad it was over and held little hope for her Scottish accent. Had it sounded authentic enough?

After the audition, and before the bus came to take her home, Ellie went into The Royal Hotel to see if she could find Jenny. She stepped into the hotel lobby and found her friend on the phone. Ellie waited. It was like coming back to The Zetland. Eventually, they had coffee together. Although Ellie could never replace Vicky, having someone she could talk with other than Harold was reassuring. She hoped to see Jenny again soon.

'Well, how did you get on?' Harold enquired as Ellie got through the front door of their new flat.

'The producer will let me know.'

'I believe that's normal, so don't worry about it.' He kissed her. 'I've made you something nice for tea. Welsh rarebit.'

Ellie laughed, it wasn't like Harold to do the cooking, but he'd mentioned he made all kinds of food in the army, even fried eggs on the top of a tank in the dessert.

'Sorry I was late. I didn't expect you home so soon.'

'The bus was early,' replied Harold.

'I had coffee with Jenny. She's really nice. She told me she and Bernie might get engaged soon. He's taken her to the jewellers to find her ring size. I suppose he wants to surprise her one day.'

'They'll make a great couple.' Harold smiled inside. 'We were friends before she met Bernie. I met her on the train. Did she tell you?'

It was then that a sudden burst of fatigue came over Harold. He couldn't explain it – he didn't want to – but he couldn't help himself. 'I'm exhausted. Do you mind if I go to bed after tea? I'm not used to being at work.'

'Bed? Hal, darling, are you okay? It's only six o'clock. I worry about you.'

'I'm all right.'

As soon as he'd eaten, he lay on the bed but couldn't sleep. His mind churned. Awful memories of the prison camp came flooding back. The day the guards had put a gun to his head, ordering him to confess all he knew and give his name, rank and number. Then later, the guilt he'd felt at being unable to contact Bruno, Agata and young Maria. She would be a pretty young woman now, in her late teens. He thought about Bernie, and how his life wouldn't have been worth living without him. What had happened to Dekkers? Perhaps he should try to find out. Hours later, he fell asleep, but the dreams didn't stop, and he woke up in a sweat when he heard Ellie getting into bed beside him.

'Hal, are you awake? You've been asleep for ages.'

In a sleepy voice, he mumbled, 'Yes. I've been thinking – there are quite a few things I want to do in my life, and I might regret it if I don't. One of them is to return to Italy, but I don't think it'll be possible if you're acting. I can't bear the thought of wondering if the Germans captured Bruno Galante and his family.'

Ellie's facial expression fell in the darkness of the room. The last thing she wanted was to stop Harold from closing down his past, but he was right. She wanted him to feel more secure. 'I haven't got the acting job yet, so don't worry, but…hang on, listen, why don't you and Bernie go back to Italy, just the two of you? I appreciate how much it means to you both.'

'What, and leave you here?'

'Yes, why not? But what about your work at the office?'

'I'm due two weeks off this year.'

'There you are, then. I'll have Jenny to go out with, and we can all make new plans by the time you get back. Maybe invite your friend Dekkers to a reunion or a party at the flat. We've put our name down for a council house, so we might get one if we're lucky. Do it while you can, and don't worry about me. This is something you must do so you can move on.'

'Oh, Ellie, you are the best! I'll speak to Bernie. Maybe next year, eh?'

Chapter Forty-Four

September 1948

Ellie spent nearly a year working in the theatre. The backstage hustle, the flickering lights, and the anticipation before each curtain call became her everyday reality. After that, she didn't know if they'd manage without her household contribution, but she hoped to continue acting as long as possible. At least they had Vicky's rent money now, thank goodness.

'Harold, love, I have news… We're expecting,' she announced.

'Oh heck, oh bloody hell, I didn't… Ellie, how wonderful.'

He kissed her, and they spent the next few hours discussing their lives and the lovely things they would do with their new baby due in March next year. They phoned Betty and Alf from the call box at the end of the street to tell them the good news. Betty sounded elated, and offered to come down to Weston nearer the time and help with the new baby, but sooner if it was convenient.

Ellie also felt it was time to write to her mother and tell her the good news. It was the right thing to do, and would give Agnes a chance to have her say and possibly make amends. Perhaps now she would see things differently. After ten days, Ellie received a reply.

Dear Ellie,

Congrats to you and Harold! So happy for you both, and I can't wait to be a granny! I would like to see you soon, and as you haven't met George, I think you should.

I'm really sorry for how I acted in these past years. Those wars really messed us all up, and it was hard to talk to you. We need to leave the past behind. There's some things I want to tell you, and we should get together. I missed you, even if you don't think I did. It took me a while to get up the nerve to talk to you. George helped me do it. We must meet soon. Please say you will – it's important.

Give George a warm welcome to the family when you meet him. He's such a charmer, and I've never been happier. Your father was a good man and he loved you, but some things weren't clear. Maybe you'll understand when we meet again.

Tommy's doing great and will be here on leave soon. I'd like to go to Weston for our holiday. How about we spend some time together then? Don't say no! Should I book a B&B? What date works for you? We're getting the train. That little car of ours isn't built for long trips.

I am looking forward to it, and best wishes to Harold.

Love,

Mam & George

Ellie reread the letter. There was a tone to the writing that she'd never felt before in her exchanges with her mother. Her dad had often complained that her mother was dramatic. Was it all just an excuse to make up with Ellie now she was expecting a baby? Well, it just wasn't good enough. She'd tell her, now that she'd married that George character. Then again, she reflected, what harm had it done if he made her mother happy? She'd given up on being angry long ago. Her mother's words now were not the same as her usual scolding, and she had at least congratulated Ellie and sent her wishes to Harold. Ellie was suspicious, though. Never had there been such warm greetings in a letter from her mother. She hadn't even attended the wedding. There was no excuse for her unreasonable and childish behaviour. Even Betty had expressed disgust at the way Agnes treated her. What was she up to? Perhaps Ellie would never understand.

Ellie accepted her mother's idea. After discussing it with Harold, she invited Agnes and George to stay. 'So, what do you think, love? Have I done the right thing?' she asked.

'Yes. Why not? She's your mother, after all. Her letter sounds cheery enough, and I'd be intrigued by her comment.'

'I suspect it's another one of her "You have to feel sorry for me, Ellie" stories, which I don't need right now.' Ellie grimaced as she said it. 'Can you put up with her for the weekend? Are you sure?'

'Yes, she's my mother-in-law.' Harold grinned. 'Anyway, we've got that other room we could use. It's small but adequate.'

Ellie sat on his knee. 'I'm a fortunate woman to have you, Harold Dean.' She kissed him long and caressed his cheeks.

The following week, Harold arrived home from work with a broad smile on his face.

'You're home early, Hal. I didn't expect you for another hour.'

He took Ellie's hand. 'Come on outside. I got a surprise for you.'

She walked down the stairs and stood at the front door.

'Okay, we're having a baby, and now we need something to carry the baby in.'

Ellie was expecting a pram, but got the shock of her life.

'See that car over there?'

Ellie stared at the green Morris Minor parked outside the house. She looked at Harold and then gazed at the car again. 'You mean…'

'Yep, I can take you and the baby all over. We can have fun together. It's ours. I got it from the garage up the road. It's brand new.'

'Brand new?! Oh, Hal, oh heck, can we afford it? That's fantastic news, but don't we need a pram first?'

'I've been saving and also borrowed the money. It's the latest model.'

'Borrowed it? From where?'

'The bank says I have a steady job now, and they let me have a loan. It won't take long to pay off. They were happy because I was putting something toward it myself.'

'But with the baby coming, we'll need every penny we can get.'

'This is the other surprise. The department wants me to manage the accounts. So I'll be getting a promotion.'

'Oh, Hal, that's wonderful, darling – clever you.' She flung her arms around him.

Harold smiled. 'I hoped you'd be pleased. It'll make a big difference in our lives. I can afford to buy a pram as well.'

'Do you need a licence to drive it? The car, I mean, not the pram.' Ellie laughed.

'I did it all in the army.'

'Oh yes, of course, I forgot. Are you taking me for a drive tonight?'

'Let's go for a drink at a pub and enjoy ourselves before your mother comes and changes everything.' Harold grinned.

'I'm not looking forward to her coming here, but let's go.' Ellie reached for her coat, locked the door, and sat in the car's front seat. If things were going to change for the better, this was it, she thought. It would be an inspiring future after all the suffering.

Chapter Forty-Five

George stepped from the train and took Agnes's hand to help her climb onto the platform. 'I hope we'll be welcome,' he said.

'Don't worry so much, love. It'll be fine. Come on, let me help you with that suitcase.'

'No, don't be silly, I'll carry it, Aggie. It's all right, don't fuss.'

Agnes's eyes searched the people waiting at the gate. Ellie waved, and Agnes waved back. George was tall and handsome for his age, with a dash of thick greying hair. He wore a smart grey tweed jacket and a blue tie.

'Hello, pet, how are you? It's kind of you to have us to stay. Hello, Harold, it's lovely to see you both again.' Agnes hugged Ellie and gave Harold a kiss on the cheek. 'Congratulations on your forthcoming event.'

Ellie looked bewildered.

'I'd like you to meet George,' Agnes continued. 'It's a pity you didn't meet before, but we can make up for it now.'

Harold and George shook hands.

'Nice to meet you,' Harold said.

George stood gazing at Ellie with a smile on his face, then shook her hand.

'Come on, Mam, let's go home. Harold has a car now.'

They all squeezed into the Morris Minor while Harold put the suitcase in the boot.

'So, do you live *in* Weston?' asked George.

'We're just on the outskirts and have a flat. We put our names down for a council house and hope to have a three-bedroom home soon. I work for the council so now and then I ask where we are on the waiting list. They are building new properties close to here that'll have lovely views out to sea. We were lucky to get this flat. Bernie's dad knew someone who owns it,' Harold said.

'Handy,' said George with a smile.

Ellie kept quiet in the car, but Agnes soon stopped the silence.

'So, Ellie, how are things?'

'Fine – they say the baby is doing well, and I go to the clinic every month for check-ups. Now we got the new National Health Service, it's great. No need to worry about paying when you get ill.'

'Hmm. Wish it had been like that in my day. You're not showing much yet.'

'Well, I'm noticing it more now that the morning sickness is easing up in these past few days. The smells and tastes are more intense. How are things with you?'

'Fine. We felt it was about time we all got together. It hasn't been an easy ride, what with the weather last year, but the year before it was terrible. How was your life in the army? I sent you letters which were returned to me. I'd no idea where you were.'

'Yes, it was a difficult time. I gather some of your letters didn't arrive.'

'I wrote to you. Perhaps not as often as I would have liked, but with the bombs and everything, none of us knew if the mail would turn up,' said Agnes.

'I was in a classified camp, meeting many interesting people. Then, of course, when we got home, the weather got in the way but we made it through thanks to Alf and Betty.' Ellie smiled at Harold as he concentrated on the road.

'Nearly there now,' he said.

Harold drew up outside the door of the flat. He retrieved the suitcase and gave it to George. Ellie climbed the stairs and showed her mother around the place. She thought it all seemed surreal, having her mother stay after all this time. How could Agnes not go to her wedding? She had written, yes, but there had been no visits. Why be so cold and controlling, and then…this? It was laughable. How could she have changed so much? Perhaps all her animosities had been left behind after the war like a distant memory. Was everything they'd said and done genuine? Could Ellie trust her, and would she and Harold throw Agnes and George out of the flat after just a few days? All these questions! It was all too much. She must accept her mother for who she was now rather than the mother she'd known before.

'You can hang your things in this wardrobe, Mam.'

'Oh, thanks. We haven't brought much, as I knew I could wash my knickers here.' Agnes gave a childish giggle.

'I miss Dad, you know,' Ellie said. 'Time stood still on the day he passed away. I was so sorry I wasn't with you.'

Agnes gave a smile. 'He was a good man and cared for us all, but life moves on, and now I hope you will enjoy having George here. I used to know him before I met your dad, but he was called to the front in the Great War, and we didn't see each other again until…a bit like you and Harold, who got married eventually. Then, unfortunately, his wife died, and he was on his own when I met him again.'

'Oh, I didn't know that.' Ellie felt she could relate to her mother's words. Something about George reminded her of dear Uncle Bert, her dad's older brother who passed away when she was twelve years old. The situation felt awkward. 'So how did you meet Dad? You never told me.' Ellie wondered at her mother's story, and was glad it had turned out well for her.

'Well, it's a long story, so perhaps I can tell you when we get settled for our holiday.'

'Aggie?' George called across the landing. 'Harold has invited me to the pub for an hour. Do you mind?'

'No, go on. Ellie and me can have a friendly chat.' Agnes looked across at Ellie. 'I'll help you make dinner for when they get back.'

'Thank you, dear,' George replied. 'You know how it is with us men. We like our pint at the pub,' he jested.

Ellie thought what a lovely man he was. Perhaps he could be her favourite uncle after all…but no. He was her new stepdad; she should get to know him better before judging his role in her life.

*

Harold drove to the pub, and George bought him a pint of beer.

'It's good of you to have us to stay. I've been pushing Agnes to make it up to Ellie for a long time.'

'Oh, right?' Harold said, nodding vaguely.

'Well, I can tell you it hasn't been easy, but she's changed since we met. When I knew her years ago, she was a sweet girl, and we were in love. Then I had to go to war.'

'Just like me.' Harold laughed. 'But I hadn't realised you two knew each other before the war.'

'It's complicated. I need Agnes to tell you about it. She has to face her own demons, you might say.'

'Oh, I see,' replied Harold, but he didn't really see, and he wondered what Agnes's demons might be. 'I'm intrigued,' he said.

George changed the subject. 'So what regiment were you in, Harold?'

'4th Battalion, Green Howards.' The words rolled off Harold's tongue once again.

'Oh yes, they were part of the East African Campaign, weren't they?'

'Well, there was my lot and several hundred thousand others from all over the place,' Harold remarked casually, and sipped his beer.

'I heard you were a prisoner of war. I know how that feels. Me too, the first time around. No one really understands how it was. I went to hell and back. I had little food and water. We came out of that prison camp like skeletons. Dreadful. I thought I was dying in there.'

'Really? You too, eh? Fortunately, my mate Bernie and I were together most of the time. I couldn't have done it without him. He lives near here – we often visit this pub together. He was one reason we moved down here. Can I get you another pint, George?'

'Yes, please. Thank you.'

Harold went to the bar to order another beer. While he waited for his turn, he wondered about Agnes. Had she come down to apologise to Ellie for everything in the past? That could be it, yes indeed. Much about her remained a puzzle: her past, her present motivations, and the expression in her eyes. He'd left Saltburn before really getting to know her, and the seaside town's charm had faded behind him as quickly as his memories of her. He sensed, however, that George held the upper hand for once; a new control that prompted Agnes's compliance, but in a way that felt positive and agreeable to her.

Harold placed the drinks on the table. 'There you go. They serve an excellent pint here. No Newcastle Brown Ale – it's all local on the hand pump. Bernie's been educating me.'

'Did I hear something about your brother?' asked George.

'Oh, young William, you mean?' Harold told him how they'd met up in the prison camp, and how William had survived his ship going down.

'Oh, poor lad, it must have been very traumatic, but how wonderful that you met up again in that way.' George swayed his head. 'I bet it made all the difference.'

'I can't tell you how overwhelming it was to see him again, but the affair changed him. He's still having nightmares, and occasionally I phone the family to talk with him. The trouble is the call is short, it's expensive ringing from a phone box but at least we have each other. His hands got severely burned, and that's what worried him most. He plays the trombone and thought perhaps he wouldn't play again.'

'It's good that you were there for each other, eh?' George looked at his watch. 'I think our hour is up. We'd best be getting back soon.'

Harold smiled. 'Yep – Ellie gets out the whip and cracks it if I'm not back on time,' he joked.

Harold liked George. He was among the few who understood his emotions, and Harold was grateful for his company.

Chapter Forty-Six

Noticing Agnes and George hadn't eaten much since lunch, Ellie decided to prepare a dinner similar to Bernie's family's guest house menu.

The rhythmic scrape of knives on peels filled the kitchen as Agnes joined her, their hands working in tandem as they scraped potatoes and carrots, a familiar scene from their Diamond Street days. 'It's been too long.' Agnes grinned, a mischievous glint in her eyes. 'You know, since we enjoyed ourselves.'

'Well, Mam,' Ellie sighed, the unspoken regret hanging heavy in the air, 'it could be said we should've done it sooner.'

Agnes, her lips pressed into a thin, straight line, replied, 'Yes, I know.' The grim reality of the war was etched onto her face. 'What do you think of George?' she whispered.

'George? He seems very nice. Why do you ask?'

'Oh, good, I'm glad you like him. He's taught me a thing or two. Look, Ellie, I'll tell you more when we have tea tonight and feel more relaxed. You were too young to understand.'

Ellie rolled her eyes. Here we go again. It wouldn't be long before her mother had one of her dramatic moments.

She made stew and dumplings, and Harold set the table. After their meal, George gave Agnes a knowing look.

Agnes took a breath, but only to say, 'Not yet.'

George glared back at her and opened the conversation. 'Your mother has something important to tell you.'

Agnes stiffened. It was now or never. 'Ellie, Harold. George is right. I have something I need to say.'

Ellie furrowed her brow.

'Before I married your dad, I went through a difficult time. This is part of the reason I was so protective of you when you and Harold got together. The trouble is, it wasn't that straightforward.' Agnes's hand shook and she kept sighing with each sentence. She looked at George.

'Go on, Aggie, you are doing fine,' he said.

She took another deep breath. 'I lost contact with George because of the war. It was a terrible time. The same as you and Harold. They told me he was missing, presumed dead. Your dad worked down the mines, and they needed him, so he never went away to war. I was pregnant and unmarried, and they would take you away from me. My mother was horrified and threatened never to have anything to do with me again. I had no one to turn to.'

Ellie tightened her lips. 'What, you? Pregnant and unmarried? Never! But what about…?'

'No, Ellie, it wasn't quite… Well, when I gave birth to you, I lived up there. The authorities had threatened to take you away from me so I ran away with you in my arms. I became desperate and went to someone I knew who I could trust. I was ill after giving birth, but she took me in for a few days and looked after me. She was a friend of Auntie Pat. The same thing happened to her and she knew what to do. It seemed she was the only person who understood. Her name was Jane Morton and she lived in Bishop Auckland. Lovely lady. I couldn't have done without her. We became friends after the war.'

Harold and Ellie looked at each other.

'Later, Jane, who was most sympathetic to my plight, arranged for me to go to a safe place when she saw how terrified I was. She said no baby should be without its mother. This nice young man she knew offered to help, and said his friend's wife would take me in as long as I worked around the house. Her husband was an officer in the army. She had severe arthritis and there were things she couldn't do. They owned a lovely home near Durham. I didn't get paid, but I had food and board. Your grandmother wanted nothing to do with me and didn't even search for me. At least while I was in service, we had a roof over our heads. They normally don't take servants with children, but she was different – she wanted a companion and couldn't have children of her own.'

'Oh, Mam, what are you saying?'

'Well, hang on, I haven't finished. After a few weeks, the young man kept visiting me, and we built a friendship, eventually leading to my marrying him. He took me on with a baby in my arms, and I felt it was most courageous. Granny Brownlee didn't approve of course, but after a while she relented.'

Harold chipped in. 'Hang on a minute – are you saying Ellie's dad wasn't her real father?'

Agnes looked at the pained expression on Ellie's face. 'I'm sorry, Ellie, I didn't mean you to know about this, but George insisted I tell you because you were bound to find out anyway, and it was better coming from me.'

George chipped in, speaking softly. 'I hope you can understand your mother's predicament, Ellie. She didn't want it to be this way, and when you and Harold were courting, the scandal would have been dreadful if you had ended up the same. Now do you understand why she was so protective of you?'

Agnes turned down her mouth at his comment.

Once again, Harold asked the questions to which he thought he knew the answer but wanted to check. 'So...who *is* Ellie's father?'

'Well, if you can't guess by now, there's no hope,' said George smiling. 'You see, we were young and naive and I had to go away to war and leave Agnes by herself. I did not know she was pregnant, and, like with you, Harold, there was no contact with anyone to tell her about me. My mother got a letter saying, "missing, presumed dead". Agnes thought I was dead too, and because of the child, she married Ernest when he asked her. That also meant she wouldn't be an outcast. No one would know because they moved house. Ernest was a good man and he took care of you. But yes, I'm your real dad, Ellie.' He smiled. 'Agnes told me all this before we got married. Tommy is not my son – he's Ernest's boy and your half-brother.'

Ellie almost fainted. Harold rushed to her side as the blood drained from her face.

'Come on, El, it's okay.'

'No, no, it's not okay,' she argued. 'You came here to tell me all this? I can't believe what you just told me.'

'It's all true, and I'm so sorry, Ellie,' said Agnes. 'I really love you, ya know. Otherwise, I wouldn't have taken so much trouble to keep you. When I stayed at Auntie Pat's house, I met up with George again and had to tell him what had happened. He was as shocked as you are, and insisted I told you. The war can do dreadful things to families.'

Tears meandered down Ellie's face. She wanted to say, "Why, why, why?", but the words wouldn't come, and she realised that perhaps Agnes *really* loved her. She'd fought to keep her, raised her, and no one knew otherwise. Had her mother loved him too? But George…her real dad? What was she supposed to say? Then came the big question. Why hadn't they come to her wedding, or at least told her about this before now?

George piped up. 'Ellie, when I saw you for the first time, I knew you were my daughter. You look so much like my mother. The way you smile, your eyes…yes, you are mine.' He smiled.

Ellie realised that her "favourite uncle" feeling went deeper than she could ever have imagined.

'I'm sorry, Ellie, it was too much for me. I didn't want to spoil your wedding day by blurting out that George is your father just before your ceremony. He wanted to be there too, but it all happened so quickly we didn't know what to do.' Agnes gazed at Harold. 'You'd just got back from a prison camp, Harold. The emotion for you and everyone else was overwhelming – how could I explain it? We didn't want to spread gossip in Saltburn which could have affected you both. I cried that day, but we decided it was for the best. When you wrote to say you were expecting a baby, we felt it was important to make it up to you. We would have told you anyway. It's not just because of the baby.'

Harold was already comforting Ellie in his arms. He was just as shocked, but seemed to understand more than she did. 'My God, this is a calamity, isn't it? I'm not sure what to say. I'm sorry, Agnes, that you had such a poor start. Life certainly wasn't kind in those days. They still do it today – it's terrible to have your child taken away from you.' He thought about William, and the time when the family feared they'd lost him.

Ellie stood and saw her reflection in the sideboard mirror; her tear-stained face made her want to run to her room and hide.

'Look, I really wanted to apologise for my behaviour, but everything just got in the way. Then it seemed I'd left it too late until George came back on the scene.' Agnes sighed. 'I regret it now. I'm sorry, Ellie.'

Harold went to Agnes and sat beside her. 'Look, we know the truth now – you did the right thing. Nowadays, society can be very cruel. Who knows where Ellie might have ended up otherwise? I certainly wouldn't have known her.'

'I'm sorry, Harold. I didn't want to be so offhand with you, it's… I just got dreadfully concerned because I didn't want you both to end up as I did. You were very young, and close – sometimes too close – and with what I'd gone through, I didn't want it to be a waste of my strength to keep Ellie safe. I hope you understand. Harold, you're a good man, and we appreciate you sticking with Ellie through all this turmoil.'

'But, Mam, if I'd been in the family way, we had Betty and Alf on our side, and they are lovely people, and what would you have done about it – thrown me out of the house?'

'True, they are, and no, I would have taken care of you, but it was the local people around us, the stigma. I only wanted to protect you from all that gossip. It's destructive,' replied Agnes. 'You cannot imagine how it was. Therefore, I had to save you, especially with the Great War. I couldn't face the workhouse.'

'You really should have told me sooner. I'd have understood. Honest, I would.'

'It was my decision not to say anything until you grew up and could understand. And then you were gone, and it was all too late.' Agnes sighed.

'So, Ellie, can you find it in your heart to hug your new dad? This is all new for me too. I mean…to find I have a daughter. It's overwhelming, isn't it?' George agreed. 'Are you happy to have me?'

With barely a moment to breathe, Ellie had little time to process the idea of having a father figure in her life again. The revelation hit her like a punch to the gut; the years spent in Saltburn, with affection for a man who wasn't her father, left her feeling both drained and furious. She reminded herself of how much she'd cared for him, despite his put-downs about her not being clever. Now she wondered what she was supposed to think, especially with the baby coming.

'Ellie, pet, your stepdad was good to you. Yes, he got sick, but he always cared for us as best he could. He was lovely, and we have much to thank him for. I mean, he was Tommy's father, don't forget.'

So, Ernest was her stepdad now? Ellie wiped her tears.

'We wanted to come down here,' said George. 'I felt it was important we were together as a family again. You have a half-sister too. I was married but, like Agnes, I was later widowed. We must all get together one day soon. None of this mess would have happened if it weren't for the war. Please don't assume that it's all our fault, Ellie. I hope we can be forgiven.'

Ellie gazed at George, searching for recognition. She could see it: she had his eyes, and felt foolish not realising there was anything familiar about him. Yes, he was her real dad, and she had to get to know him, although it might take time.

George stood and opened his arms. 'Welcome back, Ellie. I wish I'd been able to see you grow up.'

Ellie leaned toward him reluctantly, giving him a hug. Finding it in her heart to love this man like her dad would take time. At least Harold liked him, so maybe everything would be okay.

Chapter Forty-Seven

Harold and Ellie went to bed, their minds buzzing with unanswered questions, a restless energy filling the quiet room.

'Well, *that* was an enormous shock, wasn't it, El?' Harold said.

Ellie gave a deep sigh. 'What are we supposed to do now?'

'I don't know. There is nothing we can do. The baby isn't due for another five months, and I suppose we'll have time to get used to all the changes. But it's good to know our child has grandparents on both sides, and you can go back to acting once the baby is born, maybe join the local drama group for a while until the baby is older.'

'I loved my dad, you know. I mean, my real dad. No. I mean Ernest, poor man. He got so very sick. It's all been a dreadful shock for me,' Ellie said.

'Yes, I know what you mean,' Harold said. 'You're bound to be confused, love, for a while at least, but I feel George is a good man, and if he'd known about you, things would certainly have been different. It was just your mother. We never understood her, and now we do a little better. She certainly looks happier than I've ever seen her.' Harold put his hand on Ellie's belly and felt for signs of the baby kicking. So far, nothing stirred, but she'd assured him it would happen any day. He kissed her. 'Ellie, you are the best thing to happen to me. I never stopped thinking about you during the war, and every day I longed to see you again. I didn't give up when I found you were with Jack, only in the last days, and to think you found me... We were made for each other.'

'Your mam and dad are coming next month to visit. I look forward to having them stay. Let's hope they don't have more nasty surprises for us,' Ellie laughed. 'When I look back, the things we went through made us all stronger. You and me growing up, the time we…you know…down the back alley, the war, me nearly marrying the wrong man, you in prison camps in Italy and Germany. I really can't imagine how we got through it all.'

'You're right, love. It was hard, and I don't want to keep looking back.' Harold pulled the soft bedclothes over them, creating a snug cocoon, and held her close, finding solace in her presence. As he held her in his arms, he couldn't help but feel a sense of fulfilment that the woman he had longed for was finally with him. He switched off the bedside light, cuddled Ellie, and closed his eyes. 'You know, while I was a POW, I often dreamed I could fly,' he said.

'I think we can fly together now,' Ellie whispered. 'In more ways than one, at last we've made that long journey home.'

Epilogue

March 1949

Harold and Bernie's long-awaited trip to Italy finally happened weeks later.

The two men landed at Rome Airport at around three o'clock. The train ride up to the Abruzzo mountains would take a couple of hours, and they still couldn't be sure they would find their adopted family again when they reached Sulmona. Harold wasn't confident of the route. All he could remember was the shape of the mountain behind the house. Eventually, they arrived on an old bus into Sulmona town, to be greeted by the bustling sounds of people and cars. Their guide directed them to take the road toward Villavallelonga, almost the exact route they had taken during their daring escape.

'This bloody place gives me the creeps. I can still hear the German munitions echoing around the valley,' Bernie said.

'I know what you mean, but Sulmona's a pretty little town, don't you think? We never really saw it before.'

At the local bakery, they asked about a family named Galante, and a taxi driver queueing in the shop offered to take them there. It was almost half an hour from the centre and the fare wasn't expensive.

'Do you know the family?' Bernie asked the driver.

'I have not seen Signor Galante recently. He sometimes use my taxi. I *theenk* his son is working at the farm now. They bought a car, so I *theenk* that is the…reason.'

'I hope they're all safe and well,' Harold said, his voice tight with worry. He smiled at the driver's words; all very reminiscent.

On arrival, they recognised the scenery and the house. The farm had barely changed, though there was now a good road. It was quiet and eerie. Harold took a deep breath, bombarded with visions of the night when the Germans had come to search for them. The scene he'd relived many times. Was Bruno going to be there?

They ambled up the hill in the day's heat and stood at the doorstep.

'Go on, Hal,' Bernie urged, poking him in the ribs. 'Knock.'

Harold hesitated, took another breath, and wiped his forehead with his hand. He rapped on the old wooden door. After a moment, they heard footsteps and a voice crying out in Italian. A young woman opened the door.

'Maria?' Harold said.

She gazed upon the two men who stood there in all their finest clothes and she blinked. '*Oh, oh, mamma mia!* Berneee, Harold, you came back – how wonderful.'

'We came to thank your father. We came from England,' Bernie said in his best Italian. 'Oh my, how lovely you have grown, Maria – such a beautiful young lady now, huh?'

Bruno's son came to the door and stood before Maria, protecting her. Antonio Galante gazed at Harold and Bernie standing in the farmyard, unsure of what to say. 'Hello, can I help?' he said after hearing Maria's conversation.

'We're very pleased to see you,' Harold said. Then he listened as Maria told her brother that these were the men their father had mentioned.

'We have sad news,' said Maria.

Harold immediately jumped to conclusions, thinking her parents had been punished for harbouring prisoners. Still, the taxi driver had mentioned them, so what was the sad news? 'Oh dear…' he said.

'Mamma died in March this year. She got this horrible…er… sickness, and they couldn't improve her.'

'Oh… We're so sorry, Maria, Antonio,' Harold said. 'She was a wonderful mother. Our condolences.'

'Thank you,' Maria said, her eyes filling with tears. 'Papà will come soon. He is in Villavallelonga today with his friend.'

Harold placed his hand across his chest with relief. 'Oh, good, we must see him.'

Bernie spoke Italian to Antonio, but he replied in English.

'You may speak English with me. And, please...call me Toni. I was long enough in Scotland but now I'm returning there with Maria and my father. I want to open an ice-cream shop and a café with a few army friends. We are selling the farm. It is good business and I have connections there now. We made ice cream while prisoners worked on the land, and the Scottish people loved it. I have the money now, so I will return – it's a lovely country. I liked it very much, despite my wartime circumstances.'

'Your father is courageous. He risked his life for us.' Harold's speech was halting as he regained control of himself.

Maria came to him and gave him a hug.

'And you, Maria, are an excellent fibber!' Harold laughed through his tears, and squeezed her hand in play.

Bernie laughed at Harold's remark, and explained to Toni how Maria had faced the Germans. 'She was most courageous,' he said. 'We heard her saying she didn't understand them.'

'Did you know,' said Toni, 'that over 500 Italian people lost their lives in this valley and in the south? They were shot for harbouring prisoners of war. Wives were left without husbands. Fathers, sons, were taken away and children were left without parents, and there was nothing for them to live on. Can you imagine it?'

Harold lowered his gaze. 'Your father was incredible, especially on the night we left here. He gave us a chance to escape. This is one reason we had to come back, to be sure your family made it through. Of course, we both felt very guilty, but we could do nothing except wait and hope it would end. The Italian people were wonderful, and we promise never to forget them!'

Toni smiled; his voice quieted. 'Your people were good to me, too.'

After drinking strong coffee, Harold and Bernie walked around the farm and showed Toni how they'd slept. They shared their stories with Maria, who couldn't keep her eyes off them.

Bernie placed his arm around her waist and whispered in her ear. 'I must tell you I'm getting married to a lovely girl called Jenny this year, but I still love you.' He grinned.

'She is fortunate to have you,' said Maria. 'We missed you very much.'

'I'm only sorry we had to leave here so quickly,' Bernie said. 'This is why we're here today for a special thank you.'

The two men found their visit overwhelming.

'Did we really do this?' asked Harold, shading his eyes from the sun.

After a couple of hours and a few glasses of wine, an old tractor with a trailer drew up to open the main gate. They heard it at the bottom of the drive. Maria suggested they hide and surprise her father. Toni greeted him. Bruno, being Bruno, would surely know something was different by the looks on his children's faces.

'Papà, we have a wonderful surprise for you.'

'What is it, Maria?' asked Bruno as he stepped down from the tractor.

'We have visitors,' said Toni.

'Come out now,' called Maria in English.

At first, he squinted at the two men, trying to make out their faces, but then his jaw dropped in disbelief, his lips quivered with emotion, and tears streamed down his cheeks. 'Oh, how wonderful,' he said. 'You crazy men, you came back.'

Bernie hugged him. 'You saved our lives,' he said. 'Harold and me, we came to say thank you.'

Bernie took out a fresh handkerchief, and they all wept and hugged each other so tightly they didn't want to let go.

'Sorry, I'm so amazed you came back.' Bruno blew his nose.

Harold spoke. 'I'm so sorry about Agata. She was a wonderful lady, almost a mother to us.' He thought Bruno had aged a lot, and wondered how long he could work the farm. Perhaps Toni was right. It was time to move on.

They all spent the rest of the afternoon in the sun, drinking wine and discussing old times, and Harold and Bernie told Bruno, Maria and Toni what had happened to them after they'd left the farm. Harold didn't want to talk about it at first, but after a while, he realised what an immense relief it was to let go of his feelings in the presence of someone who understood. Perhaps now he could go home, get on with his life, and live happily ever after with Ellie. It was great news that the Galante family was planning to live in Scotland. They were used to mountains. The Scottish weather was another matter, he thought.

Two days later, after Harold and Bernie had spent the nights sleeping on a sofa and a mattress on the farmhouse floor, Bruno offered to take them to the station in his old 1935 Fiat 1500. He'd bought the car from a friend, the rusted chassis and faded paint hinting at its history in the valley. Toni explained he had spent hours in the garage with it, the sounds of tools and the smell of motor oil as he carefully cleaned and reconditioned the engine and bodywork. It had certainly been through the war years.

'I just bought a car, but it's nothing like this one.' Harold beamed.

They'd spent a few months in their musty, cramped hiding place on the farm, the air thick with the smell of hay and damp earth and cow dung. Now an unexpected sense of peace settled over them as they sat on the porch, the absence of fear a strange new sensation. The farmyard sounds, the howling wolves, the eagle's screech: it was as though they'd never been away. Harold found it overwhelming, and powerful memories haunted both men.

The following morning, the sun rose above the mountains. Harold rolled off his mattress and onto the floor. Now dressed in shorts and a shirt, he found Toni making breakfast in the sun.

'You might see us sooner than you think,' said Toni. 'I hope to be in Scotland within a few months.'

'It's a long way, but perhaps we can come visit you on holiday. My wife knows Scotland a lot more than I do. Sadly, we have to leave this morning,' Harold announced. 'We also want to see more of Italy and then go home to our new lives.'

Bruno finished his coffee, and soon they were ready to leave. He gave them a lift to the station. There were hugs all around.

Maria shed tears but kept a smile on her face. 'We hope to see you again soon.'

Before they left Sulmona, Bruno took a turn off the main road. He drove down a track and around a compound. Harold and Bernie recognised the mountain with the chapel on the top that stood behind the prison camp.

'I think it's important for you both to close the book on this terrible place. I do not think it will be here much longer. So now you can reflect briefly on your escape and your time with us. I brought you around the back because the camp is still in use, and the military inside may not understand what we are doing here.'

Harold and Bernie stood together, gazing through the gaps in the wall. The two men stood in eerie silence, staring at the old control towers, imagining the guards in uniform, their weapons slung over their shoulders. The huts stood silent. Harold recognised "his" hut, and the memories came flooding back. It was too much.

He turned away with watery eyes. 'We survived. We're lucky buggers, both of us.' His voice cracked, and Bernie gripped his friend's arm in support.

'We're lucky,' Bernie said with half-closed eyes. 'So fuckin' lucky to be standing here!'

Harold's thoughts turned to happier moments. The concerts, the football, playing cards outside the huts, and the camaraderie. They'd certainly had it better here than in Germany.

Bernie made a suggestion. 'Perhaps they should keep this camp open so that people can see how prisoners of war lived. People should never be allowed to forget what the Italians have done for them. Everyone back home has no idea what happened here in the freezing winters and the stifling summers.'

Finally, Harold turned away, a sigh escaping his lips as he did so.

'Now I have a girl to marry, and life must go on.' Bernie gave a smile.

Harold patted him on the back. 'Thanks for everything, mate. You were the brave one, not me.'

'Ah, but you saved someone's life under fire – that's brave!'

The Story Behind the Book

In 1995, my father, Harry Twidle, passed away. A lifetime of smoking cigarettes (a grim souvenir from the war), coupled with his already frail constitution, led to a protracted illness and his untimely death aged seventy-six. The six years he'd spent with the Green Howards Regiment had taken a heavy toll, leaving him with lasting health problems. He frequently withdrew into himself, spending hours absorbed in books about Hitler, trying to comprehend the chain of events that had led to his internment in German and Italian prison camps, the weight of the past heavy upon him. The war had left an indelible mark, and, like most of his comrades, he chose to keep his memories locked away, unspoken.

Today, post-traumatic stress disorder (PTSD) is a widely understood condition, but in 1946 the debilitating effects of trauma lacked a formal diagnosis, leaving countless individuals struggling in silence. His unsettling behaviour became clear only after further research into the condition. I chose to ignore it because 'Dad was like that' I used to say.

Along with his mood swings, he exhibited other personality traits that made him both fascinating and challenging to be around. I felt a deep sadness when his ability to communicate was lost. Like Harold in the story, his speech was halting and hesitant, a stark reminder of the trauma he'd endured.

In 1960, nestled on a shelf in a cupboard, I found a black leather box that had been passed down from my grandmother. From under the lid protruded sheets of blue writing paper, offering a tantalising glimpse of the hidden wonders inside. I asked my mother if I could see it, and to my surprise, I found stacks of letters and aerograms, each envelope adorned with stamps of the era. As a budding philatelist, I carefully examined the colourful stamps, and eagerly asked if I could have them. My mother didn't seem too bothered about the letters; they didn't seem to mean much to her, and I doubted she knew much about what they contained. She allowed me to cut the stamps from each one, which was indeed a mistake. None of us realised the significance and value of the flimsy blue aerograms. As I grew into the 1970s, I asked my mother if I could look through the box again, but by that point I had kept the letters in my parents' house for many years. I didn't read them then either! They were just 'Dad's letters', copies of which, later, I donated to the Eden Camp Modern History Museum in Malton, Yorkshire.

The rediscovery of my father's letters from an Italian prison camp didn't come until 2001, during a painstaking search of his correspondence, revealing a poignant chapter of his life that I never knew existed. Upon my return to England after fifteen years of living in the Netherlands, I delved into conducting more research with which the museum curator was most helpful.

The more I read, the more I realised my father had provided me with the basis for an absorbing novel. Most of *The Trail to Freedom* is fiction: though based on a true story, it does not follow my father's true life story. My character, Harold Dean, is pure fiction. It is only my father's account of the way things were as a prisoner of war which has been written into the story. The historical value helped me to reconstruct Harold's trail to freedom. We rarely hear of fictional novels about prisoners of war, only a few non-fiction, and I felt readers should discover more about the thoughts and feelings of our men in captivity. The Campo 78 prison camp in Sulmona, Italy, is now a place of historical interest, and you can visit the site by prior appointment. Although many of the buildings are no longer there, those that remain contain interesting wall art by prisoners of war.

I am pleased to inform my readers that my father has, in a small way, posthumously written a part of this book, inasmuch as I used some of his words to help meld the story together via the letters he wrote. I feel sure he would have been proud of this novel, and I thank you all for reading about one of the many soldiers who made a valiant attempt on a long journey home by walking the celebrated 'freedom trails' in Italy, France and other parts of Europe. Some made it: others were not so lucky.

Ellie's story is based on my mother's experiences in Strathpeffer, Scotland. My parents only met after the war in 1948. She attended clerk school in this village with the ATS, training as a secretary. She was also in the theatre, and TV in later years. I grew up in the world of acting and dancing, which was used to tell Ellie's story. Although my knowledge of my mother's life was limited to a few scant details from prior to the war, the research ahead promised a rich tapestry of untold stories.

I want to thank the following editors, writers and researchers for their help in publishing this novel:

My publisher, Helen Hart and her team at SilverWood Books; The Green Howards Museum in Richmond, North Yorkshire; Curator and researcher Steve Erskine; The Eden Camp Modern History Museum in Malton, North Yorkshire; My colleagues at the Romantic Novelists' Association; To author, Anne Harvey, whose father, Ron Williams, was also at Dunkirk. We exchanged experiences. I mentioned him in the story in memory of her dad. The late Uys Krige (pronounced 'Ace Kreeger') for his book *The Way Out*. It's an expensive, rare novel, and a fabulous read. This book helped me confirm that what my father had written in his letters matched the experiences of the author, who was also an escapee from Sulmona Campo 78. https://www.britannica.com/biography/Uys-Krige

Thank you for reading *The Trail to Freedom*. I hope you enjoyed it. Please feel free to review on Amazon and through my website https://lintreadgold.co.uk

Lin Treadgold
Author of *Goodbye Henrietta Street* and *The Tanglewood Affair*

9 781800 423046